Knot Your Princess

Pack Origins Book 1

L.A. Clyne

D1732180

Copyright © 2022 L.A. Clyne

All rights reserved.

No portion of this book may be reproduced in any form without written permission from the publisher or author, except as permitted by copyright law.

All characters in this publication are fictitious and any resemblance to real persons, living or dead, is purely coincidental.

ISBN: 978-0-6456117-1-7

Cover art: L.A. Clyne

Reach me at: www.laclyne.com

Follow me on: Facebook, Instagram, Pinterest

Join me at: L.A. Clyne's Tribe (private Facebook group)

For my husband, Pete. Who never gave up telling me I need to write a book. Then lost me to my laptop when I finally listened.

He now happily tells the world I write alien porn. Not that there's anything wrong with that. I may write a sexy alien love story one day, just for him.

This book may have been written for him, but this story was written for me.

This is a sweet, reverse harem, omegaverse romance written with multiple points of view. It features growly, protective alphas, a hot, nerdy beta, and a rebellious omega.

Maia's story will be completed in book one and can be read as a standalone. Books two and three will focus on new packs and continue the background story of the Crash.

The story contains MMFMM steamy scenes, including MM, and the heroine doesn't have to choose between her men. It's recommended for readers over 18 years old.

There are also references to past institutional abuse but no current abuse or abuse within the harem.

If any of the above isn't your jam, this probably isn't the book for you, and that's okay. Enjoy your day anyway. If it is, read on and welcome to the tribe.

One

I curled into myself tighter within the safety of my sanctuary. An old, tan leather reclining chair that had become my refuge. Sinking into its soft depths was like getting a hug from someone familiar and loved.

It was the only comfort I knew and the only place that felt like home within the high walls of the Omega Palace.

Memories consumed my thoughts today. My favorite book was lying cradled but forgotten in my arms. I'd meant to read it to help pass the hours I'd spent hiding in my secluded nook in the library. But something about today had me reminiscing.

I ran my hands over the sudden goosebumps on my arms as I remembered the day I arrived. I had been alone and feeling betrayed while bitterly grieving for my gramps, the last of my family who loved me. I had been outed as an omega at the relatively old age of twenty-one. I was a rarity, even amongst the rare.

Rage had been pounding a war cry in my head as they'd tried to drag me through the gilded doors of the Palace. I'm pretty sure one of my fingernails is still embedded in one. I was kicking and screaming like a banshee as I clung to that last doorway to my old life and a view of the slowly closing gate beyond.

Not the most serene or poised of entrances. They really should have dosed me with tranquilizers before we arrived, instead of after. So their perfect sanctum wouldn't have been disturbed by my fury.

Or maybe brought me in the back door, the way the trash goes out, just in reverse.

I remember all the pretty little shocked omegas standing and staring as I tried to claw my way to freedom back out those doors. Before the young omegas were all discreetly hustled away in case wanting freedom was contagious.

I had wanted no part of my new role as an obedient princess at the Palace to be trotted out and bought at the whims of others. I refused to cower and submit to a future I never asked for and didn't want.

My gramps knew I was an omega and had been afraid for me. He was a beta, but he had seen too much in his life and knew the ways of alphas.

Omegas were revered and coveted a long time ago. They still lived a life of luxury, but they were now powerless and enslaved. So he taught me how to hide in plain sight, and it worked. Until the day he died.

I got up from my chair, unable to sit quietly while my memories assaulted me, and paced in front of the old shelves. I watched as the dust motes lit up in the thin golden ray from the only window, shining for a brief moment before they fell to obscurity.

I stroked the spines of the precious books, looking for comfort but feeling restless. I felt an urge to run, to get as far away from here as I could, but there was no way out. I'd found that out the hard way.

This place was dangerous on a good day, but something was different today. It was too quiet in a tense, still way. As if the world was holding its breath while predators were on the prowl. So I'd been hiding here most of the afternoon.

I heard a noise in the library as the door clicked open and closed again. I dove back into my sanctuary. I was far back in the darker depths of the library, in a dusty old section nobody visits, except me.

Footsteps crept closer, and my heart stuttered like an old record player missing its groove while I held my breath. I tried desperately not to make a sound.

"Maia, are you here?" a hushed voice whispered into the stillness, and my heart started beating again.

I popped my head over the back of the chair. "Ava, you almost gave me a heart attack. Did anyone follow you?"

"Oh, thank god you're here." She rushed over. "And no, I made sure."

Ava was my only friend here. I didn't even know if she thought of me as a friend. But I didn't have any others, so I'd claimed her as mine. Palace omegas were not encouraged to make friends. We were kept apart as much as possible, even from each other.

We met when she wandered into the library one day. The only other person I'd seen in here. We started talking, hesitantly at first.

She was sweet, timid, and gentle, the perfect omega. She was also three years younger than me. She had just finished her mandatory omega training, and was about to enter her first season of the Palace's social circus.

She had long brown hair and big green eyes that begged you to protect her, like some lost waif. She was shorter than me but slim, curvy, and smelled like dark cherries. She was also stunningly beautiful and was going to get eaten alive.

As far as I knew, Ava took the usual path to the Omega Palace, although we'd never talked about it. Her awakening should have happened during puberty, her scent emerging and deepening over a few days. She would have immediately been sent here for training in how to please an alpha, the sole purpose of her new, shiny existence.

Once omegas arrived here, we were no longer allowed to have thoughts or desires of our own. We were only here to please and serve the whims of alphas, no more. We had no power and no voice, despite being rare and coveted.

The omega training wasn't pretty or pleasant behind the decadent facade of the Palace. For most, this place was more like a boot camp for omegas than the princess school they made it out to be.

Some arrived young and naive, ready to please. They managed to evade much of the darkness and corruption during training. But any omegas I had met again after their social debut had haunted eyes.

"Maia, are you okay? I haven't seen you in a few days. I was worried after I heard Ronan was here again on Saturday night. Then with everything that's happened since, I didn't know what to do."

She had sat down on an old cushion on the ground beside my chair while I was distracted with my thoughts and was now fiddling anxiously with a bluebird bracelet she wore. It had been a farewell gift from her family, and I wasn't sure how she had managed to hold onto it all these years.

She seemed stressed. She knew I regularly disappeared after an alpha got me alone, and I refused to submit. But I wouldn't tell her where I went or what they did. She didn't need to know, and I hoped she'd never find out for herself.

She was looking forward to her social debut, or so she said. All omegas attended their first social season at the Palace at twenty-one and were presented to potential, matched alphas at balls and elegant dinner parties. It sounded glamorous, but only on the surface.

I was afraid for her. Ava will be paraded around while alphas pick their poison. Sampling the goods is forbidden unless you know the right people and what motivates them, usually money. Greed has never been very inventive.

She won't get any say in mating an alpha. An omegas' scent and taste are like the most beautiful, addictive drug to alphas. Her scent will draw one in, and they will expect her to be grateful for being chosen. If she's unwilling, despite her training, the alpha will discreetly use a dominance bark to make her. Usually after money has changed hands for people to look the other way.

The alpha bark won't give her any choice. An alpha's bark works as a pure command woven through a word or sound that drives people to their knees and compels them to submit. The strength of the bark depends on the alpha's dominance level. A highly dominant alpha can even make a beta comply, but omegas are highly susceptible to an alpha's bark at any level. It was rare for an omega to resist.

It's why alphas rule the world, rather than betas, who vastly outnumber them.

So, Ava will miraculously accept with glazed, submissive eyes. And no one will say a word. Once mated, an alpha is supposed to protect their omega, but I've yet to see it happen.

Ava is still clinging to the fantasy that being chosen by an alpha is a blessing. I don't know if it's from fear or denial. But she's been here longer than I have so I try not to judge her too harshly. The omega training is insidious.

I scratched my arms absently, staring out a high window at the darkening sky, remembering the feeling of the many alpha barks directed at me and the sickly coercion that always creeps over me. But no alpha has yet managed to make me submit. Nobody knows why.

Many alphas have tried. It's almost a game or a rite of passage for new, young, cocky alphas to take a shot at me. All behind closed doors, of course, with plenty of money passing hands, just not my hands.

Every time I refused to submit, I'd get sent for correction, and I'd disappear from view, sometimes for days at a time, into the dark spaces of the Palace. Yet still, I refused to let them break me or compel me.

Ronan was the last in a long line, but he'd become the most persistent and refused to give up. There was something crazed about him more than any other alpha I had met.

To the ordinary person, he came across as handsome and charming. However, he was a little long in the face to be considered classically beautiful and looked younger than his years. He tried to overcome this by always dressing in expensive suits and slicking his hair back. It didn't work.

But when I looked into his eyes, which were so dark brown they were almost black, I saw the madness and violence within. His need to make me submit and his refusal to give up have made him unhinged and brought his insanity to the surface.

He was a highly dominant alpha from an old alpha family with powerful friends. A dangerous enemy to have. This last time, he had threatened that no one would have me if he couldn't. He wouldn't rape me. He wanted my complete submission to him. But murder, that I fully believed he would do.

I just hadn't figured out what I could do about it. I'd been trying to escape for three long years. But now, my days were numbered if I didn't get out of here.

"Maia, did Ronan do something to you? I mean, worse than usual?" Ava asked, looking concerned and trying to catch my eye.

I was startled by her voice. I was deeply lost in my thoughts today, but that was probably due to the sensory deprivation during my last correction.

It was a new tactic in their attempts to break me and was messing with my head. I was having trouble returning to myself after retreating into my mind in the endless, quiet darkness.

"Oh, you know, nothing I can't handle." I said. I tried to sound flippant but even I could hear the shake in my voice. Dammit. I was determined not to let her see me rattled.

In truth, this correction had been sickening. My handlers usually only kept me in the isolation chamber for a day or two, but I'd lost all track of time. They were determined to break me, but I was just as determined not to break.

I usually knew how long I was in by counting the meals that arrived as they were pushed through a gap in the door. But this time, the meals had stopped coming, and all the lights had gone out. I'd been alone in the empty, endless dark.

After hours or days, I'd felt my way over to the door. I'd been desperate as I'd felt my sanity start to slip and hunger pains had gnawed at me. I'd tried the handle and been stunned when it opened. I'd poked my head out tentatively, my burning eyes squinted against the light, to find nobody was there.

I'd taken my chance and blindly bolted. I'd headed straight for my sanctuary, knowing I had stolen supplies of food and water stashed here. I've been here ever since.

"Okay, if you say so," she said, looking sad and resigned. We both knew there was nothing she could do to help me.

She got up again and started poking around the shelves. "Do you have any candles or torches smuggled in here? I don't know what we'll do if the power doesn't come on soon. Everyone is freaking out, and nobody seems to know what will happen next. They're not telling us anything anymore."

"The power's out? How long has it been out for?" Electric fences surrounded the Palace. I knew because I'd checked them out extensively. A power outage could be my chance to escape.

I started throwing my things into an old duffel bag I'd stashed here. I knew the cook had an old bike stashed in the shed out the back. If I could get to it and get out, I could maybe get away.

Hope flared painfully in my chest. I looked out the tiny window. My golden beam of sunlight was a faded slice in the gathering darkness. I didn't have much time.

Ava looked at me askance. "Two days. How can you not know that?"

I sucked in a shocked breath. Two days. I'd been abandoned in the darkness, with no food or water for two days. And the door was unlocked the whole time.

I was furious. I'd been a prisoner of my complaisance for days. I was so used to hunkering down and surviving their punishments, I hadn't even questioned it.

But I needed to shake it off and focus on getting out. I forced myself to take deep, shaky breaths. I needed to know more.

"Why hasn't anyone come to fix it?"

"The power's out everywhere, Maia. It's not just us. People are calling it the Crash. It's the whole country. There's no news or radio anymore, not after the first day, and no supplies are coming in."

I just looked at her, stunned. "How can that be?"

"Nobody knows. We've been operating on generators, but I don't know how long they'll last, and I don't know how much food we have. Do you have anything to eat here? They've started rationing our supplies."

I grabbed some kind of health bar out of my bag and handed it to her distractedly while I processed what she was saying.

I was startled as the library doors banged open, letting in a gust of air. I instinctively ducked back into the chair. Ava dashed to the side and tried to stand casually, leaning against the chair and blocking me from view, surprising me.

Whoever it was, they weren't being cautious the way Ava had been. Instead, they were running straight towards us, with heavy footfalls that echoed in the silence.

I peeked around Ava, needing to know what I was facing, when Cary burst into view, breathing hard. I let out a sigh of relief, but it was short-lived.

I didn't know Cary that well, he was cautiously friendly, but he kept his distance more than Ava. He was a survivor. Being one of the few known male omegas, he was a curiosity for many alphas and an obsession for others.

He was darkly handsome, with deep brown skin and striking green eyes. He was bigger than a beta but not as big as an alpha. With well-defined muscles honed through savage workouts. He did them outside using old tires and whatever else he could find. I'd once sneakily watched through one of the library windows.

He liked to keep himself in shape, but I think it was more to stay strong than for appearances. He kept his omega instincts locked down.

He shadowed Ava intently and followed her movements whenever no one was watching. But I saw everything at the Palace.

He wasn't mated because he was a side-show attraction at the Palace's social circus. A role I didn't envy. He was rarer than me, and his position wasn't much better, but he had learned to play the game to his advantage. I was still fighting against it.

He had approached me when I was alone one day, asking how I kept denying the alpha barks and how I muted my scent before I arrived. I'd also seen him checking out the fences. He definitely wasn't buying the Omega Palace fantasy.

I had noticed him subtly run interference for me occasionally at social events with some of the more depraved alphas. He and Ava were the only things keeping me sane here.

"The guards and the dorm security have gone," he panted, catching his breath for a second, with his hands on his knees. "I don't think the trainers and staff are here anymore either."

"What do you mean gone?" Ava asked, throwing her arms up in the air. "Who's going to protect us?" Cary gave her a sideways look, seeming affronted.

"It gets worse." He straightened up and stalked around Ava to face me head-on. "The alphas are here. They're down at the front gates with a bunch of trucks."

"Which ones?" I asked, jumping out of the chair and grabbing his arm in a stranglehold. He didn't even flinch. He just stood, rock solid, like he could take on the whole world.

"All of them, and Ronan is leading them." He spun me around and started pushing me towards the door, "You have to go now."

"We all need to go," I cried, as I dodged him and rushed to grab my bag. I shoved the book that was still in my arms into it distractedly.

"No." He moved over to Ava. She was trembling as her gaze bounced between us. "You go for the bike. I know you've been eyeing it. You won't stand a chance if he finds you now.

"He doesn't care about us right now. We'll try and get some supplies quickly, and we'll follow. I can distract them if they find us, and Ava can get out."

"No." It Ava's her turn to deny. "No way. I'm not leaving you behind, Cary, not going to happen," she cried as she put her hand on his chest. He looked startled at the contact, then a look of hope stole over his face before he shut it down again. Hard.

"Ok, Ava and I are sticking together. We're going to have to walk out of here. We'll hide until we can escape. Then we'll follow you, head north, and only travel at night," he instructed, as he squared his shoulders and moved to look out the window.

Ava nodded at me with a sudden focus. "My uncle has a farm in north Greensborough, Luke Fischer. It's not too far. We could walk there in a few days.

"If you can get there, he'll keep you safe until we meet you. Give him my name and this bracelet. He'll recognize it. Tell him I'm coming." Ava ripped the bluebird charm bracelet from her wrist and stuffed it in my pocket.

"I can't–" I tried to stop her, pushing her arm away.

"Maia," she yelled, interrupting me as she forced the bracelet into my pocket and grabbed my face with her hands to get me to look at her. I'd never heard her yell before. She looked like she might slap me if I didn't listen. She had furious, desperate tears in her eyes.

"You're my only friend." Then she grabbed me in a fierce, bone-shattering hug that took my breath away.

"I know you will find me out there. You're the strongest, bravest woman I've ever met. But you're out of time. You have to go now, please, please." She begged as she pushed me away roughly.

Cary stepped back up behind her, supporting her with his solid strength. I knew from watching him all this time that he would do anything to protect her.

I didn't want to go and face this world alone. Especially now, when I knew I had a friend. But I knew they were right. What I had in my bag wouldn't be enough for the three of us, and we couldn't all take the bike. If Ronan spotted me now, I would end up mated or dead.

And so I ran without looking back, but with silent tears streaming down my face.

Two

I eyed the closed gate across the road with apprehension. It was barring me from either my salvation or my doom. I had been hiding in a big, leafy bush for hours, watching, waiting for a sign. Of what exactly, I didn't know. That it was safe somehow, that it wasn't a trap.

I could see people moving in the fields through a tiny gap in the trees beyond the gate. More details had revealed themselves to me as the world had lightened with the rosy dawn.

The gate appeared to belong to a working farm.

"Come on, Maia, move along already," I muttered, then caught myself and shook my head. I hadn't spoken to a soul in days. I didn't need to start talking to myself. It wasn't a good sign.

I needed to focus. I knew I was vulnerable here. But something drew me to this farm gate and kept me rooted to the spot. Maybe it was a glimpse of my past in the dawn light. I had grown up on a farm before I was ripped from my life and everyone I knew.

I could hear the people in the distant fields faintly calling each other. I thought I caught a hint of carefree laughter and the scent of freshly turned earth passing me by on a gentle breeze. I strained to hear more, trying to catch that elusive, mesmerizing sound again.

I tried to remember the last time I had heard genuine laughter, the spontaneous kind that came from the heart and was full of warmth.

My gramps had laughed the night before he died. That was over three years ago. I remembered it now. He was laughing at his own terrible joke so hard that he had doubled over with tears and struggled to breathe. I had just shaken my head with fond amusement at the time, but the memory tore at my heart now.

I caught a whiff of oranges and pinched a soft spot on my inner arm hard enough to bruise. Focus goddammit. My mind was wandering too easily, exhaustion making my mind fuzzy. My thoughts felt like spun cotton candy, disappearing quickly and leaving nothing on the tongue but a memory.

I forcefully returned my attention to the problem at hand. The fence. The gate.

I didn't know if this could be Ava's uncle's farm. I thought I was near Greensborough, but I wasn't sure. I'd passed some other small farms. But they'd looked poor and neglected compared to this one.

We didn't talk about our pasts, but Ava seemed like she had come from a wealthy family, and I knew Greensborough was a well-off town, so I figured his farm would be more extensive and well-kept. I was only guessing, though.

There was no giant sign anywhere announcing Luke Fischer's Farm. I mean, would that be too much to ask?

But I knew I needed to find somewhere safe soon. Every day I spent alone out here increased my chances of getting caught. I was a fluffy little bunny rabbit in the wilderness, surrounded by predators. A delicious-smelling one, too.

I had considered going over the fence when I first came across it in the early morning hours, looking for a haven to rest for the day. But when I had gotten close, I had felt, more than heard, the low electric buzz of the metal as the hairs on my skin rose.

I was intrigued by the subtle show of power. Nobody had enough electricity anymore to waste on a fence, not since the Crash. It had now been over a week since the power progressively went out around the country.

From what I had seen while hiding and watching, people with solar panels and a battery were faring better than others. But many had learned to be stealthy with how they used it.

A lit-up house at night was a beacon for trouble. People were scared. Some still thought the power was coming back, and the authorities were coming to help. For the last week, though, there has been only silence.

Things were getting bad, and I could only imagine how much worse it could get. People will need to choose between cooking their food or protecting their homes. That's if they manage to keep any power. Or find any food.

I missed food, any food. I rubbed my empty stomach absently. I was no longer picky. I'd tried to ransack a dumpster in a random town yesterday, but someone had already cleared it out.

There hadn't been any lights behind this fence last night. I had hoped it was abandoned when I came across it in the predawn darkness. At least they had learned some of the new rules of survival.

I was getting desperate. I was tired of sleeping outdoors, but I hadn't yet been desperate enough to risk trying to break into anywhere habitable.

I brushed my hair out of my face and noticed my hands. I was filthy. I didn't even want to know about the state of my hair. I'd managed to wash up quickly when I'd passed a bend in the river a day ago. But it hadn't been enough to make me feel clean.

I knew I needed to move. I'd been sitting here so long, straining for glimpses through the gate, that it was now daylight, and outside of these bushes, there was little coverage and a lot of danger.

My situation wasn't going to improve by sitting here all day, trying to capture a memory and make it real.

I stretched out my legs as far as I could inside the bush, trying to ease the burn I still felt from my days of riding through the endless darkness. I could feel a fine shake in my body, and I think burnout might be imminent.

I needed to find somewhere safe. I didn't know how long I could last without help, but trusting was hard. I had trouble trusting before the

Crash. It was way more complicated now. I didn't want to end up tied up in someone's basement or worse.

I almost swore out loud and clapped my hand over my mouth as movement at the gate caught my eye. There was someone there. A cold sweat settled over my neck.

I was trapped now. If I moved, they would see me. My options had disappeared in my hesitation. My only hope was to stay perfectly still. I took slow, shallow breaths and tried desperately to slow my racing heart as I heard a clicking noise and the gate rapidly slid open.

Three men moved through it stealthily, guns raised. They appeared to be betas, as they didn't have the stature or scent of an alpha. The middle man looked like he was in his forties, maybe. He had salt and pepper hair and was solidly built, a definite silver fox.

From watching how he moved and his steely gaze, he was either ex-military or police. The two young men flanking him were not much more than boys.

They walked in my direction, and my heart almost beat out of my chest. I could hear my blood pounding in my ears in a wild rhythm. I didn't know if they'd seen me. My best bet was to stay quiet.

At a gesture, the older man positioned himself in front of the bush, gun cocked, while the other two circled behind. I was surrounded. I had run from my doom, only to find a similar fate.

I heard movement to my side and inched my head around slightly, achingly slow, my heart in my mouth. A glint of metal on the ground caught my eye.

Shit, my bike was lying in the open next to the bush, shining brightly in the morning sun. My exhaustion had made me careless. It had been dark when I dropped it to investigate the fence, and I had forgotten to drag it under when I returned to the bushes.

I fought the urge to giggle hysterically.

"This wasn't here yesterday. I was on duty in the afternoon," the boy at my side claimed casually, kicking the bike lazily with his foot. Like this wasn't the scariest moment of my life.

Well, in reality, it probably wasn't. I've hidden from worse. But that doesn't make my current predicament any less real.

He swiveled his head to look up and down the empty road. I could see the first man still in front of me out of the corner of my eye, and his unflinching gaze was fixed directly on the bush. I would have no element of surprise if I ran.

"Are you coming out, or do we need to drag you out?" he asked as he parted the bushes in front of me with his gun and stared me directly in the eye.

"Hey Dave, have we caught a little rabbit hiding in the bushes?" a cocky young voice taunted behind me. He had me pegged right, straight off the bat. "We haven't had a fresh rabbit in a few days. I could eat rabbit for dinner tonight."

"It's a woman, and my name's 'Sir' to you," the man in front of me, who I now knew was Dave, replied as he continued staring at me steadily but not unkindly.

"What in the ever-loving fuck? What's a woman doing out here on her own?" asked the young man behind me in surprise. "Let me see."

"We don't know that she's alone, dipshit," the silver fox replied as he finally took his eyes off me and glared at the young man. "Have you checked the perimeter yet? Or is the idea of a woman enough for you to forget all your training? Pay attention," he demanded like he'd instructed cocky young guys a million times.

"Sorry, Sir," Dipshit exclaimed. I haven't caught his name and can't see him, but he will forever be Dipshit to me now. "Beck, on me," he called as he moved away. Beck appeared to roll his eyes and follow, taking a quick peek at me in the bush as he went.

"So, are you alone?" the man in front of me asked, moving his gun to his back as he kneeled and returned his attention to me. "I have no intention of hurting you unless you give me a reason to," he stated calmly, "and the idiots have gone."

I'd been caught and I wasn't sure what to do. It was never a good idea to tell a stranger you were alone, but lying might make it worse. My indecision and fear had my limbs frozen.

When I didn't respond, he sighed deeply. "My name's Dave, but you probably already figured that out. You look like a smart girl, but you also look tired and hungry, and my knees aren't what they used to be, so can we please move this along," he asked as he held out his hand.

I think he's lying about his knees. He looks fitter than most betas half his age. His eyes, which appeared stern at first, now twinkled with humor.

"Come on, sweetie," he coaxed as he smiled kindly at me.

That smile utterly transfixed me. I made an impulsive decision and took Dave's hand. He helped pull me out of the bush and steadied me when my legs wobbled.

"What can I call you?" Dave asked.

"Maia," I croaked out from my dry throat. I noted he didn't ask my name, just what he could call me. I figured he had already worked out I was running from somewhere, but I didn't have the energy to make up a fake name I would have to remember.

I was dirty, my clothing was torn, and I was sure I looked wild and half-starved. I was used to being leered at and propositioned by men, but he didn't say anything as he looked me over. He just looked like he was trying to figure me out.

It was probably hard to get a read on me under the giant men's shirt I was wearing. It was kindly donated from a store that no longer needed it, given the smashed front windows and abandoned air.

"Look, Maia, this isn't my place, and I'm breaking every protocol bringing you inside, but I don't think the boys will mind." I could tell he was trying to put me at ease, but the thought of the boys and the interest dipshit had clearly expressed before even seeing me had me rattled.

I was taking a considerable risk spending time around men behind big-ass gates, even beta men.

"I don't have anything to trade, and I'm not willing to..., to...," I stammered as I looked where the boys had gone and twisted my hands. I couldn't get the words out, but he knew what I meant. From what I'd seen, the post-Crash world wasn't kind to women, even betas.

"It's okay, honey. Nobody here will make you do anything you don't want to, but there's no free ride. You may have to work for it if you want a bed and food, and by work, I mean with your hands in the field," he elaborated and waved his hands in the general direction of the gate behind him.

"I'm looking for a farm that belongs to my friend's uncle. She told me to meet her there." I didn't want to give away too much, but I figured it wouldn't hurt to let him know someone in the area knew me and was expecting me. Plus, it would help to know where I was and if I had miraculously stumbled across the right place.

"His name is Luke Fischer. Is this his farm?"

Dave shook his head sadly. "Sorry, honey. I don't know any Luke Fischer, but I'm fairly new to the area. Someone inside might know more.

"Look, you're more than welcome to continue on your way, but I get the impression by how long you've been sitting here that you're lost and exhausted," he said while shifting restlessly on his feet.

I didn't mind people being direct, and I didn't think he meant it unkindly from the way he was still looking at me, sadly. Then it dawned on me that he knew how long I'd been sitting here.

I looked at him for a beat, before I asked, "You saw me before you came out?" I was disappointed, I had thought I was being so careful.

He shrugged indifferently. "We have infrared security cameras, and someone's always watching. We could see something out here, but I didn't know who or what."

"Who has infrared security cameras on a farm?" I blurted out rudely, then covered my mouth with my hand. My hard-taught manners obviously fled with me when I ran from the Palace.

"You'll have to come in to find out," he laughed as he turned on his heel, assuming that I would follow, "but I promise, there's nothing weird or illegal going on here."

He stopped at the gate when he realized I wasn't behind him. I was busy looking up and down the road, weighing my options, but in my heart, I knew there weren't any.

"Look, it's a sustainable farm that sells food farm-to-table. A group of friends runs it, and they had a lot of self-sufficient stuff set up even before the Crash. Not that I pretend to know what even half of it is or does."

"Seriously, worst case, you do some work, get some decent food into you, and then head on your way and continue looking for your friend. From what I've seen, the whole country's in a bad way, and it will get worse. Right now, I don't think you'll get many better offers out here." He was brutally honest, but I liked that.

I knew he was right, and I desperately needed help. But after everything I had been through, it was hard to trust. I was wary of exchanging one unbearable cage for a new one. The thought of being trapped there terrified me.

I was dying to ask if there were any alphas inside. I needed to avoid them at all costs. Dave had mentioned the military, and the military was full of alphas. But it would look suspicious if I did. Also, Dave hadn't seemed to pick up that I was an omega. I was safer trying to pass as a beta, and a beta wouldn't worry about alphas.

So I'd go in and avoid attention. I'd done it before. I'd get my strength back up, then if it wasn't right, I'd find a way to leave. I'd done that before, too, as evidenced by my mad, adrenaline-fuelled, bike-powered escape from the Palace.

I sighed and motioned towards the gate. "By all means, let's move this along then." I smirked at him before recalling my earlier urging to myself to move along and shook my head.

He laughed again as he turned and walked through the gate. Deep and rich, it was a beautiful sound, reminding me of happier days.

I decided I liked his laugh, a lot.

Three

I grabbed my bike, wheeled it inside the gate, and parked it under a tree. There was no way I was leaving my only form of transportation outside.

"You can bring that down and put it in the shed if you'd like to keep it out of the weather," he offered, gesturing down the hill.

"Thanks, but I'll just leave it here." There was no way I was putting it in a shed that was likely to get locked. If I needed to make a quick getaway, I'd need it near the only exit I knew about.

Dave narrowed his eyes at me but kept moving. He seemed to be a savvy dude. I'm pretty sure not much would get past him. I'd have to be careful.

We walked down the hill slowly, and my view of the fields opened. There were a few more workers near the gate than I'd seen earlier, but not a lot. Then we rounded a bend.

"Holy crap, this place is huge," I gasped. Dave just chuckled. Not my finest moment, my omega tutors would have given me the strap for that outburst, but the size of the place had taken me by surprise.

It was broken up into sections with fields of what looked like corn, oats, vegetables, and fruit trees. The dirt was brown and rich, and the vibrant crops stood out amongst it. Even the air smelt fresh and full of life, carried on the slight breeze.

The bounty spread down the hill and into the small valley below that also held a pond and what looked like an old mill. There appeared to be livestock barns in the distance, and I could just make out a river at the border and the forest beyond.

It was deceptive from the outside. It looked like a nothing fence surrounding a small plot of land off the road.

Yet it was a working Elysium on the inside. It was how I imagined the final resting place of heroic or pure souls would look. Who wanted a glorious and useless park to wander in eternally? Give me a picturesque farm and something to do any day. It made me yearn for a home I'd left long ago.

I sighed when I realized we'd have to walk down the hill on my shaky legs. When we reached the bottom, we walked straight into a stunning building with high ceilings, timber beams, and glass.

It was filled with beautiful dawn light and designed with a stunning mix of modern and rural tones, lots of charcoal mixed with sage greens and timber. It looked like a high-end function center for weddings and such.

We walked through it to a gorgeous commercial kitchen with every conceivable modern appliance I had ever dreamt of and a handful of women busily working. It was a dream, and I could happily hug every shiny, stainless steel surface and appliance.

But all the women stopped working and looked at me one by one as they noticed me, and all conversation tapered off. I swear I could hear crickets. I wanted to hide, but there was nowhere to go. This wasn't lying low.

A tall, statuesque woman with gorgeous dark hair approached us. She was stylishly dressed in skin-tight jeans, a very low-cut top, and wedge-heeled sandals. Who wore heels since the Crash? Seriously. What in the blazes would she do if she needed to run? I don't think she's spent much time outside the gates recently.

A scowl marred her gorgeous face as she confidently approached us, and I instantly knew she would be one to watch. I'd read about betas like this. She had mean girl written all over her face.

"What in the hell is this," she snarled at Dave while pointing at me viciously with a manicured hand. What, not who. Nice. Like I said. Mean girl. I wanted to call her out, but that would only draw more attention. She was already making a scene I didn't need.

"Ignore the skank, Maia," I muttered under my breath. But not quietly enough because Dave was still beside me and glanced at me, trying to hide his smile.

"Sirena, this is Maia. She's going to be staying for a little while." Dave moved his hands up and down in Sirena's direction, in the universal motion to 'calm your farm,' trying to defuse the situation.

"Do the boys know about this?" Sirena squawked. Seriously, she squawked like a high-pitched bird—a super annoying one. We were not going to be friends.

"I'm just about to clear it with…" Dave started to explain just before a radio I hadn't noticed on his belt started to buzz, and I heard, "Beta 6 for Beta 2, come in." Before he could reply, it buzzed again with "Beta 6 for Beta 2, we have a problem at the fence."

Dave grabbed the radio and answered, "Beta 2 here, what kind of a problem?"

"Fence down, I repeat, fence down in quadrant 4. We need you up here, now," came the reply. I recognized Dipshit's voice, even with his words tripping all over each other in his panic. Whoever he was, he wasn't a problem solver.

Dave turned and glared at me, so I put my hands up quickly and exclaimed, "It wasn't me. I heard the buzzing at the gate. There's no way I'd touch that fence. Besides, you saw me approach. I don't know where the cameras or quadrant four are, but I only went near the gate and the bush, I swear."

It was the most I'd said to him since we met. I didn't know if that made me sound suspicious or not, but I didn't like the way he was looking at me. Like I'd betrayed him.

Dave looked torn, but he had to go.

"Sirena, give her something to eat and get her cleaned up. She's welcome here but keep an eye on her until we figure out what's happening," he demanded of the woman. Then he gave me a sympathetic look, turned, and left the room.

Sirena had a smug look when she finally turned to me that I wanted to scratch off her face. But I didn't have the energy. The room started to sway after my long walk, and I didn't think a chair was in my near future if it was up to her to provide it.

"So, what do we have here?" she drawled while slowly looking me up and down. Great, we were back to what again. I didn't have the strength for any mean girl attitude, but I reminded myself that I needed to blend in and not draw more attention.

Not sure that was possible, given that every woman in the room was still openly staring at me. Great start, Maia.

So I attempted to put my nicest (cough, fakest) smile on my face and replied, "My name's Maia. I'm happy to meet you all. Dave found me out front. I passed out in a bush when I couldn't ride my bike any further."

They were all still looking at me like I was the newest exhibit at the zoo. Sirena just cocked her brow. I needed to be honest as much as possible, so I didn't get caught in a lie. That would not go down well.

I took a deep breath and continued, "I was trying to hide for the day. I got separated from my friend in the chaos out there, and I'm not quite sure where I am. I'm trying to make it to my friend's uncle's farm in Greensborough. I haven't eaten or slept in a few days. Dave said I could get something to eat and a night's sleep here before I head out again. I hope that's okay?"

A cool-looking young woman, who appeared to be about my age, spoke up in the back. She had gorgeous hair in flowing shades of purple and deep red that shouldn't work together but looked stunning on her.

"You're not far from Greensborough. It's the next big town over, but it's quite a way on foot. If you followed the main road, you were heading in the right direction. You're welcome to have something to eat. Come over here, and I'll grab you something."

I smiled at her gratefully, a genuine smile this time, and she smiled back.

"Not so fast, Lexie," Sirena sneered. "You know the rules. Nobody gets a free ride. And unless you've got something of value in your mangy backpack you're willing to trade, we'll have to figure something else out."

"The boys may offer you a bed for the night if you're willing to spread your slut legs, but from your dirty look, maybe not. Regardless, that isn't going to work for us women in the kitchen, so it looks like you're going to have to work for it another way," she railed.

Wow, I'd known her for minutes, and she was straight out of the gate slut-shaming me. Nice work. It took skill to work in a slut-shame that quickly. I was almost impressed.

"You can work in the garden outside. It needs weeding," Sirena continued, oblivious to my amused face. "I assume you can tell the difference between a weed and a vegetable. You look like you enjoy rolling around in the dirt, so you should be able to figure it out."

"And what will you be doing, Sirena, while she's working?" Lexie sassed, swinging her gorgeous hair and raising her pierced eyebrow. I wanted to straight up hug that girl right about now.

"Not that it's any of your business, Lexie, but I'll be supervising," Sirena said. "Dave left me in charge of her, and I'll put her to work how I see fit."

Lexie just looked at her smugly. "He may have left you in charge of her, but he also said to give her something to eat and let her get cleaned up." Forget the hug. I was going to squeeze the shit out of her. Then maybe sit in her lap and cry for a while. She was my new hero.

"So," Sirena shrugged nonchalantly, faking an innocent tone. "He didn't say when. She can eat after she's earned it, not before. She's going to get filthy again anyway, so no point cleaning up first either. Besides, who's to say she wouldn't eat and then take off."

"Anyway, you may be Leif's sister, but I'm Damon's girlfriend. So I'd shut up if you want to keep your easy kitchen duties, Lexie, instead of being out in the fields in the sun all day," she threatened while examining her perfectly polished red nails.

The other women stared at Lexie and discreetly moved away from Sirena as Lexie glared like she was about to throw down. I jumped in quickly to take the attention away from Lexie. No need for both of us to go down.

"It's fine. I don't mind hard work. I grew up on a farm. Just show me what you want me to do."

"Of course you did," Sirena sighed heavily as she threw her arms up in the air. Wow, the mean was strong with this one. So was the drama.

I followed Sirena straight outside but snuck a look at Lexie, who winked and mouthed, 'Find me later' behind Sirena's back. It was official. I'd found my new bestie. At least for the next day or two, before I took off. I doubt Lexie would want to come with me. Despite having to deal with Sirena, she had it good here. It was a pity I couldn't stay.

I didn't mind working outdoors, but I knew it would be tough in the sun all day, given that I hadn't drunk much water the last few days. I didn't like my chances of Sirena giving me a drink if I asked, so I didn't bother.

With filtration plants offline, drinking unknown water was a risk, but these guys seemed to have plenty to spare. I'd even spied water coming from the taps inside. Most of the water supply had stopped everywhere else days ago.

They must have ample water tanks and some kind of pump. Most people outside were desperately praying for rain.

"So here's the garden. There are tools around somewhere. I'm going to lie down under the tree and read a book," Sirena said as she waved her hand around without looking. I seethed on the inside. She didn't deserve books. Books were for nice people. I wanted to grab her book and smack her with it, but I wouldn't. I didn't want to hurt the book.

"Which section do you want me to weed?" I asked absently, rookie mistake.

"All of it, of course," she huffed over her shoulder as she walked away.

Then, she stopped, turned, and eyed me speculatively. "By the way, if you're here because you think your damsel in distress routine will seduce my alphas, think again. They're not here right now, and you'll be long gone before they get back." She flipped her hair this time as she sashayed over to the tree.

But I was too frozen to notice her trying to prove how much sexier she was than me with her swaying hips. They taught that shit at the Omega Palace, and I wasn't a fan.

Alphas. Plural. Here. My brain was stuck on those three words. "Don't panic, don't panic," I breathed. I was totally panicking. I could feel my face going numb from hyperventilating. If I were caught here by an alpha and they got a whiff of my scent, I could end up trapped, again. Stuck in an endless cycle of them trying to compel and break me.

She said they were gone now, though, which means I had dodged a bullet—a whole magazine of bullets right out of an Uzi. I needed to focus on getting some food and getting the hell out of here. I could sleep on the road again. It was safer than the risk of coming across alphas.

I forced myself to get moving before Sirena noticed I wasn't working. I grabbed some tools and headed for the first row of the garden. It was in full sun, and the kitchen garden was huge. It was going to be a long, painful day. "You've endured worse. You're tough. Just get it done," I muttered to myself as I knelt in the dirt.

I bent over but stilled when a giant dog came loping around the corner and headed straight for me. He was gorgeous, all creamy, shaggy fur with a black muzzle and paws. The dog looked like he could do some damage, though. He was as tall as me while I was kneeling, and I wasn't sure if he was friendly or not.

He approached me confidently, gave me a thorough sniffing and a lick, and then plopped down on the ground next to me. He seemed to be keeping an eye out for any movement around us. I shrugged, gave him a careful scratch behind the ear, and got to work.

I started on the corner of the garden closest to the kitchen window. I could hear the women gossiping inside, although I couldn't see them.

"I don't know what the hell Damon sees in her. He deserves better," one woman griped.

"He deserves me," another announced, sounding gleeful about it. "I know he's all stern and growly alpha, but I love the hot ones that are a little bit dark. Those lips, I bet he could do dangerous things with those lips. I reckon I could even take his knot with a bit of practice."

Uggh. I didn't understand betas being obsessed with the knot at the base of an alpha's dick that became engorged and highly sensitive during sex. Only omegas were biologically designed to take it. We had a hollow behind our pubic bone with an extra nerve that caused an intense sexual high when the knot was locked in place. But then you're stuck there until the knot deflates.

They tried to teach me at the Palace that it's the pinnacle of my existence, but being locked onto an alpha with no escape sounds like a dangerous place to be. No insane orgasm was worth it. And for a beta, it could be intensely painful.

I heard a new voice pipe up. "You know Sirena's with Hunter as well, right, and that's a damn shame. That red hair and cheeky grin, you just know he's going to be fun in bed and get up to kinky shit. She's hogging all the alphas," she complained, but not seriously. She had laughter in her voice.

"Not Leif," another one chimed in. "My god, he's hot with all those stacked muscles and long blonde hair, but he's only got eyes for Max. Leif's such a giant but a big marshmallow. He blushes so cutely when they're busted making out. I tell you, the two of them together, I'd love to be the meat in that man sandwich. Do you think they're into women too? Do we have a chance?"

"I don't know, but I hope they are," another woman giggled. She sounded younger. "I know he's not an alpha, but Max does it for me with the hot nerd look when he puts on those sexy black glasses. Yes, please," she sighed.

Finally, a voice I recognized as Lexie cut in, followed by footsteps stomping past the window like she'd just come from another room. 'Is it any of our business if they're into men, or women, or whatever they get up to in private?' she asked with a stern note in her voice.

"Sorry, Lex," a girl apologized. "I know you're tight with them."

"Look, I know they're all hot as sin, but they helped each of you when you needed a safe space and never asked for a thing in return. They gave you security, a roof over your heads, plus a great job. They deserve better than to be talked about like that."

"We know, Lex, we're sorry," another chimed in, sounding sheepish.

Lexie sighed. "Sorry, I didn't mean to jump down your throats. They're just Leif's best friends. They're all like brothers to me, and I get a bit protective.

"Julio out in the cornfield, though, he's fair game," Lexie laughed. "Man, can he swing a scythe. Anyone want to head over and ask stupid questions about corn with me while he's working later?"

The girls all laughed with her, but I couldn't hear them well anymore as I moved further down the row. I filled a bucket with weeds and pruned plants that needed it as I went—giving each one some love.

I was perplexed. The girls didn't talk about the alphas here like they feared them. I suppose they're all betas, but still. They seemed to respect them, especially Lexie. What had she meant about the alphas helping them all? I was intrigued, but there were no answers out here, only endless weeds.

Sirena briefly disappeared with a flirty, young male beta during the morning, leaving another leering middle-aged male beta to watch me for a while.

I might have been in trouble if I wasn't coated in dirt and mud. As it was, he barely took his eyes off my legs for the entire hour he watched me closely. I'm sure he could map them if he needed to.

I cursed, again, that I was wearing cut-off denim shorts that I had made from an old pair of jeans. I needed to find some warmer and less revealing clothing before the weather turned colder. For now, I at least had my borrowed check shirt on over my tank top to keep the sun off my arms and prying eyes off my chest.

Luckily my doggy companion had growled at the skeezy beta whenever he came near me, earning the good boy lots of pats and scratches behind his ear.

When Sirena returned, the beta gave her a long look, almost like a warning, before he turned and left. I had breathed easier after that, I could handle Sirena, but the strange man had given me bad vibes.

Lexie had snuck me a sandwich, some sultanas, and a bottle of water later while Sirena napped. Giving the dog an affectionate pat as she passed. I had scoffed it all gratefully, and it had kept me conscious through the afternoon, but it had barely touched the edges of my hunger or thirst.

Unfortunately, I hadn't seen Dave again. I hoped I'd see him tonight, and the fence situation had sorted itself.

I had finally done it, though. I had lasted the day and endured it all. After eight hours, my back hurt, my arms wouldn't lift, my legs wobbled dangerously, and my vision was forming black spots as I headed inside, following Sirena.

When we reached the commercial kitchen, I noticed we were the only ones there. So I couldn't count on Lexie coming to my rescue again.

Sirena turned to me haughtily and ordered, "Clean up at the far sink and get started on prepping vegetables. We need that whole tub diced. You're on kitchen duty tonight, and don't even think about stealing any food. I'm watching you, and so are others." Then she deliberately looked at a camera in the corner of the ceiling and stalked out of the room through double swinging doors.

I almost lost it. I couldn't. I was tough, but this was too much. My desperate escape from the Palace, days of little food or sleep, hiding every day terrified of being found and desperately riding every night without really knowing where I was going, now today. My body was done. It had nothing left.

I lurched over to a large metal industrial table with the tub of vegetables, ripped off my shirt, and laid my upper body across it before I collapsed on the floor. It was blessedly cool, and I needed a minute to think about what I would do next.

Four

I was frustrated. We'd not long left on a dangerous reconnaissance run and had to turn around. Luckily we weren't that far from home when we got the call, but it wasn't the point.

We didn't have enough security when we left the farm, but I hesitated to split up my team. I needed to know my teammates had my back when we were out there, and I trusted my team, Leif, Hunter, and Max, with my life.

We'd been to hell and back together, and it had formed a bond stronger than any family I'd known. Leif, Hunter, and I were alphas, while Max was a beta, but he was no less an essential and loved member of our team.

We desperately needed some more reliable security at the farm, though. We depended on an ex-army sergeant, highly trained but retired, and three untested, barely trained cadets when we weren't home.

It had been enough before the Crash, but not anymore.

We'd fixed the fence, done a sweep of the perimeter, and unloaded the truck with some supplies we scavenged while out. Last night's high winds had blown a tree onto the fence, and a whole section was down. It was in an area without cameras, so no one had noticed.

There was evidence of some animal movement through the downed fence, but no people, thankfully. We'd been lucky.

Max was going to look at rigging some alarms to alert us if the fence went down again, but it would take him some time to figure out with the limited supplies we had at hand.

Max was a geek but also a genius when it came to technology. It was mostly down to him that we were surviving the Crash. Max was what women liked to call a 'hot nerd' with his short, dark, tousled hair, caramel skin, and perfect bow lips. When he put on his black-rimmed glasses that highlighted his hazel eyes, they all sighed and fell all over themselves.

On the surface, he looked like the perfect boy next door they all wanted to corrupt, but underneath, he had the body of an athlete and the tattoos of a bad boy that drove them wild. Not that he saw himself that way. He was clueless around women and was oblivious to the attention.

It had been a long day, and now I was ready for a home-brewed beer, some hot food, and my bed, in that order.

I stalked in through the door alongside Max. I could feel a glare on my face, and I was helpless to do anything about it. It wasn't my natural expression, but it felt like an almost permanent feature these days.

My dream of a quiet life on a prosperous farm had come together beautifully, with my best friends working at my side every day. But it had all gone to hell along with the electricity.

I noticed Leif and Hunter sneak in behind us out of the corner of my eye, trying to head discretely for the bar like a couple of frat boys.

I don't know how Leif thought he could sneak anywhere. While he was generally a quiet, calm guy, the man was a giant. He was taller than me, and I was almost six-four. He was built, too, with muscles on his muscles. With all that long blond hair, pale blue eyes, and Viking good looks, he stood out wherever he went. He was our break the door down, point guy for a reason. There was nothing subtle about him.

Hunter, on the other hand, was the opposite. While his bright red hair, a smattering of freckles, cheeky green eyes, and mischievous smirk drew attention whenever he wanted, particularly around the ladies, he could shut it all down in a heartbeat and turn into a lethal predator.

He was cunning and stealthy. He was also our sniper and tracker. He was like day and night, all wrapped up in one mysterious bundle, but most only saw the light and assumed he was an entitled prince. If you saw the dark, it was often the last thing you did.

Dave headed over when he spotted me. Since the Crash, we've used the function center as an informal meeting point.

I could almost taste that beer.

I heard a screech, and Sirena ran towards me, overtaking Dave. "When did you get back?" she squealed and threw herself at me.

Dammit. Sirena and I had recently had an arrangement that we had both agreed was casual. It had been fun, briefly, until she had slowly started behaving like she was my girlfriend. I'd hired her to do the farm's marketing and events before we hooked up, which made ending our arrangement awkward.

Not my wisest decision to screw someone I paid, but she was screwing Hunter as well, and she had said she wasn't looking for anything serious. So I thought it would be fine.

I'd since called it off, and we hadn't been together recently, but she wasn't letting it go, despite everything she said at the start. Now, she was taking it way too far, and the Crash had made everything even more complicated.

I gave her a brief hug and disentangled myself. I could see Max rolling his eyes beside me. He wasn't her biggest fan, and neither was Leif. I didn't blame them. Luckily, Leif and Hunter were distracted by the delights hiding in the bar.

"You're going to have to talk to her again," Max murmured as we walked away.

I hung my head slightly and rubbed at my hair. "I know, man, but not tonight," I said. I could feel weariness dragging at me and my emotions rising. I took a deep breath and tamped them back down.

I always had to keep a tighter leash on myself when I was tired. My emotions rose more quickly, and I was less able to control them. It was an exhausting and vicious cycle. The more tired I was, the harder I had to work to keep myself contained, which made me tired.

And I could never, ever let myself go. I had a beast that lived inside me, desperate to break his chains and destroy everything in sight.

In the past week since the Crash, the intense responsibility I felt for everyone who lived and worked on the farm had left me feeling stressed and worn out. I felt like I was on the edge of something disastrous if I didn't get some sleep and control back, but it was unlikely to happen anytime soon.

We faced many problems, and survival would only get harder the longer the power stayed out.

I turned to Dave as he walked over to me, and I sighed deeply. I needed to get my head back in the game. I was tired, and my thoughts were easily distracted tonight.

Dave was likely to be just as tired. He'd been overseeing security all day while discreetly checking the whole farm for intruders, trying not to worry anyone. It had been a long day for us all.

"The fence is back up, man, and the electricity is re-connected. So you can rest easy now. Is there anything else you need to let me know before the night team takes over?" I asked. I wasn't expecting much as an answer as I clasped him on the shoulder affectionately.

Dave was usually on top of everything to do with security, despite being severely under-resourced. I don't know what we'd do without him.

Dave had been our superior at one point and had trained our punk asses when we were bratty newbies in the military. We all looked up to him and had a deep respect for him that he had earned. Dave was one of the few people we trusted outside our circle and was now more of a father figure to us. He was part of the family we chose.

Some of our field hands took turns rotating on the night security shift. It was mainly watching the cameras and a lookout on the gate. Their main job was to call one of the day team members or us if anything shady was happening. It had worked so far, but we needed a better solution. The world beyond our gates was going to hell fast. We were lucky we had evaded notice so far.

And my thoughts were straying again. Dave responded, but I hadn't heard what he was saying.

"Sorry Dave, what did you say?" I asked as I shook my head to focus my thoughts. I could feel the beast rising and pushing at me. Something was setting him off more than usual, and I was too tired to figure out what it was.

"I'll make a long story short because you know I love repeating myself." He sounded gruff, but he looked at me sheepishly, which was unusual and made me think something was up. He was usually straightforward, to the point of being abrupt, but at the moment, he looked nervous.

Sirena snickered loudly from where she was perched on the edge of a nearby table, watching us closely. "Oh, Dave's just trying to tell you about Little Miss Dirty he dragged in here earlier. It was quite a sight, let me tell you."

I didn't like her tone towards Dave. It lacked respect, which rubbed me the wrong way.

'Dave, please explain whatever Sirena just said,' I demanded. He grimaced, but he knew my ire wasn't directed at him.

"The night team saw something moving near the gate on the cameras last night, near dawn, so they called me. I checked it out on the recording, but it had moved into the bushes across the road by that time. It was too big to be an animal, though," he said.

"The night team did a great job picking it up on the infra-red cameras. It was hard to see and moving unusually," he explained further, but too slowly for my liking. It wasn't like him to drag things out.

"Great. I'll thank them later, but can we get to the point? I'm tired, and I'm not sure why I'm only hearing about this now when I've been back for hours," I snapped. I needed that beer and to stop taking my fatigue out on those around me who didn't deserve it, but I couldn't deal with much more tonight. I'd apologize tomorrow.

He got straight to the point now. "I monitored it and took the boys out at first light. We went out armed just in case. It turns out it was an exhausted, hungry woman on a bike who took shelter in the bushes. I don't think she had the energy to go any further and needed shelter."

His strange behavior was making me antsy. He didn't get nervous or waffle. I felt a faint vibration against my skin, putting me on high alert. I looked around the room but couldn't find the source of what was unsettling me. Something was different. I could sense it, something more than Dave.

"I know it's against protocol, but I couldn't leave her out there all day. She had no food or water with her, and I didn't think she'd make it another day on her own. She could barely stand. So I brought her in," he said as he looked at me in apprehension, which had me even more on edge as I returned my gaze to him.

My alpha protective instincts exploded. "Hold up a second. You found a stray woman on the side of the road on the same day we had a fence breach, and you just brought her inside? What if she was a decoy and was part of a group?" I yelled, my anger snowballing. Had he let a strange woman into the farm without vetting her? We always vetted new people coming onto the farm.

"Calm down. I didn't find out about the breach until after I had her in the kitchen. I'd sent the younguns out to do a perimeter check, just in case, but I figured it would be better to have her in here where we could keep an eye on her rather than sitting outside the front gate. So I questioned her, and I trusted her story," he said, his back straightening and squaring his shoulders as he defended himself.

"She's harmless," he clarified, maintaining eye contact with me and begging me to trust him. But I was ultimately responsible for protecting everyone inside these gates, which weighed heavily on me. I knew he had a soft spot for young women, particularly those that needed help, after the death of his daughter. But I was worried he was being manipulated.

My senses were all on high alert, and something was setting off my beast. I was struggling to keep him contained.

"Don't tell me to calm down. Where is she now?' I growled, trying not to let my dominance seep out. I could see Sirena squirming with glee, and I knew something was up.

"In the kitchen," Dave said. He looked at me with concern. He knew me well and could tell how close to the edge I was.

I exploded out of my chair. "In the kitchen, where there are knives that could be used as weapons? Who is watching her?" I demanded, losing my battle and some of my dominance leaking out. I could feel it, and fear had me lashing out at the very people I was trying to protect.

I looked around as people started backing away, which fed my fear.

"Damon, man, you need to breathe. You look like you're about to Hulk out," Max scrambled as he tried to talk me down.

I ignored Max and glared at Dave. I could feel my dominance starting to batter him.

"I left her with Sirena and the other ladies. Lexie was there, and you know she can take care of herself and anyone else too."

"Sirena and Lexie are both in here," I growled, louder this time, as darkness crept into my voice.

Dave started to sweat as he looked around, belatedly noticing both Sirena and Lexie. "Who do you have watching her, Sirena?"

I was on the move before I heard her answer. "Everyone stay here."

Five

I could hear a commotion in the next room through the buzzing in my ears. A loud, gruff voice was yelling. Maybe this was my chance to grab the tub of vegetables and flee. The farm was huge. Surely I could hide somewhere for a few hours, eat and rest, then sneak out when it was quiet in the middle of the night. It was a long shot, but it was my best plan.

I heaved myself off the table, quickly scrubbed some water from the tap next to me over my face, hands, and arms, filled my water bottle, and reached for the tub. But my exhausted arms wouldn't lift it, no matter how hard I strained. So I shoved a few carrots in my backpack, grabbed my shirt, and turned towards the back door.

Before I could take more than a lumbering step, I heard the swinging doors smash open behind me, banging heavily against the wall. Heavy footsteps stride through quickly.

I spun around. How could I get caught so quickly? I had thought Sirena was only pranking about someone watching through the camera in the corner.

It was my last thought before all of my attention was taken by the stunning man striding through the doors. He was tall and solidly built. I could see his muscles bulging through a tight black shirt that outlined his broad shoulders and trim waist. His hair was so dark it was almost black, short on the sides but longer on the top, perfect for running hands through and tugging on hard.

His face looked chiseled from marble, all cut jaw, high cheekbones, and a stern, full mouth. He looked like a Greek god come to life. He was too perfect to be mortal. Surely he had been cut from stone.

Not a god, though, I realized belatedly, an alpha, an incredibly dominant alpha. I could feel his restrained dominance crawling over my skin like it was seeking me out. But it didn't make me tremble in fear for once. It lit me up.

He also had the most piercing pale gray eyes I had ever seen, and they were currently cutting right through me. It was too late to run.

"What are you doing there?" he demanded to know, his voice a low deep growl that made me shiver.

The dog appeared from behind me and stopped between us. He faced the alpha like he was going to protect me from him. Although he wasn't barking or growling, he was just observing.

Dominance rolled off the alpha in waves as he strode towards me. Again, I was frozen to the spot. Seriously, I had never frozen in my life as much as I had this day. This shit was getting old.

My body was overwhelmed by his presence. It screamed at me to succumb, to desire, to rage. A wildness I had never known rose in me. I had never reacted so viscerally to an alpha before. It had to be my exhaustion.

As I struggled to breathe and form words, he neared me, and I got a lungful of his scent. It was like lightning in the air, rain in the wind, and the baked earth after a hot day.

The tumultuous, overwhelming scents of a raging storm electrified my body. It was too much when I had so little consciousness left. I saw the black spots in my vision widen and felt my body fall. I fought to stay aware with everything I had, but it was no use.

He reached for me, and the last thing I heard was a roar ripped from his throat as he grabbed me. The world exploded with a flare of white light before something snapped into place in my chest and pulled hard. I was finally caught. Then there was nothing but darkness.

Six

I noticed the woman as soon as I entered the room. She was filthy, Sirena hadn't been lying about that, and she was barely standing as she wavered on her feet. Yet, even with the dirt, I couldn't deny she was an effortless beauty. The word beauty even seemed too dull for this rare vision.

Her blonde wavy hair was a riotous mess, half in and half out of a ponytail. She had the face of an angel, with full luscious pink lips and the tiniest beauty spot dotting above her full upper lip like a guiding star.

She was slim but curvy in a way that made men groan and covet her, and a fair few boys too, I was sure. She looked like something out of a swimsuit calendar. The type that was hiding under mattresses all over the country and pulled out during private moments. Or a farm calendar, maybe, with her cut-off denim shorts and tank top. Her legs went on for days.

Her eyes were a deep, mesmerizing blue, but they looked glazed and unfocused right now, like they might roll back into her head at any moment.

My heart was beating a pounding rhythm, and I felt my chest constrict like the moment before death.

"What are you doing there?" I demanded as I stalked toward her, anger, fear, and adrenaline driving me. My dominance was rising in response and aimed directly at her.

I noticed Bear move out from around the bench and stand between us, watching me with an intent expression. I didn't know what to make of it. Why was he watching me and not her? As if I was the threat when he had long been a fixture at Lexie's side and knew me well.

She faltered as her gaze fixed on me, her eyes widened, and she took a shocked breath. She didn't look afraid, though. She looked electrified.

She opened her mouth as if she was going to speak, but then her eyes rolled back into her head, and she started to drop.

I lunged for her, operating on pure instinct.

As I grabbed her and pulled her towards me, sinking to the floor as I tried to protect her head, my whole body went rigid. A burning light exploded inside my chest that brought no pain, only intense joy and a deep connection to the woman in my arms. The kind of light that transformed everything and re-made you anew.

Her scent exploded into the room, sweet and achingly bright, like summer fruits grown in the sun, oranges, and pineapple, with a hint of cake. She smelt fresh and delicious but also somehow familiar.

She smelt like life, and it cut right through my dark scent. I felt like it was designed just for me as my cock immediately went rigid in my pants, and I felt an overwhelming protectiveness.

Oh dear god, she was an omega, and I was fucked. Why had nobody warned me? Did they not know? How could they not tell?

And not just any omega. Fear sliced me like an arrow, my true mate—someone who was vulnerable to my beast and whose death I wouldn't survive.

I could hear a noise roaring in the room, that I didn't realize was me, and footsteps running.

What the hell was I going to do?

Seven

T he second the roar from the kitchen split the air, Leif and Hunter spun into action from behind the bar they had been raiding. A single glance had them both moving in opposite directions.

Leif barrelled directly towards the double doors, whiskey bottle in one hand and knife in the other, nodding to me on the way. At the same time, Hunter leaped over the counter. He was like a jungle cat, all intense focus and ferocious, explosive speed. He darted towards the front doors, gun already in his hand, aiming to circle to the back of the kitchen and the only other exit.

I didn't need to ask what they were doing or what I needed to do. We all knew our roles well and each other's strengths. We had honed them through countless missions. We worked together on instinct now and almost without thought.

"Dave, move the women behind the bar and get your boys to cover them," I ordered over the gut-wrenching roar from the kitchen.

"Everyone else, grab anything that can be used as a weapon and split up to defend the three doors, including this one. Don't stand down until one of the guys or I tell you. The only current threat is from the kitchen, so your families outside should be safe for now," I explained, trying to keep everyone calm.

I quickly took in everyone in the room and noticed the grim, stern faces, all nodding. Our farm hands, primarily immigrants, had been working together for years and had become a tight-knit community that looked to us for leadership and protection.

Dave was already on the move. 'Dave, if we're not back out in ten minutes, scope out the front doors, then evacuate everyone to the cave." I whisper-yelled over my shoulder as the roar cut off abruptly.

The sudden quiet was eerie in the aftermath as if every sentient creature knew a dangerous predator was nearby.

I headed cautiously for the double doors, grabbing an empty silver serving tray on my way.

"Go, I got this," Dave hissed as he started guiding the women to safety behind the bar.

"I'm coming with you," Lexie whispered, as she dodged Dave and followed behind me, despite my glare. "That girl looks like she's been through enough crap already and may need help. I'm not staying behind."

I sighed in frustration, but I didn't fight her on it. I knew Lexie could take care of herself and would defend any woman at risk, even from us.

The echoes of that roar were still causing shivers up and down my spine. I had never heard agony and rage like it. It could only have come from one person. I needed to know what was happening with my guys.

The kitchen was eerily quiet now. I couldn't hear Damon or Leif, so I needed to try and be covert until I knew what was happening. I edged closer to the far door and pulled it open towards me slowly. I couldn't push it forwards and risk someone on the other side taking me by surprise.

I handed the tray to Lexie and gestured for her to hold it up in the doorway. She figured out what I wanted quickly. She held the shiny tray up in a way that showed me a reflection of the room, but I couldn't make sense of what I saw.

I gestured for Lexie to move back. She put the tray quietly on the ground as I peeked my head around the corner, gun at the ready. It wasn't ideal or exceptionally stealthy, and the guys would kick my ass later.

But I didn't have a choice. As the rear guard in our unit, I usually focussed on the subtle sounds and movements of the guys to lead my actions. The devastating quiet was unnerving me.

What I saw confused the hell out of me. Damon was kneeling on the floor, holding a woman tightly to his chest. I noticed long, dirty legs and a pair of muddy sneakers, but not much else. His head was hanging low. He looked almost defeated, but he was also curled around her protectively.

Leif was on his knees before him, looking intensely at Damon, or was it the girl in his arms? He was breathing shallowly and holding himself very still. I could see Hunter out of the corner of my eye gazing through the back door, watching the woman intently too.

Leif made a discrete stay and guard motion to Hunter but motioned me forward. Hunter shifted to keep the woman and the garden in view, gun at the ready, covering our backs.

I crept through the kitchen, skirting cabinets, trying not to move too suddenly and spook anyone. Lexie was behind me, her hand resting on my back so I'd know where she was. She was calm in a crisis and used to unpredictable situations; I'd give her that.

"Damon, can you hear me?" Leif asked as he kept his eyes on Damon. His posture was tense and watchful. He was ready to move at a moment's notice and defend his friend with his body, with his life, if Damon needed it. And it was no small offer. Leif was towering and deadly, even kneeling, but only to those that endangered his loved ones. For us, he was squishy on the inside.

Damon let out a deep, shuddering breath. He raised his head to look at Leif as I moved around the side of him, keeping Lexie behind me. Damon's face was a surging mix of emotions. Grief, despair, fear, and joy all battling each other. More emotions than he could handle. For as long as I had known him, Damon had kept everything locked down, even with us.

"I need Max to look at the girl, make sure she's okay. Can you let her go, Alpha?" Leif urged. Damon just growled and shook his head, then looked down at her intensely.

The use of the term alpha concerned me. An alpha didn't usually address another alpha that way, and I'd never heard Leif do it. Something was off.

I knelt closer to Damon, and Lexie moved behind Leif. I wasn't sure if Lexie should be here. Damon's mess of emotions seemed intensely private. She never took any shit from Damon, though, and he had a grudging respect for her. We all did. I also knew we might need her from the look of the woman in Damon's arms.

Damon had her face pressed into his neck, and her long, wavy blonde hair covered what little I could see. It was lighter and brighter than Leif's, like spun golden silk. But it was also knotted, only half in a ponytail. It appeared to have bits of leaves in it, like she had been sleeping rough. I had the strangest urge to reach out and touch it.

"Damon, it's me, man. There's only your friends here. Did she hurt you?" I asked, trying to keep my voice gentle and not spook him.

"No," he all but growled. His voice was low and rumbling, startling and aggressive in the eerie quiet. He was barely in control, and it worried me.

"Did you hurt her?" I asked, leaning forward slightly, trying to scan what I could see. I knew it was a dick question. Damon would never hurt a woman, but I needed to know what was happening.

"No," he growled low and shot me a threatening glare. I needed to get him to use more than one-word answers.

"Has she passed out?" I tried next, taking a different tack. "Did she hurt herself?"

The question caused Damon to look panicked as he switched his gaze back to her. He seemed shaken.

"I don't know. I came in and yelled at her. She seemed frozen, and her eyes were glazed. Then her eyes rolled back in her head, and she dropped. I caught her," he rasped, like his voice was raw.

He relaxed his hold on her subconsciously and looked at me with total trust. I'd never seen him rattled before. He seemed almost lost.

"Have you checked her pulse? Is she clammy or feverish?" I asked. I wanted to check her myself but didn't want to exacerbate the situation. Damon looked half wild. He shook his head hesitantly.

"Can I do it for you? I want to make sure she's okay." I checked with him before moving. He seemed highly protective of her, despite his confusing emotions. An alpha in protective mode over an omega was rare in our modern world and wasn't to be messed with, especially one as dominant as Damon.

I inched forward slowly, careful not to spook him, when I heard another low growl and noticed Bear move out from under the bench beside him and stand protectively in front of them. I don't know how I missed the giant dog.

"It's okay, Bear. You know me. I'm going to help, okay?" Bear stopped growling as if he understood. He gave me a long look before moving to Lexie's side, and I had the distinct impression he had just warned me.

I moved her hair aside, trying not to shudder as small electric shocks raced up my arm when I touched it. My eyes zeroed in on her exposed throat, and I had to force myself not to stroke it as I checked her pulse. It was beating steadily.

Her skin was warm and alive under my fingers. I took a deep breath, trying to control my breathing and racing heart.

That's when I caught her scent. I'd been too distracted when I came into the room to think about the strong, summery, citrus smell, unconsciously assuming the kitchen hands had been making jam or cakes earlier.

But it was her, and the scent sent all the blood in my body straight to my dick. I shifted uncomfortably and looked at Damon. He narrowed his eyes at me, and I quickly looked away.

I gasped as I realized what it meant. "She's an omega?" I choked out in disbelief, suddenly unable to breathe at all. Betas didn't have such strong or unique scents, only omegas, and alphas. "Where the hell did she come from?"

"Omega?" Lexie asked abruptly, startling me. "I didn't get very close to her earlier, but I didn't notice any strong scent. Sirena didn't mention one either."

Damon glanced at Lexie at the mention of Sirena, then quickly looked back at the girl in his arms with a pained expression. Things with Sirena would get ugly fast if something happened between Damon and this omega.

I had to think quickly. "Was anyone else in here when you came in, Damon?" He shook his head again.

"Okay, here's what we're going to do." I tried to look only at my team. Not the omega who was trying to steal all my attention, even while unconscious. They weren't faring any better. All of them were fixated on the omega, even Hunter by the door.

"Her pulse seems fine, but we need to move her somewhere safer so I can fully check her out."

"Hunter, stand down. Let Dave know he can stand down too. Just give us a few minutes to move out. Lexie will signal you when we're clear.

"Oh, and watch out for the guys behind the door," I amended as Hunter blended into the shadows. He looked over his shoulder in question. "I told them to grab what weapons they could find and guard the doors and the women behind the bar. They may be a bit jumpy," I said.

He nodded and moved away, giving the woman one last lingering glance as he went. He seemed tense in a way that was unlike him and hadn't yet spoken. He was usually the group's comedian, but a calm, deadly side always came out when violence was in the air or when his team was in danger.

Technically, I shouldn't be directing alphas. That shit can get you killed. But my guys didn't operate like that. So I was going to take care of them and figure this out. I mentally shook myself.

I turned to Leif and Lexie. Leif was back to staring at Damon and the woman. And from what I could see now that Damon had relaxed his grasp a little, she was all woman. She had curves for days.

I shook my head to clear my thoughts. That was inappropriate right now. I mentally slapped myself up the back of the head and shifted back to get some distance. I kept my eyes firmly on Damon's face.

"We're going out the back. We need to move quickly and keep the omega's scent away from other people, so we'll take the pond path."

"Lexie, spray the place quickly with a strong smelling disinfectant, then move over to the double doors. Once we're out, pop your head out and signal Hunter. Then meet us on the path. We're headed for our place."

"Damon, do you want Leif to carry her, or can you manage it?" I asked.

"I can manage, pup," he growled at me as he glared. He was three days older than me and liked to rub it in now and again.

"Okay then, old dog," I replied, trying to lighten the mood. "As long as you don't drop her or pop your hip out, it's a long walk by the pond, you know."

He growled at me again, but he shot me a grateful glance. He knew I was trying to get him to ease up. He trusted me to have his back while he was vulnerable. He knew in his heart we always did. He just needed to learn to let us when we weren't on a mission.

Damon rose off his knees and raised the woman in a deadlift before adjusting her in his arms.

"Yeah, yeah, studmuffin. We know you're strong and manly. No need to show off," I teased.

"Leif, can you wait at the back door for Lexie and make sure she meets us on the path safely," I suggested.

He seemed startled when I spoke to him, like he was coming out of a trance. "Are you sure Lexie needs to come with us? Why was she even back here in the first place?" he asked. I knew he wasn't being unkind. He was just very protective of his sister.

"Right over here, big guy," Lexie hissed from the other side of the kitchen, by the double doors to the dining room.

I glanced at her and smiled. "You know Lexie. She would never hang back if a woman was in trouble. Plus, the omega needs to be cleaned before I can properly check her over. Are you going to do it while she's unconscious?"

Leif blushed and shook his head rapidly. He would never dream of taking advantage of an unconscious woman. None of us would.

"Not on my watch," Lexie challenged under her breath.

"Okay, smartypants, good points." Leif grinned lovingly at me.

I was glad the guys were starting to relax again. They had freaked me out with all their weird tension and intense staring earlier.

"Okay, we're moving out," I said. "Time to get this shitshow on the road, or the path, whatever." I spied a bag the girl seemed to have dropped. It was as dirty as she was, so I grabbed it for her and followed Leif out the door.

"'Is that whiskey?" I asked as I spotted the bottle he was still carrying.

He gave me a smirk. "Don't be a nark," he whispered. "Besides, I think we're going to need it tonight.' He nodded discretely towards Damon, who was disappearing into the gloom.

'Okay, sexy pants," I smirked back at him. "Good point."

He groaned and pinned me up against the wall beside the door before grabbing my chin with his free hand and kissing me in a sudden frenzy.

He nipped at my lips and aggressively thrust his tongue into my mouth while grinding his rock-hard dick against mine. I was still half-hard from my first whiff of the woman's scent, and my cock was instantly rigid again.

I kissed him back just as passionately, moaning out loud. My body was trapped deliciously between the wall and Leif.

Leif wasn't usually so forward or sexually aggressive, but this was getting heated fast. I was seriously into it. I didn't think his reaction was all from me, though. I think he was as worked up about the omega as I was, and I didn't mind a bit.

"Ewwww, no. I don't need to see that. Or is this supposed to be a distraction? If it is, I can give the signal to Hunter and grab some girls who would love a front row seat?" Lexie said from the doorway.

Crap, we hadn't noticed she had wandered over to the back door to double-check Damon was clear. Leif blushed as he adjusted himself. I stumbled into the darkness, following Damon, while Lexie laughed at us. Damn, it's hard to run away with a hard-on.

Eight

"**Y**ou're up, Lexie," I announced as Damon gently placed the woman on the bed in our spare bedroom. Bear hopped up and lay down next to her, which surprised me.

Damon had wanted to take her to his room, but I convinced him a strong alpha scent on the bed might freak her out when she woke up. There was already enough of his scent on her skin and clothes.

The guys were all hovering like they intended to stay, casually leaning on walls and door frames, but I suspected a room full of strange alphas could also freak the omega out. "Everyone out but Lexie," I ordered.

Damon looked torn, like it physically hurt him to leave her here. But he turned and went with Leif shadowing him like a gentle, protective giant.

Hunter hesitated at the door. "You got this, Lexie?" he asked, even though he knew it was unnecessary. Lexie had helped numerous women escape abusive situations. I was sure she'd seen worse.

As well as working on the farm, Lexie taught self-defense lessons at our local gym. She had an informal network of contacts who directed her to women who needed and were ready to accept help.

She'd approached us one day and calmly informed us we were going to give a woman she was helping a job, and we weren't going to be assholes about it. We'd agreed instantly, and the woman started work the next day. We all had a lot of respect for Lexie.

It was how many of the women here had started working on the farm. It was also one of the reasons why we had a lot of security, even before the Crash.

As the farm had grown, we'd built simple cabins dotted around the hills for staff and their families. Farm work involved a lot of early hours, and many of our workers were single mums or young families.

It made sense to provide housing so they weren't far away and were comfortable leaving their kids in the mornings. The women had also banded together and formed an informal creche for the younger kids, where they all took turns, and we were happy to roster work, so someone was always there.

She rolled her eyes at him. "Of course, I do."

"Thanks, Lex," he murmured as he returned, giving her a gentle hug before he followed the other guys out. We all supported Lexie as much as we could, but Hunter was the one who worked the closest with her. So he spent the most time with Lexie and the women she regularly brought home, often shaken and badly afraid.

Despite being an alpha, Hunter's normally easy-going and fun personality put them at ease. He came across as a friendly big brother. He was also a favorite 'uncle' to many farm kids, who often hadn't had great male role models.

To his dismay, Leif initially seemed scary to many of the women. Damon's intensity caused much the same reaction. So they kept their distance until the women were more settled. Leif was also a big hit with the kids, though. They could always sense his soft center. I helped with a lot of tech support, getting the women new phones, bank accounts, and sometimes, new identities.

Lexie approached me hesitantly where I was leaning against the dresser. I'd put the woman's bag on top, knowing she'd probably want it nearby when she woke up.

"I know you guys would never hurt a woman. You've proven that over the years, but Damon looks like he's lost the plot, while Leif and Hunter are both acting weird and hyper-focused on her." She looked over her shoulder at the woman, then back at me with a question in her eyes.

"Are we good here, or do I need to be concerned?" She watched me as she worriedly bit her lip.

"You've just never seen the guys respond to a serious threat before. They went into military mode, and it takes a while to snap back out of it sometimes," I assured her while I fiddled with my rings, even though I didn't believe that myself. Something was up.

She tilted her head and raised an eyebrow at me, calling me on my shit without saying a word.

I never got anything past Lexie. "Look, that's partly true," I told her, knowing Lexie deserved complete honesty from me. She'd earned it. "I've never heard Damon sound like or react like that. I've also never seen Hunter or Leif instantly fixate on someone like that. And I've seen them around other omegas, so it's not just that."

"I don't know what's going on yet, but I'm going to find out. I know in my heart, though, that woman is in no danger from them," I insisted, needing Lexie to understand that my guys would never hurt her.

Lexie sighed deeply, willing to trust me but still not entirely sure. "Yeah, okay, just keep me in the loop. I mean it," she implored as she rubbed my arm affectionately.

The guys and I were very tactile. It surprised a lot of people, but it felt natural for us. Lexie had picked up the habit after spending time around us.

"It's not just her I'm worried about, though. You and Leif are tight, but what does it mean for you that he's so affected by her? And what does it mean for the guys if they're *all* reacting to her?

"You guys are all like my big annoying brothers. You drive me stark raving mad, but you mean the world to me. You're the only family I know."

Lexie hesitated, looking away briefly like she was considering what she would say next. "I'll make sure she's okay, no matter what, but I'll get her out of here in a heartbeat if she's going to come between you all."

I'd never heard Lexie talk about us as brothers before, and it hit me right in the feels. I didn't have a lot of friends. I fixated on things and could sometimes be a bit oblivious to anyone outside our team. So her friendship and acceptance meant a lot to me.

"Awwww, Lex. You love us," I replied as I grabbed her in a half headlock, half hug, and gave her a noogie. Hunter always did it to her, and I knew it drove her insane.

"Get off, you big goofball," she groaned but smiled at me. "Don't you start that shit. You're supposed to be the sensible one." I smiled back at that.

"Seriously though, Lex. I love that you're worried about us, and we love you, too," I said earnestly.

But she just raised an eyebrow at me again. I'm telling you, her eyebrow-raising skills were next level. She was going to make a fantastic mother one day. Her future kids were already screwed.

"Not like that. Like, an annoying little sister who gets under our feet and follows us around begging for attention. That kind of love," I said, using her analogy but taking it just that little bit further.

"Whatever, dork-a-saurus," she said. "Go do your magic voodoo shit and sort those guys out."

This time it was me raising two eyebrows in confusion. "What the hell are you talking about?"

She gave me that look that girls give guys when they're being stupid.

"I know you're clueless about your charms most of the time, but you've got to know you're the glue that holds those guys together and keeps their alpha shit in check. Without you, they wouldn't function as well as they do. They need you, and they listen to you. Even Damon, and he doesn't listen to anyone else," she said.

I was shocked and stared at her. I knew the guys and I always worked well together, but I was a beta and not in their league. I'd called Lexie the annoying little sister, but I'd always seen myself the same way. The pesky little brother type who idolized them, and they let me hang around because they were nice guys.

"Clearly, you need to process that a bit, but we don't have time right now," she laughed in exasperation and gave me a rough, quick hug.

I let her distract me. She knew me and that my brain would fixate and try and puzzle it out otherwise. Probably while I stood and stared uselessly at her for an hour, saying something brilliant, like "uhhhhh."

Seriously. I knew I was a smart guy, but I swear I turned into Homer Simpson with a donut sometimes. Truthfully, most guys do, usually around girls at some point. They're so much more emotionally aware than we are.

I turned around and stilled when I noticed the woman on the bed watching us warily. We hadn't noticed her wake up while we'd been talking.

"Uh, hi," I mumbled, unsure how long she'd been awake and how much she had heard. She had the most beautiful, dark blue eyes. Like deep pools you could dive into, and they were watching me intently. She just gave me a small, unsure smile and looked at Lexie.

"Oh, hey, girlfriend, glad to see you're back with us," she greeted the woman warmly like they were old friends. The woman sat up quickly and then clutched her head.

I sprang towards her, but Bear beat me to it. He sat up and propped his head and shoulder under her arm, holding her up. She lay her head on him. "Headspin?" Lexie asked with a note of concern, and the woman nodded gingerly.

Lexie took charge instantly, grabbing more pillows and creating a cozy pile behind the woman. "Lie back for a minute, sweetie. You don't want to rush moving too quickly.

"Max, can you get me a few washcloths and a bucket of water? We're going to have a quick sponge bath. I don't think she should be standing up in a shower, but I'm sure she wants to clean up a bit."

I dashed into the bathroom, grabbed what Lexie needed, and brought it to the bed hesitantly. I didn't want to get too close and make the omega uncomfortable.

I wet one of the washcloths, folded it up and handed it to Lexie. "Here, put this on her head for a sec. It will help with the dizziness."

"Good idea. Thanks, Max." Lexie sat on the bed and put the washcloth on the woman's head as Bear lay back down again.

I just stood there awkwardly, not sure what to do with my hands all of a sudden, so I shoved them in my pockets.

"I, uh. I don't know what happened earlier, but I'm a trained field medic, and I'd like to give you a quick check-over if that's ok?"

She nodded slightly, so I pressed on. "Is it okay if I touch you, I just want to check your eyesight and make sure you didn't hit your head."

She nodded again, so I moved closer and crouched next to her, trying not to crowd her. I reached up and gently pulled her hair out of her ragged ponytail, letting it fall over my hands. Then I ran my fingers along her scalp, through her long blonde locks.

She seemed to relax and lean into my touch, and I struggled not to prolong it more than necessary because even that slight touch felt so damn good. I tried to keep my breathing even and not pant all over her. I also tried to stop my dick twitching in interest, but I had a distinct lack of control around her.

She just watched me intently the whole time, not saying a word. Completely disarming me with those stormy, blue eyes, I'm sure could see right through me. She had me completely mesmerized until Lexie coughed pointedly.

Act professionally, man. She's a patient. I tried to tell myself. I let her go before Lexie chopped off my balls for messing with a vulnerable woman. Rightly so.

I held up one finger. "Can you follow this with your eyes?" I asked.

I moved my finger around in front of her, glad for a moment to have that intent gaze on something else. She followed it fine.

"You didn't get bitten by anything in the garden today that you know of?" She shook her head.

"Okay, let me know if you see any suspicious marks when you wash off. Besides that, you seem fine, although you don't say much, do you?" I asked curiously.

She just shrugged and gave me a small, almost secret, smile. Deep blue eyes watched my face again as I stared back at her, impossibly drawn to her and trying to figure out why. The need to touch her again was overwhelming, even just a casual touch.

"Okay, out now, Romeo," Lexie snapped, and I jumped to my feet, not realizing she had moved right behind me. I'd forgotten for a minute she was even in the room.

"Uh, sure, okay," I stammered. Romeo had nothing on my lines.

"I don't know what the hell's gotten into them all today," I heard her mutter as I turned to head out the door.

"Oh, help yourself to anything you need. There should be plenty of stuff in the bathroom. But yell if you need anything," I told Lexie, turning around, my brain finally coming back online. "We're right outside in the living room."

"I was planning on it," she said as she shot me a smug grin. "Now get. You too, Bear, out." She pointed at the door, but Bear looked up at her balefully before resting his head on the bed again, clearly going nowhere. The omega absently stroked between his ears, and he moved his giant head onto her lap.

"Yes, ma'am," I snickered as I turned to the door again. I heard Lexie sigh as I closed the door behind me. We made her do that a lot. I could hear her faintly talking to the omega as I walked away.

I headed for the living room and found the guys staring at each other. They turned and looked at me in unison. Okay then, maybe there was something to what Lexie was saying. It felt good to think the guys needed me, even a little bit.

They had done so much for me, not the least was building my confidence in my tech skills. Leif had all but adopted me way back in basic training. Damon and Hunter had been senior officers on our first mission, but they quickly took us both under their wings.

We'd all been together ever since. Eventually, we all moved on to special forces, even though betas were never usually accepted into the elite ranks.

We'd also retired together and planned this farm. They'd given me a life and a family. I wouldn't be the man I was today without them, and I would always have their backs any way I could.

"I think we all need whiskey," I started saying, and Hunter perked up immediately.

"Whiskey, who has whiskey?" he asked as he looked around.

It was his go-to drink, he'd always loved it, and we had all developed a taste for it after meeting him.

He finally spied it hidden partly behind Leif's broad back, where he was sprawled on our oversized, u-shaped, sectional sofa. It was a gorgeously soft, buttery yellow leather monstrosity. Leif had it custom made to fit our sunken living room, as well as fit three giant alphas and a tall beta.

It probably wasn't what you would expect for a bachelor pad, but we all loved it. It was where we all tended to gather at the end of the day, and on the rare lazy Sunday we had no chores.

"Dude, are you holding out on me? I can't believe you still have that," he laughed.

If you wanted to play hide and seek, the best spot was behind Leif. He had muscles on his muscles. You could hide anything back there. I'd once seen one of the farm kids hide back there when Leif was having a siesta under a tree. It took ages for his friends to find him. I'm pretty sure the kid had a nap back there too. Leif was great as a nap partner. He gave the best cuddles.

"Did you manage to smuggle some ice too? Please tell me you have some hidden back there. Just not in your butt cheeks. I don't want butt ice," he laughed uproariously at his butt joke, like a five-year-old.

Leif just shook his head at him, but I could tell he was trying not to smile at Hunter's ridiculousness.

"I did, but it melted," Leif deadpanned, which set Hunter off laughing again. Even Damon's lips tilted slightly. The guys being themselves, idiots that they were, always calmed him.

"At least you'll be nice and wet for Max later," Hunter teased as Leif blushed and I groaned.

I think half the appeal of us for Damon was that we never cowered around him. He only exuded a fraction of his true dominance, but even that intimidated people, including other alphas.

But it wasn't who he was. He was a caring, protective and loyal guy. People just couldn't get past the dominance to see it.

"I guess it's whiskey neat then," I said as I grabbed four glasses from the kitchen and brought them back to the lounge for Leif to pour. He expertly poured out three glasses and handed them to us.

Damon immediately skulled his straight, even though it had to burn. I absently took his empty glass and handed him mine, my eyes on Leif. Damon drank that too. Hunter just sipped his slowly. He was serious about his whiskey.

"What about you?" I asked, noticing Leif hadn't poured any for himself yet. He was just fidgeting with his empty glass, rolling it between his hands.

"I know she came in alone, and we worked out that the storm brought the tree down, but I'm still on edge. I need to check the gates and ensure they're safe tonight."

"Dave's going to have his hands full calming people down, and the word's going to spread. I want people to know we're on top of this so they can sleep easy. It won't help if we've all disappeared," he said. It was typical of Leif, always thinking protectively about others.

Hunter looked at Leif like he had betrayed him. "Man, you suck. I was enjoying this," he moaned as he put his whiskey down. Nothing would make him skull it the way Damon had.

"I'll come with you as far as the dining hall and help Dave out. Let him know you're at the gate, so he doesn't have to rush back up there. I'll bring some dinner back later, too, so Damon doesn't have to go back down just yet, and we've got some for the omega if she wakes up. She looked like she could use a good meal."

He pointed at his drink and glared at both Damon and me. "This had better be here when I get back," he threatened half-heartedly as he climbed directly over the back of the sunken couch, "and the bottle better not be empty. Who knows when we'll get any more," he called over his shoulder.

Damon didn't even raise his eyes. He was staring at his empty glass, lost in thought.

"Buzz me on the gate channel if you need to *talk* to me," Leif said. Emphasizing the word talk and jerking his head in Damon's direction before he headed out of the sunken living room using the steps, like an adult.

I just nodded. I may be oblivious at times, but I could tell the guys were leaving me to talk to Damon and try to see if I could get him to open up where they hadn't been able to earlier.

Leif and Hunter looked longingly towards the spare room when they reached the door as if they could see through the wall to the woman inside before heading out the door in resignation.

I got the feeling both would rather stay here, but we had responsibilities to this farm and all the people within it. I didn't know what to make of it or my intense reaction to the woman.

I waited until they had left out the front door before pressing Damon gently. "Look, a lot went down with the woman back there, and you don't owe me anything, but I'm here if you need me."

"I know," he said, still looking at his glass and not at me. I needed a different approach. Maybe if I focus on something other than the strange omega, we could lead into it.

"You were all riled up before you even saw her. What set you off?"

"Are you kidding me?" he growled, instantly angry, slapping his hands down on the couch. "We'd just had a fence breach, and a stranger was inside the fence. I had every right to be furious and suspicious."

I didn't let his anger bother me. I knew it wasn't about me.

"We've brought plenty of women into the farm before, especially ones in distress. The farm is full of them, and none have ever meant us any harm, so what's going on?" I probed.

"That was before," he hissed, "before we lost power and the country descended into chaos within days."

"You've trusted Dave's instincts for a long time, and with good reason. So try again," I said, casually leaning my arm across the back of the couch like I didn't have a care in the world.

"Everything's different now," Damon sighed, the fight leaving him. He braced his arms on his knees and closed his eyes like he could block out whatever he felt.

"You trusted Dave enough to look after the farm while we were gone, after the Crash, with all the craziness worsening rapidly. So that excuse isn't going to fly either. Try again," I repeated. I wasn't going to let him fool himself or me.

"People are different now. You saw it yourself out there. People are doing shit they would never have even considered a few weeks ago." He stared out the sliding doors into the darkness, remembering the shit we had seen that we'd all rather forget.

"People are desperate and trying to survive any way they can," Damon tried to explain as he got up and started pacing around the room. He ran his hands through his hair in agitation.

I poured myself a new drink and sat quietly, relaxing on the couch, trying to encourage him silently to continue.

"It's not even just looting anymore. People are dying. And it's not just criminals in a free-for-all. It's at the hands of their neighbors and friends. Everyone's turning on each other out there. And there's no one stopping them."

"I know that," I sighed, "but we're not different, not before tonight at least."

"You're saying I wouldn't have behaved like that before the Crash?" he asked, scrunching his eyebrows up and looking confused.

"I'm saying you wouldn't have behaved like that before tonight, even after the Crash," I elaborated, sitting forward slowly, still trying to figure out my thoughts on this, and his.

"I don't know what to say," he sighed, as he slumped back onto the couch across from me. He picked up his empty whiskey glass and fiddled with it, circling the edge of the cut crystal with his finger.

His erratic behavior worried me. Damon had been our rock, our leader, through covert missions so dangerous everyone else had refused. He had always been calm and in control, dealing with threats and rapidly evolving situations in the field. He had always led us out again.

"What's changed with you? What is it about her?" I asked, sitting up straighter and deciding to be blunt. The gentle approach was getting me nowhere. Sometimes Damon needed pushing to get him to open up.

"That woman could have been up to anything in here, all day, especially alone in the kitchen," he yelled this time, deflecting again. "She could be working with anyone. She could have sabotaged something."

"The safety of everyone here is our responsibility, and we're vulnerable," he continued yelling, getting louder and more worked up.

He still had the whisky glass in his hand, and I was worried he would throw it at something. He seemed angry, but I couldn't tell at what.

"We've been lucky so far, we've escaped notice, but that's not going to last. Don't you get that?" He asked in a sudden rage.

That was true, and we all knew it. Damon had stressed out about it since the Crash. We'd been in enough warzones to know the types of things people did when they were desperate. But that wasn't what had gone down tonight. We both knew it, but he dodged it, hiding something, and I didn't like it.

Before I could call him out on it, he jumped up again as Lexie entered the room.

"What is it, what's wrong?" he growled, instantly on edge.

"Oh, I don't know, a couple of yelling assholes freaking a scared chick out," she goaded him snappily as she stopped at the top of the steps. She had no fear of the big bad alpha.

She turned to me quickly before he could respond. "We've gotten the worst of the grime off, and she's resting. I want to get her some food before I let her have a proper bath, or she may pass out again."

She looked at Damon, hesitant for a second, unsure what to reveal in front of him in his volatile state. "She has a lot of bruises," she reluctantly said. Damon went rigid, going on alert.

Lexie sat on the step and put her head in her hands. Helping women was her life's work, and she always took it hard when she came across one who appeared to be suffering abuse.

"I think she's been on the run for a few days, given the color of some of them. When she came in this morning, it was at first light, and I thought she would drop then. I tried to help her, but Sirena stepped in and refused." She huffed and squinted as if imagining what she wanted to say, or do, to Sirena.

"Sirena took her straight out into the garden and sat under the tree while she worked all day weeding the garden in the heat, without food or water." Lexie looked pointedly at Damon, and he cocked his head, confused.

"We're going to talk about Sirena at some point, you and me, but that's a whole other story," she declared while pointing her finger between Damon and herself. He looked rightly concerned.

"But I can tell you now, I heard a little of what you said, and you couldn't be more wrong. Dave discreetly asked me to keep an eye on her, and I did. Not to spy on her, to make sure she was safe. I watched her from the kitchen and the hill when my shift was over.

"She worked hard to earn some food and water. She didn't slack off when Sirena fell asleep or when Sirena took off with one of only two farm hands in this place I don't trust and left her with the other one. He was drooling over her like a piece of meat the whole time.

"Bear arrived not long after she went into the garden and stayed with her all day. He watched everyone but her as if he was guarding her."

Lexie got up and started pacing at the end of the couch, in front of the useless television.

"And what's more. When Sirena was getting ready to stick her claws into me, she diverted attention from me. She was exhausted, and in a room full of people she didn't know, but she instinctively tried to protect me. She's a good egg.

'I managed to *sneak* her a little bit of food and a drink of water, but it wasn't anywhere near enough," she emphasized the word sneak so that it would sink in.

"None of the girls in the kitchen liked what was going on, but none of us felt like we could intervene further, and that shit is going to change," she glared at Damon angrily. Damon looked startled and looked at me, but I shrugged helplessly.

It seemed something was happening with Sirena and the other women we didn't know about. We were going to have to look into it sooner rather than later. I wasn't Sirena's biggest fan, but I hadn't heard she had been causing any problems.

"Oh, and by the way," she continued relentlessly, "not that any of you have bothered to ask, but she has a name, it's Maia, so you can all stop calling her the woman."

And we'd just had our asses served to us.

I hung my head before I looked up at Lexie again. "I'm sorry, Lex, you're right. We should have asked when you said you were around her this morning. Or asked Dave. We're not thinking right."

Lexie shrugged, hands on her hips and was not mollified by my apology. "I'm not the one you all need to apologize to, she may be in a bad spot and looking rough right now, but she's a human being." Lexie was utterly unimpressed with us.

"Max, can you grab that bruise cream you swear by and see if she'll let you put some on? It will let you check them out. Some of them look pretty nasty."

"Sure, no problem. Do you want to come back with me and watch while I do it?" I queried over my shoulder as I hustled into the kitchen to grab the first aid box.

Lexie's tone was softer now. "I trust you, Max. I know you'd never do anything to hurt her. So you go ahead, and I'll be in, in a sec.

"Besides, I want to have a quick chat with Damon." I saw her turn to him and raise her eyebrow out of the corner of my eye.

"Uh oh, someone's in trouble," I sang as I left the room, chuckling to myself. Glad the eyebrow of doom had turned on someone other than me. I had my guys' backs in some pretty dangerous situations, but when it came to Lexie, they were on their own if they had messed up.

I continued chuckling until I entered the bedroom door and noticed the empty bed. I headed quickly for the adjacent bathroom and knocked on the door. "Maia, are you okay?" I called out, concerned.

There was no answer, and I was worried she'd passed out again, so I turned the handle and opened the door slowly. "If you're in here, I'm coming in, alright? I just want to make sure you're okay," I tried to reassure her.

The bathroom was empty.

I spun around wildly, scanning every inch of the bedroom before I noticed the bag I'd left on the dresser was gone, and the sliding door to the deck was cracked open. Shit, I'd forgotten this room had another exit. I felt my stomach drop instantly.

"Damon," I yelled, as my body strung tight and panic set in. Damon came crashing through the door, closely followed by Lexie.

"She's gone, and so's Bear." Before I could say another word, Damon had raced back out of the room.

Nine

I gun the quad bike as fast as I dare in the dark, thankful it's electric and quiet. I'm unsure what time it is or how long I was out. It was nearing dusk when I entered the kitchen, and it was full dark now. The moon is low in the sky, and I can vaguely see people moving near some buildings, so I didn't think I was out too long.

All I know is that there's at least one alpha behind me. When I woke up I felt raw and exposed, my chest aching like I was somehow bruised inside. I couldn't get my scent under control either, no matter how much I discreetly tried to pinch myself.

I could sense the alpha nearby and I heard him after Max left. I recognised the deep growly voice from last night in the kitchen. It vibrated through me even from a room away. My instinctive, visceral response to him scared the hell out of me.

The alpha sounded angry and yelled about 'that woman,' which I assumed was me. And Sirena had said there were more. I don't know what the hell happened last night, but it was time to leave now. I had never backed down from an alpha, and I wasn't about to start now, but I also wasn't stupid enough to put myself in one's way if I had an option to run.

When Lexie said she would check what was going on and get the "barbarians to pipe down and cut out the testosterone shit," her words, not mine, I took my chances and escaped out the door. Bear had looked at me quietly, then gotten up and followed me with a soft "whuf."

I ordered him back to the bed, but he ignored me. For a dog that appeared to be highly trained, he was terrible at taking orders. But I figured he could come along as long as he wasn't barking.

Luckily, I'd been able to grab my bag when I spied it on a dresser next to the bed, along with my shoes and socks I'd dropped on the floor while giving myself a quick sponge bath. I hadn't even stopped to put them on. I just grabbed them and ran.

I wish I'd had time to find some food or at least fill my water bottle, but I didn't dare stop. I was an unmated omega with a dangerous alpha nearby. I couldn't take any chances if I wanted to get out of here without getting barked into submission or, even worse, unwillingly bitten and claimed.

I felt bad about bailing on Lexie. She'd been nice to me. Besides, BFFs didn't bail on each other, or so movies told me. I'd never had one in real life. But I had to go now. Lexie had told Max they were like brothers to her, so I didn't want to put her in a position of having to choose between her loyalty to them or helping me.

My luck had held earlier when I had rounded the corner of the building while fleeing and spied the quad bike. We'd had quads on my grandpa's farm growing up. I'd been driving them most of my life, since way before it was legal, or probably safe, to do so.

I spied a dirt path and figured anything uphill had to lead to the main gate. I didn't have time to scout for another exit in the dark.

So I made a sharp turn, two of my wheels leaving the path and making me gasp a quick breath. I stifled the urge to whoop like I would have while racing quads with my brothers, imagining my grandpa's grin and how he used to high-five us behind my mum's back when we got caught.

I yelped as a tree branch hit me in the face and almost knocked me off the quad. I needed to focus now, or I was never getting out of here. My face stung like a bitch. Bear barked once, low and sharp, but kept pace alongside the quad bike.

Was it just me, or was the quad slowing down? We were on the hill now, but I should have more power. I looked down to the gauge, noticing the single red bar.

"Shit," I swore. I knew swearing was unladylike and unbecoming for a proper omega, but I firmly believed a little swearing now and again was good for the soul. I'd be lucky if I made the gate, and I was in no condition to run. I needed to at least get to my push bike.

"Come on, baby, you can do it," I whispered to the quad bike, stroking the wheel. Luckily there was no one around to judge me because I was desperate. If I thought standing on the seat and doing a shaman dance to whatever gods still existed would help, I'd do it right now.

I turned the final corner, the quad slowing to a crawl, before stopping only meters from the closed gate. I breathed a deep sigh of relief before levering my exhausted body off the bike and patting her. 'Thanks, girl, you did great.'

I knew she wasn't getting me any further, but I wanted her to know I appreciated her giving it her all. I think fatigue was making me a little delirious.

Bear just watched me with his head tilted, like he couldn't work out what I was doing. Me either, Bear. I have no idea.

I grabbed my bag, shoes and socks and turned for my push bike. Just as a giant, hulking figure dropped from the tree right in front of it. Two shorter figures appeared out of the shadows behind it.

I screamed and quickly stepped backward, colliding with the quad and almost going down. Bear moved in front of me again and gave a low menacing growl.

One of the short figures lunged toward me, and I screamed again before the giant grabbed him and hauled him back.

"Don't touch her," he growled deep in his throat. "Get back to your post. I've got this."

The two shorter figures melted back into the shadows, which left the giant. I almost wished I could go with them.

He stepped towards me slowly, moving out of the tree's shadow and into the moonlight on the path in front of me as I gasped and stared with my mouth hanging open. Real classy.

He was magnificent, with long, messy blonde hair, high cheekbones and a short beard. I had the strongest urge to reach out and run my hands through all that glorious hair. I could picture it with tiny plaits, like an old Viking warrior or a Norse god.

He had the build of a Viking too. He wore dark pants and a tight black t-shirt that showed off his broad chest, snug waist, and thick, muscled legs. Every curve in his biceps and forearms was highlighted to distraction, caught between the shadows and the moonlight that seemed to make his fair skin glow, adding to the aura of a mythical creature from legend. I was a little unsure if I was awake or still passed out and dreaming right now.

He looked like he should have an ax over his shoulder as he raided a small village. I had never seen a more dangerous-looking man. But he wasn't a man, or a god. He was all alpha.

The hairs on my arms rose. I was awake, and he was very real.

I couldn't breathe, and it wasn't from fear. It should have been, but that wasn't the emotion I felt. It was desire, a desperate, all-consuming desire, that burned through me. I felt pulled to this alpha on a level that was beyond carnal. It was a soul-deep need.

I held it in check, barely. This was the second alpha in a matter of hours to incite an extreme reaction in me. But I was a survivor and had yet to meet an alpha I could trust. I wasn't blindly putting myself in an alpha's power, especially not a huge beast that could snap me in two with a finger.

Or maybe make me come with it, slowly, for hours.

"Bear, stand down," he said, and the dog lay down at my feet, watching us both but no longer on guard.

The alpha took another step closer to me, tentatively, like he was trying not to spook me as he moved into my personal space. "You need to breathe," he murmured, and his deep, rumbling voice was a caress across my heated skin.

I took the tiniest of breaths, and his scent, this close, almost crushed all my resolve. It was a smoky scent, with overtones of chocolate and marshmallows. It reminded me of nights spent around campfires as a kid, huddled in a blanket and toasting s'mores with my gramps and brothers. His scent was like a giant hug wrapped up in happy memories. It drew me towards him instinctively.

I closed my eyes briefly, trying to shut out some of the stimuli overwhelming my senses and the feelings that flooded me, taking tiny, controlled breaths. I had never scented an alpha that smelt so good before tonight, or one that pulled such a reaction from me.

When I opened my eyes, I saw he'd reached over my shoulder as his gaze shifted to my hair. I felt a gentle tug, then a whisper of a touch, like he had run a finger down a curl, before he pulled his hand away, with a small, green leaf in it.

My body shook lightly, even though it had been the barest of caresses. I used all my strength and fortitude to turn my head away slightly, trying to avoid the intensity of his gaze as it returned to my face. I refused to be at his mercy.

I heard an intake of breath, and he moved impossibly closer still as he gasped, "You're bleeding." His finger ran the gentlest of lines down my cheek, and he groaned softly. His other hand landed lightly yet possessively on my hip, anchoring me to this world as my body tried to float away.

Another deep breath had him swaying towards me, his chest lightly rubbed against mine, and my nipples were instantly hard and aching. I could see him subtly angle his head toward my neck before jerking backwards and stepping away.

For alphas and omegas, the crook of the neck was highly erotic. It was where our scent was strongest and often where mates bit each other in claiming. Sniffing or touching the neck was considered intensely intimate. By turning my head when he was so close, I had unconsciously presented it to him.

I felt oddly empty when he moved away. Like I had lost something important that had almost been in my grasp.

"I'm sorry," he choked out, breathing rapidly like he was desperately trying to get himself under control. I whipped my head around. I'd never heard an alpha apologize before or show any kind of restraint.

He raised his arms and clutched the back of his head like he was physically trying to hold himself back. But it only made his biceps bulge further, and his shirt raised slightly, exposing his perfectly toned six-pack and a hint of his adonis belt.

It was my turn to choke and try to calm my breathing. I grabbed the frame of the quad basket behind my back, locking my arms in place, which unfortunately caused my chest to thrust forward. The alpha's gaze darted down before he dragged it away with what looked like superhuman strength.

"Your scent, it's intoxicating," he rasped. "It's like the upside-down orange and pineapple cake my nanna used to make me. It was heaven. It feels like every good, happy memory I've ever had rolled up into one breath. I want to drown in it.

"But at the same time it sucker punches me and turns my dick...fudge, sorry, I need to shut up," he said as he looked away awkwardly and lowered his arms to adjust himself. I tried not to look down, but I failed miserably.

It was too dark to see much with his black jeans on, which was probably for the best, considering how little hold I had over myself right now. I had a death grip on the quad, though.

Then what he said registered. "Did you just say fudge?" I blurted as I cocked my head.

He looked startled for a minute, then sheepishly nodded.

"I'm not a big swearer. My nanna hated it, and it feels disrespectful to her if I do it consciously, so I've never gotten into the habit. Other inane words pop out randomly sometimes, though," he admitted adorably.

I couldn't see him very well with the moonlight and all that wild hair around his face, but I swear he was blushing. This alpha was not what he appeared at first sight. He had me confused. I had never known an alpha to explain themselves, or hold back from something they wanted.

"I'm uh, I'm Leif, by the way," he said as he held his hand out to me without looking directly at me. It was kinda how you would approach a spooked animal you were trying to calm.

"Maia," I replied as I stared at his hand. It would be rude not to shake it. My gramps would kick my butt if he were here. But to do it, I had to let the quad bike go.

Leif kept his hand out patiently, not making any comment or showing any impatience, just leaving it to me to decide what I wanted to do.

I looked to Bear, and he "whuffed" gently at me like he was encouraging me.

I reluctantly prised my arms off the quad. This situation was so beyond anything I could process right now. But I figured I would just go with it, and maybe this alpha would help me get out of here.

Although, I suddenly wasn't so sure I wanted to leave. The instinctive draw I felt to this alpha intrigued me, despite my past experiences. But there were more alphas here. Was it worth the risk for one alpha who seemed decent? What if it was all a ploy?

It was ridiculous to continue staring at his hand like a scared little mouse. I was no mouse. I had never backed down to an alpha, even ones who treated me much worse than this one. So I stepped closer, faking confidence and shook his hand. Every nerve ending in my hand lit up at the contact, and I could see him shiver, his eyes finally flicking back up to mine.

I yanked my hand back and discreetly stretched it out while he rubbed his hand through his beard and gazed at me with that look in his eye, like he wanted to devour me.

Why was that so hot? A man rubbing his beard or his jaw. It didn't work the same when women did it. Not that I knew many women with beards, except for the old librarian in my hometown. Her chin hairs were epic and came pretty close. I'd never seen her rub them, though.

And I was rambling in my head again. What was I doing before I got distracted by the gorgeous man mountain? Oh, that's right, escaping.

"I take it I'm not a prisoner?" I asked, suddenly feeling bold.

Leif looked startled. "No, absolutely not," he exclaimed, "why would you think you're a prisoner?"

"Uhhhh, big ass fences, yelling alphas accusing me of shit I didn't do, punishment chores, no food or water, kinda the definition of a prison if you ask me. Even if it is a gorgeous one," I sighed as I stared longingly over my shoulder.

Now that my eyes had adjusted, I could see some of the fields bathed in moonlight, and I recalled the beautiful, modern farm buildings I'd glimpsed earlier. I wish I could have explored more. This place could be a dream and not be any more perfect.

"I've lived in a prison before," I said, turning my head back to him but looking at the ground and keeping my voice low. "They called it a palace, but it was still a prison. They don't always look like what you think, and I'm never living in one again."

Bear suddenly got up and pressed himself into my leg. I reached down and absently stroked his head. I could get used to him being around.

"Maia," Leif said my name reverently and reached his hand out before hesitating. I liked how my name sounded when he said it in his deep, sexy voice. I was screwed. I needed to get a grip and leave now.

"You're free to do whatever you want. I guarantee nobody here will hurt you. Not if I have anything to do with it. I'm sorry nobody looked after you when you arrived, but we can fix that. We'll do better. We're not bad people here, and you're safe behind these fences. Can you say the same out there?" he implored, jerking his thumb over his shoulder to indicate the gate.

When I didn't reply, he crouched down to look up at my face and continued gently, "Do you even have anywhere to go?"

"Nobody's asked me to stay," I said, feeling awkward at having to admit that. "I'm looking for my friends. We got separated. Dave was sweet and offered me a quick respite, but the other intense alpha from earlier didn't exactly seem happy I was here.

"Plus, Sirena was downright awful to me. She told me I had to go before you guys got back. Lexie was the only person who has been kind to me. She snuck me some food and water. Can you thank her for that, by the way, if you see her? Promise me she won't get in trouble. I probably shouldn't have told you that."

Christ almighty on a cracker, I was rambling on the outside now. I was suddenly so very tired. Not just with physical exhaustion, which was rapidly catching up with me again now that the adrenaline of my escape was wearing off. But I was tired in my soul, tired of trying to survive on my own, against all the odds. I was so very tired of being alone. I slouched backward, leaning into the quad bike, suddenly unable to bear the weight of my own life.

Leif stood slowly before moving towards me and gently lifting my chin, looking me searchingly in the eyes. He seemed to see what he needed as he straightened and stood proudly before me, with the confidence of a man who knew what he had to do. I couldn't tear my eyes away from him.

"I'm asking," he replied simply.

"What?" I was so confused and wasn't sure what part of my long rambling meltdown he was answering.

"I'm asking you to stay, please," he implored.

I just stared at him again. "Why? Why do you want me to stay?" I asked. I suddenly, desperately, needed to know. I was hanging on for his answer like my life depended on it, and maybe it did. My chances of surviving out there on my own weren't great, and were getting worse every day. I knew that, it was why I had taken the risk of coming inside.

I suddenly felt like I was at a crossroads, and whatever I did here, at this moment, would be important.

"Because I need you," he said plainly, but with intense feeling, "because if you go, I'm coming with you, and I've got a lot I'll be leaving behind. There's no way in hell I'm letting you go out those gates alone. It's not safe, but I'm also not going to keep you prisoner.

"So I'm asking you to stay, but if you're sure going is what you need, we'll go. I just need you to give me a day, so I can put things in place here and make sure it's protected, too. And say goodbye to some important people," he tripped up a little over that last bit, but then he squared his shoulders further, and he seemed resolved.

"They'll be upset, but they'll understand. They love me, and real love never limits."

"Why would you do that for me, for someone you just met, give all of this up?" I couldn't understand. I'd lived in a world of black and white, and it felt like he was suddenly offering me colors, and I didn't know why.

Nobody had ever given up anything for me, not even something worthless. So I had no frame of reference to understand.

"Because of this," was all he said before he wrapped me gently in his arms, lowered his face to mine, and searched my eyes for permission. I tensed as I kept my eyes on his, waiting for his bark, but all I saw was restrained need and care. There was no anger, no arrogance, and no compulsion.

Having his arms around me sent tingling shockwaves through my body, and his scent, this close, saturated my senses. It was like a siren's call, tempting me to draw even closer to him. His eyes widened and his pupils dilated, so I knew he felt it too. Yet, he was holding back.

He wasn't barking at me or trying to force me in any way. He was silently asking and waiting patiently. I got the feeling if I shook my head even slightly he would back away.

No alpha had ever cared about my willingness before. I wanted to know what it felt like to give into the desire I could suddenly feel lighting me up. The sensation was so new. I had met plenty of alphas but never wanted any before tonight.

It felt like a calm rightness was slowly unfurling inside me, as if I had arrived at a place I didn't even know I had been seeking. Could I walk away from this intriguing alpha without figuring out what was between us? Was it alphas I hated, or just when they tried to take away my choices?

I knew in my heart I would regret it forever if I let fear win and this moment passed. As terrifying as it was, I suddenly realized I wanted to make a choice for myself, even if it was a mistake. I'd had so few real choices in my life. Mistakes were a privilege I'd rarely had.

Linked together in this moment I knew the emotions I could see in this alpha's eyes were different. They drew me in and promised safety. I trembled as I nodded slightly, and held my breath.

He inched impossibly closer, searching my gaze and giving me every chance to change my mind. I closed my eyes on a sigh as he kissed me gently and tenderly, feathering the lightest of kisses along my lips until I opened for him on a moan. Then he devoured me. He kissed me with his whole soul, with a passion and intensity I had never known.

The kiss shattered my heart into so many tiny pieces I would never recognise it again. It blasted all the cold, the fear, the loss and the loneliness away in a blazing rush of warmth and light. Then he took all the pieces and turned my heart into something new, something more potent. A thing of beauty that beat for him but was capable of so much more.

I gasped within his embrace as I felt an echo of his heartbeat, as though it was beating within mine. Like his had shattered too, and we shared a heart now.

He pulled his head back slowly, easing away while continuing to pepper me with tiny kisses along my jaw like he couldn't bear to stop.

"Because you're my true mate," he whispered in my ear. Before running his fingers down my arm and taking my hand gently, entwining it with his and raising them together to rest over his heart. "Now that I've found you, I'm never letting you go, and I'm never letting anyone hurt you again."

True mate. The words reverberated through me. True mates were rare in our world, a myth almost. The way he said mate so softly, too, made it mean something entirely different to the way I had always heard it used. He said it with reverence, rather than with sneering, derogatory possession.

I was exhausted, hadn't showered in days, and was dirty, despite the quick rinse-offs I'd done, but the way he looked at me as he smiled made me feel like the most beautiful woman in the world. Like I was the most perfect thing that ever existed.

Leif had just blown apart everything I thought I knew about our world and myself. He was an alpha, but I suddenly felt an intense need to protect this gentle giant and keep him close.

Before I could respond, a deep voice growled, "What the hell is going on here?"

Ten

I looked up without fear and stared at Damon, who was standing with his hands on his hips and sweating. Hunter and Max flanked him. Max eyed me curiously while Hunter had a cheeky smirk on his face.

Bear got up and moved around to a spot between us all, head swiveling back and forth like he wanted to watch the show.

"About time you guys got here," I challenged, with an easy smile, while holding Maia's hand to my chest.

"No fair man, you had a head start," Hunter groused, but shot me a small smile.

"Are you okay, Maia?" Max asked as he stepped forward cautiously. 'You shouldn't be up and about so soon after passing out. I was worried.'

Maia nodded to Max, mumbling, "I'm okay," before shifting to watch Damon warily. She attempted to step away from me, but I wouldn't let her, snaking my other arm possessively around her waist to keep her close. I didn't want her to disappear. Not now, not ever again.

"We may have gotten here sooner if you hadn't turned your damn radio off," Damon growled, ignoring Max. "Or if you had bothered to tell us you had her, we heard her scream from down the hill."

"But if you had gotten here sooner, you would have been too early and scared her away," I said, trying to tease him a little. I know he felt responsible for everyone on this farm, especially since the Crash, and it was such a heavy weight on his shoulders. But I didn't like his attitude right now, and I was hoping I could calm him down like our teasing usually seemed to do.

"Scared her away? She ran away like she had something to hide." He flung his accusation angrily, his dominance roiling in the air with the scent of lightning, and Maia tensed in my arms. I was naturally a gentle person, but I was also a highly trained killer. The fear I could sense rolling off her had me going still.

"Did Maia have a reason to run away from you, Damon?" I asked, a deadly note creeping into my voice. "What did you do?" I accused. Damon was one of my best friends, but if he had hurt or scared her, he would deal with me.

I was rapidly descending into the void, the mental space I'd developed to survive in the military. I shut down my emotions and became intensely focused and lethal when I needed to be.

The difference between Damon and me was that I could turn it off again. Damon had less of a handle on his emotions and his alpha instincts.

"Me?" Damon growled as he stepped forward, eyeing how I was holding her. 'That's rich. You're the one mauling her,' he snarled.

I shifted Maia behind my back, holding her in place with one arm, and got ready to defend her. Damon wasn't thinking right now, and I knew he would regret the way he was behaving later, but there was no way I would let him intimidate or scare her any further. I could feel her trembling behind my back.

I'd never seen Damon behave like this around a woman, especially a vulnerable omega. He was usually more protective than me. But he was losing his shit, and I wasn't about to stand here and let him take it out on Maia.

Damon was naturally a lot more dominant than I was, which confused people because I was physically bigger. But true dominance had nothing to do with size.

Regardless, I could and would stand up to him if needed. So I squared my shoulders, took deep, measured breaths and widened my stance, ready for his next move.

"Hand her over, Leif," he growled again, low and dangerous, as he took an aggressive step towards me while clenching his fists.

This was going sideways fast. If it came to blows, Maia could get hurt while standing so close to me. And she didn't need to see this. It was going to get bloody.

"Max, I need you to take Maia and keep her safe," I asked as I risked a sideways glance at him while still keeping Damon in my line of sight. I knew he'd do it. I saw him move toward me instantly. He wasn't taking sides, I'd never ask him to do that, but there was no way he'd let a woman get hurt.

Bear let out a low whine like he could feel the tension between us.

Hunter had lost his cocky smirk and watched the two of us warily, taking a step closer to Damon, ready to intervene if he had to. He didn't like what was going down either.

"Maia, I need you to go with Max," I urged. "It's okay. You can trust him." But I felt Maia straighten behind me. She quickly dodged Max.

"Oh, hell no," she snarled, to my utter shock. "You're not laying a hand on Leif when he's done nothing wrong."

She put one hand on my chest reassuringly and pointed the other one right at Damon, not a speck of fear showing on her face now. "Back off, or I'll make you," she growled lightly. "And don't even think about trying to alpha bark at me. That shit's not going to fly."

She looked gorgeously fierce and wild, standing barefoot like a warrior goddess in the moonlight, ready to defend what was hers with her bare hands. Her scent flared brightly and flooded my senses. But it had an underlying tartness that hadn't been there before, like a warning.

Damon was so startled that he took a step backward. Bear whined at him. His eyes fixed on Maia.

"One of you is going to open the gate," she said, "and Leif and I are going to leave. I don't know what is happening here, but I'm not letting you hurt Leif."

I snapped back into myself as I realized Maia was defending me against another alpha. Just like an omega would her true mate in the old stories my nanna had told me, from long ago.

A warm glow radiated out from the spot she was touching my chest, and I placed my hand back over hers, weaving our fingers back together and holding them to me. I stared at her in wonder.

True mates were found through scent, but they were now so scarce in our world. A natural, true mate connection can't be forced. It has to be willingly accepted on all sides. The way omegas are forced into matings now makes it almost impossible to find one. Once a forced mating happens, it changes an omegas scent, so their true mate will no longer recognize them.

I didn't dare hope I would ever find my true mate. So many people didn't even believe in them anymore, thinking they were just a fairytale.

But I did, and the thought of her being out there somewhere, forced to mate another alpha, has always made me unbearably sad.

How Maia had made it so long without forcefully being mated was beyond me.

"Maia, it's okay," I implored as I tried to turn her towards me, but she wasn't turning her back on Damon or letting him out of her sight. My sweet, lonely omega had hidden teeth.

"Maia, sunshine, look at me," she startled at the endearment and turned to me. I could see Max moving behind her with a look of shock, but he was instinctively defending her back.

I could also see Damon out of the corner of my eye looking devastated, all of his anger and dominance bleeding away. Hunter had moved closer to put a hand on his shoulder in silent support.

"Leif, I can't stay here if I don't feel safe. I've been in that space before. I'd rather take my chances out there," she said, sounding earnest. "If you don't mean what you said just before, I'll understand, but I don't want to see you staying anywhere you don't feel safe either."

I chuckled at that. "Damon's being an ass right now, but he's the brother I chose. All three of these guys are. We may try and knock some sense into each other now and again, but they would never seriously hurt you or me. I trust them with my life."

"But if you feel you can't be here, we'll go," I reassured her, stroking her hand on my chest lightly with my thumb. "I meant what I said, all of it."

"What the hell, Leif? You're leaving?" Damon asked. He sounded agonized. "How could you leave us?"

"I don't *want* to leave, but I will if she doesn't feel safe here." I stared Damon down.

"I would never hurt her," Damon declared quietly into the sudden silence.

"That's not what you made her think or feel, Damon," I returned.

I looked at Max over Maia's shoulder; unlike Damon, he smiled joyously at me. I knew it wasn't because I'd said I was leaving but because he knew and was happy for me. My heart burned with love for him. I knew I had room for them both, for them all.

"Can't you feel it?" Max whispered while he looked at Maia with reverence. He turned to Damon and Hunter, who both looked confused. "She's his true mate. They've started a bond."

Damon dropped to his knees, looking destroyed. As if his whole world had just burnt to the ground, and all he was looking at was ashes. "She can't be," he whispered.

"Damon, man, talk to me," Hunter begged as he crouched down next to Damon. Bear moved over to him and whined low in his throat.

"I know you're freaking out, but this is a good thing for Leif," he urged, glancing at me with genuine warmth, while patting Bear with his other hand, trying to reassure him too.

"You don't understand," Damon insisted. "She can't be his mate," his voice was raw and desperate.

Hunter wrapped Damon in his arms, offering him comfort. We'd never bought into the whole men can't hug each other bullshit.

"We'll figure it out together like we always do," he said while resting his forehead lightly against the side of Damon's.

Damon took a deep, shuddering breath and closed his eyes. Grabbing Hunter's arm draped across his chest and hanging on tight as if it were a lifeline. Bear pushed his nose under their arms until his head popped through, and Damon nuzzled into him.

I couldn't stand to see Damon's pain. I suspected what was causing it, but this wasn't a conversation Maia needed to hear right now.

"Maia, I know you don't feel safe right now, but I told you I would protect you, and I meant it. So I'm asking you, again, to give me a day, can you do that? Then if you still want to leave, we'll go, but we'll do it safely and with supplies, okay?"

"Fuck," she muttered quietly to herself, clearly torn. She looked at the gate over my shoulder, then turned her head and looked hesitantly at the other three guys and Bear. Max stood protectively behind her, and Hunter cradled Damon in his arms while they knelt on the ground.

I could see all the adrenaline from her second surge of the night was wearing off rapidly, and she was running on fumes. She could see Damon was no danger to either of us right now. He looked broken and couldn't even look at us. It was breaking my heart. Max gave her a reassuring smile, and Hunter winked at her. She smiled hesitantly back.

She turned back to me, looking into my eyes, and seemed to see something there that settled her. She took a deep breath and nodded firmly. That's my girl.

Her trust in me made me feel, for the first time, like my strength and size were something good. Like I could use it to shelter and protect her, rather than maim and destroy as the military had taught me. And that was more than okay.

I felt worthy, like a good man for the first time in my life. As though my alpha status finally fit, where it had always sat uncomfortably on me before. I felt like I could take on the world for her.

"I'm going to take Maia back to the cabin on the quad bike," I directed, taking charge for once. "It's out of power, but I can coast down the hill. I should make it most of the way to the cabin. She's in no condition to walk back down right now. Not without some food, water and more sleep, I insisted.

"Can you two take care of Damon and walk him back down? We'll discuss this later after I get Maia settled back in her room."

Hunter and Max both nodded at me. I knew they'd take care of Damon right now. He was breaking my heart, and I desperately wanted to reassure him, but Maia had to be my priority right now.

"Jack, you're back on as lead gate guard tonight," I called out. "If you need backup, buzz Dave."

"Yes, Sir," came the abrupt reply from the darkness of the tree behind me.

"And whatever you heard or saw tonight never happened," I ordered gruffly.

"Aye, captain," came a cocky reply from the younger guard before I heard what I assumed was a smack on the back of his head, and he yelped. "Do you have a death wish?" Jack whispered.

I chuckled. I knew containing this was a long shot and what went down tonight was likely to be all over the farm before the morning.

We were a small community, and people were all in each other's business on a good day. But it was worth a try. I wasn't worried for myself. I planned to make it clear to everyone here that Maia was my mate if she agreed to stay. But Damon liked to keep his emotions shut down and people at arm's length. His messy display of emotions tonight was intensely personal, and he wouldn't be happy with people talking about it.

I turned Maia away and moved her gently onto the quad bike, keeping a hand on her at all times in case she stumbled or dropped. Her legs were trembling lightly, as though her crash was imminent now that the danger had passed, and it was taking everything she had just to move.

I settled her across my lap. "Put your arms around me," I urged. "Don't let go. This will be fast and I'm not going to have much control."

"That's what he said," Hunter shouted, and I rolled my eyes at him.

I released the brake and used my feet to maneuver the bike in a circle to point back downhill. Luckily these electric quads were light and easy to move.

Hunter disentangled himself from Damon and hustled over, but Bear kept nuzzling into Damon. "Hang on a sec, big man. I'll give you a push."

"Thanks, Hunt, are you guys okay with this?" I whispered to him. I wasn't used to making decisions for us or giving orders.

"Yeah, man, you take care of our girl. We'll see you soon," he whispered back. Maia looked up at him confused, but he just gave her his cocky, signature smirk.

"I meant with taking care of Damon, you jerk," I growled as I took a playful swipe at him, and he laughed as he dodged me.

"I know, but I'm okay with the rest too, just so you know," he remarked, giving me a more casual grin like his support didn't mean the world to me. Before I could say anything, he moved to crouch slightly behind the bike and pushed off, using the massive strength in his legs to get us moving quickly.

"Hang on tight," he said as he ran with us and continued pushing us faster around the bend before he suddenly let go with a whoop. So much for our rule of being quiet around the gate at night. We'd blown that rule big time tonight.

Maia started to giggle in my arms as we hit the straight downwards stretch and then laughed out loud as I fought furiously to make the tight turns towards the bottom of the path without braking and risking losing our momentum. Our girl was a daredevil, it seemed.

I threw on the handbrake, and we slid to a screeching, sideways halt beside the cabin. I threw myself to the side, and Maia leaned backwards as I tried desperately to stop the bike from tipping when two wheels briefly left the ground.

My heart jumped into my throat before the wheels settled back down again, and I sighed in relief.

"That was fun. Can we do it again?" Maia laughed, trying to catch her breath as she looked up at me.

I just stared at her, already knowing I would adore this woman. "Yeah, no," I said. "I'm going to kill Hunt, that was insane."

"Don't kill him. He's too cute," Maia said, then blushed as she realized what had just slipped out. She looked at me like she thought I'd be mad.

"Oh really, I'm going to tell him you said that," I said, liking that I could tease her. It was a big part of our group dynamic. If we were going to stay, she'd have to be able to handle a little back and forth with the guys.

"Oh god, please don't. I've known Hunter for five minutes, and I already know he has a huge ego," she sighed.

"Hunt's actually quite sweet and very caring. You'll see when you get to know him," I told her, wanting Maia to like him. "He's flirty, sure, but sweet."

"We'll see," she said, still blushing, and I was okay with that. I was happy she was considering getting to know Hunter because it meant she was also thinking about staying.

"Can you stand?" I asked as I straightened up, but she continued sitting in my lap.

"Nope," she replied with a cheeky sparkle in her eyes as she popped the "p" loudly. "I think you're going to have to carry me."

She smiled up at me tiredly, and I was gone.

"Can do, ma'am," I replied in a serious, gentlemanly tone as I easily lifted her in my arms.

She gasped and giggled simultaneously, exclaiming, "I was joking, Leif. Put me down. I'm too heavy," as she grabbed my neck and pressed her body into me. I would happily carry her everywhere if she held onto me like that. But my sudden hard-on was making it difficult to walk.

I looked down at her in astonishment. "Are you seriously doubting my ability to carry you? Do I need to do two hundred push-ups to prove my strength? I'll do it," I promised, sounding way too eager.

"No, of course not. I just, you know, I'm not light," Maia explained, ducking her head as if she were embarrassed. 'I'm tall for an omega and grew up on a farm. So I'm not some little princess who diets and watches her weight.

"They kept telling me at the Palace that I was too big to be a good omega and had to custom make my clothes to fit. Most of the other omegas were tiny and obedient. I wasn't either," she rambled as she yawned suddenly and rested her head on my shoulder.

She was exhausted, and it seemed her thoughts were wandering, or she was delirious. But that was the most I'd gotten out of her about herself all night.

"That's rubbish. You're perfect, just as you are. Perfect for me, anyway," I huffed.

"Hang on. You grew up on a farm?" I asked, much more interested in that little tidbit, as I walked into the house, straight through the front door, which was wide open with all the lights on inside. We were breaking every security rule tonight. I kicked the door closed behind me.

She squinted and covered her eyes at the sudden bright light, and I reluctantly put her down on the big island bench in our kitchen. She squealed and shifted round a little as her exposed legs met the cool, natural stone of the benchtop.

I moved to turn off all of the downlights and just left the decorative pendant lights on over the bench, so it wasn't so bright. They gave off a soft, warm glow. We often used just them at night when we were winding down.

Our kitchen was big and spacious to accommodate four big men. We naturally tended to congregate together when we were home. So if one of us was cooking, the others were generally in here too. Pretending to help, but mostly just stealing food during prep.

The dining area in the open plan kitchen, living, and dining space had a big ten-seater reclaimed timber table for the same reason.

The kitchen was also reclaimed timber, with polished concrete floors, stainless steel appliances, and pops of yellow to match the couch.

"Yeah, my grandpa had a farm. He pretty much raised us," she sighed, answering my earlier question while lilting to her side on the bench. "Are we there yet?" she asked, yawning wide enough to crack her jaw.

I spied a tray of pies on the bench behind her, with some hand-cut chips. Hunter must have dropped them off and then taken off quickly when he realized everyone was gone. They weren't hot anymore but would taste okay.

'Here, eat some of this before you pass out again, sunshine. If you don't eat a little something before you sleep, your body will keep waking you up because you're hungry,' I coaxed. I'd learnt that the hard way in the military.

I grabbed a big glass and poured her some water, handing it to her as she grabbed a pie with her other hand. She took turns gulping the water and munching on the pie while I rested my hands on either side of her on the cool bench, making sure she didn't slide off.

I eyed the scratch on her cheek and decided it didn't need bandaging but some antiseptic would be a good idea. I grabbed some from a kitchen drawer quickly and told her to hold still while I cleaned off the dried blood and applied the salve. She didn't even flinch. Either she was too tired for the sting to register, or she'd been fixed up a lot. The idea made me a little crazy and I tried not to tense.

I focused back on her eating, making sure she finished it all. "Good?" I asked.

"Mmmmm, so good," she moaned as she ate the last of it and licked her lips. Jesus, she was going to be the death of me. My dick was still hard from earlier and was now a steel rod in my jeans watching her tongue slide across her full lips. I tried to adjust myself discreetly and think unsexy thoughts like shoveling manure. It didn't work, though. Even scooping poop, Maia would be sexy as hell.

"Okay, time for bed, ma'am," I ordered in desperation, but it was the wrong thing to say.

"Yes, Sir," she giggled as she shuffled closer to me on her butt, threw her arms around my neck and pulled herself up so she could wrap her long, gorgeous legs around my waist.

"I'm going to ride the cowboy to bed," she whooped as I picked her up and started walking towards her room. I put my hands underneath her to hold her up while trying desperately not to cop a feel.

"Uh oh, are you smuggling something illegal in your pants cowboy," she laughed as she ground herself against me and it was my turn to moan. She felt so damn good all wrapped around me.

"Feels like you've got something big and hard down here. Let me check it out," Maia suggested and her voice lowered, along with one of her hands, as she ran it down my chest. I almost dropped her.

"Nope. All hands must remain in the upright position, or this ride won't commence," I instructed in a hostess's voice as I wrangled her hand back up around my neck and tried valiantly to keep her still before I exploded in my pants from her grinding on me.

It wouldn't take much, I was so turned on. Between her scent surrounding me and the heat of her body pressed firmly against me, I was a goner. I wasn't going to take advantage of her in this state, though.

"Cow poop, cow poop, cow poop," I muttered under my breath desperately.

"Did you just say cow poop?" She laughed out loud. "Is that your bedroom talk? We're going to have to work on that," she instructed as she ground down on me again, and I almost ran into the wall.

"Nope, nope, nope, this ride is over," I exclaimed as I dumped her on the bed, and she pouted at me. It was the sexiest damn thing I had ever seen as she lay all rumpled and splayed out.

"Do you want a shower, or just want to sleep?" I asked, trying for a distraction.

It worked to a degree. It distracted Maia, just not me, as she rolled over and started crawling up the bed, waving her ass in the air. It was like waving a red flag at a bull. I had to cross my arms over my head and grab the timber frame of the canopy bed to stop from reaching for her again.

"Too tired. I'll sleep on top of the covers and shower in the morning," she mumbled.

Maia turned at the top and flopped down onto the pillow, closing her eyes and letting out a long moan of contentment, snuggling into the down comforter on top of the bed. It had a blue, bamboo blend cover that was incredibly soft and silky. I noticed it also matched her eyes.

I heard the timber of the bed frame groan as I gripped it hard, almost snapping it, imagining her moaning like that as I thrust my hard dick inside her wet heat. It was time to go before she caught me mumbling unsexy crap again and decided I was certifiable.

She opened her eyes sleepily and looked at me through hooded lashes. "Can you do that again in the morning?" she asked through a yawn.

"Do what?" I asked, confused as hell.

"Whenever you lift your arms, I get a sneak peek of your abs. It's hot as hell watching you do it at the end of my bed," she sighed. My willpower was at its limits hearing her talk about me like that. Note to self, half asleep Maia was a chatterbox and extremely horny. Very different from her earlier quiet reserve.

"Go to sleep, sunshine, and I'll do whatever you want in the morning," I promised as I walked over to the door.

"Where are you going?" I heard her mumble, almost asleep.

"To my room, it's upstairs," I told her, keeping my voice quiet, not sure how awake she was at the moment.

She struggled to open her eyes again and tried to lift herself off the bed.

"Please, I feel safer with you here. Can you stay? Please, Leif," she begged. "I don't want to be alone in here in the dark right now."

"Of course." There was no way I could deny her anything. I got the impression from her stiff posture, that she wasn't used to asking for things. She never had to beg with me, though. I'd give her anything she needed.

I looked around the room. "Do you want me to lay on the floor?" I asked as I grabbed a throw blanket from the dresser beside her bed.

"No, I want to see you if I wake up," she mumbled again.

"Okay, I need to talk to the guys when they get back, but until then, I'm just going to lay down over here where you can see me," I told her as I draped the soft throw over her and lay down on the other edge of the bed.

I tried to stay as far away from her as possible, but I was a big guy and took up more than half of the bed. I tucked my arm under my head to try and give her more room.

She smiled sleepily as she grabbed the blanket and shuffled over to me, curling herself into my side, throwing one leg over me and pulling the blanket across me before settling her arm around my waist and her head on my chest.

She took a deep breath and let it out slowly, her body feeling heavier against me as she relaxed.

"You smell so good. I was terrified of mating an alpha from my past experiences, but you're nothing like I've ever known or dared to imagine," Maia mumbled. "Thank you."

"What for?" I whispered, stunned that she'd referred to me as her mate, even if she was mostly asleep at this point. I brought my arm down and settled it over her, hugging her to me gently like she was precious, which she was. She had no idea how much.

"Being you," she murmured one last time, and then she was out. I hadn't thought my heart could get more full tonight, but I was wrong.

Eleven

Damon

The guys were a quiet, supportive presence at my side as we walked back down the hill, and I appreciated it. I needed time to process everything that had just gone down, and they seemed to get that.

The farm was a hive of activity during the day, but it became almost magical at night. Especially on a bright moonlit night like tonight.

I took a deep breath of the sweetly perfumed air from the nearby strawberry field and stopped to look at everything we had built, some of it with our own hands.

I could see the flowing fields interspersed with quaint cabins where our friends spent downtime with their families.

The glittering pond and old mill offset by the modern function center, which had been a labor of love, glowed in the moonlight. The river wound gently through the bottom of the valley, surrounded by old-growth forest that stretched into the distance.

I could hear crickets and insects chirping and the cool breeze rustling through the trees. An owl hooted in the distance. It was peaceful.

What we had created here was something to be proud of, and I had almost destroyed it in one night through fear. The thought caused an ache in my heart.

These men, the family we had created together, and this community meant everything to me. We'd lost a lot when we threw our old lives out the window and built the life we wanted, but we'd gained so much more.

Bear nudged my leg as we reached the house. "Find Lexie," I ordered him after giving him a quick scratch.

I dropped down into the sunken couch as soon as we walked back into the cabin, still lost in thought. The aftermath of so many intense feelings had left me drained and exhausted. I felt extremely vulnerable and didn't know what to do with that.

"Do you want some pies and chips? They're not hot, but they're ok," Max asked, breaking the silence as he wandered over with the platter of food. "It would be a shame to waste it."

I don't know how long we'll be able to make things like chips once essentials we don't make or grow on the farm run out, like oil and sugar. If we can't find more, we'll have to adapt—one of the many things I've thought about since the Crash.

"Give them here. I'll heat them up for a minute. I think we all need some comfort food right now, and I'm sure we can spare a little bit of power tonight," Hunter suggested as he grabbed the tray and his earlier glass of whiskey and wandered into the kitchen.

I nodded at him absently. I knew they were trying to take care of me, and I loved them for it. I wasn't hungry but knew I had to eat, especially after throwing back whiskey earlier and then running up the hill at full speed.

I'd burned a lot of energy. I'd be useless if there was an emergency tonight, and I hadn't re-fuelled.

How had I gotten so far from myself, so quickly? I kept my dominance on a tight leash. It often made me seem stern, but I wasn't usually an asshole.

I wasn't as in control of myself as I thought I was. One moment, one woman had brought me wholly undone.

Fear of the beast inside me being unleashed and hurting people had overwhelmed me, and I had lashed out angrily. I had wanted her gone until she went. Then the thought of never seeing her again filled me with blind panic.

I had watched her defend Leif as her mate against me. I could still feel the broken shards of my walls as they had crumbled, raking me raw and leaving me in rubble-strewn devastation. I didn't know if I could fix the damage I had caused.

"I can hear you thinking from the other room," Leif mumbled as he entered, strolling over and stretching out on the couch opposite me. He had a contented smile on his face, and I was jealous as hell.

Not because he had the girl, but because he hadn't epically screwed up meeting her.

"Is she okay?" I asked. I could feel the tension in every line of my body, and I couldn't make eye contact with him.

"She's okay. She's sleeping."

"I'm sorry," I rasped out, the words feeling like razor blades in my throat. I knew I had messed everything up and was terrified I had broken us when these guys held the strings to my sanity.

"What are you sorry for exactly?" Hunter called out from the kitchen. He never let me get away with shit.

"The meltdown, the temper tantrum or the sulking afterwards?" he asked as he leant casually against the breakfast bench and sipped his drink. He looked straight out of a whiskey commercial photo shoot, all gorgeous, relaxed arrogance with his signature smirk.

"All of it," I breathed out, still watching the floor as if it would suddenly open and I'd tumble into a dark void.

"Damon, man, look at me," Leif asked, sitting up, so he could look at me straight on. I looked up slowly, painfully, grinding my jaw. "We're good, okay?"

I just nodded. I was relieved, but it didn't ease the tension in my body.

"What's going on, Damon?" Max asked from where he'd dropped opposite me on the couch in his usual quiet but direct way. He was always getting to the heart of what was happening with us.

"You've never been this emotional or irrational about anyone before, and you're usually so protective of women. Like all of us are."

"I don't know." I evaded the question, changing my focus to stare at the door. I wanted to escape this conversation so much that I felt my skin itching.

"I call bullshit," Hunter said. "Do better. We don't lie to each other."

"You said she couldn't be Leif's mate earlier. Why?" Max pressed, always trying to figure people and things out, like a bloodhound.

"Let it be, Max. Just this once, leave it alone," I snapped at him.

"No, this will only tear us apart if we let it," he said, ignoring my tone completely.

"I know, okay. I know," I groaned. "I'll apologize to Maia in the morning. I'll make it right. I don't know how, but I'll figure it out."

"We'll figure it out," Max said, "because that's how this works."

He was a good man. They all were. I nodded and looked down at my feet, feeling a heaviness settle over me, despite his words.

"You still haven't answered the question," Max persisted. He could never let anything go until he figured it out. It would drive him insane.

I sighed, a frown returning to my face as I got up to pace around the couch.

"Because she's Damon's true mate," Leif said lightly, answering the question for me as he headed back out of the kitchen.

I whipped around and glared at him. Max looked to be in shock.

Hunter didn't look surprised. He just continued sipping his whiskey as he flopped down next to Leif on the couch and put the tray of warmed food in front of him. He casually picked up a pie and handed one over to Max before grabbing one himself and started munching on it.

I felt lost in a sea of emotion, without an anchor. I tried desperately to build up some walls. Leif just looked smug, with one eyebrow raised. Like he was waiting for me to try and deny it.

The silence stretched out. Max was swiveling his head between the two of us and Hunter. The warmed-up pie he'd automatically reached for already forgotten in his hand.

"Why would you say that?" I was trying for a casual tone and failing. My voice was far too low and my body tense. "You've openly acknowledged her as your mate. I wouldn't go after your girl," I insisted roughly.

"Our girl," Hunter said, in a calm tone, completely unfazed.

Leif just chuckled, and Max looked like his brain was exploding. "What am I missing here?" Max complained.

"Damon, it was written all over your face earlier. I suspected as soon as I ran into the room," Leif said. "I didn't call you out on it because you were royally losing your shit."

I stood very still, not acknowledging what he was saying but bracing for whatever would come next. I felt like the prey for the first time in my life instead of the predator.

"The second I got a good lungful of her scent, I knew she was my true mate, too. She called to me in a way I've never felt before, like every cell in my body was screaming 'mine,' loud and clear."

Leif paused, unsure if he should keep going, but he looked over at Hunter, who nodded.

"Then, when I kissed her, I felt it snap into place. I could feel her emotions, and a faint bond instantly connected us. It's tenuous and new but vibrant, and it feels so damn good. It needs time to develop, though, to deepen, I think."

I sat down heavily on the steps, staring at him intensely. I wanted him to keep talking and shut the hell up at the same time. I could feel my heart pound in my chest, and I tried futilely to rebuild some of my shattered walls.

"You can feel her in the bond? That shouldn't be possible. Feeling emotions through a bond is a myth," Hunter said, sounding intrigued. Leif just shrugged.

"Hang on, but if she's your true mate, how can she be Damon's true mate?" Max asked, looking between us all. He seemed perplexed.

"Our true mate," Hunter said. Both Max and I whipped our heads toward him this time.

"I figured as much," Leif said, "from how you zeroed in on her, not Damon, when you stopped at the back door. You looked like I felt."

Hunter nodded at him again. "Her scent, man. That orange and pineapple shit is potent. It went straight to my dick, and I was hard as a rock instantly. I felt like I was going to come in my pants on the spot," he declared as he chuckled, shaking his head.

"I'm half afraid to touch her, given how I reacted just to her scent. I don't want to lose it like a fifteen-year-old boy copping his first feel. I have a reputation to uphold." Max rolled his eyes at him.

Leif just stretched out, cupping his junk casually and probably unconsciously, very comfortable around us after all this time. Not at all bothered by what was going down.

"But I'm drawn to her in a way I've never felt before. I just knew, instantly," Hunter said, completely unapologetic. He looked relaxed, too, lounging on the couch like we were discussing a football game or tomorrow's weather. Not something that was going to change everything and put us all in danger.

"Holy shit. I just, I didn't see that coming. You guys are sneaky as shit," Max said. "Is that why you went up to the gate, Leif?"

Leif grabbed Max's hand and squeezed it. "Yeah, things happened so fast. I felt she was going to run, so I waited at the gate."

"When she turned up, she seemed lost, alone and scared. She needs us. I just wanted to give her a safe space. The kiss and the true mate bond, they just happened." Leif looked at me intently as he talked.

"I don't plan on doing anything about it," I said gruffly. I needed Leif to know I had his back no matter what it cost me.

"I do," Hunter interjected with a confident grin as he raised his glass in a salute. Max chuckled, and Hunter winked at him.

"I plan on starting something. Not right this second. A hell of a lot went down tonight, and she's exhausted," he said as he casually leaned back and stretched his arm out along the back of the couch.

"So I'll give her time. Maybe even until tomorrow," Hunter added with a casual, cheeky shrug as he turned to Leif, "but I'm not walking away."

I stared at him, feeling my chest getting tight. I was on the edge of losing my shit again, desperately trying to hold the sharp shards of my wall together, making me bleed. But Leif just calmly replied, "I expected no less."

"Hang on, do you guys understand what you're talking about?" I wanted to know if they were saying what I thought.

"Yep," they both answered quickly, without having to check-in with each other.

"I've never really been into sharing a partner at the same time, like a threesome. I'll leave that up to her, Leif and Max," Hunter said, and Max laughed out loud while Leif muttered, "'Oh heck, yeah."

"But I'm cool with her having a relationship with any of you, too. Or all of you."

His arms were splayed out wide on the couch while he cocked his head at Leif and Max with a small smile, completely comfortable with the situation and discussion.

"That's not how our society works. What you're talking about will be considered a pack," I said harshly. I couldn't believe what I was hearing, and I was desperate to get the guys to understand.

"Do you not remember what happened when I visited the Omega Palace? When they tried to force me to take a mate, I refused. We were accused of being a pack then, and we almost lost everything," I said, my voice getting louder, begging them to understand what they were considering doing.

My gaze darted between them all as my forearms strained where I was gripping the edge of the couch while breathing heavily. This was bad.

I gritted my teeth against my beast, who wanted to break down the cage I held him in.

"What happened back then was a vindictive, spoiled alpha trying to get his way and spreading lies when he felt threatened by you. This situation is not the same," Leif said with a determined glint in his eye.

"And all the stuff about packs being dangerous is phooey anyway." He wasn't backing down.

I couldn't believe what I was hearing and that they were so casual about it. I thought this night couldn't get any worse, but we'd taken a left turn into hell. And I was terrified I wouldn't be able to protect them or save them from the people who would come for us.

"I won't do that to you guys, not again," I vowed as I exhaled fiercely and tried to get my breathing back under control. My blood was pounding in my ears.

Max dropped in front of me out of nowhere and grabbed my wrists, holding them in his hands and anchoring me.

"You're not doing anything to us, Damon. You need to slow your breathing down. You're spiraling," he said calmly but with worry tightening his eyes.

"Are you telling me you're okay with this? Seriously, Max, you're the sensible one. Do you not remember?" I asked, squeezing my hands into fists. Not that I would ever hit Max, but I needed to hold onto myself any way I could.

I felt like a floodgate had opened in the darkness when I touched Maia earlier, and a torrent of black, inky water was drowning me. I had been closed off from my emotions for so long that I didn't know how to process them in a way that wouldn't hurt the people I loved.

"I remember how it changed you. You've never really come back to us. You've locked everything inside since then, trying to protect everyone."

"But we're a team, Damon, a family. You have to let us in and let us have your back, too. It's not all on you. I know you're struggling with your emotions now, but I'd rather have you out of control and here with us than the locked down version we've been getting lately."

"Are you hearing me, Damon?" His voice was getting louder now, too. He wasn't backing down either.

I latched onto his voice and his touch. They were like the moon hovering above me in the dark depths, guiding me back to the surface.

"What do I do, Max? How do I make this okay? I don't know how to do this," I begged, feeling ragged and worn out.

"Just listen to what Leif and Hunter are saying." Max looked at them as they sat together, watching me worriedly. Hunter's earlier cockiness was gone. They both moved over and sat beside me. Hunter gently leaned his arm across my back, and Leif pressed his leg against mine to anchor me further.

"They're not being flippant or careless. Hunter and Leif are telling you honestly what they feel and need. Trust them. Trust their instincts. You always have before. What they're asking for feels right to them, and they need you to back them up," Max said.

"I know you worry about protecting us, Damon," Max continued. "But you've seen outside our gates. The world as we knew it is gone. It's just us now and the community we've built here."

"The power could come back, it could all come back, and it'll be like the Crash never happened." I said, but I knew, weirdly, that I'd be happier if it never did.

"It's not coming back, not in the way it was before. I know people are still hoping it will. But it's not. We know that. From everything we've seen on the satellite feeds and every government agency I've hacked, it's gone," Max said with feeling, leaning forward, trying desperately to get through to me.

"I don't know what happened yet, but I will figure it out. What I know is that this thing is everywhere, and everything has changed.

"The world will be what we make it from this point on. Us. Together.

"You've always led us from the middle, listening to what we needed to happen, then getting us there and making it work.

"That's all we're asking you to do again now," he said. "Listen to your family and help us get where we need to go. You're our center."

I took a few moments to breathe deeply, trying to hear everything he said and move past my fear, so it wasn't choking me. I realized, in a moment of clarity, that he was right. They needed me, and I haven't been there for them in a while, not wholly.

I'd locked them out, as well as my emotions. I looked at each of them, remembering how each had been there for me over the years.

I knew I needed to do better for myself and them. And I needed to start now.

"That's where you're wrong," I replied roughly as I straightened, letting his strength and belief in me wash out the darkness and the rubble.

I could feel his words deep in my heart. Max has always had this way with us. Whenever we doubted ourselves or got lost, our alpha instincts pulling at us in a way that stopped us from thinking clearly, Max has always been there to pick us up, dust us off, put us back together again and point us home.

"Don't misunderstand me, Max. Everything you said about me is right, and I needed to hear it. Thank you," I said huskily and meant it. I felt suddenly clearer than I had in a long time. Like the surging waters threatening to drown me had ebbed, and I was standing under a moonlit sky with a clear path to follow.

We had never fit into the old world. Maybe it was time to make a new one. The thought made me feel lighter, surer, almost hopeful. I could breathe again.

"But you're wrong about one thing." Max tilted his head in confusion, sneaking a look at Leif, then Hunter, who both shrugged.

"You're our center, always have been, always will be," I said.

Max shook his head and tried to back away, but I grabbed his hands firmly in my own, anchoring him like he had done to me moments ago.

"Ha ha, real funny," Max tried to joke and laugh it off like we were playing around.

"He's right," Leif said with a softness to his voice he only seemed to use with Max.

"Of course, he is," Hunter agreed, his voice had humour in it, but his eyes were serious.

"Damon is our growly leader, but he's too emotionally stunted to be our center. He's got some growing up to do," Hunter said as he ruffled my hair affectionately. I sighed and rolled my eyes. But I knew this was his way, easing tension with jokes.

Hunter looked back to Max and seemed to get serious for a moment, though. "I know you sometimes feel like you're not as important as the rest of us, or some bullshit, because you're a beta. But without you, we'd fall apart."

"I don't know what to say to that," Max finally said, being honest and direct, like he always was.

"You don't have to," I said, taking over, but leading from the middle, just like he said. I was starting with what I knew to be true.

"But I need to know if you're in too?" I asked, needing to know exactly what we were dealing with here. "With Maia."

"Me?" he asked, a little stunned.

"Hunt's okay with you being part of this arrangement he has all planned out." I flashed Hunter a smirk over my shoulder, a darker mirror of the one he usually gave me, and Hunter grinned back at me.

"And Leif is okay with the idea of you and Maia together, preferably with himself in the mix somewhere," I cocked my eyebrow at him, and he nodded vigorously, like a big, over-excited puppy.

I laughed abruptly, and it felt good. I could feel my beast receding now that the tempest had passed. I didn't know what I'd do without these guys, and I never planned on finding out.

"Are you interested in Maia?" I asked directly, getting to the point in a way I knew he'd understand.

"I, uh, don't think she'd be interested. I mean, I'm a beta. We don't feel the mate thing. But if she were, then I'd have to say that I'm attracted to her," he blushed, fidgeting nervously. He was always clear about what was happening with us but clueless about himself.

"Whoa, back up a little, dude. Don't sound so keen," Hunter teased, putting his hands up like he was trying to hold Max back. Max pulled his hands out of mine, then leaned over and punched Hunter in the leg before he could scramble over the back of the couch laughing.

"Does this mean we're going to do this then?" Leif asked, rubbing his hands and leaning forward in anticipation.

I sighed, getting serious for a minute again. "I won't deny anything you guys have said tonight, but I'm not there yet."

They all looked disappointed and were about to protest at once.

"I just mean about me," I cut in quickly. "I'm not trying to talk you out of anything. If you say you want and need this, then fine. Max is right. We'll find a way to make it happen and figure it out together.

"I just need some time to sort my shit out." I didn't want to hurt her more than I already had.

"Plus," I sighed again, settling back into the couch. "I want to make sure we do it right. This isn't some fling or quick, casual fuck," I said. I needed them all to hear me this time. "This is complicated."

"Leif," I said as I turned to face him, "did you even talk to her about Max and your existing relationship? How do you know she'll be okay with you two being together? Multiple partners might shock her, and you've already put her in the middle without giving her a choice."

Leif shook his head. "No, I didn't even think about it. I was just in the moment."

"I'm sorry, Max." Leif said with genuine feeling, turning and grabbing Max's hand.

"I just assumed you'd be a part of it because you're a part of me. But I should have been clear with Maia about you from the start. We're a package deal.

"You know when I said I would leave with her if she went, I didn't mean I was leaving you, and I didn't mean for good. I just needed to make sure she was safe until I could get her to trust me, then trust us," Leif said.

"Leif, you don't have to apologize and don't owe me an explanation. We always knew this was a possibility, we're good." Max soothed Leif while stroking his scruffy face lovingly. "I'll take whatever part of you I can get."

"You get all of me, Max. Never doubt it." Leif grabbed the back of Max's head and leaned his forehead against Max's in a move that seemed more intimate than a kiss.

I knew there was much more to be said between those two, but it was private. I'd been worried when Leif and Max first got together, about what it would do to the team if it ended, but they had their shit sorted and were solid. Maybe I should take some notes.

I turned to see Hunter lying on the floor behind my head. "Hunt, don't take this wrong, but you've never wanted a serious relationship. So what happens if you change your mind or feel trapped?"

Hunter dropped the smirk and looked at me seriously. "I hear you. I know I don't have the best track record, but that's because nobody has ever felt right before. It's always just been fun.

"I'm ready for this. I've been waiting for her. I'm all in, Damon."

He hesitated for a beat before continuing. "I was just practicing while waiting. But I think I've mastered the art of sexy times now. I'm all hers," he said, trademark smirk firmly back on his face.

"Bloody hell, man," I groaned as Leif leaned back and slapped Hunter up the back of the head. "Please, never say that in front of her."

"We just need to be careful about this, is all I'm saying. We don't need to rush it if we're in it for the long haul. But, we need to make sure Maia wants this and understands what she's getting into, okay?"

"Okay," they all said together, before, as one, they all leaned forward and hugged me.

I breathed deeply, feeling more settled than I had in a long time, even without my walls. Now I just needed to convince Maia to stay.

Twelve

I stretched like a cat in the sun as I came awake slowly. My body was stiff and sore, but I felt more relaxed and refreshed than I had in a long time. Like some of my worries had been lifted.

As I opened my eyes, I realized I was lying in a shaft of soft sunlight. I blinked, cleared my vision, and looked out the sliding door. I remembered this room, but it was dark the last time I was in it, and I had escaped out that door.

Then, everything that had happened last night came rushing back, how my life had changed overnight.

I rolled over suddenly and came face to face with a book. I put my finger to the top, lowered it, and Leif's gorgeous face came into view. He smiled at me slowly.

"Hi," he said, almost shyly. "I like to wake up with the sunrise and watch as the world wakes up. So, I usually open the curtains up after I turn out the light when I come to bed. I hope you don't mind?"

"Hi. Uh, sure. That sounds nice. I don't mean to be rude, but I have to go, and I have to go now," I said as I climbed across Leif rapidly.

"Wait. We need to talk. I can fix this," Leif said, seeming panicked as he tried to get up, but I slipped away and cut him off by shutting the bathroom door.

When I opened it again, he was lying back on the bed, eyeing me and the door warily.

"Sorry about that. I said I had to go," I explained as I stood awkwardly in the bathroom doorway.

"Yeah, I figured that out when I heard the waterfall and the long, relieved groan coming from the bathroom," he said, relaxing his big body on the bed. "I thought you meant you were leaving again."

"Nope," I said without elaborating. "And it's rude to comment on a lady's morning ablutions," I stated primly.

"Sorry, ma'am. I...oomph, you know you can go around, right," he complained as I climbed back over the top of him and lay down on his other side again.

I rolled my eyes at him. "Yeah, but it's more fun that way."

"Oh, is that how it's going to go? Two can play that game. I think I need to check something on the sliding door," Leif said as he moved his arm and upper body over me like he would climb across but pinned me to the bed instead.

"No fair, uncle, uncle," I squealed breathlessly. "You have a size advantage."

"I'm just working with what I've got, same as you were, little miss rubbing her body all over me,' he teased. 'Don't think I didn't notice that."

"Are you seriously complaining?" I giggled. Since our kiss last night, something about Leif had me completely relaxed around him, which was unusual. I'd never been relaxed around any men, especially alphas.

I probably should be more worried about that, but I'd decided last night to trust him and see where this would go, so that's what I was going to do. If it went badly, I'd deal with it and call it a learning experience.

I was a hell of a lot better off right now than when I woke up yesterday, or any day over the last three years, so I wasn't going to second guess everything.

"Nope, you can climb on me or over me anytime you want. Consider me your personal man mountain," he said as he settled back in at my side but left his arm over my waist.

"Okay," I replied simply, rolling over to face him. "Your eyes are the lightest blue. I couldn't see the color in the dark last night. They're beautiful."

"Okaaaay," he parroted me but drew it out. "You're very agreeable this morning. I wasn't expecting that."

"What were you expecting?" I asked in surprise.

"I don't know. More of last night, I guess?" he replied, a little confused.

"The dramatic passing out, panicked running or overtired babbling?" I asked while watching him, trying not to grin.

He smiled slowly, like he had a secret. "I liked the overtired babbling personally. It was very informative."

"Crap," I groaned, "that bit is a little fuzzy. Do I need to be worried?"

"Nope, your secrets are safe with me. Pinky promise," he said as he crossed his heart like a schoolgirl and held out his pinky finger for me to grab, which was adorable on this giant alpha.

"You're ridiculous, but I like it," I laughed, giving in to the moment, as I grabbed his pinky finger with mine. He held onto it, then moved his fingers across mine and cupped my hand, bringing it over his heart and holding it there.

I remembered him doing the same thing last night. I'd loved it then, and I loved it now. I threaded my fingers through his, and he smiled softly. He instinctively made me feel safe and protected in a way I'd never known, and I would enjoy him for as long as possible.

I desperately needed a shower and food, but I just wanted to snuggle into this feeling and him for a little while first. Before the moment was gone, I knew the hard way that good things never lasted.

"I have to talk to you about something," he said, suddenly serious. And there it went.

"Uh oh, nothing good ever started with that sentence," I said as I felt suddenly wary. "Can I shower and get properly cleaned first, in case I have to run again?"

"It's nothing bad. Well I don't think it's bad, but if you do, we can work it out," Leif said, rambling like he was flustered. "I stand by what I said last night. You're safe with me. Do you still trust me?"

"I don't know. You're freaking me out," I blurted out. "Just say it."

"Ok, here goes. Before I kissed you, I should have mentioned that I'm in a committed relationship with Max," Leif said, a frown marring his beautiful face.

"I'm sorry. It wasn't fair to you or Max. I've apologized to him already, so I'm saying it to you now. I stand by everything I said last night. I will leave with you, if you need to go, because I need to make sure you're safe." Leif continued frowning and watching me carefully. I could tell he was apprehensive about this.

"But Max has my heart and always will. The other guys do as well but in a different way. There's plenty of room for you in there, too. You're already in there now." He hesitated for a beat, watching me and searching my face, trying to gauge my reaction, then kept going when I didn't react.

"I don't buy into the lie we've been sold that love has boundaries and limitations. I think love is endless, ageless and capable of encompassing many things and people.

"I just need to know if this will be a problem for you because it's not for either Max or me. Or the other guys, for that matter. You don't have to agree to anything or do anything you don't want to do. This is a safe place, and I'll fight anyone to make sure it stays that way.

"I'm just asking you to keep an open mind while we figure out how this works and communicate with us about how you're feeling if anything bothers or upsets you, and we'll do the same, okay?" He finally came to a rambling halt and held his breath, watching me.

"Okay," I replied.

Leif's mouth dropped open as he stared at me for a minute, dumbfounded. "I just poured my heart out and dropped a bomb on you, and all you can say is okay?"

"Yep," I shrugged, stroking his chest gently with my thumb, trying to reassure him with my touch, the same way he had for me last night.

Leif just blinked at me, so I made an effort to try and explain myself better. "Sorry, I thought it was going to be something bad. But I knew about Max, and I already agreed to stay and give you a day to convince me I'm safe here."

"I figured being open-minded was part of what I agreed to, and I think communicating honestly and openly is a great idea."

"You knew about Max?" he asked, shaking his head in confusion. "How?"

I sighed. I hadn't wanted to tell him this. "I overheard some women talking in the kitchen while I was working in the garden yesterday morning, and you and Max came up. Some of them would like to be 'the meat in that man sandwich,' that's a direct quote, in case you're wondering."

A spurt of jealousy churned in my gut now that I knew him, and his frown intensified. I didn't like them talking about Leif, or Max, like that. I mean, at the time, I had just been curious. But now I knew they were talking about my mate, our partially formed bond made me feel a little insecure.

This was all new territory for me. I'd never been jealous of anyone in my life and didn't know what to do with it, so I kept going.

"They weren't sure if you guys were into women as well. They're hoping you are. I don't judge who anyone loves. I think love is love. I don't know how the whole meat in the man sandwich thing works. I'm not that experienced, but it sounds tasty."

He just looked at me in astonishment, eyebrows raised. Clearly, it was my turn to ramble nervously.

"Plus, when you kissed me, it felt like a bond snapped into place...I mean, you felt that as well, right?" I held my breath, but he nodded when he realized I was waiting for a response.

"Okay, good, because I wasn't sure if that was just me for a second." I was relieved I hadn't imagined the whole thing in my fatigue and just made a fool of myself.

"So when I first felt it, I didn't just feel you. I felt echoes of Max. It's all subtle, like a shadow, but when Max arrived, I could pick up enough to know how you felt about him and me.

"It's one of the reasons why I agreed to stay. There's so much joy and love in your heart for Max."

"I didn't know a mate bond lets you feel each other like that. All I ever heard about alphas and mate bonds growing up was how terrible they were—my time at the Palace reinforced that idea too. So I wanted to know more, and I wanted to feel this a little longer. It's been so long since I've felt love, even just feeling someone else's. It's nice."

I ground to a halt, watching him tentatively now. He looked like he was trying to process everything I said and was failing.

"So, you're telling me you can feel how I'm feeling through our bond, and you can feel Max in there as well?" he finally asked. The frown was back on his face. It was making me nervous.

"Yep, I mean, that's normal, right?" Leif just shook his head.

"You can feel me too, though, right?" I asked, feeling confused. He just nodded, and continued frowning.

"Oh," was all I had in response. That was a mind-fuck I couldn't process right now.

We both watched each other uneasily. Then, Leif grinned at me, his smile growing progressively wider.

I laughed nervously. "What?"

"I don't know what in the heck is going on, but I like it. I really like it," Leif said, still grinning like a loon with my hand over his heart. I'd take the grinning over the frowning any day. It lit his whole, beautiful face up and put a sparkle in those gorgeous pale blue eyes.

I brushed his messy golden hair back over his face with my free hand, feeling my heart swell. "Me too."

"And for the record, we're both definitely into women, just in case that needed clarifying," he said cheekily.

I had been so scared of alphas for the longest time, but Leif was nothing like what I had been told. I couldn't believe I had only met him yesterday. It felt like he'd always been there, just waiting for me to find him.

The cold, empty feeling I'd had since my grandpa died and my brother betrayed me was dissipating and being replaced with light and warmth in a way I'd never dared hope to feel again.

It was all tentative and new but also felt solid and stable simultaneously. I could run from it, or I could embrace it. I was choosing to embrace it. I'd made an instinctive decision on the hill last night to trust Leif, and nothing had changed my mind so far.

"Why can't I feel anyone else through my bond to you?" he asked tentatively.

I shrugged, faking nonchalance. I was a big shrugger. A good shrug was easier than words and sometimes more effective, especially for me. But

Leif kept looking at me steadily. I knew it was a trick to get people to fill the silence, but I always fell for it anyway.

"Maybe because there's nobody left alive who loves me?" I replied honestly. The frown returned to his face, and I thought he might be angry, but I felt a hint of sadness through the bond—his, not mine. I felt like the connection was getting stronger just by spending time together.

Leif looked like he wanted to ask questions, but instead he leaned forward and kissed me gently and sweetly, a mere brush of my lips with his, to let me know he was here and cared. Like he knew I needed gentle contact. I felt like I was glowing as his contentment flowed through to me.

Huh, this bond could come in handy.

At that moment, there was a knock at the door. "Come in," Leif spoke against my lips like he was comfortable with anyone it could be in this house, even though he was kissing me.

The door opened, and Max popped his head inside. "Hi," he said. His eyes darted towards us and away again.

"Hi," I replied, turning my head towards Max and ending the kiss. My witty banter skills were on point this morning.

"Speak of the devil," Leif teased, rolling onto his back but still holding my hand over his heart. His shirt had ridden up, and a peek of his abs was on show again, and I may have gotten a little distracted at the slice of heaven.

"Oh, um, I can go, I just...," he stammered.

"No," I said. "Ignore Ragnarok here. Come in." I was trying to put him at ease.

"Ragnarok? Really? Is that going to be a thing?" Leif chuckled in disbelief, while Max opened the door fully and took a single step into the room.

"Maybe. I haven't decided," I teased.

"Ragnarok? Isn't that the epic Norse legend of a world-ending battle between the gods, giants and demons that leads to the death of all gods? I like it." Max joined in on the joke.

I smiled at him. "Yes, am I right? Totally fits," I laughed softly, and Max smiled back at me shyly.

He adjusted his glasses and nervously put his hands in the back pocket of his tight blue jeans like he didn't quite know what to do with them while he was still hovering in the doorway. Only it made his biceps pop and stretched his shirt across his chest. He wasn't as big as the other guys, but he was beautifully proportioned, and I could happily lie here and watch the show.

Leif turned his head and smirked at me like he could tell what I was thinking, and I blushed. Could he read my thoughts? I was going to have to figure out how this bond worked.

"We just got back, and I heard voices, so I figured you were awake. We were just discussing what we're going to do for dinner, bring food up here or head down to the dining hall. Are you hungry, Maia?" Max asked, blushing furiously.

Could he read my mind too, or was I just being obvious in my ogling? I'd have to discreetly check a mirror and see if there was drool on my chin. Was it okay to ogle both of them within minutes? Leif had asked me to be open-minded and honest, hadn't he? So surely it was okay.

Then, my brain came back online in a rush.

"Dinner? Isn't it mid-morning?" I asked, confused, turning to look at the gentle light coming through the sliding glass door.

Leif chuckled. "Uh, no, you slept all night and most of the day, sunshine."

"And since you only gave me a day to convince you to stay, and then you slept through it, you owe me another day," he smirked.

"Okay, wow," I mumbled as my stomach gave an embarrassingly loud growl.

"I think I need to feed my girl," Leif announced pointedly, getting up off the bed and letting my hand go.

"Our girl," came a voice from the hallway, and Hunter popped his head around the door. Both Max and Leif grinned fondly.

"Hi," he said eloquently.

"Hi," I replied just as eloquently and laughed lightly again. I didn't know what was happening with me and all the laughing today. I was a grown-ass woman, not a six-year-old girl. I couldn't remember the last time I had felt so light-hearted.

"Why don't you let our girl have a shower and get cleaned up while we figure out dinner," Hunter suggested.

I didn't know what was with all the "our" girl talk, but I couldn't say I minded. It made me feel wanted and included. Two other things I hadn't felt in a while.

"Then, we can all hang out and get to know each other."

"Sounds like a good plan to me," I said. Although I was nervous about facing Damon, I wanted to get to know Max. And maybe Hunter. He seemed fun. "I'm starving, and I probably smell."

Leif pulled me off the bed and then pulled me into him, leaning close to my neck and inhaling deeply.

"Yep, you smell," he said.

"Hey, not nice," I said and slapped him ineffectually on the arm. I should do that again, slowly, rubbing a little maybe. It was a nice arm.

"I didn't say you smelt bad, sunshine," he smirked before swatting me on the ass and walking out the door. So, it was going to be like that. Game on. I could get handsy too.

I turned to Max and Hunter, who were still hanging around the door.

"Uh, there's towels and toiletries in the bathroom that are all yours now, and I grabbed some of my clothes and Leif put them in the dresser. They'll be big, but I figured I'm closer to your size than the others. They should be comfy for tonight."

"We'll ask the other girls tomorrow if you can borrow some clothes until we can sort something out for you. I know Lexie will be happy to help out. If you're here tomorrow, I mean. No pressure," he stammered, suddenly realizing what he was saying and not wanting to come on too strong. Hunter just smirked at him.

"Take your time and come out when you're ready, okay? No rush."

"Okay, thanks, Max," I wandered over and gave him a quick kiss on the cheek, then headed for the bathroom.

He didn't reply. He just stared at me in speechless amazement while Hunter grabbed him by the hand and led him out of the room.

"Smooth man, real smooth," I heard Hunter tease him.

Max groaned, "Shut up, man," before they disappeared down the hallway.

I smiled to myself as I headed for the bathroom. I liked Hunter and Max's dynamic. There was a lot of love there —a different kind of love, but it was love all the same.

Thirteen

The boys and I were all sitting quietly in the living room when we heard Maia come out of the bathroom. The thought of her naked and drying herself off in the next room had me all hot and bothered.

I was lying on the couch upside down, with my legs resting on the upper floor, bouncing a soft ball off the ceiling. It usually drove Damon nuts, but he was fixated on the hallway to Maia's room.

I watched Max get up and move towards the kitchen, then change his mind, come back and sit back down again. He was bouncing his leg up and down anxiously.

"Chill, dude," I drawled.

"I am," he muttered as he sat forward on the edge of his seat and fiddled with the silver rings on his fingers. His nervousness was making him flustered, much to my delight. Leif was just smiling gently at him. It wasn't like Max to be so nervous. He was usually our calm center.

I looked up when I noticed all the guys had stilled and realized I'd missed her entrance. I looked towards the door and lost all the breath in my lungs as I swiveled to sit upright.

She was fresh out of the shower, her hair still wet and skin damp, like she had rushed getting dried. She was wearing Max's clothes, and I liked how right that looked.

She had twisted his t-shirt and tucked the loose section up through the neck, so it fitted to her body. She wasn't wearing a bra, so the shirt molded directly to her full breasts in a way that made my hands ache to caress them through the soft fabric. I wanted to tease them until her nipples turned hard and ached in the same way my cock did right now.

She'd also put on a pair of soft, light pants Max usually used for yoga, but they were swimming on her, so she'd rolled the top down a few times until they sat low on her curvy hips. The effect was casual and natural yet stunning. She looked like the hotter, sexier version of the girl next door every guy fantasized about as a teenager.

The outfit left much of her stomach tantalizingly bare. I wanted to lick a trail from her breasts to the edge of those pants and then continue down. I should stop staring, but I couldn't look away.

Leif fake coughed, which made both Damon and Max startle. I snickered lightly at them, knowing full well I was just as transfixed.

Max went to stand up but realized he had a giant tent in his sweats. He sat down again, grabbing a cushion to cover his lap, making me laugh harder. I guess he also liked the sight of her in his clothes. I'm glad I was wearing heavy jeans, so my hard-on wasn't so obvious.

Damon took a deep breath and stood up to walk toward her. I tensed and sat up, fully alert, sensing trouble. I knew Damon wouldn't hurt her, but he could freak her out and make her run again, and I wasn't ready for her to leave. I also felt incredibly protective of her already.

I'd told the guys I would wait until she was comfortable, and I'd meant it. I was as keen to get to know her as Leif and Max, but I didn't want us all to rush her at once. We were a lot and she was jumpy.

Plus, I wanted to give Max, Leif and Maia a chance to figure out their dynamic. Max and Leif were one of the most solid relationships I had ever known and I would be devastated if that changed.

"Stand down, Hunt. We're all good," Damon said as he passed me and ruffled my hair affectionately.

I mock-scowled at him, smoothed my hair back into place, then relaxed back into the cushions, still wary. "Just don't be a dick to her, man."

'I have no intention of being a dick. I just want to apologize,' he assured me.

I noticed she looked at Leif in concern, and he nodded in reassurance. I liked that she trusted Leif already. He had that effect on people once they got past his size and their preconceptions. He was like a giant protective teddy bear. It would be easier to convince her to stay if she trusted one of us.

Damon stood straight and tall before her, where we could all see and hear him. I knew he wanted to include us in this. Then, he got straight to the point. "Maia, I'm sorry for my behavior last night."

"I treated you harshly, and it was unjustified. You didn't deserve it, and I'm ashamed of how I behaved. I could give you many reasons or excuses, but there aren't any."

He hesitated and looked away for a moment and I held my breath. It looked like he wasn't sure what to say next, even though I knew he'd been practicing in his head all day.

He sounded too formal and I was worried he was messing this up. Maia was just watching him carefully.

He ran his hands through his hair restlessly before he looked back at her and he seemed to force himself to relax slightly. I breathed a little easier as he continued, sounding a little more chill.

"The guys and I talked last night, and they made me realize I was acting out of fear over my own issues. I won't ask you to forgive me right now because I believe actions count more than words. I know I will have to prove I'm not what you saw of me last night.

"I swear to you, though, that I'll do better. I want you to feel safe here for as long as you need or want to stay. The idea that I made you, of all people, feel unsafe," he shook his head and growled quietly, like he was trying to dislodge something from his brain, "that's on me."

"I am going to ask two things of you, though," Damon said, pausing and making heavy eye contact like he needed to make this bit clear.

Maia raised her eyebrow and cocked her head at that, squaring her shoulders in challenge, which was hot as fuck. I liked that she had some sass. It made my dick hard. Plus it meant that she wouldn't put up with any shit from us and would keep us on our toes. She'd need to be strong to deal with all of us and our crap.

She crossed her arms under her chest while she waited for Damon to list his requests, unintentionally pushing her luscious breasts up. I had to force myself to keep looking at her face.

"Please don't hold my actions against Leif, Max, Hunter or anyone else here. They don't deserve it. They're good people."

"And, please give Leif another day because I want to fix this, and I can't do that if you leave tonight."

Damon paused and waited for her reaction because she'd given him nothing so far. I held my breath to see what she would say. I could see Leif and Max shifting anxiously across from me.

"Okay," she said as she relaxed her posture, releasing her arms and putting her hands casually into her pockets. Leif burst out laughing, and Damon spun to look at him in confusion.

"That's Maia code for 'thanks for the awesome speech. I appreciate it because you freaked the poop out of me, acting like the insane alphas I've been warned about. I like everything you said, so you're off the hook for now. Just don't mess up again, you idiot. Oh, and I already agreed to give Leif another day,' " Leif chuckled, and Maia rolled her eyes at him.

Damon turned back to her expectantly, he seemed unsure what to make of that. I'd never seen him look so wary around someone, like her response meant something to him.

"What he said,' was all she gave him, jerking her head in Leif's direction, 'but my version had the words shit and asshole in it." She looked pointedly at Damon and smiled sweetly, making my dick jerk in my pants.

"Ooookkkayyyy," Damon drawled, not quite sure but willing to go with it. I figured he wasn't going to get any more just yet. She seemed to have connected to Leif instantly and instinctively, but she was justifiably wary of Damon.

They both stood near the top of the steps looking awkward, and seemed unsure of what to do. Luckily Max stepped in and rescued them. He must have gotten himself under control.

"You weren't in the shower long, Maia. We thought you'd be in there for ages. Is everything okay?"

"I didn't know how much hot water you had, and I didn't want to use it all," she replied.

"That's very considerate of you. Most people wouldn't have cared after going so long without one," I said, not mocking her, just being honest.

She shrugged. "I'm not most people," she said as she grinned at me. Oh yeah, she was going to be fun.

She started running her fingers through knots in her hair, and my fingers itched to touch the long strands.

"Do you need help with your hair?" Leif asked.

"I couldn't find a hairbrush, and I couldn't get out all the knots," she sighed as she grabbed a piece of her gorgeous long blond hair and tried to run her fingers through it. She seemed nervous and hadn't asked for help or a brush. Instead, she just tried to deal with it herself.

From what Lexie and Dave had said today, she hadn't asked for help from them either and had only accepted it hesitantly after agreeing to work for it. I got the impression she was used to doing things for herself without help.

"I've got a detangling hairbrush. Take a seat, and I'll grab it for you," Leif instructed as he ran up the stairs to his bedroom two at a time. Damon walked back down the steps and headed towards the back end of the couch, where he'd been sitting earlier. I gave him a fist bump when he raised his fist as he passed.

Maia calmly walked down the steps after him but went to sit next to Max, crossing her legs up on the couch. He shifted in his seat nervously.

"Thanks for the clothes, Max," she said as she turned to him and smiled more genuinely this time.

"Oh, yeah. No problem, they uh, look great on you," he managed to get out. I couldn't help but grin at his nervousness. He was adorably flustered.

She looked down at his lap, still covered by a cushion, then back up at him and smirked, raising an eyebrow. He looked away, embarrassed as I sniggered quietly. He was so busted.

Thankfully Leif came bounding down the stairs, like a giant puppy, so eager to get back that he jumped the railing over the landing instead of walking the last flight. She turned at the thud as he hit the ground, and her face lit up with a grin when she saw him.

The way she looked at him made my heart pound in my chest. I was so happy for him. I could only hope she'd look at me like that one day.

"Bad hulk, no smash," I said to tease him. Damon lunged and tried to grab me in a headlock, but I evaded him as we wrestled briefly on the couch, laughing wildly.

"Hulk get hairbrush for pretty girl," Leif growled playfully, exaggeratingly flexing his muscles.

"Thank you," she said. Damon and I settled down and I noticed she eyed Leif's huge, flexed biceps and unconsciously bit her lip as she held out her hand for the brush.

"Uh, can I do it?" Leif asked her, blushing and fidgeting with the brush. Man, he was so gone for her.

She looked flustered at that. "Oh, okay, sure." I had a feeling it had been a long time since anyone had brushed her hair, if ever.

Leif sat down on the floor behind her, draping his legs down either side of her. Then he carefully grabbed sections of golden hair and started brushing it out gently.

"Oh," she said, as she leant into him a little more and closed her eyes. "That feels good. I don't think anyone has brushed my hair since my older brother got kicked out of home when I was a kid."

We all stilled and watched as she sighed dreamily and tilted her head forward with her eyes closed. I could watch Leif brush her hair all day.

"I'm happy to brush your hair anytime you let me, sunshine. I used to brush my sister's all the time when I was younger," Leif mumbled while focussing on her hair, spending as much time stroking it with his fingers as brushing it.

I think he used to brush his sister's hair a little differently. He was incredibly gentle whenever he came across a snag, though. I know because I was watching it intently, wishing I could have a turn.

I'd never been interested in anything so mundane as brushing a woman's hair before, but with Maia, I was desperate to touch her in any way I could. I was willing to bide my time though. I wanted to make sure we got this right, because for me, this was going to be forever and we only had one shot at it.

I got up and headed for the kitchen to grab some snacks. I was willing to hang back in pursuing her, but I could still make damn sure she got what she needed in the meantime.

"Here, you need to eat something. We can grab some dinner from the dining hall soon, but this should help until then," I said as I handed Maia some snacks in a bowl, being careful not to make physical contact.

I knew Damon and Leif had both had intense reactions after touching her for the first time and I didn't want to trigger anything before I was ready.

"Thanks, Hunter. I'm not fussy, I'll take anything I can get." She smiled gratefully at me as she grabbed an energy bar and a juicy green apple and put the bowl on the coffee table. My heart almost stopped beating as her smile shone my way. I had to force myself to keep moving and back away.

"Why was your older brother kicked out of home?" I asked, watching her closely as she ripped open the energy bar and devoured it in three bites, before moving on to the apple.

"Hunt, man, you can't ask that," Max said, shaking his head at me. I knew it was a personal question, but if I couldn't touch her I was desperate to hear more about her.

"No, it's okay. We said tonight was a getting to know you night. I don't mind." Maia said gently, opening her eyes to look at me across from her on the couch. Man, her eyes, when she looked at me intently like that. I didn't know how long I was going to be able to hold out. It was like she'd lassoed me and was drawing me closer with just a look.

"I'm sure you guys have a lot of questions," she added.

I had a tonne of questions. I wanted to know everything about Maia. Where she had come from, where she was going, and who I had to kill for hurting her. Because she was clearly on the run from someone. The idea made ice run through my veins.

I was a killer, but I didn't kill gladly or wantonly. I made damn sure the person in my crosshairs deserved it before I ever pulled a trigger. Whoever put those shadows in her eyes though, they deserved everything that was coming to them.

I noticed Damon move out of the corner of my eye. I knew him, and I knew he'd try to leave after apologizing, feeling like he hadn't earned a spot in this getting to know you chat. I grabbed his shirt and pulled him back down, subtly shaking my head at him. He needed to be here if we were going to make this work.

"My gramps always warned us about alphas growing up and how they treated omegas. He never gave us details, but I think maybe he secretly loved an omega once and it ended badly at the hands of an alpha. Gramps was ex-military, and he saw a lot of abuse from alphas," she said.

We all looked at each other. We'd seen a lot of bad alphas in our time too, but it wasn't who we were. We'd have to prove that to her over time, though. For now, all we could do was listen.

"Anyway," she continued, "Sam started shooting up and filling out young, probably around the age of twelve or so, and gramps started watching him all the time. Soon after, he presented as an alpha, and I was worried for him. I don't know what happened, but I came home one day, and Sam was gone."

She tried to play it off like it wasn't a big deal, but I could hear the pain in her voice, and it felt like tiny splinters embedding in my heart with every word.

"Gramps just told me it was necessary, and Sam wasn't coming back to the farm. He never talked about him again. I know Sam didn't go willingly. He loved me."

"Sam and Ben, my younger brother, didn't always get along. But Sam was my best friend. Gramps was always busy with the farm, so Sam took care of me, even though he was only two years older. He always brushed my hair, made my breakfast, and read me bedtime stories."

"Things were different after Sam left. I had to learn to be more independent, fast. It fell to me to look after Ben, and he had a lot of anger issues."

Maia had closed her eyes again. I wasn't sure if it was because the story was painful or if she was enjoying Leif brushing her hair. I think it was a bit of both.

The guys all looked at Max this time, and he nodded solemnly without us having to ask. He'd do some hacking and see if he could find anything out about Sam. It was harder to do after the Crash, but I knew he'd do what he could. I didn't know what we'd do without him and his tech skills.

"Is that why you were so freaked out and ran last night after we arrived back here?' I asked. 'Because you'd been told so many bad things about alphas as a kid and your brother became an alpha then disappeared?"

Maia nodded. "That and personal experience." She didn't elaborate further, and I didn't push. I didn't want to remind her of bad experiences with alphas right now, but I'd get her to open up to me about it eventually.

"Where were your parents?" I asked gently. The guys were all sitting still, completely mesmerized by her while she talked, hanging on every word.

"Dad died in a car crash when we were young. I only have vague memories of him. I don't think he was around all that much before he died."

"Mum took us to live on the farm with gramps when we got evicted. But after a few months, she decided she wanted to go off and find herself. She said we were holding her back. We never heard from her again." Maia was quiet after that. Leif had all the knots in her hair out now, but he kept brushing her hair gently. I was glad one of us was able to touch her right now.

So many people had left her. No wonder she seemed so lonely and happy with any little attention.

"We get it. None of us had great home lives either." I told her honestly as I lay down along the couch to get more comfortable. I wasn't one for sitting upright with correct posture.

"I grew up in foster care," Max said, sharing part of his story, "then went straight into the military when I aged out. It was the only way I could get the education I wanted. I didn't know what family was until I met these guys." He looked at us all warmly and I nodded at him in encouragement. He didn't like talking about his early years.

She opened her eyes and took his hand, giving it a gentle squeeze. He seemed a little startled but kept hold of her hand. Max began stroking it lightly with his thumb, almost unconsciously. Leif was very tactile with her as well. She seemed to soak up small touches. It made my hands itch to touch her.

"I grew up with only my dad and my sister," Leif said gently, still focusing on her hair. "Mum died giving birth to her. My nana was my rock when I was young, but my dad banished her and the rest of my mum's family after mum died."

Maia reached up with her other hand and grasped his, bringing it around and kissing his knuckles before placing their joined hands over her heart together. I'd seen him do this with her last night, and my heart warmed seeing her returning the gesture. Leif had so much love to give and deserved the same in return.

Leif gently kissed her forehead when she looked up backwards at him.

"Dad was so happy when I presented as an alpha," Leif continued, "he'd always thought I was too soft and that I needed toughening up."

"I took a lot of abuse to try and shield Lexie. He never forgave her for our mother's death. But, after I presented as an alpha, it got worse. He thought my size should make me mean and aggressive. He didn't like it when I wouldn't bully people for him."

"He was a politician and pulled strings to get me all but drafted when I turned eighteen. I don't know if I would have survived the military with my soul intact if I hadn't found these guys."

He looked around fondly at us, and I noticed Maia's eyes were misty.

"I was an unwanted 'oh shit' late in life baby for my parents," I said simply, watching Maia, Leif and Max interact on the other side of the couch. "I had an older brother I never met. He was the beloved heir, but he died young. They had no interest in me when I turned up unexpectedly. I was raised mostly by a revolving door of nannies."

"I met Damon in high school and spent most of my time at his house after that. My parents rarely even noticed if I was there or not. They always seemed surprised if they saw me around the house."

I fiddled with the cushions on the couch, picking a small one up and spinning it around. I hated talking about my childhood, but I knew I needed to open up to Maia if I wanted her to trust me.

"I joined the military when Damon did. There was no way I was letting him go through that alone."

Maia looked at Damon expectantly, and Leif disentangled his hand so he could continue brushing her hair.

I knew Damon was reluctant to share any part of his story. I dropped the cushion and put my arm around his back in silent support. Touch was so important for us both. He reached up, grabbed my hand and squeezed it gently.

"My Dad was a big-shot CEO and a psychopath. My mum was a society wife and alcoholic. They were never around much, but things were bad when they were."

"My dad had big plans for me. He insisted that having a high-ranking military son would help him get military contracts, and he didn't care what I wanted. He'd been trying hard to break me ever since I hit puberty and started showing signs of strong dominance. If Hunter hadn't come along, I don't know if I would have survived."

It was only a hint of what we had gone through growing up, but I knew it was as much as he could give right now. He wasn't used to dealing with his emotions instead of pushing them back behind walls. His emotions were messy and so close to the surface at the moment, he was genuinely terrified of them.

"That's how we became a team and eventually a family, Leif, Max, Hunter and me," Damon continued. "We bonded in basic training and had each other's backs from the start, against the people who raised us and what the military tried to turn us into.

"We kept each other grounded and stopped each other from spiraling when things got tough. It's been us against the world for a long time."

We were all quiet for a moment. Maia was watching Damon intently, but he wasn't meeting her eyes.

"I think that's heavy enough for one night, guys," I said casually. Damon squeezed my hand gratefully.

"Do you want to come and grab some food from the dining hall with me before there's none left?" I asked Damon. I wanted to give Max some time alone with Leif and Maia.

"Good call, let's go." He knew what I was up to.

"I'm starving, and we promised this girl some proper food to eat," I added, getting up slowly and heading for the stairs.

"We'll be at least fifteen minutes, maybe more, which is plenty of time for getting to know each other," I smirked and opened my eyes wide at Maia before looking exaggeratedly at Leif and Max, trying to lighten the moment in my usual way. With teasing.

Damon grabbed a cushion from the couch and launched it at me, but I dodged it, leaping over the back and racing to the door. "Last one there has to–"

"No fair," Damon yelled, cutting me off and racing after me out the door. He knew whatever I'd come up with, he didn't want to be doing it.

Fourteen

I didn't know what was wrong with me. I was behaving like a teenage boy that had never spoken to a girl before. It wasn't even my first time talking with Maia. I'd spoken to her ten minutes ago.

She had kissed me on the cheek earlier, and my brain had turned to mush, while my dick unilaterally decided it was party time. As a beta, I didn't have the instant scent reaction Leif, Hunter, and Damon had. But I knew without a doubt, I wanted her to be mine.

When I saw her step forward and defend Leif from Damon, looking like an avenging angel, I had instantly realized she was his mate. I was struck dumb, then so damn happy for him. I hadn't thought at the time about what it might mean for us, nor had Leif until Damon mentioned it. Even then, I had brushed it off. Confident everything would happen the way it was supposed to. I knew Leif and I were solid.

It wasn't until I saw them lying in bed together that it suddenly got very real. I hadn't been jealous. It was the exact opposite. I realized how badly I wanted to be in there with Leif and Maia, and I wasn't sure how to make that happen.

I felt nervous around someone for the first time, knowing she was important. If Maia had Leif, Hunter and eventually Damon all chasing her and claiming her as a mate, what could she need from me? And if I messed this up, what would it mean for Leif and me?

She was still holding my hand right now. I didn't want to move or make a sound in case she realized and pulled her hand away. So I just kept stroking it gently with my thumb.

I was hyper-aware of her body alongside mine. Seeing her come out of her room in my clothes earlier had almost exploded my brain and my pants. Knowing my shirt was pressed against her naked body was doing stupid things to mine.

I was so embarrassed she'd spotted my hard-on, but I still wanted to shift closer to her and feel her soft heat through my clothes. Man, I had it bad. I needed to snap out of it, or I would embarrass myself even more.

I looked to Leif nervously, unsure how to break the silence or even if I should. I was pretty happy just sitting here watching her.

"All done." Leif announced as he picked up the section of golden hair lying over her shoulder and brought it back with the rest, smoothing it all down. I looked down at the motion, watching her hair move like liquid silk through his fingers.

But I also noticed that her wet hair had soaked through my shirt and left it almost transparent over her breast. I could see her hard nipple clearly through the material, and I forgot to breathe.

It was one of the most erotic things I had ever seen, and she was completely clothed. My dick had definite ideas about what to do. It was stiff and aching in my pants.

"I think Max might need a hand with something Leif," she murmured, and my eyes snapped to hers to see her watching me with raw curiosity.

I gulped and looked at Leif, who smiled sweetly at me. "Always happy to lend a hand," he said as he slid down onto the couch behind her, somehow managing to maneuver her onto his lap and turn her sideways, so she was facing me.

She shifted one of her legs, so it was thrown across mine. The heat of her skin through the thin cotton fabric burned a path across my lap.

Leif then leaned slowly down towards me. He grazed his lips across mine tenderly, encouraging me to open to him.

I could never deny him anything. I parted my lips slightly, and he took the opportunity to deepen the kiss, slipping his tongue into my mouth and stroking mine reverently. All the while, Maia was still holding my hand.

He pulled back slowly, and we both looked toward Maia, not knowing how she would react. My breathing had sped up, and I could feel my heart pounding anxiously. Knowing she was watching made my dick impossibly harder.

Her lips parted, and she breathed heavier while watching us with hooded eyes. She shifted slightly in Leif's lap and subtly pushed her chest out further, straining the fabric like she was seeking some friction against her nipples.

"Fuck, that was hot," she said slowly, desire clear in her husky voice.

Leif groaned as she shifted restlessly on his lap, unconsciously grinding her ass into him. He snaked his arm around her waist and clamped his hand on her hip, squeezing hard.

She looked at him with molten heat, then glanced coyly at me before looking back to Leif again.

"You know how you asked me to keep an open mind about Max?" she asked huskily. He nodded slowly as he subtly shifted his hips upwards to grind against her in return.

She breathed heavily, a sigh escaping her gorgeous mouth and his eyes immediately went to it, watching intently as she licked her lips, making them wet and glossy. I could relate to both of them at that moment.

Leif's dick was the same as the rest of him, giant-sized, and I knew what it felt like grinding into me. It was impossible to miss or resist. I was just as mesmerized by her mouth now as he was.

Sitting here with a hard-on while they grinded against each other and talked about me had me almost coming in my pants. My teenage fantasies had nothing on this reality.

I was hanging on her next words, hardly able to breathe. If she didn't get to the point quickly, I was likely to pass out.

"Does that include tasting him?"

Leif groaned louder this time and thrust harder like he couldn't hold himself back. "Heck, yeah."

She smiled slowly at him. He was adorable and incredibly sexy at the same time. She reached up and caressed his face slowly, then turned her attention to me.

It was like being lit up with electricity. My body immediately buzzed with an intense need to taste Maia, to feel her. I just needed more. Anything she would give me.

I waited, feeling like I was pinned between heaven and hell, unable to move as she gently leaned toward me. Those deep, blue eyes branded me.

She lifted her hand and reached up to gently caress my hair, and I shifted my head into it, letting out a deep exhale. She ran her hand slowly down to my face, leaving sparks behind, before she leaned forward, stopping a breath away and looking into my eyes.

"Is this okay?"

It was so very okay. I think I would honestly shoot someone if they interrupted us right now. "Yes, you can have anything you want from me, Maia."

I couldn't see or hear Leif. I think he was holding his breath, but I knew he was right there with us, hanging on to this moment that would change everything between us and make it so much better.

She smiled a sexy little grin and closed the final distance between us. Her lips grazed mine as gently as Leif's had done. They were so very soft, much softer than his. The contrast had me panting, needing more.

I could taste the sweetness of the apple on her breath. It mixed with her naturally fruity scent into an intoxicating mix that had all my senses on overload. It was like tasting and breathing in sunshine and summer. But it now had a deep, sweet undertone of cake from her arousal.

She pressed more firmly, moving her lips over mine, exploring the shape of my mouth, before parting her lips gently. I took it as an invitation, and it broke my stasis. I reached out with both hands, running them up the soft, damp skin of her arms and into her hair like I'd been longing to do all night.

Wrapping the silky, wet strands around my fingers, I yanked her harder against me and thrust my tongue into her mouth, making her moan and driving me wild. I lost all restraint as I kissed her passionately and fervently, exploring every inch of her mouth and making it mine.

I could feel her moving slightly, as though Leif was grinding into her ass harder, and the thought tipped me over the edge. I ravaged her mouth desperately until I pulled back suddenly, breathing hard, worried I had gone too far.

She looked at me dazedly, her eyes glazed. "Wow," was all she said.

"Tell me how he tastes," Leif begged.

She turned to him and shrugged. "Or, I could show you."

She leaned towards him and placed her lips over his, parting them instantly and thrusting her tongue into his open mouth as he panted, devouring her while still grinding against her ass, only harder now and much more obviously.

She pulled back and curled an eyebrow at him sexily, with her hair all mussed up and her lips slightly swollen from two brutal kisses. "So, Leif, how does he taste?"

"His sweetness, mixed with your natural fruitiness, it's everything I never knew I wanted," he answered honestly, and her face lit up.

My heart melted, and when Leif turned to look at me, I knew he felt the same. We had never felt anything was missing in our relationship, but we had never dared to hope of finding someone who would complete us in this way and be so accepting of both of us.

Leif leaned over and rested his forehead against mine, bringing her in against us in a gentle hug. She reached up and put her arms around us while leaning against our chests. I could feel a faint echo of their contentment and joy. It filled me with awe. I had never dared to dream I would ever feel a mate bond, even an echo of one.

At that moment, it felt like in the utter chaos and darkness of the world, we had managed to find something perfect and pure.

I would do anything, and everything, to protect her, and I knew Leif would do the same. She was ours. Forever.

We stayed like that, just sitting in the moment until a feminine voice asked, "Well, what do we have here?" and Maia stiffened between us.

Fifteen

I went on high alert, not liking another woman around right now in such an intimate moment with my mate, until I recognised the voice as Lexie's.

"It smells like orange and chocolate cake in here. Has someone been baking?" She was all sass with a cheeky grin.

I hopped off Leif's lap, flipping my hair back over my chest, so I didn't give everyone an eyeful of my nipple, as Leif blushed furiously.

I headed over towards Lexie, keen to say hi and get to know her better. Especially now that I knew she was Leif's baby sister, and he'd come to mean so much to me, so quickly.

"It looks like we interrupted playtime, and we didn't even get an invite," Hunter said as he wandered over and eyed the two men on the couch.

"Well, considering every dick in this room falls into the category of brother dick for me, I'm not looking for an invite."

The horrified look on Hunter's face had Lexie lighting up with glee. "Well, that's one sure way to get a dick to deflate quickly. Can we please never hear the term brother dick coming out of your mouth ever again?"

"Well, there's two different types of brother dick, you know. One refers to the dick of your brother, and the other to the dicks of two or more brothers unrelated to you. Do we have to ban both of them? Because I'd be happy to see some brother dick if it's the second one."

I kept a straight face at Lexie's antics. If teasing Hunter was on the cards, I was all in.

"Well, technically, the second one should be brother's dicks, because there are two of them, so that may clear things up," I said as I reached Lexie. She had pulled up a chair at the dining table and made herself at home. I put my hand up for a high five. She grinned and slapped my hand, turning to wink at Hunter playfully.

'Ugggh, please, someone make them stop saying brother dick,' Hunter begged, dropping his bags and throwing himself on the couch dramatically. With a glint in his eye, he turned and tried to steal the cushion off Leif's lap, knocking the empty whiskey glass off the huge coffee table in the center of the living room as he tussled with Leif.

"Knock it off, you guys. Put the dinner on the table, Hunter, not on the floor, and put the glass in the sink," Damon instructed, sounding stern, but when he turned away, I saw his lips curve slightly like he was trying to hide a smile.

"Where's Bear?" Leif asked Lexie.

"Off sniffing shit and chasing night creatures. You know, important doggy stuff. He often disappears at this time of night."

Damon brought back a stack of plates from the kitchen as Hunter reluctantly got up and picked up the bags. "We usually eat on the couch or around the breakfast bench, but we can eat at the dining table if you'd prefer, Maia?"

Lexie shook her head at him, popping up from her chair and grabbing my hand before leading me towards the door. "Sorry, those bags are for you guys. This one's for Maia and me. I'm stealing her for some girl time. We're going to watch movies at my place, try on all my clothes, eat food and talk shit about all of you." I loved this girl so much already.

"Hang on, wait a sec," Leif jumped up quickly.

Lexie turned and put her hand up. "No way. Sorry bro, you can't come. My clothes won't fit you."

Leif rolled his eyes at her. I got the feeling these five all liked pushing each other's buttons, but they did it affectionately.

"I wasn't asking to come, Lex, but before you drag Maia out the door, maybe let her put on a pair of shoes and a hoodie. It's cool out there once the sun goes down."

Max jumped up and headed for the spare room, talking over his shoulder. "I'll grab her shoes out of her bedroom and a pair of my socks out of the dresser."

I was momentarily distracted by him calling it my room as I watched him walk away. Did he mean it as my room permanently, or just as in the room I had been using earlier? And hot damn, he had a gorgeous ass in those jeans.

I was distracted from my ogling of Max by Leif. As he walked over to me, he pulled his hoodie over his head, which pulled his shirt up, exposing that ripped stomach that made my insides clench with need. I couldn't tear my gaze away. It felt almost pornographic, just watching him take his hoodie off.

My scent intensified sharply, and I could hear Lexie snicker at me while waving her hand in front of her face pointedly, but I didn't care. I wasn't missing a second of this show.

"Here, sunshine, take mine. It will be nice and warm for you already. Lift your arms."

I did what Leif asked without thinking, entirely on autopilot, since my brain was currently off-line. He slipped the hoodie over my arms and down my body, managing to caress my sides and graze my boobs as he did it. The tiny caress had me instantly wet with need, and a slight whimper escaped me.

"How the hell can putting clothes on someone be sexier than taking them off?" Hunter asked with a rasp in his voice as he watched with his head resting on his arms on the back of the couch, mesmerized.

Damon was standing still, with the plates in his hand, as if he had completely forgotten what he was doing.

The hoodie was blissfully warm as it swamped my body, and smelt strongly of Leif's irresistible scent. I looked up at him gratefully. "Thanks, Leif." He just watched me intently.

"Here you go...uh, what did I miss?" Max asked as he stepped back into the room, looking around at all of us curiously.

"The opening scene of a porno," Lexie quipped.

"Have you watched any porn, Lexie? The clothes come off thirty seconds in, not on." Hunter said as he returned her wink from earlier. "That was hot, Leif, but can you demonstrate to Lexie how porn actually works, please."

Leif blushed furiously again, and I smiled at him, taking his hand and giving it a gentle squeeze.

I noticed Max appear at his side, holding out my shoes. "Thanks, Max." I dropped Leif's hand reluctantly and reached for my shoes, sitting down in Lexie's vacated chair to put them on.

Leif grudgingly turned his attention to his sister. "Keep to the main paths, Lex. Don't circle out by the fence. Take my radio and buzz Damon when you're done, and we'll come to pick Maia up. Or, let us know if you're turning it into a sleepover, okay? One of us will come to keep watch."

Before I could say anything in reply, Lexie jumped straight in. "You know you taught me how to take care of myself, big bro, and I'm pretty sure Maia can handle herself. She spent three days alone in the big bad world and survived."

Damn right I did. I've never needed anyone to rescue me. I didn't even need Lexie jumping in, but I appreciated her trying to pull her brother into line, especially while I was hormone-addled.

I mean, seriously. I'd gone from being slightly curious about guys in my late teens and fooling around with a beta secretly on my gramps farm to being completely turned off by any of the men at the Palace, alpha or beta.

My libido had been missing in action for three years. Now it felt like a giant switch had flipped, and I was a lusty, panting mess anytime one of these four guys came anywhere near me.

Even Hunter affected me, and he hadn't even laid a finger on me. I didn't want to think about my instant, intense draw to Damon the first night before I dramatically passed out.

I'd worried for a hot minute earlier that maybe being out of the Palace had brought my omega instincts back online, and I was reacting to any man I came across. But I'd been around Dave and some of the guards since I'd been here, and they hadn't raised even a passing interest from my girl parts, not a tingle or aching nipple in sight.

Plus, I'd dodged a few men on the road, even an alpha at one point. I'd come around a corner in the dark and spotted an alpha standing in the street like he had no fear of anyone. His buttered popcorn scent had been all wrong, not off-putting and not gag-inducing like others I'd been subjected to at the Palace, but just not for me.

The mysterious alpha had sent all my prey instincts into overdrive. Watching from the shadows, I could sense he was looking for something. He had stiffened and started scenting the air, turning around and looking for the source.

I'd jammed my finger between the handlebar of my bike and the brake, hard, to cause enough pain to dull my scent, and backed away slowly. So, I knew it wasn't just any alpha that had me so hot and bothered. It was the three in this room and one hot beta.

When I looked up, Leif was looking at his sister with a note of pride. "I know, Lex, I'm not doubting you, and I fully expect you to pull me, or any other guy, back from any line we cross."

He looked at me quickly, then back at his sister. "Can you just humor me a little, just for a bit, while I figure this out? This whole mate bond thing is new for me. I'm a little on edge having her out of my sight right now while I haven't claimed her, and I'm trying hard not to turn into a possessive jerk."

Oh, be still, my beating heart. I was trying hard not to swoon.

Lexie smiled softly at him but said sternly, "You get a little lee-way because I know you're a good guy. But, I will bust your balls if you start telling her what she can or can't do."

I liked Lexie's fierce spirit, but I could talk for myself.

I grabbed his hand again as I stood up, to reassure us both. "Right here, guys. I appreciate you both being concerned for me, but I have a voice, and I'm not afraid to use it. I'm not a cowering princess hiding in a palace tower." Not that there was anything wrong with princesses, I just preferred the kick-ass kind who saved themselves.

I turned and faced Leif fully. "This is new for me as well. I was terrified of being mated, but you've made it feel like something beautiful. Before you even kissed me, you made me feel safe."

"I know we haven't claimed each other yet, but realizing you're my mate is already the best thing that has ever happened to me. So relax, and we'll figure it out together."

Leif's face split into the biggest smile I'd ever seen, and he moved our joined hands up to his heart in a move I was quickly growing to love. I realized he did it whenever he was feeling a strong emotion for me.

I'd loved his smile earlier, but this one lit him up from within.

"Are you claiming me as your mate in front of my family?" he asked with a note of wonder.

I didn't even hesitate, which was a whole revelation in itself for me.

"Yes." It was simple but from the heart. I already knew I'd be a fool if fear led me to let this big, beautiful man go.

I'd been alone long enough. Leif was mine. I'd fight to keep him if I had to.

I knew I was attracted to the other guys as well. I'd figure out what that meant later. No matter what, though, I knew I'd never come between them. I wanted to be part of this family they'd built, in whatever way they'd let me. I'd never been more sure of anything.

Lief picked me up with his other arm, like I weighed nothing, and spun me around, whooping loudly, almost knocking his sister over. She just jumped clear, laughing with tears shining in her eyes.

When he finally stopped, I glimpsed Max, standing just behind us and reached out my other hand for him. He stepped into me instantly, and Leif let go of my waist to put his other arm around him. "You're part of this, Max. I know you're not an alpha, and we can't form a bond, but I can feel how important you are to Leif."

"I can feel you in here," I said as I placed Max's hand under ours, over Leif's chest. While Leif stared at me in awe, Max looked like he was about to cry. "And, I already know you're going to be important to me, too."

I hadn't had as much time with Max as with Leif yet, but I knew he had a big heart and cared for everyone here, always noticing what they needed.

I could also tell he hung back sometimes, thinking he wasn't as essential or wanted as the other guys. I was going to prove him wrong.

"I don't know how we got so lucky that you stumbled into our life," Max said quietly, "but we're going to make it the best life for you." Leif just nodded, and I smiled at them both, standing so strong, side by side.

We were all silent for a moment. I suspected if Leif asked to bite and permanently claim me right now, I'd say yes. I had an overwhelming urge to claim him right back. But I looked around and realized the moment wasn't right.

I hadn't noticed Hunter move earlier, but he had gotten up from the couch and moved a few steps toward us. Like he wanted to be a part of it and couldn't stay away, but also didn't want to interrupt us. He watched us intently. The usual cheeky humor was temporarily gone like he knew this moment was significant.

Damon was still standing with the forgotten plates in his hand. He'd tilted his head quizzically like he was trying to puzzle something out.

It was Lexie who finally broke the silence.

"So, girl's night, or an orgy. Those are your two options. Where are you at?"

I chuckled, shaking my head. "While I would be down for an orgy," Hunter's ears perked up at that, and a sexy grin lit his face. He was a shameless flirt. "I think some girl time would be perfect right now."

I was so happy at this moment, despite the Crash and the nightmare going on outside these fences, but the last two days had been a lot, and we were moving fast. I was ready for some downtime and some girl-talk with a new friend.

"All right, let's go before this food gets cold. I'm starving," Lexie said, bouncing on her feet impatiently.

"I'll be back in a few hours." I promised Leif and Max, who were both still holding my hand.

"You have to let her go, if you're going to let her go, bro," Lexie said with her typical sass.

Leif relaxed and released me. "If you're spending the evening with Lexie, that means you owe me another day."

He either hadn't figured out that I wasn't planning on leaving anytime soon, or he was teasing me. I figured I'd string him along a little more and see what happened.

"Okay," I said, but I gave him a quick, gentle kiss, which said so much more, then leaned over and gave Max one as well.

I headed out the door as Lexie asked, "One more day, what's that about? Are you going somewhere?"

I grinned. "I'll tell you later." Seriously, my cheeks were going to hurt from all the grinning I'd done this afternoon. It felt weird but good. I don't remember ever smiling this much. Even back on my gramps' farm, which I had loved, I never smiled much, especially after Sam left. Farm life had been tough, and so had my gramps, and there had always been more work.

The path was dark, but I had become used to the dark this week. I knew there were more monsters in the daylight than could ever be hiding in the dark bushes. What was usually hiding back there were scared people like me.

True predators didn't need to hide. They ruled the world in plain sight.

Besides, the moon was still full and letting off a beautiful silvery glow once you let your eyes adjust.

We wandered the path quietly until we reached her cabin, not awkwardly, just in companionable silence, which I liked. I didn't feel the need to fill every moment with words, and it was nice when I met someone who felt the same.

Her cabin was cute, like a little log cabin with a porch. When she unlocked the door, she motioned me inside and shut the door behind us before I sensed her moving away, and a small lamp came on that lit the place with a warm glow.

"Sorry," she said. "We have a policy of no light shining outside at night. So the door needs to be shut before the light goes on. The guys have always been pretty big on security, but even more so now. They're trying not to attract too much attention to our set-up here."

"I get it. It's smart. You'll get no complaints from me. I saw what went on out there to people who flaunted having power at night. They didn't seem to keep it long."

"The guys redesigned this place to be self-sustainable when Damon inherited it. We're completely off the grid, but with a lot of mod-cons thanks to Max's tech genius."

'Every cabin has energy efficiency stuff, like the block-out curtains to keep heat out in summer and warmth inside in winter. Things like that have made it easy to conceal our electricity usage from each cabin's solar panels and batteries.'

"The biggest problem is the main building because it's all glass, which is why we prepare dinner early right now. The guys are getting around to blocking it up so we can use it more at night."

"We used to cook and eat in our cabins. But we've started preparing all the meals for everyone in the main kitchen to track how much food we're using. It's kinda nice, having meals together as a group."

I nodded and looked around. I realized it was a studio, with a big bed covered in a funky art print quilt and a small functional kitchen with bright yellow cabinets that I loved. A giant blue, squishy couch and a TV unit created a small lounge area. There appeared to be a white, tiled bathroom through a doorway.

Around all the walls were large framed photos. Many appeared to be taken around the farm, some showing people hard at work, while others were landscapes or macros of water and flowers. They were gorgeous.

She put the bag on her kitchen bench, grabbed some cutlery and plates, and started doling out food. It looked like some kind of stew. "Help yourself," she said around a mouthful. Lexi hadn't lied. She was hungry.

I sat on a barstool next to her and dug in. The lightly spiced beef gravy and root vegetables smelt divine and tasted just as good.

Between mouthfuls, Lexie asked, "Do you want to try on some of my clothes and see what fits, so you can borrow some stuff? We're almost the same size, although you're curvier than I am. You didn't look like you had much with you when you arrived."

I shook my head. "That's very sweet, thank you. I'm good for now, though."

"Don't want to take his hoodie off, huh? Does it smell that good?"

I laughed, feeling both carefree and seen. Lexie was spot on, and she knew it.

She grinned at me. "I hope I find someone who makes me feel that way someday."

Then, she shook her head, frowning as if trying to dislodge a thought. I cocked my head to the side, contemplating her odd reaction.

"Don't mind me," she said, "I'm a little strange on a good day," as she pointed to her coloured hair and eyebrow ring with her spoon.

I didn't like to see her putting herself down. "Don't say that. You're beautiful just the way you are. I love your hair. Maybe you could color mine for me one day. I've never had the chance to do anything like that."

"Oh, don't tease," she said as she put the spoon down and rubbed her hands together. "I'm scheduling a pamper day as soon as I can find some supplies."

"Until then, I've got some new underwear and basics in different sizes in a box in one of our storage sheds. I teach self-defense classes for women. I often work with women who are escaping abusive situations, so I like to keep some emergency stuff on hand."

"I'll grab you some things in the morning. You look like you're a DD, is that about right?"

"You're good," I said around a mouthful. Lexie had slowed down, but I had missed a lot of meals and wasn't letting any of this hot deliciousness go to waste.

"As I said, it's not my first rodeo. Is there anything I need to know about why you're running? I'm not trying to pry. It just helps if I know what to keep an eye out for, for your safety and mine."

I shook my head. "I was living at the Omega Palace. I took the Crash as the opportunity I'd been looking for to escape."

"Not a fan of forced matings?" she asked with an open expression, no judgment there.

It sounded like Lexie had seen a lot, and I'm sure she'd known her share of women who found it easier to stay with what they knew, no matter how bad. We each coped the best we could.

I shook my head again, deciding to give her my sad, sorry tale in as brief a version as possible.

"I was a late addition to the gang. My gramps hid me until he died when I was twenty-one. I was lucky my scent was subtle, and we found ways to hide it. My brother ratted me out to the Palace, so he could inherit our farm.

"I was there for three years. A lot of alphas tried to bark me into submission, but none of them could. I don't know why I could resist them, but it didn't make me very popular."

Lexie opened her mouth as if to say something and then closed it abruptly again. She looked deep in thought.

"I'm sorry that happened to you," she finally said. I knew it was a lot to take in. But, while my circumstances may have been unusual, my treatment at the hands of men wasn't, and I'm sure she'd seen worse.

"Thanks." I got up and stretched. A change of subject was needed.

"Do you want any more?" she asked as she picked up the containers.

"Nope, my food baby is fine right now," I said, pulling up the hoodie, poking out my rounded belly and slapping it.

She laughed, smoothing down her shirt and poking out her belly. "Looks like we're due at the same time."

I grinned back at her before wandering over to one of the photos that had caught my eye. It was a close-up of an older man with a massive smile on his wrinkled face while he leaned on a pitchfork. It was black and white and stunningly beautiful.

"Who took these photos?" I asked. There was no name on them to identify the photographer.

"I did," Lexie said simply.

I was in awe of her talent. "They're beautiful, Lexie."

She seemed embarrassed and moved over to the couch. "Thanks. I haven't shown them to many people. I don't usually have a lot of visitors here."

"Seriously? They should be in a gallery. You could sell them for a fortune. I mean, if you wanted to. I know some people are particular about not wanting to sell their art, and that's just as cool."

She just shrugged—a girl after my own heart.

"Do you have any photos of the guys?" I asked.

"Tonnes. Some compromising ones. Are you after blackmail material or just curious?" Lexi rubbed her hands together and arched her brow like she was excited for some blackmail.

I laughed as I sat down next to her on the couch. I loved the way her mind worked. "Just curious, but if I need to blackmail them, you're the first person I'll come to."

She popped up and went to a bookcase she used to divide her bed from the living space, pulling down a big blue box and lugging it over to the couch. She plopped it down between us and popped off the lid. It was full of photos. They didn't appear to be in any order.

Lots were of the women and kids around the farm, but there were plenty of the guys, and their photos seemed to go back in time.

I pulled out a picture of the guys in uniform. They appeared to be standing in the middle of a military camp, with no shirts on, looking all hot. Lickable hot, not sweaty hot.

"I sent Leif one of those instant polaroid cameras while he was on tour. The years he was away were hard for us both. It helped when I could see him and what he was doing. The guys were in many of the photos he sent back. He also told me all about them in his letters. So, I felt like I got to know them all."

She smiled at a photo of Leif with Hunter in a headlock, and I chuckled.

"He told me nobody ever wrote to the guys. So, he read them all my letters, and they all looked forward to them. I started putting in comments and notes for them. I sent them little things sometimes as well, and they'd send me messages through Leif. Occasionally, they'd write me letters to add to Leif's."

She paused, deep in her memories, as she shuffled through photos, handing me funny ones. "I think they all needed a connection to a home, any home, not necessarily their own, which were all pretty crappy. Just something real."

"When they retired early and came back together, they all greeted me like a sister, and I've treated them all as brothers ever since. They're Leif's home, so they're mine now, too."

I stayed quiet, letting her talk, happy to hear stories and look at the photos. I wish I had known them longer and been a part of their lives. They had built something special together. They were different from all the other alphas I had met, or my gramps had described.

Many photos showed how they transformed the farm, building cabins and planting crops. They were filled with hugs and laughter. It seemed to be a theme with them. Although there were plenty of them trying to get a stern-faced Damon to laugh.

I held one up. "Is Damon always such a frowny-face?"

She looked thoughtful for a moment. "Damon's had it tough, and he feels a lot of responsibility. He doesn't let people in easily, with good reason. That's his story to tell, though."

"Oh, of course. I wasn't looking for gossip. I was only wondering if it was just me or the whole world Damon hated?"

She shook her head and smiled. "He's a good guy, Maia. Just give him time and a chance."

"I don't think that's an issue. Damon's with Sirena, right? So is Hunter? I don't go after other girls' guys."

She laughed loudly at that. I liked her ready humor, but I wasn't sure what was so funny in this case.

"She wishes. She may be screwing them both and may like to make out that it's something more, but it's not. I have a feeling even that's going to change very soon."

"Besides, I didn't say a chance at dating or sex. I just meant a chance to show you he's a good guy. You're the one who went there. And, who said anything about Hunter?" Lexie asked as she narrowed her eyes at me. "Are you getting greedy, girl? Do you want the whole team?"

I blushed at that. I didn't know what to say.

"It looks like you already caught two, so you're off to a great start."

"I wouldn't say I've caught two. There's only been kissing so far."

"Kissing, and you've publicly claimed my brother, if not officially mated him. He seems pretty happy about it. They both do."

"I know it's moving fast."

"It's moving fast?"

"Well, I'm guessing from a normal perspective, it's moving fast. I don't know. I'm not very experienced in this sort of thing. I just know what I feel." I sighed.

"But I just want to let you know I'm not messing around with your brother or Max. They both mean something to me already. I don't know how to explain it, and I wasn't looking for it, but I already feel connected to them. They're important to me. I would never knowingly or intentionally hurt either of them."

Lexie gave me a long look. When I didn't say anything more, that was already a lot for me, she put me out of my misery.

"We're good, Maia. If I thought you were messing with either of them, I would have kicked your ass already." She leaped up and made some over-the-top kung-fu moves. She was hamming it up, but I could tell she had a lot of natural grace in her movements. She seemed strong and centered, both emotionally and physically.

I smiled, and she came back to flop on the couch. "The guys have all had it tough, in different ways. They chose each other as a family because they all needed one. I've been lucky that they've included me, so I'm protective."

"It's just. All four are essential to each other. Unfortunately, some girls have found that problematic over the years, trying to come between them or resenting all the time they spend together.

"I can tell it means a lot to them that you've accepted Max as part of Leif's life so quickly. I think you're going to be good for them."

I shrugged, not knowing what to say. Lexie seemed to figure out that talking about myself made me feel awkward, so she let it drop.

We were silent for a moment, both lost in thought, but it was comfortable until I remembered why I had wanted to talk to her.

"Oh, I never thanked you for sneaking me the food the first day while I was weeding the garden. So, thank you. It meant a lot."

"Please don't thank me for that, I shouldn't have had to sneak it to you, and you shouldn't have had to work for it. Sirena is way out of control. I should have done something about that a while ago. It was never that bad before the crash, but it seems to have brought out the worst in her, and you definitely set something off in her."

I shrugged. "People react to stress differently."

"Yeah, I know, but there's no call for how she's treating people, and it needs to stop. I'm going to talk to Damon."

"No, please, don't do that for me. I don't want to cause trouble. Besides, if we combine our evil genius, I'm sure we can come up with some revenge ourselves and have some fun with it."

"Oh hell yes, you're officially my BFF. I'm all in for some mean girl smack down." She was bouncing up and down on the couch, spilling photos everywhere.

I grabbed as many as possible, trying to save them while smiling at her antics. "I think we need some movie motivation. Did you say you had access to movies?"

"Great idea, we need some great female villains. Who are you thinking?"

"Well, I don't think you can go past Hela. She was so much fun."

"Yeah, she's one of my favorites. Let's do it. I have a laptop with hundreds of movies on it. Let me set it up." She jumped up and ran over to the bookshelf again, coming back with her laptop and plonking down almost on my lap. "Grab that throw blanket. It's movie snuggle time."

I grabbed the throw blanket off the back of the couch. It was so incredibly soft. I felt the urge to roll myself up in it like a big snuggly burrito, but I didn't want to hog it. I pulled it over both of us and snuggled under it while Lexie set up the movie.

"I called your brother Ragnarok earlier today, and he was a bit miffed. So the movie's been on my mind ever since."

"Oh, that's perfect because he looks a bit like an Asgardian god?"

"Uh, no, because of the giant monster that keeps growing bigger and destroys Asgard," I said.

She laughed so hard that I thought she was going to pee herself.

"Ragnarok, that's a keeper." Her laughter petered off as she settled under the blanket with me for the opening scenes, giggling over the monster with me when he appeared. "We have to make Leif a giant crown that looks like eyebrows for Halloween," she laughed.

We were only a few minutes into the movie when the radio suddenly came to life. "Beta 1 to all, fence alarm tripped, east side. All guards on alert."

Lexie flung off the blanket and jumped to her feet. She grabbed the radio from the kitchen bench where she'd left it earlier while I paused the movie.

"I'm sure it's fine," she said, trying to reassure me. "The guys are super cautious with security while we figure out what's happening. They're worried people will want what we have and take desperate measures to get it. It's a general alert."

"Sure, I get it. I spent time out there. It's justified, and it's going to get worse the longer this goes on," I replied as I headed for one of the windows, curious to look outside even though I knew I wouldn't see anything.

She flopped down on the couch, put the radio on the coffee table, and hopped under the covers again. Before she could restart the movie, the radio erupted again.

"Beta 1 to Alpha 1. Movement behind fence. Single person. Moving stealthily. Out." Which was quickly followed by, "Alpha 1 to all units. Code red for everyone until further notice. Out."

"Don't open the curtains," Lexie said in a rush. "You'll let the light out." My hand was hovering over the curtains, so I dropped it quickly. At the same time, the radio announced something more about cameras.

Lexie jumped up from the couch again, looking around nervously. "Wait a sec and open them after I turn the light off, it's not a big space, but I don't want you falling over something in the dark."

She quickly grabbed a bottle of water from the kitchen bench, and a baseball bat I hadn't noticed was resting up against the back of the door jamb. She nodded at me and then flipped the lamp off, and I pulled the curtains wide.

"Shit, the laptop," she said as we both noticed the light coming from the screen behind us. I lunged over to the coffee table and snapped it closed.

"Nice move, girlfriend. You're quick on your feet in the dark," she said as she walked back over to the couch while I snuggled under the blanket for comfort.

I just shrugged. "I've spent a lot of time in the dark."

"Sorry," she said as she put the water between us on the coffee table and snuggled back under the blanket, "but code red means no light and no sound, so going dark it is."

She placed the baseball bat in her lap and looked out the open window.

I could feel anxiety pulling at me, but I wasn't sure if it was Leif or me.

"Fuck, I hate the dark," I heard her mutter with a shake in her voice. I reached out and grabbed her hand, squeezing tightly. I figured we shared some similar trauma, but now was not the time to ask.

"Me too." But at least this time, I had the moon and a friend in the darkness. I could feel Leif as well through our burgeoning bond. He seemed to be feeling anxious but was pushing reassurance at me. It was faint, and it was hard to tell his emotions apart from mine, but I could feel it. He seemed to be getting closer.

"It's okay, Leif's coming." We sat quietly together, holding hands and waiting for more news until we heard movement outside. We looked at each other in the darkness.

Then, I heard a quiet knock on the door in a strange pattern. Lexie had put her finger to her mouth in a shushing motion, but a huge grin quickly spread across her face.

She pulled me up by the hand and whispered, "It's Leif. It's a code we used when we were young, and he had me stashed around the house, hiding from my dad. It means to come out, but quietly."

It made my heart ache to think of a young Leif hiding his sister from someone who was supposed to protect them. And it happened so often that they had a system for it. No wonder they were so close. It sounded like they were all each other had growing up.

Lexie cracked the door open slightly, then flung it open and all but jumped at Leif, dragging me with her as she still had hold of my hand. I decided to join in. No way was I missing out on a group hug, so I snuggled in on his other side.

I peeked up at Leif, and he wore a massive smile. It lit him up from the inside. He squeezed us both tightly.

"As much as I love the greeting, can we move this inside where sound won't travel as easily?" he said in a whisper, looking over his shoulder.

Lexie and I quickly let him go and dropped our hands. We moved back inside so he could come in. Leif looked around, noticing our nest on the couch, and motioned us towards it. He took a quick look out the open window before he joined us. We pushed him into the middle so we could sit on either side of him. He went willingly.

"What's going on?" Lexie asked.

"Max checked the camera feeds when he got a perimeter alarm."

I tilted my head curiously. I didn't think phones were still working. Leif noticed my movement, even in the dark.

"Max has a military satellite phone he reconfigured, which still works. He's connected it to a closed network he built here that includes our cameras."

I was surprised at that, and Leif could tell. I could see him faintly smirk at me in the dark.

"Most people lost their internet connection because their wireless modems wouldn't work without electricity, and neither would most of the private hosting servers.

"But the internet originally started with the military, so most of it is still there. The satellites are still orbiting as well."

"We're lucky Max had a lot of tech set-up here, and our network was locked down for security reasons before the Crash, so we didn't go offline like everyone else did."

"Max is a tech genius and is endlessly curious. He's trying to figure out what happened to the military and why they haven't mobilized, so he's been hacking whatever he can find in his spare time," he said.

Wow, I was impressed. If Max still had access to satellites, maybe he could help me find Ava and Cary and work out what had been happening with all the trucks and alphas at the Palace before I fled. I'd have to talk to him soon.

"Yeah, yeah, dork-a-saurus is a genius. We get it. You can brag to Maia about your boyfriend later. What's happening out there right now?" Her words sounded harsh, but I could hear the humor and affection in her voice. I was sure she was smiling as she said it.

"Max picked up movement behind the fence. The person was military trained but probably didn't realize our cameras were still operational. We think whoever it was may have been tuned into our radio channel because they spooked and left when Max alerted us to them."

"So they're gone?"

"Hunter, Damon, Dave, and some of the day guards are doing a quick sweep of the perimeter to make sure, and Max is keeping an eye on the cameras up at his security office with one of the young guys he's training.

"We switched radio channels,'" he said as he picked up our radio off the coffee table and fiddled with it.

"We haven't lifted the code red over the radios, though, in case the person is still in range. There are only so many channels available, and they can easily flick through them. We don't want to encourage them to come back tonight.'"

He leaned back onto the couch and put an arm around each of us. "We shouldn't be moving around much tonight, so is it okay if I hang out with you girls for a while?"

"Shouldn't you be out on perimeter check?" Lexie asked.

He shifted as though he was a little embarrassed, and I could feel he was still a little tense. "No, I started to run here as soon as I heard there was a potential intruder. Damon told me to stay put once I got here and watch you both."

He had said earlier that the bond made it hard to be away from me. I could only imagine his instincts had been tearing at him, thinking I was possibly in danger and out of reach.

"I know it was girls' night, so I can go and sit outside if you'd prefer?" He seemed genuine, like he wouldn't mind and would do it if we asked.

I leaned up and put my hand over his chest, feeling its steady rhythm as I nuzzled into his neck, breathing deeply and taking comfort from him in the same way I sensed he needed to. I could feel him relax underneath me and take a deep breath.

"It's fine with me if Lexie doesn't mind."

"Whatever, big guy," she said. I could still hear the smile in her voice, and I think she was comforted by his presence after being forced into the dark.

"What were you guys doing?" he asked.

"Watching Ragnarok," Lexie said, and I could hear the laugh this time.

Leif groaned. "That's going to be a thing now, isn't it?"

"Yup," was all she said.

"Whatever, little mouse." He leaned over and gave her an affectionate kiss on her head. I think he could sense she needed him.

"I can't believe you girls are watching an action movie without me. That's low."

Lexie snickered. "Are we clear to keep watching if we close the blinds?"

"Yeah, we're good." Lexie hopped up straight away and grabbed the laptop on her way back, settling it in front of us all and pulling the blanket back up over our laps.

"I like this movie, but it bothers me a little that one of the only acknowledged female alphas you see portrayed in movies was cast as the villain. I know female alphas are rare, and I think it casts them in a bad light. They have a hard enough time being accepted by society as it is," Leif said.

"I know, but I like that they kept the redhead a beta in all the movies. They always make women alphas or turn them into superhumans if they have any action scenes. But she's a badass beta and holds her own."

Bear scratched at the door while they discussed movie characters and their designations, and Lexie jumped up to let him in. He trotted to the couch and jumped up alongside me, draping himself over my tucked-up legs. He was like a big heated blanket.

I listened quietly to Leif and Lexie talking while I yawned. With the darkness, food in my belly, Leif's scent in my nose, and warm bodies snuggled around me, it didn't take long for me to feel drowsy.

"Sleep sunshine, I've got you," I heard Leif whisper as I drifted off, feeling a sense of contentment I hadn't known in a long time.

Sixteen

I woke lazily to a pale, rosy dawn light gently filtering through the open door. The curtains were open, and I could hear insects buzzing outside, excitedly greeting the new day and a soft, gentle snore that wasn't coming from me.

There was a firm weight over my midsection, but it wasn't uncomfortable, more a cozy weight that was familiar and made me feel safe. Until a hand moved slowly up my abdomen, gently grasped my breast, and stayed there.

I tensed as a body shifted behind me, desperately trying to remember where I was and who was in bed with me. I vaguely remembered falling asleep against Leif at Lexie's cabin last night and the feeling of being carried later.

"Are you okay?" a husky voice asked quietly. I glanced over and saw Max watching me carefully while he was sprawled out on the other side of my bed. "He's asleep, you know, but I can move his hand if you'd like."

I assumed it was Leif behind me then, snoring softly. Where one went, the other usually followed. "It's okay. I don't mind. I don't want to wake him," I answered truthfully, which surprised me. If I was honest, talking to Max with Leif's hand on my breast felt naughty in the nicest way. I had been aching for one of them to touch me intimately since we'd all kissed yesterday. Or maybe both of them. Would all of them be so greedy?

Max was only wearing sweatpants, and his gorgeous golden chest was on full display. He had tattoos that I hadn't noticed before and a nipple ring that intrigued me. They contrasted his geeky good looks but suited him. As if he was hiding an inner bad boy.

The idea had my libido perking up with interest. Max wasn't as big as the other guys, being a beta, but he had a lean athlete's body that I found I liked. It was more sculptured and came with a killer six-pack that made my mouth water.

I leaned in slightly closer to look at the tattoo on his chest, partly as an excuse to move closer to him, but I also wanted to see the tattoo up close. It was a small wing across one side of his chest, over his heart, that was incredibly detailed. Underneath and showing through was a rainbow of colors in vibrant splashes. It looked like a watercolor painting, and it was spectacular.

Next to it was some kind of script I couldn't read. I touched the wing, lightly brushing my fingertips across it. It looked so beautiful that I couldn't help myself.

"Oh, so we're at the chest-touching stage for everyone, are we?" he smirked at me, and I blushed furiously. There was something infinitely more intimate about mornings in bed with a man than anything you did the night before.

"What does it say?" I asked while pulling my hand back, unsure what his reaction would be if I continued touching him.

"The ones you love will set you free," he murmured, deep in thought suddenly as he stared down at his chest.

"What does it mean to you?"

He continued staring at his chest, not meeting my eye.

"I told you I grew up in foster homes, but I was luckier than most. From about the age of eight, I lived with the same couple until I aged out of the system at eighteen. They never adopted me, and I never asked why. I figured it was because they got paid to be my foster parents. I didn't mind. I was just grateful to have a consistent roof over my head.

"They were old hippies and had a chilled, hands-off style of parenting. I was very independent early on, but I liked it that way. We didn't have much in common. I was a tech geek from a young age."

I could imagine a young, curious Max pulling things apart and figuring out how they worked. I wanted to go back in time and give him a giant hug.

"Anyway, I had this old neighbor who lived alone next door during that time. I used to wander over to tell him all the random, useless shit that filled my brain when I got obsessed with trying to figure out something new. He was patient and would listen to me for hours. Then, the next time I went, he'd tell me he found a book about that very thing in his study and ask if I wanted to read it.

"It wasn't until I was older that I realized the books he gave me were always new. He'd gone out and bought them for me so that I could explore my new interest. He always encouraged my need to figure things out, even things beyond my age level."

I pictured a lonely guy, living on his own, happy to indulge the vibrant, intelligent little kid next door who brightened his day. I wanted to find his neighbor one day and add him to my hug list.

"So many people didn't get me as a kid or didn't bother to spend any time figuring me out. They just wanted me to fit in with their idea of who I should be, or be the way that made life easier for them, even my teachers. It's all just another form of a cage. But my neighbor cared and always encouraged me to spread my wings.

"He set me free and let me know it was okay to be myself. The tattoo is kind of an homage to him and a reminder to me to treat the people I love the same. It doesn't matter if I care about someone romantically or in friendship. I want to set them free, not cage them, and I expect the same in return.

'Life is much easier when people love and celebrate you for who you are, even if it's just one person.'

I'd been lying completely still, enraptured with his story and hardly daring to breathe in case I spooked him. I didn't want him to stop talking.

His words and how he felt about them hit me deeply, what he said about caging people resonated with me painfully. I'd lived in a cage in some form or another most of my life, never able to be myself.

Max was a rare soul.

I leaned over and gently lifted his chin so he could look me in the eye. His eyes found mine willingly, but there was nervousness in them. I could see this was important to him.

"I love that," I responded simply, with a smile spreading across my face that correlated with the warmth I felt in my chest. I wasn't good at expressing myself with words, but I sensed Max knew that.

"It's kind of how the farm came about," he told me honestly, as he looked me in the eye this time. He reached up, entwined my fingers with his, and kissed them gently. 'It feeds something in all of us we weren't getting elsewhere, even though, for the guys, it's not considered a suitable job for an alpha.

"There's something here we each needed, though, and we supported and loved each other enough to do it together in a way that worked for all of us, despite what everyone else thought."

"It shows. This farm, the way you care for the people and the land, it's all love. Every part of it," I said.

His smile grew at my words, and he leaned forwards subtly as his eyes moved down my face towards my mouth, like he was about to kiss me much less gently.

Max stilled when I let out a startled gasp and jerked. He seemed concerned until he looked over my shoulder and laughed.

"Found some morning wood, did you?"he smirked.

Leif had snuggled closer in his sleep, re-established his grasp on my breast, and thrust his dick into my ass.

"More like a morning baseball bat."

At that moment, Hunter stuck his tousled head up from the end of the bed. "I've got some nice morning wood if you're looking for some," he said as he rubbed his face sleepily.

"Oh my freaking god," I shrieked, breathing hard and whipping my head around. "You scared me half to death. I didn't know you were there."

"I know a god-like man who likes to get freaky if that's more your thing right now," he mumbled with a cheeky smile and jerked his head over his shoulder at the doorway.

"I think you're up, Damon," he called out as he stretched his arms out.

"Shut up, man," came a disembodied voice from the hallway.

I inched up slightly, and I could see a large pair of feet through the door, pointing upwards like someone was lying on the floor.

It occurred to me that they were all in, or almost in, my room and had been while I was sleeping.

"What are you all doing in here?" I blurted out, startled.

"You were screaming and thrashing in your sleep, and we all came running," Max said. "You seemed to settle when we all got in here, and Leif and I hopped on the bed and hugged you."

"You mumbled 'stay' when we went to leave, and we didn't know who you meant, so we all did," Hunter said as he shrugged like it was no big deal.

My heart had been glowing warmly at his words earlier, but now it exploded with sunshine. I was speechless and didn't know what to say until Leif broke the awkward tension I could see settling over the guys when I didn't respond.

"Can you all shut up and let me pretend to sleep a little longer?" he grumbled as he ground into me again and massaged my breast lightly.

The other guys all laughed, and I groaned, not in disgust, though. If I was honest, it was really more of a moan. His hard cock against my ass felt amazing. I wanted to explore him further, and the idea of them all watching had me suddenly hot all over.

"Is it just me, or is watching Leif grope her hot as hell?" Hunter mumbled, suddenly being serious as his eyes locked onto Leif's hand, which was still massaging my breast, causing my back to arch and my breast to push further into his hand. So, it wasn't just me then.

"I'm kinda getting the appeal of the sharing thing. I think you're onto something, Max," he stated as he rubbed the stubble on his jaw and ran his eyes down my exposed legs.

I had kicked the blankets off at some point during the night, probably due to the heat from Leif's body, and I was only wearing Leif's t-shirt. It had ridden up and was barely covering my ass.

"You're going to have to explore the idea another time, Hunter. You too, Leif and Max. We've got chores to do," Damon said as he rose into view and stood in the doorway. His gaze flitted between us, then settled on me when he noticed me watching him before he turned abruptly and disappeared down the hallway.

The boys groaned in unison as Leif rolled away from me, and Max got off the bed with a longing glance in my direction.

"Man, that was a hell of a nice way to wake up, though," Leif said, still half asleep and rubbing his eyes.

I suddenly felt empty, like all the warmth had left me. Until Max smiled at me and held out his hand, he seemed to know what I was feeling. For a geek, he was remarkably intuitive.

"Let's go, sunshine. We've got work to do, the kind that's not going to get done in bed," Leif said, looking me up and down like he'd like that option, despite his words.

"You may need to give Leif a few minutes," Hunter said as he rolled up off the floor and stretched out some more, reaching his arms up to the roof. "He needs to hit a home run with that baseball bat before he can get to work."

I found myself blushing furiously. Where had all my confidence from last night gone? When I got caught kissing both Max and Leif on the couch?

"You may need to chop some wood yourself," Max laughed while eyeing the noticeable tent in Hunter's sweatpants as he took my hand.

"No, just no. No mention of chopping or cutting when referring to my dick, dude. Not cool," Hunter said while covering his junk with his hands and backing out of the room.

I laughed loudly. Not all guys could get away with using the word dude without sounding like a douche, but Hunter managed it. It suited his cocky, playful personality.

I loved how open and comfortable the guys all were with each other. I let Max pull me off the bed and into his arms as he finally leaned in and kissed me sweetly while I wound my arms around his neck.

"I have to agree, it was a hell of a nice way to wake up," he whispered as he nuzzled into my neck and took a deep breath. With the attention of all the guys this morning, my scent was drenching the room. He pulled me in closer, and I could feel his cock hard against my leg.

"Do you need to deal with some wood too, or do you want a hand with that," I asked as I ran my hands down his delectable back, feeling his muscles flex under my hands as he curved his back into my touch. I wasn't usually so forward, but all the casual touches and kissing had left me in a heightened state of arousal.

"Max, move it, man," Damon yelled from the living room. "We need to check those cameras that were glitching last night. You've got two minutes."

"Fuck, I'm going to have a serious chat with him about his cock blocking," Max swore lightly, giving me a light squeeze on the butt before he moved away and adjusted his cock in his pants.

"Get dressed and meet us out front in two minutes. We'll take you over to the dining hall,' he said. 'We'll have some breakfast, then all head out for chores.'

"You know, I have two legs and know how to walk on my own," I called out to him as he left the room.

He poked his head back around the door and said, "Believe me, I know all about those legs." He ran his eyes over them and bit his lower lip before yelling at Damon, "Make it five minutes, man, I've got to deal with some wood."

I got dressed quickly in my shorts, which someone had washed, and one of Max's t-shirts that I knotted in the front. Knowing that three of them were probably jacking off right now because of me made me feel desired in a way I had never known, and I loved every minute of it.

Seventeen

The walk down to the dining hall was gorgeous, with the world just waking up in the early morning light and plants bursting into life around me, smelling fresh and vibrant. I could hear the river burbling quietly in the background and animals saying their good mornings to each other and the world.

The farm sounded like it had small herds of cows, goats, and sheep. I could hear a few dogs barking somewhere in the distance. I wanted to find them and pet them all.

The world inside the farm felt crisp, clean, and full of life and possibilities, despite all the trauma outside, or maybe because of it. I don't remember ever waking up and feeling this happy. It felt like a well-loved home, and I realized I wanted to stay and see if it could become mine.

I was used to early mornings on a farm, but my gramps' farm had been on a dry plain, and it was a hard, thankless life getting anything to grow well. We had always struggled. Yet this farm was a paradise, with deep red soil and plenty of bees around helping to propagate the plants.

"How do you irrigate the fields on the hill?" I asked, my curiosity getting the better of me as we walked. I wasn't usually one to ask a lot of questions, especially with new people. Yet, I was already more comfortable with these four men than most people I had known in my life. Even Damon, despite his gruffness and reserve around me.

Leif held my hand as we walked. I'd never felt so secure or connected to another person. Hunter and Max were sticking close behind us, but Damon was hanging back.

"That's thanks to Max," Hunter said. "He's an engineering genius as well as a tech one." He grabbed Max in an affectionate headlock and ruffled his hair. Max pushed him off in embarrassment.

"Max set up a system where the water wheel at the pond pumps water up the hill, and then it flows through a series of irrigation pipes before moving through the reed beds, which naturally purifies the remaining water."

"It makes the water in the pond drinkable, so it acts like a dam. The whole system also generates electricity for us, so we have multiple sources and aren't reliant on one. We have a closed solar system linked to industrial batteries, and we also have wind power from small windmills placed along the far border," Hunter said.

I shook my head in amazement. It was seriously impressive.

"Wow, no wonder you're not suffering from a lack of electricity. I wondered how you had enough for the fences when I was outside."

"Why did you stop outside?" Max asked, not insinuating anything sinister, just endlessly curious and probably wanting to change the subject away from him. I was onto him already. He was very modest about his abilities.

"You can't see a lot from the road when the gates are closed, and we took all the signage down advertising the farm the day before you arrived."

"Exhaustion and desperation," I said. "Sometimes in life, you have to pick a place or a person, make your stand, and then hope for the best. I felt the electricity in the fences as soon as I got near them and knew people were inside. I didn't know what kind of people, but I knew I couldn't go much further."

I stopped and turned to look up the hill toward the gate, where my bike still rested.

"Something drew me to that spot and wouldn't let me leave. I'd told myself to move on for at least an hour, but I couldn't seem to do it. I'd been avoiding all contact with people for days, but something in me felt this spot was important.

"When Dave came and called me out, I was still debating whether to try and run, but he was so gentle, calm, yet forthright. I decided to make my stand and trust him."

"I'll have to thank him later," Leif said as he squeezed my hand. 'I hate to think what would have happened if you'd kept going and made it to the next town, or worse, passed out on the road.'

I smiled at Leif and got moving again, shaking off my reverie. Damon was standing at a distance but watching me with an intentness that seemed to sharpen whenever I talked about myself. He'd done it last night while we were all getting to know each other. It made my whole body come alive like he stroked my skin without touching me. His intensity unnerved me a little.

"I was trying to make it to Greensborough, which I think is the next town," I said. "I was supposed to meet up with a friend at her uncle's farm. I'll have to figure out what to do about that soon."

I could feel all the guys looking at each other. I guessed they were drawing mental straws to see who would ask me more about it.

We reached the dining hall just then, and my nervousness returned. I'd met some of these people the first night, but I hadn't been at my best, and I wasn't sure what kind of impression I'd made.

I'd also been posing as a beta. I pulled Leif to a stop again, and he looked at me in confusion. The other guys all slowly noticed we had stopped and turned around.

"Maybe this isn't such a good idea," I blurted out. "I was pretending to be a beta when I got here. I've only ever been able to mask my scent for short periods, though, and that's when it was much more subtle. It usually worked best when I was afraid or causing myself pain.

'My scent has been much stronger since I met Leif. Well, technically, since I met Damon." Damon glanced at me quickly with a light in his eyes I couldn't decipher, but looked away when he saw me looking at him. "I don't know if I can keep it up now, especially in a room full of people while I'm eating or while Leif is with me."

Max stepped closer to me, concern on his face. "You kept your scent at bay through fear and pain?" He didn't look happy at that, and neither did Hunter. I glanced over at Damon. He looked murderous but was looking away from me like he was struggling to contain himself.

Leif swung me around to face him and put his finger under my chin, directing my gaze to his. A mixed look of adoration and concern crossed his face.

"I have no problem letting everyone in that room know you are mine. I don't want you living in fear or hurting yourself to stay hidden. Not anymore."

"I promised you this place wasn't another cage for you, and I'm going to keep that promise." Damon looked at him sharply at the use of the word cage, then turned to look at me carefully. I could see he was dying to ask me questions but was holding himself back.

Leif turned to the others. "Do any of you have an issue with Maia letting her omega free while she's here at the farm?" Both Hunter and Max quickly answered, "No," while Damon just shook his head without taking his eyes off me.

"Good. Problem solved. Let's eat." I smiled at Leif at that. He was so confident in his ability to defend and protect me. So sure about the way he felt about me, even though he had barely known me for two days.

Max looked at me questioningly, seeming to want to get my take on Leif's declaration, checking in with me as he did with everyone. I just shrugged at him and said, "Okay, let's eat already."

I realized it was easier said than done, though, when we walked through the doors, and all conversation slowly stopped while everyone turned to look at us. Just great. Here we go again.

Only this time, I had Leif firmly holding my hand, with Max standing protectively at my back. Hunter and Damon followed closely behind as we headed for a long table that had breakfast food laid out on it. It looked like bacon, eggs, some kind of veggie patties, and even some hash browns. My mouth salivated instantly.

I wasn't sure what their food situation was like long-term, but they seemed to have plenty of it right now. I could smell toast and eggs, but I also spied cereal and some muffins. The sight of fresh orange juice made my mouth water.

Dave got up immediately and came towards us. I let go of Leif's hand and stepped into him, giving him a big hug that knocked him back a step. I don't think he'd been expecting it. He was a burly guy and, I imagine, not easy to shift if he didn't want to budge. He let out an 'oof,' followed by a chuckle.

"Hi," I said as I looked up at him.

"Hi," he said, clearly surprised by my affectionate greeting. Then, he stilled, took a deeper breath, and turned to look at the guys with shocked, wide eyes.

I looked over my shoulder. Both Leif and Damon were glaring at him with deadly intent, while Hunter was trying hard not to laugh, and Max just looked confused. None of them, to their credit, tried to pull me back, although it looked like Leif and Damon both wanted to.

Lexie came barrelling out of the kitchen at that moment with a tray of hot food and stopped short, tilting her head.

"You work fast, but leave some for the rest of us," she said as she winked at me, and Dave gently extracted himself, glancing at both Lexie and the boys.

I let him go abruptly. I'd never had anyone be jealous over me before, and that was the feeling I was getting through the bond with Leif.

Damon looked the same, and that confused the hell out of me. He'd been angry and volatile when I met him, then reserved and distant with me since. He was very open and affectionate with the guys, though. I couldn't work him out.

"I knew there was something you weren't telling me when I found you," Dave said, bringing my attention back to him. "I figured you were running from someone because you were scared and skittish as hell," he said in the straightforward way that had put me at ease the day we met.

"I would never have guessed you were an omega, and you were trying to hide from us in plain sight. How the hell did you pull that off?"

"It's a long story, one I'll tell you another day. You weren't wrong, though. I was running from someone if that makes you feel better."

I could feel all the guys watching me intently, and I almost felt a low growl coming from Damon. I would have to talk to them about my past. So far, they hadn't asked, but I owed them honesty.

Lexie was busying herself with nothing at the food table, fussing and moving things around but really just eavesdropping. I couldn't blame her. My life was a bit of a soap opera at the moment.

I turned my attention back to Dave. "I just wanted to thank you for finding me and convincing me to come inside the other day. You could have sent me packing, but you didn't. You're a good guy."

"Sorry to take you by surprise with the hug," I said, feeling awkward. I wasn't used to explaining my actions or impulsively hugging people. This was new for me.

I had a suspicion my omega instincts were rioting now that my suppressed pheromones had fully awakened. Omegas were known to be tactile, and my appetite for touch appeared to be ravenous.

Especially when it came to the four guys shadowing me, I wanted them all within easy reach. I didn't want to second guess why right now. I just wanted to enjoy the sensation when they were all near.

I moved back over to Leif. He pulled me to him, bringing my back to his chest, so he could wrap his arms around me and take a deep breath of my hair. I could feel he needed the contact right now as much as I did.

I sighed happily as I gave my hand to Max, who took it willingly. He brought our hands up so he could kiss the back of mine. I felt grounded when they were with me.

Hunter was watching us longingly, his earlier laughter gone, and Damon was clenching and unclenching his fists. He didn't appear to be angry, more like he needed something to do with his hands. I felt like Damon was on the precipice of something, but I didn't know what. Finally, he moved over to the food table and away from us.

"Anytime, sweetheart. I never knock back a hug. It was more your scent and realizing you were an omega that took me by surprise," Dave said, watching us all interact with open curiosity.

"How hungry are you, Maia? I can grab you a plate of food if you let me know what you like," Hunter asked.

"Already on it," Damon said, to my immense surprise. From what I had read in the old books from the Palace library, feeding an omega was something a true mate felt compelled to do. But so far, Hunter and Damon had brought me food, not Leif.

At that moment, the kitchen door swung open, and Sirena stomped out. She spotted Lexie at the table and started on her straight away, sounding annoyed. "Lexie, what is taking you so long?"

I could feel Leif stiffen behind me. Given how close they were, I didn't think he'd like to hear anyone talk to his sister like that. Judging from Max's face, he wasn't Sirena's biggest fan either.

Lexie looked sideways at Damon, who was on the other side of her, and raised an eyebrow. He popped his head up and looked at Sirena with a polite, detached expression.

"Is there a problem, Sirena?" Sirena's entire demeanor changed the instant she spotted him. The scowl disappeared, and she popped her chest out while smoothing her hand down her hip in a suggestive motion. "Oh, Damon, I didn't see you there, honey."

It was my turn to stiffen. Damon wasn't mine, but hearing her call him honey made me feel a little ragey.

She strutted over to him, no more stomping now. "No problem, I was looking for Lexie. I wanted to see if she needed help." A smooth yet blatant lie.

She put her hand on Damon's chest, and all my hackles rose like a wolf protecting her pack. Max glanced at me in concern, and Leif tightened his arms around me in support.

"Did I thank you properly for coming over to check on me last night? It was so sweet of you to worry about me."

Hunter took a step closer to Damon, but Damon was already in motion, picking her hand off his chest and turning back to the plate he was piling high on the table.

"I wasn't checking on you, Sirena. I was telling you to close your curtains. I could see your light from the bottom of the hill, and we had a perimeter alert. This isn't the first time I have warned you. I'll have to remove your access to electricity at night if we can't trust you with it. I made that clear last night."

I figured from his tone that she'd been leaving her curtains open at night in a ploy to get him to come to her cabin. Sneaky, but not very smart. It was a risky play.

Sirena looked a little flustered. I don't think she expected Damon to call her out in front of other people. Lexie coughed loudly, trying to cover her laughter.

Sirena persisted, despite Damon's apparent coolness. "Well, you know, we would save a lot of electricity if I came to stay with you. It's ridiculous wasting so much with me in my cabin when I could be nearby whenever you need me."

She was trying for a playful, sexy tone. She was twirling strands of her long hair around her finger near her chest like she was trying to draw attention to her boobs. It was clumsy, though, like she had seen someone else do it and tried to mimic it but was just coming across as desperate.

My anger cooled now that her hand was off Damon, and I realized it was obvious she was trying to play him, like Lexie had said, but wasn't all that good at it.

Before Damon could say anything, Hunter jumped in. "Well, that might be a little awkward, Sirena. I don't think I'd be comfortable having an ex-fling living in my house."

"What?" she squawked, like a crazed parrot, looking at him with a bewildered expression. I was getting more amused with each passing moment. I needed some popcorn for this show, so I relaxed back against Leif and squeezed Max's hand. "What do you mean, ex-fling?" she persisted.

"Well, ex, as in, it was a fun fling, but I have no intention of ever being with you again, so we're no longer having a fling," he said. Sirena just looked at him, so he kept going.

"It was hardly even a fling, more like a few one-night stands. So, maybe an ex-one-nighter is more appropriate. Sorry, I didn't mean to overstate things and presume. I'm okay with not calling it a fling, if it makes you more comfortable?"

Lexie was almost choking, so Hunter walked over and patted her on the back cheekily while giving me a wink. I could have hugged him right then. Maybe I would later.

"You okay, Lex?" he asked innocently.

"Yuh, huh," she said, deliberately not looking at Sirena, who was still standing with her mouth open. It wasn't a very attractive look. I wasn't sure I should point that out, though.

"Actually, that's an excellent idea, Sirena," Damon said, halting what he was doing and turning to her. I held my breath, and so did the other guys. He wouldn't, would he?

"Sofia and Isabella share a three-bedroom cabin, so they have an empty room. Moving in with them will reduce electricity, and they can help you keep on top of things like closing the curtains."

"Plus, it would help our badly under-resourced security team. Would that work better for you Dave?" He looked over at Dave, who nodded calmly. Dave was leaning against the food table with his legs crossed casually, looking like he was enjoying the show as much as I was.

"There's nobody else living over on the east side in the guest cabins, we could lock them all down if Sirena moved. She'll be much safer bunking with the others if she's going to stay for a while and work around the farm rather than being a guest," Dave said.

Ooh. That was a well-executed burn. This show was getting good. It sounded like Sirena would get a proper farm job, as well as new cabin mates. Dave was getting another hug.

"No, I...," Sirena started to say, looking like she was frantically trying to back-pedal so she could keep her cushy little guest cabin.

"Great points, Dave. Thanks. Sirena, grab all your stuff and shift it to the other cabin. I'll let them know you're coming," Damon said, not giving her a chance to intervene. "I appreciate you thinking about the group as a whole like that and how we're using our resources."

Damon was damn good. I was impressed. I felt like I should be taking notes on how to execute a perfect take-down.

He turned to Dave, effectively dismissing Sirena. "I think we should have a community meeting here tonight. Other people here may have good ideas for managing our resources."

"Plus, we can use up some of the perishables we have stocked in the function center cold room that can't be frozen and are about to expire. We can make it a fun evening, maybe get all the board games out afterwards and have a few drinks? As long as we put up the storm shelter panels over the windows this afternoon and keep it fairly quiet."

"I think it will help our people feel connected and safer if we come together as a community right now. What do you think? Do you have any issue with that from a security perspective, Dave?"

I could see everyone perk up at that idea and Dave nodded his head. "No issue with me, Damon. I think it's a great idea. I'll rotate my guys so they can all have some time down here."

"Great. Done. The guys and I will make it happen, spread the word," Damon said, turning back to the food table.

I had to admit, for all his reserve toward me, Damon treated the people around him with care. I'd never seen a dominant alpha defer to a beta for input before now.

Sirena wasn't done yet, though. She tapped him on the shoulder, and he turned around, his frustration clearly on show. She wasn't one to give up easily. I'd give her that.

"Can we go somewhere and talk alone, honey?" She was all up in his personal space. She'd gotten her footing back and seemed to have a new play in mind.

"No, I'm sorry. I've got a list of things to get done today." He said firmly, yet not unkindly. He wasn't being a jerk. He was just attempting to clarify his boundaries, and I had to respect that, even if she didn't.

Sirena gave him a long-suffering look like he was being unreasonable. "I agree with what you're saying, honey, but I still think it will be easier for us at your place. We'll have no privacy when you want to come over if I'm bunking with the other girls," she said.

"Besides, like Hunt said, what he and I had was barely even a fling, so he couldn't be that upset at my staying with you guys? It was more a friends with benefits thing, and we're still friends, aren't we, Hunt?"

She gave Hunter her most winning smile, trying to get him back onside, before she moved even closer to Damon. She pushed her boobs against his arm and looked up at him coquettishly as she batted her fake eyelashes, completely ignoring the rest of us watching.

Seriously, I'm pretty sure we were firmly in apocalypse territory now, and she was still wearing huge fake eyelashes. I didn't even own any make-up anymore. It had been as much as I could do to keep clean-ish this last week.

"I can stay in the spare room if it makes everyone more comfortable," she said, playing what she thought was her trump card. Easy access for a quick fuck without the pressure of sharing a bed every night.

Damon picked up the plate he'd been carefully filling, taking a step back. "Sorry Sirena. Even if Hunt, Leif and Max were okay with it," he said as he looked at each of the guys and made it obvious they were a family of four, not two, "the room's already taken."

Damon walked over to me and casually handed me the plate. I nodded my thanks to him, trying not to read too much into the gesture. He gave me a small, polite smile, then immediately returned for another plate.

"By who?" she asked, looking at me suspiciously and eyeing the way I was standing, being held by both Leif and Max.

"Maia, of course," Hunter said, backing Damon up as he brought me over some cutlery and a glass of juice. I smiled my thanks at him, letting go of Max's hand to take the cutlery from Hunter carefully while Max grabbed my juice for me.

Sirena heaved out a frustrated breath as she glared at me. I was a little nervous about where she would go with that information. I wasn't worried about myself. I knew I could handle Sirena, but there were a lot of people in this room I hadn't met yet, and I didn't want a public spectacle before I got to know them.

I noticed a quick movement and saw Lexie give me the thumbs up and a cheeky grin in the background, mouthing 'mean girl smackdown' at me, and I remembered our pact from the night before.

I grinned as she nodded eagerly at me and gave her an awkward thumbs up with my hand holding the cutlery.

"Have you had any breakfast yet, Lex?" Dave asked her familiarly as if he did it every morning. She looked startled but shook her head. He turned and started gathering a plate.

"Damon, honey," Sirena said, fixing a fake smile back on her face, determined to have one last try.

I almost sighed out loud. I wanted to eat my breakfast. The hot, buttery toast smelt divine. My stomach growled loudly, and Hunter raised his eyebrows at me. I put my cutlery on the side of my plate and picked up a piece with my fingers, devouring it quickly, and I'm sure, not very gracefully.

If I had to watch this show, I would make it dinner and a show. Or, breakfast and a show, as it were. Hunter just smiled broadly at me. He was standing casually next to Lexie, who wasn't even pretending to fiddle with stuff anymore.

Sirena continued, thinking fast on her feet now. "I don't think it's appropriate to have a woman you hardly know living in your house with you. Especially when it appears, she's already messing with Leif and Max's relationship."

Oh no, she didn't. If this went as I suspected, I would get all up in her face in about thirty seconds.

"People talk and everyone knows we're together, you need to think about both of our reputations. I think it would be best if you moved the stray girl into the shared cabin where the other girls can keep an eye on her." She looked at me smugly. I raised an eyebrow at her. Read the room, wench.

"Sirena," Damon said darkly, with a warning clear in his voice. She turned to him eagerly, thinking she'd won, clearly not listening to his tone. She was delusional.

"Are you attempting to slut-shame Maia right now? Think about that for a moment because you just admitted to having a casual arrangement with two men at the same time." It was official. Damon just earned a spot on my hug list.

"Damon, honey, you can't call what we have casual," Sirena said, moving towards him and attempting to touch him, again, by placing her hand on his arm.

Damon narrowed his eyes at her and stepped back, quickly this time, before she could make contact. I almost laughed out loud as she stumbled slightly. I had a feeling it was strike three, and she was out. Buh-bye.

He squared his shoulders, widened his stance and stared her down, while shoving his hands in his pockets with a casual arrogance that was hot as hell.

"Sirena, this was fun at first and convenient for both of us, and we agreed it would be casual upfront. At no point has it been anything more, but lately, it has come to my attention that you have been behaving as though it was something more, and not just to me, but also to others."

Damon was suddenly in full alpha, master of his domain, mode. His tone was firm, deep and slightly growly. It was making me all kinds of hot. His natural rain scent had deepened like an impending storm, and it woke my omega hormones up in a way that created an intense response in me.

If he talked to me like that while standing and focusing all that intensity on me, I think I would fall to my knees and moan out a 'yes, alpha. I've been a naughty girl.' I didn't even care at this point what he was saying.

"It shouldn't have started, given our working relationship. I will own up to that mistake," Damon said, trying to remain fair, despite his anger and rising dominance.

"Damon, honey," she tried again, a wheedling note in her voice that was not attractive. She must have thought she could see an in because he was still holding back to a degree. Was she for real? Was she still not getting it?

"I didn't want to do this here in front of everyone, but you have left me no choice, Sirena." We all took a collective breath in and waited for it eagerly.

"You are not respecting any boundaries I have been trying to set or the people I care about." A deeper growl entered his voice, and his dominance rose even further. Along with his scent, a hint of lightning seared the air.

He crossed his arms over his chest, getting angry now, which flexed his arms and stretched his shirt deliciously over his thick biceps. His dominance was unleashed and rising steadily, but he wasn't using his alpha bark on her. If he hadn't done it yet, I didn't think he would.

I could feel his dominance heating my blood and caressing my skin like it wanted to play. Alpha dominance displays usually made me anxious, but Damon's was like a direct line to my clit, which was suddenly swollen and aching.

I stirred restlessly on my feet, trying to ease the sensations. I didn't think I had ever been this aroused by someone, and he wasn't even touching me.

"Let me make myself clear. We have never had the kind of relationship you are trying to imply, and we haven't had a casual arrangement for some time. We are done," Damon said firmly.

"Stop calling me honey and trying to touch me inappropriately when it's clear I'm not interested. If a man did that to you, it would be considered harassment. I'd like to be treated with the same respect you would expect to be shown to you."

"You also need to start treating the other people who live and work here with the respect they deserve. I won't tolerate you trying to claim some kind of authority that you don't have over them."

I think my panties were about to melt and my scent was spiking. Leif leaned down to whisper in my ear. "Do you like it when Damon goes all dominant alpha, Maia? Your scent is intoxicating. My dick is hard as a rock."

Just hearing Leif whisper Damon's name in my ear while I was so aroused had me shivering and almost moaning. I needed to get out of here before I embarrassed myself. Hunter was smirking at me openly.

When Leif thrust into me subtly from behind, I nearly dropped my plate. Max, ever the observant one, grabbed my loaded plate in his other hand and shifted slightly to block me from the room.

"Dave," Damon said with a low growl, his voice full of authority with just that one word. It made me shake with need, and his attention wasn't even on me.

"Yes, sir," Dave answered quickly. See, even he got it. He had moved from casually leaning against the food table to fully alert as soon as Damon eased the leash on his beast.

"Assign someone to help Sirena pack up her cabin and escort her to her new dwelling. Let me know if she refuses to do so or gives you any trouble."

"Damon," she tried yet again. She started to fake cry, trying to get sympathy as she looked at Hunter and Dave, but there was none. She had tried to insinuate and trap Damon into publicly accepting a relationship that didn't exist, and it had backfired dramatically.

Dave stepped up and Sirena turned to glare threateningly at me, like this was all my fault, her mean girl showing through the carefully crafted facade she usually showed the guys. It didn't matter though, I wasn't paying her any attention. All my focus was on Damon and the dominant alpha pheromones he was giving off in waves.

Sirena gritted her teeth as she looked past me and seemed to flinch at all the people watching, before dropping her act. "Fine," she said.

"Fine," Damon said. "As long as you don't try to renew any physical relationship with me, we can work out a way to move past this and get along."

"Or me," Hunter piped in, and she narrowed her eyes at him.

"Let's go," Dave said and escorted her out of the room. "Lincoln, you're with me."

The young guy I knew as dipshit got up from the table next to where we were standing, and mumbled, "Shit, why me," as his friends watched Damon warily.

"Max and I are going to take Maia for a walk," Leif announced into the silence.

At my name, Damon whipped around and faced me. The moment he saw me and registered my scent flooding the room, his eyes dilated until they were almost black. He took a small, involuntary step toward me and Hunter jumped up in front of him, his forgotten plate crashing to the ground.

"Whoa, Damon, not the right time. I get it but don't do something you're going to regret. Leif, get her out of here, man."

Damon went rigid like he was holding himself back through sheer force of will, but his eyes only left mine to run all over my body.

I was openly panting, and my gaze locked on Damon. He was breathing just as hard, and I could tell he was barely in control. I could feel his desire for me like it had been sitting below the surface, building slowly, but was suddenly ripped free in one burst of pure, intense need that couldn't be denied.

It was hammering me, both physically and through a tenuous bond I hadn't even realized was there, sitting next to Leif's. It felt like he was touching every inch of my body at once, even though he was nowhere near me.

My nipples were hard, my panties were soaking wet, and my clit was aching with need. I was halfway to orgasm just from Damon's stare and his dominance. I let out a moan, unable to keep it inside with so much sensation coursing over my skin.

I heard another plate hit the ground and felt Max take my hand, but I was gone. Maia, the rational person, wasn't in charge anymore. My omega had taken over completely and was running on pure instinct. What she wanted more than anything right now was Damon. She didn't care that he was off limits.

My focus narrowed even further to the pulse beating a wild rhythm in Damon's neck. I started to take a step towards him, despite Leif's arms around me, happy for him to come with me. I got no resistance from Leif. It felt like he moved with me, as if he was in a trance. Damon strained towards me as well, as Hunter braced his hands against Damon's chest.

"Max," I heard Leif beg, his voice ripping from his throat.

"Max, you're going to have to do it. Get her out. They're both gone," Hunter demanded. I could vaguely sense people getting up and moving away from us, and I could hear Lexie yelling at Leif.

So Max did the only thing he could do, he bodily picked me up, threw me over his shoulder and sprinted for the kitchen exit. Leif followed close behind us, with his hand laying possessively on my back. I could feel Damon's roar vibrating through the air between us, and singing through my blood, as we rushed past the shocked women and fled out the door.

Eighteen

Maia

The cool breeze outside hit my overheated skin like a caress, making me shiver and moan even more. Every sensation felt carnal.

Max sprinted past a washing line behind the kitchen and pointed to a quilt airing out in the sun, yelling, "Leif, grab that."

I heard a protest, but we quickly left whoever it was behind. I thought Max would take us back to the house, but he veered off and headed for the bush near the lower guest cabins.

He rounded a bend and took a faint path I would have missed up a rise that wound around a small rocky outcrop. I was bouncing around with my ass in the air, and I couldn't take it anymore. I desperately needed friction.

I pushed myself up off Max's shoulder and moaned his name. He grabbed me and pulled me lower down his body as I slid my legs around his waist and started grinding on his pecs, my tits all but pressed into his face. He groaned loudly but kept running, and my moans intensified as I rubbed against him with the movement.

Everything lit up inside me, and I felt like an explosion waiting for a spark. I was out of control, and I didn't care. I wanted this more than I'd ever wanted anything in my life.

I dropped down further and started licking Max's neck and biting his ear, needing to taste his salty sweetness. He started shaking, not with exertion, but with raw need.

We rounded a final bend in the small path, and I felt shade cover us as he stopped under a large, low-hanging tree that gave us shelter and some privacy. I was grinding on him furiously and sucking on his neck hard enough to bruise when I felt myself being lowered, and I landed on the quilt on my back. I hadn't even noticed Leif had thrown it down behind me.

Leif followed us down quickly, grabbing my face between his giant hands and kissing me brutally, holding nothing back. He invaded me with a desperate desire to be inside me any way he could. I bit his lip savagely, letting him know I needed more, and he moaned loudly.

I needed his weight on me, pushing me into the blanket. I needed to feel his skin now. I started pulling at his shirt, trying to get it off, moaning 'need skin' like a wanton cavewoman.

Leif pulled back suddenly, took my t-shirt between his two strong hands and ripped it down the middle. My bra quickly followed, being torn in two forcefully with his alpha strength. I almost passed out at the overwhelming sensation of being ravaged with complete abandon, no thought to consequences.

He fell on my exposed breasts licking and sucking fervently, and my vision went white. I held his head to my chest, whimpering and begging, but not knowing what for, just wanting it all, now.

My hips were grinding against nothing as I felt Max run his hands up my legs and jerk my shorts and panties down in one motion. I felt the air hit my pussy as my legs fell apart, and I felt empty. I needed to be filled.

My scent exploded in the clearing and mixed with Leif's in a way that drove our need higher, merging and becoming something new, like chocolate oranges melting on my tongue.

Leif looked at me, the barest hint of restraint left and growled deeply. 'Need to be inside you. Can we fuck you?' All traces of my gentle giant were gone, but I loved this version of him just as much. He was holding out for permission with the last of his control, almost unable to form the words but still including Max.

I nodded wildly at him, needing him desperately, too, and begging, "Please" in a deep breathy voice I hardly recognised as my own.

I reached out to Max, needing him just as much. He didn't hesitate, lying beside me and hoisting my leg over his hip to give Leif better access. Then he bent over and started lathing his tongue across my nipples before sucking and biting them gently in turns like they were his favorite lollipop.

Leif smoothly pulled his shirt over his head and dove between my thighs. He devoured me with deep licks, parting my folds and exposing me to him completely, then thrust his tongue aggressively inside me. I rode his face from below with wild abandon, driving myself onto him.

Max crept his hand up my thigh and flicked his finger over my slippery clit, rubbing lightly in teasing strokes. I was so primed that I exploded instantly, coming hard and fast all over Leif's face, crying out at the sharp intensity of my orgasm.

As mind-blowing as it was, it wasn't nearly enough. I still felt empty. I whimpered until Leif delivered on exactly what I needed. He reared up, and I saw his jeans had also disappeared at some point. He'd been busy while eating me out.

I only got a glimpse of his enormous dick, erect and proud, and had no time to panic before he lifted my hips off the ground and thrust into me mid-orgasm.

I screamed out as my orgasm doubled in sensation at the intrusion. Not in pain, in pure, undiluted pleasure. Leif was thick. I doubted I could have fit him without prep if my muscles hadn't already been convulsing madly, desperately pulling him in. I stretched around him in a glorious, hedonistic burn.

I rode him hard through my orgasm, thrusting up as Leif groaned loudly, his eyes rolling back in his head. Max lifted his head to watch Leif sliding in and out of me, Leif's dick glistening, while Max pinched my nipples roughly with each of Leif's furious thrusts, prolonging my orgasm to the point of exquisite pain.

Leif was grinding his teeth hard, desperately trying not to lose all control. "Max, need you. Can't bite her, yet."

Max was up in an instant, and Leif bent Max to him, kissing him forcefully while thrusting into me, before he pulled out and slipped Max between us, facing me.

He ripped off Max's shirt and pulled his jeans down roughly, in the fastest yet most erotic strip I had ever seen. Max was almost vibrating with need. I don't know how he had held back from touching himself this long.

Max's tattoos and his gloriously toned body were on full display, as were his long, fully erect dick and the surprising Jacobs Ladder piercings running up it. I'd heard about it but had never seen one or felt one before. I wanted it now. I wanted to lick and suck, but that would have to wait for another day. I had an empty ache, and he would fill it nicely.

Max knelt and went to lean over me, but I pushed him back onto his heels, getting up and grabbing his face between my hands, kissing him passionately, making sure he knew this part was about him and that he was nobody's stand-in.

I straddled his lap and dropped down onto that glorious, long, studded dick, not even hesitating for a second, still driven mad with desire for these men. He groaned, long and low, as I settled myself onto him, feeling every ridge of his pierced perfection. My nipples brushed his chest as I bounced up and down on him desperately, making me moan along with him.

"I can feel her slick on my balls," Max moaned.

"Fuck yes," I heard Leif swear as he reached up between us to collect the slick that only omegas produced and only when incredibly turned on. It was like manna to alphas. It drove them insane. But with the cruel way most omegas were treated, it was a rarity, almost a myth, in our modern world.

Leif shoved his fingers in his mouth, sucking on them and groaning, before reaching down to collect more and running his hands along his dick and Max's ass, coating them both. I could see him thrusting into his hand. He was so impatient to be buried in us.

He nudged Max forward slightly while gripping his waist to keep him steady, and the movement had me almost hanging from Max. It was a delicious sensation to feel myself swinging lightly as Max thrust into me, held up only by the strength of his arms as he wrapped them tightly around me. I was entirely at his mercy and he was at Leif's.

I felt Max shudder as Leif breached him with his fingers, the sensation making him moan again. I could feel the vibration through his chest where I had plastered myself against him.

"Fuck, her slick is opening you up. It's like a magic lube," he said eagerly as he withdrew his fingers, raised himself on his knees slightly and thrust into Max from behind. He held us both steady with his brute strength.

I felt it in my core as Leif's thrust shoved Max's dick further into me. The sensation of Leif fucking me using Max's dick was almost too much. I started to whimper as I held onto Max's neck and thrust myself lightly onto Max to meet each of Leif's more powerful thrusts.

It was a sensation overload. I could feel Leif's pleasure and wild abandon through our growing bond. It seemed to intensify with each thrust into Max sandwiched between us. Max's mouth was open on a savage yet silent cry, and I could feel Leif's overwhelming need to lay a possessive claim on us both, but I knew, as did Leif, that it wasn't our time yet.

I met Leif's eyes over Max's neck as a feral need came over me that I saw reflected in his eyes and felt through our bond. My teeth ached to claim these men with a ferocity that made me feverish. I pulled myself higher as Leif lost all control, spurred on by my need, thrusting wildly in complete abandon. Our desire fuelling each other into a frenzy, with Max, lost to sensation between us.

"Fuck. My knot. He's taken my knot," Leif growled low, his voice shaking with intense pleasure.

I let my instincts rule as another orgasm rushed me in a moment so intense that I couldn't tell if it was my body or my soul alight.

"Need to bite you," I growled at Max and he panted, "Fuck, yes."

I pulled up and bit the crook of Max's neck. I felt Leif do the same as an orgasm exploded through Max, which set me spinning into a ravening so deep I felt it written into my very bones. It changed everything and blew the last of my hold over my omega instincts wide open.

I felt set free.

Nineteen

I woke up on my side, facing Maia, and I could feel Leif lying curled behind me. It was like a repeat of this morning, only we were all naked, and I was the one in the middle, being groped. Maia's hand was on my pec, over my tattoo, where she was snuggling into my chest, and Leif's hand was possessively covering my dick.

If I had known where we would end up less than an hour later, I probably wouldn't have bothered jacking off before we left.

I could still feel Leif hard and buried deep inside me, I was locked onto his knot, and it felt deliriously sensual as it pressed against sensitive nerves. I took a moment to marvel at the sensation. We'd never managed it before. While the sex had still been great, I had sometimes wondered if I was enough for him. I had always loved him but knew there was a possibility I may have to let him go, if he found an omega.

I had been genuinely happy for him when he instantly connected to Maia and over the moon when I realized she might accept me as well. I had never imagined I might be so included in their relationship. The sensation of them both using my body to bring us all to climax had almost felt like more than I could bear.

Maia had brought so much to my life so quickly, but I didn't just want her so I could keep Leif. She already meant the world to me. She was so generous with herself after suffering and losing so much. She was so very easy to love.

They weren't words I could say to her just yet, but my feelings for her were growing quickly. Just days ago, I had been worrying about the Crash, what it would mean for the country and how we would get it all back. Now, I knew I would do anything to build a new world out of the ruin of this one, where she could be safe and free. She deserved no less.

Our old world was broken if someone like Maia could be treated so heartlessly, as though she meant nothing when she meant everything.

I gently brushed a tendril of her golden hair off her face. She looked so peaceful and content, curled up in my arms like she was where she belonged. My heart pounded a steady rhythm in my chest, wanting to keep her like this for as long as I could.

She stirred gently, smiling to herself and rubbed her cheek against my chest.

"I'm so glad you grabbed this quilt, Leif, great thinking," Maia mumbled as she stretched out. It appeared as though we'd all taken a little nap. I wasn't surprised. What we had just done together had been mind-blowingly intense, for me at least.

Leif chuckled behind me. "Best sex of my life and all I get is, 'great quilt, Leif.' Wow, I need to work on my skills."

Maia giggled, and it was a sound I wanted to hear more. She had been so skittish and wary when she had first arrived and so obviously shut down and alone.

In only a matter of days, with some genuine warmth and care from Leif and a little teasing from Hunter, she had lightened into a ray of sunshine in all our lives.

"It's a perfect quilt. I think I'm going to keep it," Maia said as she stroked it.

I smiled at their antics. I could feel Leif and Maia's joy thrumming lightly through my chest, along with quiet contentment from Leif. It felt glorious.

I stilled in shock, and they both eyed me in concern, Leif leaning up onto his elbow so that he could see me.

"Max, what's wrong?" he asked softly. I could feel his concern, which had me spiraling into a freakout. My heart was racing as I tried not to let the sensation overwhelm me.

I could feel their emotions. I could feel two bright, joyful bonds in my chest that felt so right and natural, like they had always been there, that I hadn't even noticed the change.

"I think we broke him, Leif," Maia said, in a cautious whisper, like she was trying not to startle me.

"I can feel you," I said in wonder, reaching up and feeling Leif's bite mark on my neck, then Maia's on the other side. "You claimed me, both of you."

They both just watched me closely as I closed my eyes, feeling joy so intense I felt my heart might explode like a glitter bomb all over the grass.

"How is this even possible?" I asked, desperately hoping I wasn't dreaming or that it wasn't some kind of trick that would disappear. Now that I had this connection with them both, I never wanted to let it go.

I felt complete for the first time in my life. Like the constant need to figure everything out and my endless curiosity about the world that had driven me for so long, had been leading me to this moment. So I could find this.

I took a deep breath as I felt them both push reassurance at me. Realizing Maia and Leif could feel what I felt as well, I pushed my joy back at them. Both of their faces lit up with huge smiles.

"I don't know how it's possible, but I think it has something to do with Maia. I knew from the first moment I saw her that she was mine, but also more than that. Knowing I get to share her with you makes me feel complete in a way I never expected or thought to want," Leif said.

Maia looked awkward at having us both stare at her so reverently. She went to say something, then stopped and took a small breath. Her brow was creased like she was puzzling something out.

"There's nothing special about me, but I think there may be something special about us," she said, with hesitation halting her voice.

"I can't explain it easily. It's something I have to show you, but I need the other guys to be there too. Is that okay?"

Leif and I looked at each other. That felt right to both of us, so we simply nodded at her.

She took a deeper breath like she'd been worried about how we would react. Leif leaned over me, entwined his fingers with hers, and then brought their hands up to rest over my chest, where they could feel the steady beat of my heart.

"It's more than okay," Leif said.

"Okay," she said, in her usual, simple and honest way. She wasn't big on using a hundred words when one would do, and I loved that about her.

A leaf from the sprawling tree that sheltered us floated down and landed in Maia's hair, almost like a natural blessing. Leif let go of her hand and reached up to pluck it out of her hair.

She looked up into the tree and smiled at the dappled light flowing through gaps in the branches. 'This spot is so beautiful, and it's so warm here. It's heavenly.'

"The hot spring heats the air around it," I said.

She jerked her head back to me with wide eyes and said, "The what, now?"

I smiled and pointed behind her. "The hot spring, behind you."

She whipped her head around to see where I was pointing so fast it was almost comical, but all you could see from our angle was some rocks, with ferns around them and a faint haze of steam in the air. I figured the faint mineral odor would have given it away earlier, but it seems she had been distracted by other scents when we arrived.

"Are you freaking kidding me?" she said as she jumped up and dashed over.

"It's a hot spring," she said incredulously.

"I know," I smirked at her. She was adorably bewildered. And hot as all hell, standing naked, her lush curves in full view, wholly uninhibited and surrounded by nature. In the morning light, she looked like an incarnation of Gaia, the earth goddess.

"I've never bathed in a hot spring, but I've always wanted to. Is it safe to swim in?"

"It's safe. It's not a magma spring. A geothermal gradient heats it, so the warm temperature is consistent and doesn't have dangerous fluctuations. It's deep, though. We haven't found the bottom in some sections, so stay close to the edge if you're not a great swimmer."

"I'm good. There was a fairly deep dam on gramps' farm that wasn't fenced, so he made sure we could all swim when we went to live with him. Is anything going to bite me on the ass, though?"

"Only me when I come and join you," Leif said with a wicked grin.

"It's fine, nothing bigger than bacteria lives in there, and none of it is harmful. I check the water regularly."

"Okay." She looked at both of us, still lying on the quilt. "You're not coming in now?"

"No, uh, we're kind of stuck for a bit yet," Leif said, and I could see him blushing furiously out of the corner of my eye.

She looked confused for a minute, but then it dawned on her. She looked down towards my dick like she could somehow see his knot using x-ray vision.

"Oh, the knot. I remember Leif feeling amazed when he knotted you. What did it feel like?"

I groaned. "It felt incredible, but if you keep staring at my dick while talking about his knot while it's still locked in my ass, we'll be here a lot longer."

I could feel Leif's arousal while watching her, through the bond and his dick as it twitched hotly inside me. I bit back a moan with great effort.

She smiled wickedly, and I knew she was up to no good. "Fine, I'll just bathe naked by myself then."

It was Leif's turn to groan, and he thrust shallowly behind me as she bent over in front of us to steady herself on a large rock at the edge as she tentatively stepped into the pool. She moaned loudly when she walked in, and the warm water rose slowly up her legs and over her waist.

Maia turned towards us with her eyes closed and her head thrown back as she sluiced handfuls of water over her breasts. They were high and naturally round. Way more than a handful, with perky, pink nipples. I was developing a rapid obsession with them. I wanted them in my mouth again, now.

I knew she was taunting us when she started lazily stroking them, but I didn't care. It was one of the sexiest things I had ever seen. She was completely confident with her body around us, which was a massive turn-on.

Leif didn't care either as he started thrusting into me shallowly, his dick firm and rigid inside me. We didn't have much range of motion, but the shallow thrusts were causing building friction against the bundle of nerves inside me and caused my dick to harden instantly.

Leif reached over and started stroking me leisurely, in contrast to the rough grinding behind me, and the difference in motion was driving me mad. I wanted him to grip me hard and squeeze, but he was teasing me as effectively as Maia was.

My eyes rolled back in my head for a moment. I was still so raw from my explosive orgasm earlier that it didn't take much to bring me back to the edge again. I unconsciously lifted my leg over his, opening myself up to him and trying to give him more access.

When I opened my eyes again, I noticed Maia watching us through heavy lids. One hand was still roving over her breasts while the other disappeared into the water, moving up and down gently.

I didn't think this could get any hotter, but she was masturbating while watching us, and I was gone. I moaned loudly, watching her while Leif ground on my ass. He started dragging his big, strong hand up and down my length harder, squeezing my tip at each upstroke.

I wasn't going to last long. I didn't think Maia was going to either, as her hand started moving faster while she watched Leif's hand with hunger.

"Come with us, Maia." I heard Leif demand in a rough, gravelly voice.

At his words, she spread her legs wider under the water and started thrusting harder, jerking her body in time with Leif's hand on my dick, and her tits started bouncing against her chest. It was decadent and carnal. The sight drove me over the edge.

If she was Gaia earlier, she was all Aphrodite now, as her gaze raked brazenly over my body while I was fully exposed to her.

She started to tremble, and I was right there with her as Leif's grinding became wild and his grip on my dick grew erratic. He began to mutter, "Fuck," repeatedly, with his eyes glued on her.

We all came together, the feel of Maia's intense orgasm reverberating through our chests and pushing us over the edge, too.

I came all over my stomach and the quilt in hot bursts, and I could feel Leif emptying himself inside me, his dick twitching hotly. I was breathing hard and completely spent when she raised one eyebrow and said breathlessly, "Well, that answers that question then."

"What was the question?" Leif asked, with a hint of a growl still in his voice.

"If you have a potty mouth during sex," she said with a wicked grin. "I thought I just imagined it earlier. Wait until I tell the other guys."

"Don't you dare," he growled, but with laughter in his voice. He slipped free from me finally and leapt up, giving me a quick, affectionate, squeeze of my ass before he helped me up. I watched him leap over the rocks and into the pool, knowing where the safe spots were and splashing Maia while she squealed.

He then picked her up and kissed her thoroughly yet gently, worshiping her rather than devouring her. She sighed and melted into him as I followed him into the pool.

He finally let her go and said, "You're evil, sunshine, but you're mine, and I wouldn't have it any other way."

"Ours," I said as I eased into the water alongside them, and she reached for me, bringing me into their arms.

I twined her hair around my hand, pulling it away from the water and trying to drape it over her shoulder. 'We'll have to condition your hair later. The magnesium and calcium in the water are good for our bodies but bad for hair. They'll dry it out. We'll have to tie it up next time."

I could feel a soft emotion from her coming through our bond, but she didn't say anything. I don't think she was used to people caring about her or wanting to take care of her. We would have to take it slow, so we didn't overwhelm her.

"We should wash up quickly and head back to the guys," Leif said."I want to check in on Damon."

Maia stiffened a little at that and looked away from us. Anxiety came through the bond. Leif looked over at me, not sure what to do.

"It's going to be fine, Maia." I tried to reassure her. "I know this morning was a lot, but we'll work through it together. That's how we operate."

She looked at us hesitantly. "It's just, I know he doesn't like me, and now I've gone and claimed Max. I don't know what he's going to think about that. He's very protective of you guys. You're such a solid unit, I don't want to come between you all."

"You think he doesn't like you?" I asked while Leif's mouth hung open incredulously. He ran his hand up and down her arms, unconsciously trying to comfort her while his brain misfired.

She just nodded and shrugged simultaneously, like she had mixed emotions about the question.

"What about this morning makes you think he doesn't like you? I think it was obvious to everyone in the room that he's insanely attracted to you."

She glanced at me nervously. "There's a difference between attraction and liking, Max. He's an alpha, and I'm an omega. Of course he's attracted to me, but that doesn't mean he likes the idea. He's trying to fight it, which can only mean he doesn't like me."

"I mean, I get it. I'm not an ideal omega. I don't fit the compliant princess mold. I'm tall, graceless and refuse to submit. I'm kind of wild."

She couldn't be more wrong. "You're perfect, exactly as you are, so I don't want to hear that bullshit. The ideal omega thing is just a way to brainwash you into compliance with a system that abuses you. I like your spirit, and I'm so fucking grateful that the world hasn't stamped it out."

"You're strong and beautiful, inside and out, Maia. I hope you never change. Anyone who can't see how amazing you are is an idiot and doesn't deserve you."

Leif nodded his head and added, "What he said." I rolled my eyes at him.

"Damon has issues that have nothing to do with you, Maia. He just needs some time. So, please keep an open mind, okay?"

She glanced up at Leif and sighed. "Leif asked me to keep an open mind about you, and that worked out okay."

I gasped and sputtered, "Okay?" as I leaned back to look her in the face.

She smirked at me as she turned and wrapped her arms around me affectionately. She murmured into my chest as Leif moved in to cuddle her from behind.

"I can tell Damon's a good guy. He just seems to be keeping himself distant by choice. I'm too used to people leaving. I won't risk myself with someone who isn't sure if they want to be in my life. Especially if I feel they could be important. I just can't."

I could tell that confession hadn't been easy for her. She wasn't used to opening up to people.

Leif and I looked at each other over her shoulder, he was struggling to contain his emotions and stop them from reaching her, but he looked worried. We knew Damon was trying to keep her safe rather than push her away, but if that wasn't what she was seeing, it could end badly for us all.

"We're not asking you to do that, Maia. We just don't want you to write him off just yet, please."

She shrugged, seemingly unconvinced but willing to wait it out. I could feel her sudden sadness at the situation, and it broke my heart.

We needed time, but I had a bad feeling we wouldn't get it.

Twenty

I noticed Damon and Hunter sitting on the steps to the sunken lounge as soon as I stepped onto the deck. They were quietly watching us as we approached.

The way they were sitting, Damon leaning into Hunter and Hunter hugging him from behind, was so rare but seemed so natural to them. Their relationship appeared purely platonic, but they were very comfortable showing affection to each other.

The image was so sweet that I took a mental picture to keep it tucked up in my heart. I had never seen anything like it before between men. Alpha or beta. It gave me warm fuzzies all over, like a shot of sunshine straight to my heart, even through my nervousness. Hunter was clearly supporting Damon, who had a slight frown marring his gorgeous face but was more relaxed than I was expecting after our fireworks this morning.

"Hi," I said, feeling a little awkward. I almost felt like I was intruding on this moment.

"Hi." Hunter parroted with his trademark smirk on full display. He and Damon watched me closely as I stood just inside the door. I was holding Max's hand while Leif stood protectively, slightly behind me.

I needed to get a larger vocabulary and figure out a better way of greeting people.

Max, Leif and I were pretty rumpled and damp from our swim. Leif had the quilt draped over his shoulder, and Max was carrying his ripped shirt. While I had tied the front of my shirt together to protect my modesty. My torn, useless bra was hanging from Leif's pocket.

It was pretty obvious what we had been doing.

Nobody said anything for what felt like an eternity, as if nobody knew how to start this conversation. Until Max absently reached up with his free hand and rubbed at his neck.

I saw the moment both Damon and Hunter noticed the marks. Their eyes bugged out, and I faintly felt Damon's shock.

"One bite not enough for you, Max?" Hunter asked as he got up from the steps and strode over to us to look at Max's neck more closely.

"You bit him?" He looked directly at Leif. No judgment in his voice, just curiosity. Leif nodded, waiting to see where Hunter was going with his inquisition.

Hunter looked at the other side of Max's neck, at the different bite marks, one smaller than the other.

"You bit him as well?" he asked me, putting it together quickly. I nodded and bit my lip.

"At the same time?" I nodded again. I was starting to feel like one of those bobblehead dolls.

He gave Max a sniff. "You smell like chocolate oranges." Max nodded with a knowing smile, joining our bobblehead doll line-up.

Hunter smirked, eyeing off my torn shirt and Max's in his hand. "Well, hot damn. I would have liked to watch that. Give me a heads up next time, will you?"

Max straightened his shoulders, and I could feel a new confidence coming from him, along with humor and affection. "You're going to have to up your game, man, if you want in on this action."

Hunter laughed, then slapped Max on the shoulder, smiling broadly. "I can't believe we're really doing this." He was almost bouncing. I was used to his smirk and even his wicked smile. He had so many different smiles, and he used them well. But this one was new. It looked like pure joy.

He seemed excited, and I was bewildered. It wasn't the reaction I was expecting coming back here. I looked over my shoulder at Leif, hoping for an explanation, but Leif was watching Damon intently.

Damon still hadn't moved from his perch on the stairs. He didn't look mad or like he was about to lose his shit. He just looked like he was processing a million different emotions at once.

It seemed as though his dominance had been stilled. As if he'd gotten it back under control again, which made me a little sad for him. I knew what it was like to shut down my instincts and hide in plain sight.

My omega instincts were currently curled up in a contented ball and not looking to cause a scene right now.

When Damon noticed me watching him, he got up quickly. Smoothing his hands through his hair as he walked over to us.

He stopped in front of Max, avoiding me for the moment, and asked, hesitantly, "Is it a mate bond? Can you feel them both like Leif said he could earlier?"

Max nodded jerkily, as if he was unsure how Damon would react. Despite that, he was still standing tall and proud next to me.

A genuine smile broke across Damon's face as he looked Max over. He grabbed Max suddenly and gave him a fierce hug, pulling him tight and wrapping his arms around him. Max stilled for a moment before he melted into Damon and hugged him back just as tightly with his free arm.

I felt awkward standing attached to Max while they hugged. I tried to pull my hand away, but he wouldn't let me. Leif stepped into me from behind, a solid presence supporting me and helping keep me in place.

"I'm so happy for you, man." Damon said with feeling, sounding a little choked up. Max looked like he was glowing. He was all lit up from the inside, like one of those teddy bears that glow when you squeeze them. I squeezed his hand gently to see if I could get him to light up more, and he looked down at me with a grin.

Damon moved over to Leif and gave him the same bone-crushing hug, but with more back-slapping. Max tugged me out of the way, so I wouldn't get squished. Leif had a huge, smug grin, and Damon laughed lightly, stepping back again.

"Yeah, we know, big guy. You've got all the moves."

Leif started gyrating his hips back and forth to imaginary music, pretending to hold onto a pole. "You mean this one? This is my best one." Damon laughed again, a deep, rich sound that sent goosebumps skittering over my exposed skin. It was like manna coming from someone who was usually so intense and stern.

Leif was pretty smooth with those hip thrusts. I'd pay to see that show.

"Smack me on the ass, you know you want to," Leif said, sticking his butt out and shaking it in Damon's direction. Damon shook his head, grinning.

"I'll do it." Hunter leapt forward before I could volunteer as tribute. Leif yelped as he moved away and covered his butt.

"No way, you're too rough, man. You left a handprint on my ass last time."

"It's like my calling card," Hunter said proudly. Remind me never to shake my ass anywhere near Hunter. Or maybe, a little near Hunter. He seemed like he would be wicked fun in bed and was hot as sin.

Damon turned to me, and I took a deep breath and held it. Having him this close after the way we had reacted to each other this morning had me on edge. It felt like the whole world held its breath along with me.

Hunter and Leif dropped their antics and turned to us with a wary watchfulness, like lions watching over their pride. I noticed Damon taking a big swallow like he was nervous too.

"Thank you. I don't know what you did or how you did it, but thank you," he said, a sexy gruffness to his voice that did all kinds of tingly things to me.

"Oh, I, uh. It wasn't me," I choked out.

I was so lame. I could hardly get words out when Damon looked at me so intently. His raw, male beauty, coupled with those intense gray eyes, was disarming, especially this close when you had his full attention. He almost felt otherworldly.

Was it hot in here? I was tempted to fan my top to give me some air. It was hanging precariously though, and I didn't want to give the guys an accidental show.

Damon was still watching me, so I started babbling, which was an improvement on my inane stuttering.

"I mean, I bit him. I know that may seem like a weird thing for an omega to do, but I didn't do anything special. It wasn't me. I told the guys that, but they don't believe me."

Oh god. I was acting like a thirteen-year-old school girl around her first crush, and there was no school bell to save me.

"Yeah, she did," Leif butted in. "She'll deny it, but it was all her. I've bitten Max before, sometimes soft, sometimes hard. It's never left a claiming mark like that before."

Damon continued to stare intently like I was a rare nymph he'd caught in his net. A half-naked nymph. I felt exposed and breathless. I couldn't meet his eyes.

"Can I give you a hug?" Damon asked with a soft gruffness that washed over me and had my gaze jerking back up to meet his.

That was not at all what I was expecting Damon to say. That was definitely not keeping his distance. Maybe he just didn't want me to feel left out?

"Oh, uh, sure?" I was so confused right now, and he must have picked up on that because he hesitated. He suddenly looked as nervous as I felt.

Leif jumped in to break the awkwardness. "She thinks you don't like her, man."

I swiveled and glared at Leif. How could he betray me like that? He raised his eyebrows at me innocently, but Leif knew he was in the doghouse.

"You think I don't like you?" It was a dark rumble from a confused god.

I just shrugged—one of my classic comebacks.

"Maia," he groaned roughly. "You couldn't be more wrong if you think that. You just scare the hell out of me, and I'm not sure what to do with that."

I stilled, hardly daring to breathe in case I spooked him. I was hanging on every word.

Damon went to run his hands through his hair but changed course and stuck his hands in his pockets instead. As if he didn't know what to do with them now. He was being brutally honest with me, and I was here for it. I had front-row seats booked.

"You're one of us. I knew that the first moment I saw you and your scent slammed into me. You and Leif biting Max just solidified that," he said as he watched my reactions carefully.

'The only problem is, I'm not good at processing my emotions. I've been locking them down for a long time, but you've cracked all my walls. Now my emotions intensify whenever I'm around you, and I seem to react instinctively.

"I'm trying to keep my distance. But I'm constantly drawn to you. It's a tug-of-war with myself I seem to be losing."

"Why do you need to lock them down?" I asked quietly.

He looked searchingly at each of the guys, and they all nodded at him encouragingly. Max squeezed my hand again, subtly.

"My leash on my dominance slips when I feel out of control, and that's bad for everyone. You need to trust me on that. I don't ever want to hurt you." He was grinding his jaw and he looked suddenly tormented.

It was his turn to hold his breath, and mine came out in a giant whoosh. I felt lightheaded.

I couldn't stand Damon's suffering. It was pulling at me. I responded instinctively, moving like I was on a string being yanked. I threw my arms around his neck and hugged him tightly.

It felt like he was vibrating in my arms. In a jerky movement, he bent slightly and lifted me. I nestled my head into his neck, and he did the same to mine. He took a deep breath as I wrapped my legs around his waist and the subtle vibration intensified.

"Sorry, is this okay?" I whispered into his neck. It was way more contact than the simple hug he had requested. We barely knew each other, and I clung to him like a baby monkey.

"Tell me if it's too much. It's just that meeting you guys blew away all my defenses as well. My omega instincts are pulling at me constantly now. I can't seem to shut them down anymore. I feel an intense need to touch you all, all the time."

"So I get it, Damon. I understand. You scare the hell out of me, too."

It almost sounded like he was purring, and it felt divine. It soothed every raw nerve in my soul. His scent filled my senses; it was a soft hint of rain, like a sunshower. It seemed elusive and vaguely familiar, yet comforting.

He nuzzled my neck in response, and I arched into him as Leif, Max, and Hunter stepped forward in unison and joined us. They wrapped us tightly in the middle and put their foreheads against ours.

"I want you to tell us if there's something you need, Maia. I don't want you hurting or struggling if there's something we can help with," Damon said quietly. I nodded into his neck.

"That goes both ways, Damon. Tell me if you need me to back off." He nodded and I could feel his tension ebbing away.

It felt like coming home, when you had been away for a long time, and finding all the people who cared about you had gathered to greet you. Well, this was how I imagined that felt, never having experienced it before.

This home felt better than anything I had ever known. Even my time spent on my gramps' farm was only a fraction of this. This felt like where I truly belonged.

I realized my fear wasn't of Damon. It was of the feelings he brought out in me and the possibility he, and all the guys, may disappear.

We stayed like that for minutes or an eternity. I wasn't quite sure. I didn't want it to end.

Twenty-One

"C an I just say, about fucking time," Hunter groused loudly, pressed up behind Damon with his arms around us all. I felt Damon smile against my neck.

"You talk a big game, but I don't see you rushing the girl" Damon growled lightly, teasing him. Every word was like a caress against my skin, driving me insane.

Wait. Was Hunter interested in me? I certainly felt a draw towards him, like the other guys. But despite all Hunter's flirtation, he hadn't made a single move on me.

I needed all these guys in my life, but I wasn't sure if Hunter and Damon wanted friendship or something more. They were intense at times, but they were the same way about each other too. I wasn't sure how I fit into their dynamic beyond my connection to Leif, and now Max.

Hunter was hot as sin, though. I was more than happy to flirt with him.

"Well, you should always leave the best to last," he said, winking at me as I turned my head slightly to see him. "Besides, I didn't want to outshine your attempts to woo her."

Leif and Max chuckled while Damon kept smiling against my neck like he couldn't stop now that he had started.

"There's wooing?" I asked, a cheeky, teasing grin on my face. "I haven't noticed any wooing."

"Hey," Leif said in mock exasperation. "I grabbed you a blanket earlier for our romantic picnic."

"Picnic? If it was a picnic, there would have been food, but the way I remember it, I was the only thing getting eaten."

Damon groaned loudly as he put me down suddenly and jumped away from me like I was burning him.

"Nope, too much. You can't give me a visual like that with your legs wrapped around me."

"Watch out. Maia's wicked. We found that out the hard way," Leif said as he winked at me.

"Yeah, very hard. Max was definitely hard, and from the way I could see Max panting while you had him locked on your knot, it seemed like you were pretty hard yourself." I winked back at him. I'd never felt comfortable enough around any men to tease them, but these guys had shredded all my inhibitions along with my defenses.

"Dude, you got knotted? Nice," Hunter said and held his hand up to Max for a high five. Max laughingly obliged, slapping his hand hard.

"Can everyone please stop saying words like eat, knot and hard right now, or this is going to go in a direction I don't think we're ready for just yet." Damon growled, a dark threat in his voice that sent delicious shivers up my spine.

Before I could say anything about my clear state of readiness, which I figured should be pretty obvious to him with the way my hard nipples were waving hello, Hunter jumped in.

"Speaking of food and eating, I brought you some breakfast after Max so rudely dropped yours, Maia. I figured you would be hungry when you eventually showed up again," Hunter said.

He disentangled himself from our group hug and headed for the kitchen, shouting over his shoulder, "It's called wooing, guys. Take notes."

Max let go as he jumped onto the couch, picked up a cushion and threw it at Hunter, who managed to dodge it while laughing delightedly. I loved how much these guys laughed and smiled when they were at home together. They brought out the best in each other.

Damon was such a different guy around them, more open and relaxed. I hoped he would include me in that now and not shut down on me, again. I just needed to respect his boundaries.

I patted Leif's arm that was still around me, so he'd let go. I ducked into my bedroom, coming out with my bag. Leif had settled on the couch, but he jumped up as soon as he spotted it.

"Are you planning on going somewhere?" he asked with a hint of panic.

"No." I smiled softly at him. "I want to show you what I was talking about earlier."

"Oh, okay, sure," Leif said, sounding relieved.

"Although technically you only have until tonight to convince me to stay," I chided him, plopping down next to him.

"We're not being convincing?" Leif asked with an eyebrow raised as he grabbed me and pulled me onto his lap. "We need to work harder, guys."

"Yeah," I said, wriggling on his lap. "Work harder."

Leif grabbed my hips and kept me still as Damon growled, "Bad kitty" from my other side.

"Kitty?" I asked, surprised. I loved it when Leif called me sunshine, but I wasn't sure about kitty.

"Yeah," he seemed almost embarrassed. Like he had blurted that out without meaning to. "You seem all soft and cuddly and like being petted, but you have hidden claws."

I laughed out loud as Hunter leaned across and handed me a plate of food, which I grabbed thankfully. I was starving. He passed the guys some, too.

Hunter couldn't help adding, "I'll happily pet your pussy anytime, Maia."

No, just no. It was my turn to throw a cushion at Hunter, but I missed. He just chuckled, caught it and put it on his lap under his plate. "Thanks, babe, I needed a cushion."

"Babe? What, are you fourteen and in high school?" I liked that I could join in their lighthearted teasing, and they didn't blink an eye. They seemed to delight in it.

"Yep," Max jumped in. "Couldn't you tell from the pussy remark?"

Damon groaned again as his head fell back against the couch. "Please. I'm begging you all, no more pussy talk."

Hunter and Max both laughed together, and the sound filled me with joy. Nobody here told me to be anything but exactly who I was, which was such a revelation.

At gramps' farm, I'd had to hide so much of myself. At the Palace, they had tried to break me and mold me into something else. Here, I felt like I could finally be free to do whatever felt comfortable, and the guys would be perfectly okay with it.

So, I just smiled my thanks at Leif as I shoved a piece of toast half in my mouth and put my plate on the table. If the guys wanted me around and were happy with me as I was, I wasn't going to pretend to be something else.

I was a farm girl. I grew up grabbing food when I could and eating on the run, or I didn't eat.

I pulled the old, leather-bound book out of my bag. The one I had intended to read the evening I had fled the Palace and unconsciously stuffed in my bag in my panicked flight. It was one of my favorites, and I had read it cover to cover more times than I could count.

I chewed my toast furiously and swallowed. I could feel Damon fixating on my mouth as I licked my lips. I may have done it again, just to make sure I got all the butter and crumbs.

"I came across this book a while ago. It's old, like really old. It's all about packs and pack dynamics. It was written before packs were banned, and it talks about lots of really cool and amazing stuff."

"I think the whole thing about packs being dangerous is a crock of shit made up by lone alphas to get more influence and control."

"Told you," Leif jumped in, looking smug as shit.

"You guys have talked about packs?" I asked. I was curious, most people didn't even mention the word anymore, but these guys hadn't even batted an eyelash at the word or my old, illegal book.

"Briefly," Damon said, looking at the book on my lap and stroking the leather lightly and reverently. I could tell from the motion that he was a book nerd, like me.

"We were once accused of being a pack by an asshole trying to take Damon down. It got nasty, but they had no proof and had to drop it," Max said. I had a feeling there was a lot more to it than that.

"Huh, when I think about it, that doesn't surprise me. The way you all move in sync with each other, even when you're just walking, and do that silent conversation thing when you look at each other. I can see how someone might think that. It's obvious you guys have a bond beyond friendship."

I realized this might be nothing new to them. "You know all about packs then?" I was a little disappointed.

"No," Damon said, still looking intently at the book. "We know nothing beyond the word and the concept that it involves multiple alphas and usually an omega."

"Can you tell us more, Maia?" Leif asked, looking intrigued.

I nodded. There was so much to tell, but I wasn't sure where to start.

"Can I look at it, Maia, while you talk?" Damon asked.

I handed it over, and he took it gently. Max was eyeing the book avidly as well. His thirst for knowledge was probably driving him hard right now.

"Max is actually the key," I blurted out. They all looked up at me in confusion.

"I'm what, now?" Max asked, squishing his eyebrows together and looking adorably befuddled.

"It's not all about alphas and omegas. According to the book, traditionally strong, successful packs also had a beta who was linked in by an omega and an alpha."

"The omega seems to be the heart and binds everyone together, but the beta is the center, if that makes sense."

There was a mix of sharp breaths and open mouths as they all stilled and looked at each other. They were doing that silent communication thing, again. I got a faint sense of recognition through the bond. It sent a chill up my spine.

"Yeah, uh, that makes sense. Keep going," Hunter rasped. He was the first to find his voice again after the emotionally laden moment.

"According to the book, the beta is usually tuned into everyone's emotions and helps keep everyone level when alpha and omega pheromones and instincts make them erratic. They're key to the pack staying strong. Without them, packs seem to self-combust."

I looked down to the book lying in Damon's lap, suddenly understanding why I had been so comfortable with these guys, despite my initial fear of Damon. I had unconsciously recognised their dynamic that first night up at the gate. I had spent years fantasizing about meeting people like them.

"I honestly wasn't sure if the book was a reference book or more like a mythology before now."

"All I know is that I was incredibly drawn to this book like I am to you guys. The idea of a pack and real bonds that go both ways sang to something inside me when I felt so alone at the Palace."

"I didn't intend for this to happen, though. Biting Max just felt so right to me at that moment. I hadn't planned it or even thought about it before then, but when all three of us were moving together, it was so beautiful and real.

"I felt powerful and connected for the first time in my life. I wanted it to last forever. The bite came from a place of pure instinct and emotion. A place I've never felt before because I've suppressed my omega instincts for so long."

But was it unintended? What if I had unconsciously made this happen because I wanted a family so badly?

I suddenly realized I may have pulled these guys into something without asking if it was what they wanted. The thought that I had just trapped Max and Leif into something permanent, possibly against their will, had my heart racing and my pulse spiking.

"I'm sorry. I should have shown you this, or talked to you, before I bit Max."

I felt them all pushing comfort and need at me, Max most strongly, but I thought I could also feel Damon, and even Hunter in there faintly, and it was honestly a little overwhelming.

Damon must have sensed that because he put the book down, pulled me into his lap and gave me a full-body hug, settling me against his chest and starting that vibration again that instantly relaxed me.

"Maia, you and Leif claiming me felt like a part of me that has always been missing fell into place," Max said, moving around to sit next to me and taking my hand. "Please don't even think about apologizing for it, or I'm going to get upset."

Hunter, Leif and Max were watching me with a quiet intensity that disarmed me. I snuggled in closer to Damon, and as his vibration intensified, my whole body went boneless. I was really on board with this new hugging thing with Damon. It made me feel like I was part of their group with the way they all touched each other constantly.

"What the hell are you doing over there, Damon?" Hunter asked.

Damon looked startled. "What do you mean?"

"I can hear you buzzing from over here, and that's the most relaxed I've ever seen her. So I say again, what the hell are you doing and how do we turn it on more often?"

I barked out a startled laugh, and Damon looked confused like he didn't even realize he was doing anything.

"I think he's purring. That's what the book calls it," I said.

Hunter burst out laughing, too. "Purring, like a cat??"

"Shut up, man." Damon growled, but I looked up and he had an affectionate smile on his face.

"I can feel it through the shared bond," Leif said, and Max nodded. "It's beautiful. It feels like pure comfort and love, makes you want to lean into it."

"Man, you guys all suck. I'm regretting my decision to wait for my turn so we didn't overwhelm her."

Hunter was interested in me? The revelation made my omega do a happy dance. But I smiled at him with a cheeky grin. I was nobody's sure bet. "Turn? Am I a toy to be shared? Maybe you just don't have Leif's killer moves," I said, winking at him this time.

"Oh no, you didn't," he laughed. "Challenge accepted. Now you're going to see some real action." He jumped over the coffee table ready to bust some moves and shake his ass in my face. Max leaped up and pulled him down, wrestling him back onto the couch, laughing.

"Knock it off, you idiot. We're supposed to be talking about the priceless book you almost kicked onto the floor. We don't need you shaking your ass in our face right now," Max said.

"Okay, later then. There will be ass shaking later, lots of shaking." Hunter said, pulling Max into a hug that Max seemed happy to settle into.

I smiled at their antics, feeling their love, even when they were teasing each other.

"What causes the purring? Can we all do it?" Leif asked, watching Damon and me with his head tilted curiously. He ignored the other two, who seemed to have started a poke war on the couch.

"I don't think so. I think it's specific to Damon."

"How so? Does it have to do with his dominance levels?"

"Kinda, the book describes a prime alpha, and I think Damon may be one."

Everyone in the room froze.

Twenty-Two

Hunter and Max instantly stopped their play war and were frozen where they were. Hunter looked awkward where he was lying half off the couch and half on the floor. He tried to sit up straight, and Max helped to pull him up.

"What's a prime alpha?" Hunter asked, direct, with no messing around.

He was suddenly very serious, which had me on edge. I could feel electricity building in the air. Something was coming, and I knew I couldn't run from it. Not this time. There was too much at stake if I messed this up for the guys.

"It was a type of alpha that could dominate any other alphas and not just one at a time. Groups of alphas, omegas, betas, basically everyone. They were the top of the power structure."

I couldn't breathe, and Hunter was laser focused on me while Maia was talking. There was an edge of stress in her voice and her body, where she still sat on my lap. Like she could see the way we were reacting to what she was saying, but she wasn't sure why.

Whatever the purring was that Maia had been talking about before had stopped abruptly. It had been instinctive. I hadn't noticed I was doing it until the others pointed it out. It had never happened before, but my alpha had been enjoying how she reacted to it. She instantly seemed to melt into me.

Now, there was only tension vibrating through my body and hers.

She looked at Leif uncertainly but he was watching me warily, as was Max. They could both feel the change in the air and through the bond. They were sitting on the edge of their seats, so they could move quickly if needed.

"What happened to them? Why aren't they around anymore if they were so powerful?" Max asked, always needing to know more.

"The book doesn't say. I assume it was written before they died out or went into hiding. But prime alphas were incredibly rare, even then."

"How did it work, prime alpha dominance?" Hunter asked with a terse note in his voice that wasn't like him.

Maia looked up at me nervously before she spoke. "Other alphas were drawn to them, the same way they are to omegas, I guess. When pushed, they would send out a powerful dominance wave. It would send everyone who was a threat to their knees, or everyone except their pack."

"Damon," was all Hunter said in response, eyes locked on me.

"No," I growled at him lightly.

"You have to tell them."

"No," I growled again, low and dangerously. Maia tried to shift on my lap as if she was going to get up and move away, but I clutched onto her harder. If she left me right now, I felt like I would blow apart and disappear. My body vibrated with tension, and I could feel myself leaking dominance all over the place.

Memories started assaulting me. I could hear Hunter yelling, "Shit, Damon. Snap out of it," while Leif yelled, "Let go of her, Damon." They both sounded frantic.

Through it all, I could hear Maia yelling, too, "No, stop. Everyone be quiet."

But they were all overlaid by other voices, my father screaming at me. "Do it. Do it now. I won't have a coward as a son."

I could see the kitchen in my father's mansion, the staff looking horrified. A boy not much younger than me clinging onto his father, who was our butler. He looked torn. Wanting to defend his son but not wanting to defy my father and lose his job, or worse. Hunter looked devastated as he watched on, unable to help me.

I could scent terror in the air. The need to dominate was building in me rapidly, but I couldn't do what he asked. I was desperately trying to hold on to my control and failing.

The scents and the sounds of that kitchen were more real to me than my own surroundings at the moment. The smell of food burning, neglected on the stove. The escalating rage of my father as everyone else was silent. The sobbing of the boy.

"Do it, you worthless piece of shit, dominate him now, or what good are you? Do it, or I'll make him suffer myself, and it will be so much worse. You know I will."

The boy's terror escalated sharply, and I snapped. I let out a wave of dominance into the room, dropping everyone to their knees. Even my father, who was glaring at me in cold fury.

My terror replaced everyone else's as I realized what I had done. Hunter was the only one still standing. He discretely moved behind me and placed his hand on my back. I could feel reassurance and love pour into me, enough that I could release my dominance and shove it back down deep. I caged it so deep, it would never come out again.

I was shaking as my father got up. He was instantly in my face. He yelled, spittle flying everywhere, "You'll pay for this. Follow me, now." I gave Hunter one look and mouthed, "Go." He shook his head, but I glared at him over my shoulder. I didn't want him here for this part. Hunter sighed in defeat and nodded at me as I left the room and followed my father. Better I suffer my father's wrath than anyone else.

I didn't want to remember what came after, and I tried to focus on a soft voice calling, "Damon. Damon, come back to us. We're right here."

The tangy smell of oranges and pineapples slowly seeped in and overlaid the burning smells. I could suddenly feel soft hands on my cheeks. I forced myself to focus on the hands and the feeling of calm reassurance flowing into me. The hands were quickly joined by others on my arms and back, and someone hugged me from behind.

I blinked, and Maia came into focus in front of me. I stared at her, feeling gutted. I'd had flashbacks after that day; sometimes, my dominance would leak out while I was stuck in my memories. It usually took Hunter hours to get me back.

"How long was I gone? Did I hurt anyone?" I asked in a ragged voice. That was always my biggest fear and why I kept everything locked down so hard.

"No, you would never hurt us, Damon," Maia said, watching me intently, pure conviction in her tone. "And it was only minutes at most."

Minutes? Did she get me out in minutes?

"I got flashes of that through the bond. It was like you were pushing it at me. Was that your father?'

I just nodded, feeling broken, unable to meet her eyes. But she shifted one hand down under my chin and raised my head.

"Did you all see?" I asked as I finally looked up.

Max and Leif both mumbled "yes," quietly. Hunter said, "I was there. I remember."

"I can sense your guilt. But you were a child, Damon. Nothing that happened there was your fault," Maia said.

"It doesn't matter. They were still my actions. I hurt people because I didn't have control."

"Who did you hurt, Damon?" Maia asked.

I was confused. Maia said she got flashes of what happened.

"Who did you hurt that day?" she repeated calmly.

"Everyone in the room. I dropped them all to their knees, Maia. I took away their independence. I controlled them. They were terrified. Of me." The thought of ever doing that again horrified me. Just talking about it made me feel like a monster.

"They weren't terrified of you, Damon. They were terrified of your father. Could you not feel the difference?"

"Prime alphas used their dominance to protect, not attack. It's part of who they were. They kept the worst excesses of other lone alphas in line and protected people from them."

"What you did was directed at your father, but you dropped everyone so he wouldn't realize, and no one would get hurt. You only let your dominance loose when your father threatened the boy. You were protecting him and everyone else in the room."

I remember being so angry at my father. He was pushing me so hard to do something that felt unnatural to me. My instincts kicked in when he threatened the boy, but I hadn't wanted to hurt anyone except my father. And, even then, I only wanted to stop him.

"He was asking you to dominate the boy, but you couldn't do it, could you?"

I shook my head, unable to find my voice. Was she right? She couldn't be right.

"Have you gone all this time thinking you hurt everyone that day?"

I couldn't breathe, so I gave the barest nod.

"Oh, Damon," she said and wrapped her arms around me, between Hunter's legs on either side of me. "Didn't you talk to any of them after that?"

I shook my head. "My father made them all disappear after he took his rage out on me. I never knew what had happened to any of them. I don't even know if they're alive." I felt broken at the thought. I had betrayed them all.

"Dammit, Damon. Why didn't you talk to me? You refused to talk about it. You shut me down every time I brought it up. I didn't push because you were in such a bad state afterward. It took you months to heal. If I'd known you thought that, I would have insisted you talk to me. I would have told you the truth."

"What truth?" I asked. I was so very confused.

"Your father didn't make the staff disappear. I did. My parents gave me so much 'shut up and go away' money, and I never had any use for it. So, I used it to help everyone there that day disappear into new lives. I knew you would never forgive yourself if anything happened to them."

"I talked to them all before they left, and Maia's right. They weren't scared of you, Damon. They were scared of your dad. They all asked me if you were going to be okay."

I started to shake. Hunter gripped me tighter, sliding down behind me on the couch to give me a full-body hug. Maia swiveled around so she was straddling me while Leif and Max hugged me from the sides.

They all held me as I fell apart at the relief of realizing I hadn't hurt innocent people that day, or gotten them killed. My father had threatened to kill every one of them for dominating him in front of them, and I thought he had followed through. He had held the belief over me for years, and I had never used my full dominance on anyone again, not even him.

I was surrounded by my family, my pack, as they let me purge my emotions, pouring reassurance and love into me. They didn't rush me, and I didn't try and push the feelings away or back down into a box.

I just let it all out, and it felt cathartic. I felt free for the first time. Like all my fear washed away while my pack held me.

They finally pulled away one by one, and Maia said quietly.

"Prime alphas need a pack to stabilize them. One person isn't enough. Your dominance and power are so immense, that they can tear you apart. It's not just your dominance that's higher. It's all your emotions. You feel things deeply, especially the need to protect."

"That's how packs first came about, according to the book anyway. They're a support network for the prime and each other. They have the prime's back, and they help him come back down and level out."

"You've been unconsciously building your pack all this time because you instinctively knew you needed one. Despite the fact you've also been trying to shut down your emotions."

I knew she was right about that. I needed my guys, and I'd known for some time that they kept me sane. My emotions were so volatile sometimes. Like a dark tempest that came out of nowhere and quickly made me feel out of control. But my guys always grounded me.

I had always just thought I was broken. I had never considered that maybe it was part of my nature and natural for me. The idea was a revelation. I needed to find out more.

"I really need to read this book," Max said a little dryly, and I cracked a small smile. I figured his thoughts were on the same path. I had no doubt he'd read it cover to cover by tomorrow morning.

"Didn't you ever wonder how you always seem to be able to pick up on each other's emotions?" Maia asked.

"We just kind of figured we were super awesome and empathetic people?" Hunter said, but there was a question in his voice.

"Oh, you're all undeniably awesome."

"She missed the super part," Hunter stage whispered to Leif, and I felt affection rising in the bond. And we were back.

After a few minutes of quiet, all of us happy to just be together, Max cleared his throat.

"I hate to break up this heartwarming moment," Max said, sounding hesitant, "but we announced this morning that we were holding a community meeting tonight and then left Lexie alone to sort it all out. We've been gone for hours."

"Oh shit, you do not want to leave Lexie in charge of a party," Leif said as he jumped up from the couch and turned for the door.

"Oh, wait up," Maia called to Leif. "I've never hosted a party before. I'd love to help her." She gave Max a quick kiss before she hopped up and followed Leif.

Dammit, I was done with the keeping my distance crap. I needed to move us to the kissing stage. My dick was rock hard watching her kiss Max, even briefly, while sitting on my lap.

"It's not a party. It's a community meeting," I yelled at them.

"Wait for me. I love party planning. I'm awesome at it. Do we have any disco balls?" Hunter asked Leif as he jumped up and followed them.

"It's not a party," I said again, looking at them all frantically. "We're in the middle of an apocalypse. We can't have a party."

"Oh man, read the room." Max chuckled as he leaned over to grab the book off the coffee table and settled into the couch, while the others headed out the door.

"Shit. Someone needs to get Maia some clothes that aren't ripped to bits, and I need to make sure this thing doesn't get out of control."

"Yeah, good luck with that," Max said as he chuckled lightly, already turning the pages.

What have I done? I thought as I chased after them. I really didn't mind, though. I figured we all needed a night of fun after all the heavy today.

The apocalypse could go to hell for one night. I wanted to watch our girl shake her ass.

Twenty-Three

"**W**hat the hell is she doing?" Damon asked, dumbfounded but with a rare smile on his face. He was much more relaxed tonight after all the morning revelations. He seemed far more settled and open. He'd been moving about the room, smiling and talking to people.

I knew it wasn't all going to be that easy. Damon's dad had left a lot of scars, but I was so damn happy to see him relax, even a little.

"I think she's dancing," Leif surmised, chuckling.

I looked over my shoulder to see what they were talking about and spotted Maia dancing with Lexie. Damon had finally relented and let them have some music after the community meeting earlier, as long as it was down low and we had gotten all the storm shutters up.

We had busted our asses getting the dining hall locked down, so no light and hardly any sound was escaping.

"Is that the sprinkler?" I asked, amused. "Man, I love that crazy chick already," I sighed. "I'm tagging in."

"Can you do that, tag in? Is that a thing we're doing with her?" Leif asked excitedly. "Because if it is, I'm giving you five minutes, then I'm tagging in."

"Hey, maybe we can tag team?" he asked as he turned to Max, who was cuddled at his side.

Max just laughed. "Sure, why not."

"From the way she looks at the both of you when you're together, I think she'd be all over that," I said as I nudged his shoulder.

"Oh, she was definitely all over that this morning." Leif smirked, and I groaned.

"One of you needs to tag in and save someone from an injury. She almost took Dave's eye out with that Saturday Night Fever move she just pulled," Damon said. "I'm going to go and relieve some of the boys at the gate, so they can come down and hang out for a while."

"I'm awesome at the Fever. I'm definitely in," I boasted as I took off. I could hear Damon chuckling behind me, and I loved the sound. I wanted to hear more.

I had been more than patient, but I was done waiting. Maia was going to find out tonight that she was mine.

I grabbed her from behind, whirling her around. She squealed, then laughed when she realized it was me.

"Hi," she said, a little breathlessly. God, she was adorable. She was also sexy as sin in a tight, pale blue denim skirt, tan wedge heels that showed off those long, long legs, and a pale yellow, loose camisole top that looked like it should be illegal with the way it shifted over her curves when she moved.

With her long golden hair rippling around her in waves, she looked like sunshine incarnate.

Up close, the camisole looked silky, and I wanted to run my hands all over it as it slid over her skin. I could see the outline of a lacy bra underneath it. I desperately wanted to see it up close, preferably as I peeled it off with my teeth.

I assumed she had gotten the clothes from Lexie. They had disappeared earlier to raid the supplies Lexie kept stocked for the women she tended to rescue, who often arrived with nothing but bruises.

It seemed she had found some other girly stuff, too. Her hair was curled in luscious waves, and she was wearing light make-up with pink lipstick. She suddenly looked like she belonged at the Palace, and I didn't know how I felt about that. She was stunning, but I think I preferred her natural, with her hair all mussed up and wearing one of our t-shirts.

"Hi," I said, pulling her into me and pressing her close in a classic slow dance move. I felt her shiver as I ran my hand down her back slowly and then slipped it under her top to rest against her skin.

It was the first time I had touched her, even casually. I'd kept a strict hands-off policy so far, knowing that Damon and Leif had both lost their shit the first time they had touched her. I knew I would be no different.

Her eyes dilated instantly, and she moaned quietly, thrusting her chest into mine instinctively. Shit, why the hell did I think it was a good idea to touch her for the first time in a crowded room. I could smell her scent rising already. The sweet smell of oranges and pineapples, with a hint of cake, filled my senses and made my already rock-hard dick weep.

I needed to get her alone for a minute, or maybe an hour. "Come with me," I whispered into her ear, giving it a quick lick along the rim with my tongue. She just nodded, looking a little dazed.

I was okay with that. I didn't need a lot of words. I just needed her consent and active participation.

I kept hold of her hand and swung her behind me, shielding her from the curious looks around us. Plenty of people had seen her react strongly to Damon in this very room this morning, and Leif and Max had been handsy with her all night.

I'm sure they were all curious about what was going on. We were going to have to address that soon. But, right now, Maia was all mine.

I was glad Sirena had decided to skip the community meeting tonight, so we were spared more drama.

I ducked through the kitchen and made for the cool room. Maia was sticking so close behind me that she was almost plastered to my back. I grabbed a can of whipped cream off the shelf, then turned and headed straight out again.

Maia looked adorably confused. "What are you doing?"

I stopped and looked her up and down as I licked my lips and raised an eyebrow cockily. 'Do you want to have some fun?' Her eyes widened, but she nodded.

"Do you trust me?" I asked next. She nodded again. Good. I'd never given a woman a reason not to trust me, and I didn't intend to start now.

"Let's go," I said, hearing a little gruffness creeping into my voice. I was so primed for this.

The way she followed me willingly anywhere I wanted to take her made my alpha pheromones go crazy. I wasn't macho in the way some alphas were. I mean, I could more than hold my own, but I didn't feel the need to throw my weight around aggressively. Maia trusting me implicitly, though, made me want to beat my chest and roar, "MINE" at anyone who came near us.

But, I reined it in. I had a much better outlet in mind for my alpha instincts. I turned the kitchen lights off before heading out the back door. There were two young farm hands outside, smoking. I could smell the noxious smoke and see the cigarette butts light up as they took a drag. They needed to enjoy those sparingly. Who knew when they would get more?

"Evening, boys," I tipped an imaginary hat at them, but I had the can of whipped cream in my hand, and I could see their smirks. Maia just giggled behind me.

"We're going down by the pond, but if anyone is looking for us, tell them we went up to the treehouse." The boys nodded at me and snickered to themselves.

"You have a treehouse?" Maia asked.

"Yeah." I looked over my shoulder when she didn't say anything. She was looking at me in surprise. "I mean, come on. This farm was rebuilt by a bunch of single guys. You've met us. There was always going to be a tree house."

Maia clutched her side and laughed out loud at that, a free and easy sound that was so different from when she first arrived. I wanted to hear more of it. I needed to make her laugh every day. It was my new mission in life.

I felt her stumble slightly and remembered she was wearing wedge heels in the dark on a gravel path. I crouched down in front of her. "Here, hop on."

She snorted. "Yeah, right. I'm wearing a tight skirt. I'd have to hoist it up, and my ass would be hanging out."

"Fine with me. I'm the only one here, but if you feel more comfortable, I'm good with this, too." I jumped up, turned quickly, and picked her up in a bridal hold. I carried her down the path at a jog. My night vision was excellent, and the moon was still fairly bright tonight.

"Are we in a hurry?" she giggled as she nuzzled into my neck and took a deep breath of my scent.

"We are now," I groaned. My dick felt like it was about to snap off. It was so hard, just from feeling her breath on my neck, let alone feeling her in my arms.

"Hunter, you smell so good," she moaned suddenly. "Like fresh oak with a hint of zingy juniper that buzzes on my tongue. I can smell honey creeping in, too. I want to bite you and see if I can make it stronger."

We had both been patient, but she was as ready as I was to take the next step. Hearing her talk about biting me while moaning like that had me upping my pace even more.

"Near enough," I mumbled to myself as we rounded the bend. I veered off the path and headed under the branches of an old fig tree that sat alongside the pond. I wasn't going to make it to the private nook with the bench further down the path.

I knew the view behind me was spectacular in the moonlight, but the sight in front of me was even better.

It was darker under the tree. We used to have solar fairy lights all through it, but we'd disconnected them. Maybe one day we could turn them on again. I hoped so.

I let go of her gently and slid her body down mine, torturing us both. She kept one leg wrapped around my waist as I pushed her back against the tree and dropped the whipped cream on the ground.

Her nose was still buried in my neck, and she started licking my skin right over the most sensitive spot where a bite would often go, then sucked on it aggressively.

I almost came in my pants on the spot. "Jesus," I groaned, bucking into her and grinding against her hip.

"No, Maia," she said, with a laugh in her voice. Oh, the little minx.

"Two can play that game," I said, a dangerous note entering my voice. Maia was triggering my alpha instincts, and my pheromones were going crazy.

Our scents were mingling under the tree branches. Maia's sweet fruity scents balanced out my more woody tones. Together we smelt fresh and natural. The more turned on we got, the more her cake and my honey rose to the surface, though, driving us wild and turning the dark space into a bakery.

My night vision was improving every second I spent under the tree, and her pale skin was almost glowing in the filtered moonlight.

I pulled my neck away from her mouth, and she was panting almost as badly as I was. It was time to take this up a notch.

She licked her lips in expectation of a kiss, and who was I to leave her hanging? But I wasn't going to be that easy to direct.

I bent down slightly, burying my nose in her hair and then her neck. I returned the favor, sucking and kissing a light trail down her neck as she moaned louder. I continued over her clavicle and down into her cleavage, making my kisses progressively lighter to tease her.

She thrust her chest forward as I pulled my head back slightly, blowing over the wet trail I had left. She shivered, pushing her hips into me where we were still connected.

I ran my hands lightly up her arms, leaving goosebumps in my wake.

"Are you cold? Do you want to go?" I asked her, my voice husky in the quietness.

I could see her shaking her head in the shadows.

"Good," was all I said in reply.

My hands reached her shoulders, and I slipped two fingers underneath the thin straps of her camisole. I was sorely tempted to snap them off, but I knew Max and Leif had already destroyed one shirt and bra. I knew she didn't have many.

I gently grasped them and slipped them down her shoulders, tugging when the fabric caught on her full breasts. The slow reveal as they came into view, encased in pale yellow lace, almost made me lose it.

I groaned, and she arched an eyebrow at me. I didn't know who I was teasing more as I let the fabric pool around her waist. I trailed my hands back up slowly, with only the barest graze against her breasts.

"Hunter, please," she groaned, thrusting her breasts and grinding against me, begging for my touch and driving my alpha wild.

She tried to reach up and touch me, but her hands were trapped by her camisole straps. Before she could free herself, I repeated the motion with her bra straps. Easing them slowly down her arms, tempted to forget my plans and just devour her right now as her breasts popped free, ripe and begging for my mouth.

I looped her bra straps around her wrists, securing her more effectively in place. Then I picked up the canned whipped cream from the ground.

I had been waiting patiently, and I was going to enjoy this treat.

"Are you ready?" She nodded, breathing hard, her nipples pointing at me in the moonlight and bouncing slightly with her breaths. It was a gorgeous sight.

"Here we go." I shook the bottle and squirted whipped cream straight onto her nipples, and she gasped loudly.

"Oh god, it's cold," she exclaimed, a hitch in her breath. "Hunter, touch me please," she begged when I just stood there watching her writhe in place. I knew the cold sensation, after so much teasing, would drive her wild.

"Yes, ma'am," I said as I leaned my head down and licked once over her nipple, my tongue making the barest contact. She bucked again, moaning long and low.

"More," she begged, her voice husky and sexy as fuck.

"Yes, ma'am," I repeated while licking the other breast slowly and gently.

"More, now," she insisted, and my resolve broke. I dropped the can and descended on her breasts, licking and sucking furiously, alternating teasing a gorgeous nipple with my mouth and rolling the other between my fingers.

She was bucking against me. Her need driving her into a frenzy. I dropped to my knees, hoisted her skirt to join her camisole around her waist, and tore her underwear down and off completely. I was past teasing or even being particularly gentle.

She lifted her leg over my shoulder and thrust her dripping wet pussy at my face, and I was lost. I licked long strokes through her folds, and her honey taste tipped me into a frenzy. I ate her like a starving man, thrusting my tongue roughly inside her while I rubbed light circles over her engorged clit.

She came quickly, on a cry, before I could even finger fuck her, bucking wildly against my face. I loved every minute of it. I licked her clean before standing and pulling my shirt over my head in one quick motion.

"Yes, please," she begged. I could listen to her beg all day. "I need to touch you."

I released her hands, and she sprung at me, licking and kissing my chest, running her hands all over me until she reached my jeans, she tore them open, and I'm pretty sure I heard the button hit the tree. She shoved my pants down and went to drop to her knees, but I grabbed her.

"I need to taste you, Hunter," she moaned, half wild.

"No time, won't last. Need you." It was my turn to beg, and I wasn't above it. I could hardly even get out the words, my beast so near the surface.

She jumped up using my shoulders as leverage, all but climbing my body, as I leaned her back against the tree, keeping my arms behind her so she wouldn't scrape against any bark.

I thrust into her, driving through her gushing slick, and growling deeply. She was so hot and wet I had to focus not to lose it instantly. The muscles in her tight channel were squeezing me and pulling me in deeper with every thrust until my knot hit her opening.

The sensation as the edge of my swollen knot hit her wet heat almost had me seeing stars. I didn't want to force myself into her, though. I fought to keep myself steady, but Maia had other ideas.

"More," she growled at me, almost feral, as she grabbed my ass and thrust me into her while she ground down. My knot slid home as she rammed me into her forcefully, and we locked into place at the exact moment her lips finally met mine, and my whole world exploded into light.

I felt a bond snap into place in my chest as a powerful climax ripped through me. Her body clamped down on my knot in a delicious, strangled possession as she came hard and fast with me.

The force of our orgasms reverberated in our bond, building off each other until it felt almost painful as we continued wildly grinding against each other. It felt endless as sparks of light kept setting off new tremors through my body.

My teeth ached with the need to bite and claim her, but I knew it wasn't our time yet. I instinctively knew why Leif had held off, too. We wanted to claim her together. So I continued ravaging her mouth with my own, thrusting my tongue and caressing hers in time with my still grinding hips.

Her hands were still on my ass, but they slipped up my back and fastened into my hair, holding me to her as I continued to kiss her through the last of our orgasm as it finally ebbed, leaving tiny little aftershocks in its wake.

I could feel small scratches on my arms from the bark of the tree, but I didn't mind. I'd rather get scratched up than have it happen to her through my carelessness. They were nothing compared to the pure rapture of feeling her bond thrumming lightly in my chest.

She sighed softly and went limp against me. We weren't going anywhere just now, while she was locked to me with my knot still buried deep inside her.

I hoisted her more steadily in my arms while making sure my knot didn't pull on her too much, but she still moaned lightly and shivered against me.

I turned us and walked carefully over to a hammock that was hanging nearby, attached to the branches of the tree. Each step shifted my still-hard dick inside her and made me groan. She started instinctively grinding against me again, and I could feel another climax building quickly.

I stumbled to the hammock turning and dropping into it so I wouldn't crush her under me. She came down with me, pulling her legs up and bracing her knees on either side of me. She then pushed up against my chest and started grinding against me, rubbing her clit against my pubic bone.

She was riding me without shame with her magnificent tits swaying lightly and her golden hair flowing over her arched back. Her head was thrown back in ecstasy while I thrust into her roughly from below. She was fucking glorious.

The moonlight chased shadows over her alabaster skin, and she was in complete control of her own needs, taking what she wanted. She was a goddess, and I was lost in her spell.

She came again, hard, with a loud cry, as she forced another short, sharp orgasm from my body. Then she collapsed against me. We were both breathing hard, happy to just lay in each other's arms for the moment, letting the evening breeze cool our overheated, sweaty bodies. I could feel our shared contentment faintly through the bond.

The feel of the woven hammock as it curled slightly around our naked bodies, gently swaying us, the dark outline of sprawling branches over us, and the quiet noises of night creatures and insects nearby, made it feel like we were cocooned in nature. I couldn't think of a more perfect place to spend time alone with Maia.

"That was nice," she said as she snuggled into me.

"Nice? I'm pretty sure I have nail marks on my ass. That was more than nice."

"It's like my calling card," she said. I could feel her grin against my neck as she mimicked what I had told Leif this morning.

I laughed. "Touché pussycat."

"Pussycat? Really?" She propped her head up on one arm so she could glare at me.

I shrugged, mimicking her signature move. "Damon's right. You do have claws."

She shrugged back at me. "Damon seems to be right about a lot of things."

"He's also wrong about a lot of things too."

"Like what?" I could feel curiosity flowing through the bond from her. It was faint, but from what Leif had told me, the sensation would grow the more time we spent together. We hoped it would solidify when we all eventually claimed her. Leif's had increased drastically when they both claimed Max, as though he was a link.

I couldn't wait to know what that felt like. The faint flashes I was already getting made me feel intimately connected to Maia, more so than with my dick still buried inside her. I looked up, lost in my thoughts, and she watched me carefully. She cocked an eyebrow in question.

"Sorry, what was your question again?"

"Glad to know I'm so fascinating you can forget I'm here when I'm sitting on your dick," she said with dry humor.

I stilled beneath her. "I didn't forget you were here." How could she think that? Did I make her feel that? I could feel panic rising, and I closed my eyes as old sensations rushed at me. I tried to push them away. They weren't a part of my life now.

"Hey, it's okay. It was just a joke." I could faintly feel her pushing reassurance at me. She stroked my face tenderly, trying to get me to calm down and come back to her. She was remarkably good at calming other people for someone who had been so alone all her life. Or maybe just good at calming us.

"Look at me, Hunter." I opened my eyes, and she was watching me carefully but tenderly.

"I would never do that to you, Maia. You have to believe me. That's one thing I would never do."

"Okay," she said, simply and plainly. She leaned in and kissed me gently. It was a kiss of comfort and affection, with maybe a hint of growing love.

I could kiss her all night and be perfectly happy, but it wasn't helping my dick go down.

"Tell me about the forgetting."

"You don't want to hear about my sad old tale, especially while my dick is inside you."

"Hunt, if you can't talk to me about something personal while your dick is inside me, you'll never be able to do it."

It was the first time she called me Hunt like the guys did, and I liked it. I also liked her calling me out. It showed she was comfortable with me and had trust in me. I know Maia said she did earlier, but actions spoke louder than words. I had been given plenty of words in my childhood but little action.

I swallowed hard. It was never easy having this conversation, not that I'd had it a lot. I just wished I had a nicer story to tell her.

"It's one of the things Damon's wrong about," I said, remembering her earlier question.

"He thinks I keep him sane, but he doesn't realize he delivered me back my sanity." I paused, not knowing what to say. She just waited patiently, not pushing.

I looked past her shoulder, through the tree branches swaying lightly in the breeze and caressed with moonlight. I remembered the ancient tree outside my bedroom window as a kid. I had sat endlessly watching it, noticing its movements and the creatures living in it.

At times, it felt like I slowed my own rhythms to match that of the tree. It was also a reminder that life existed outside my home if only I could one day reach for it.

If I could have picked that tree up and taken it with me when I left, I would have. It was the only thing I regretted leaving behind, but it had existed there before me and would exist long after I was gone.

I think it was one of the reasons I was so drawn to this farm, with its surrounding trees, some of them ancient, too, like this one. When Damon brought us here the first time, I fell instantly in love. It had felt like home, even before we made it everything it is today.

"I grew up in a cold, lonely house. My parents conveniently forgot I existed most of the time. They didn't want to bother with me until they knew if I would become an alpha or not. Even then, it was only as a status symbol, proof of their superiority.

"There was staff around, of course, but they were paid to do chores, not watch me. They all took my parent's example and ignored me. Sometimes they'd even forget to feed me because I wasn't allowed to eat with my parents. I learned to fend for myself when I was young."

I remembered the nanny who gave me the bare essentials when I was a toddler, but she was dismissed when I turned school-age. She had never shown me any affection, not even giving me a backward glance when she left.

"My early schooling had been done online. My tutor was the best in the country, but I only had contact with him directly a few times a week to check in on the tasks he had set me. The only reason I excelled was because I had nothing else to do. I didn't even have any toys.

"The giant tree out my window was my only friend and solace, but I'd lose hours watching it, sometimes days. So, I applied myself to anything he set me to do and always asked for more."

Maia looked over her shoulder at my words and smiled at the tree sheltering us. I sensed she got it. I knew it was strange to talk about getting strength and companionship from a tree, but it wasn't that different from little kids with a security blanket or teddy. I just didn't have access to anything I could hug or hold.

I sighed. Here was the hardest part, though. I was grateful Maia was just listening without asking questions because this was tough for me to share. Damon was the only person who knew the full extent of my trauma.

"It got so bad at home that I started to doubt my existence. I thought maybe I had died at some point and had become a ghost. I could walk around the entire house and not have a single person react to me.

"My sanity was slipping, and I started to waste away. I stopped feeding myself. My parents finally noticed how skinny I was one day and called a doctor. The doctor suggested I be sent to boarding school to be socialized, but my first day was overwhelming. I didn't know how to interact with other kids. To them, I was a tall, skinny, quiet kid who didn't push back. I was a perfect target for all their own issues."

I still remember the overwhelming confusion, the din and musky smell of a big group of pre-teen boys in a confined space. So many people were looking at me that it felt like a weight pushing me to the ground. All of them expected me to interact with them, but I didn't know how to at the time.

"Damon came to my rescue when he saw my freak-out developing on that very first day. He got me away somewhere quiet and talked me down. Damon never let any other kids bully me after that day either. Even before we hit puberty and presented as alphas, and even though he was new money, they were either drawn to Damon or scared of him. He was protective, even then. I felt like he was the only person to have ever seen me. Damon made me feel real.

"Without Damon, I'm pretty sure I would have become a statistic. I would have ended up dead or insane. He gave me a life. He taught me how to interact with people. I learned to use humor to deflect attention until it became a natural part of me. I loved the feeling when I could get people to laugh.

"Damon took me home for the holidays so I wouldn't regress spending time alone in my parents' house. His dad allowed it because I was from an old money, alpha family. He wanted the social connection. If I ever went home, Damon would come with me. He made it fun, sliding down banisters and getting up to mischief. It was like a holiday for him, away from his dad. It was the same at school. Damon made life fun."

I smiled fondly at the memory of those days, but they didn't last.

"He shut down a lot when he was older and became closed off after everything that went down with his dad. But, in our early years, Damon helped me find myself. My coping mechanisms came in handy as we got older. I later used the humor I had learned, to shield him when he needed it.

"When Damon was sent to the military to try and break him and to become a tool for his father, I went with him." The only place I had wanted to be was wherever Damon was. I still felt that way. "We met Leif, then Max there, and the rest is history."

Maia was quiet for a moment, taking it all in. She had rested her head back onto my shoulder while I talked and absently drew patterns on my arm and chest with her finger. Her fruity scent mixed with the tree's fresh, green scent and enveloped me in comfort. It was nice. Really nice.

"So that's why you guys are so close? Because you saved each other as kids?"

"Yeah. People think it's weird that we're so tactile with each other. Some people thought we were gay when we were teenagers." Damon and I never corrected them because it didn't bother us what people thought.

"I learned quickly that it grounded Damon to have physical contact when his emotions were building, and it anchored me. It reminds me that I'm actually here, even now."

"It never bothered Max or Leif. They quickly picked up that we both needed it, and they're cool with some manly hugging."

I remembered how it had helped deflect attention in the military, too, if all four of us were doing it. It meant nobody focussed on us too much individually. It was clear we were a natural team from the start. We were more effective and even more focused when they left us alone. So they mostly did.

"Damon's dad's plan backfired to a degree. Joining the military and building our team gave Damon the power and courage to escape him. We eventually realized that the military was not the right place for us. We couldn't stomach the things they wanted us to do, so we got out as soon as we could."

She was quiet for a beat, again. I could hear and feel her gentle breathing as I stroked my hands down her back, loving the feeling as she shivered lightly when I stroked a sensitive spot.

"I'm so glad you guys found each other. I love watching the way you all interact with each other. There's so much joy and love. It's what drew me to you all when Leif was trying to convince me to stay."

"I won't pretend to understand what any of you went through, but I can relate to the not feeling seen, in some small part. I had to hide who I was for so long, even around my family. It made me feel disconnected from myself," she said.

"Even when they took me to the Omega Palace, I couldn't be myself because it didn't fit what they wanted me to be. They tried to break me to fit their mold, but I refused. I couldn't lose more of myself because I didn't know what would be left. Ironically, I had to hide and learn to become invisible to not lose myself."

She paused for a minute, looking up at me and searching my face to gauge something. I'm not sure what, but she seemed to see what she needed and kept talking as she looked up at the tree again.

"It messes with my head sometimes. I think it's why I don't always talk a lot. I always had to be careful about what I said or how I presented myself, so it was easier to not say much at all."

"I had one friend at the Palace, Ava. We weren't close in the way you and Damon are. We could only meet occasionally and in secret. Cary sometimes watched out for me, but he kept himself aloof."

"Ava was the only friend I had ever had. There were no other kids on my gramps' farm. We were homeschooled by the wife of one of the older workers. I'd always had to keep myself apart from people in my teen years."

"There was a young beta guy who delivered supplies and helped around the farm sometimes. I, uh, fooled around with him growing up, but trying to keep my scent at bay was so hard when he got me worked up. I'm pretty sure he knew and just didn't say anything because he didn't want it to stop, but I never asked."

"Fooled around?" I asked, feeling a hot flare of jealousy—a new feeling for me.

"Yeah, you know," she ground on my dick to demonstrate, and I groaned.

"No. No talking about fucking other guys while I'm knotted to you. New rule." I growled lightly at her and nipped her ear lightly.

She yelped and smirked at me, and I wanted to kiss that cheekiness right out of her, but I didn't want to interrupt her story.

"Anyway, my point was, I didn't have a lot of people growing up. An old, beaten-up leather chair became my sanctuary at the Palace, hidden in the dusty back-end of the library. My gramps had one like it. That chair was the only comfort I knew. So I get your connection with your tree. My chair became my home in that hell hole."

"Just that small comfort helped keep me sane. You can never underestimate the impact a person, an object you connect with, or a small act of kindness, can have on someone's life."

"I see you, Maia. You're a strong, caring, beautiful woman who refused to let the world break you. I'm proud to call you mine. I don't care how much or how little you say. I'm just fucking glad you stopped outside our fence."

I felt incredibly close to her right now, with our newly awakened bond still glowing faintly in my chest.

I kissed her gently on the head and continued stroking her back while we enjoyed spending time quietly in each other's company, snuggled together into the hammock in the moonlight. There was nowhere else I wanted to be right now.

"At least we've learned one thing tonight. Deep and meaningful conversation makes my dick go limp."

She giggled, and I loved that sound. The movement made my dick slip from her, and I already missed the feeling of being inside her. My knot and my dick had slowly softened while we were talking. They had finally figured no more sexy times were happening just now.

"So, have we convinced you to stay?" I asked her as I tucked her into my side more comfortably. "We had until tonight, right?"

"I don't know," she sighed melodramatically, running her hand up and down my stomach, making the muscles jump and flex. "I may need some more convincing."

I grinned wickedly at her. I was on board for more convincing and was about to show her when she started talking again.

"Seriously, though. I love spending time with you guys, but I'm also worried about the number of days I've been here. I was supposed to meet up with Ava at a farm that I think may be in the next town. I need to know that she and Cary made it out okay. I can't settle in anything until I know.

"Not knowing what happened to Ava is like a splinter in my mind that's festering. I feel guilty that I'm living here in comfort with you, not knowing if she's in danger or not."

I picked up her hand to stop it from wandering further and brought it to my lips for a kiss. I needed her to hear me without distraction.

"Maia, if you need something, you just need to let us know, and we'll make it happen. Okay?"

She was suddenly quiet, more than usual, and it worried me. We couldn't lose her now.

"Maia, look at me." I echoed her earlier demand when I'd been lost in my head.

She looked up, and her eyes were glassy. It made my heart bleed.

"Tell me you hear me."

"I hear you, Hunt. I'm just not used to asking for or relying on anyone for help. I've done everything by myself most of my life because everyone who was ever supposed to be there for me has left.

"When I was little, I asked my dad for a glass of milk. He went to the shop and never came back. I knew it wasn't his fault. He was drunk and had an accident, but that's the connection my young brain made." Maia was getting agitated, and her breathing sped up.

"Not long after, I asked my mother for help with the cows one day. She said she'd get changed and never came back. When I went to look, the car and her handbag were gone.

"I asked my brother Sam to read me a bedtime story, like he usually did every night, because he hadn't come in, and I'd been waiting. He said he'd read me two tomorrow. I woke up the next morning, and he was gone.

"I was like a mother to my younger brother Ben, but his leaving was the worst. He didn't just leave. He betrayed me to the Palace so he could take gramps' farm when it was left to me in the will. He banished me from my safe space and fed me to the monsters for his own gain without a lick of remorse.

"I can keep going. There's more. Those are just the big ones."

Silent tears were running down her face now, and I frantically tried to brush them away, not knowing how to make them stop.

"I hear you, Hunt, but even hearing you say that makes me panic that you'll leave if I ask you for something. Everyone who was ever supposed to be there for me has left."

"Even claiming Max and being with you all, I'm letting myself enjoy being in the moment for the first time in my life. But a small part of my brain says I'm being selfish and asking too much, which will make you all disappear."

I pulled her in tight, feeling every tear echo in a drop of blood from my torn heart. "I hear you, Maia."

"Just give us more time to prove we're not going anywhere, and to help you figure it out, and honesty if you need something. Can you give me those two things, time and honesty? That's all I'm asking."

I was worried. I was supposed to be the fun one, and we had unloaded a lot of heavy shit on each other tonight instead. But I felt like we had both opened ourselves up in hard ways tonight, and we understood each other better now. It brought us closer after dancing around each other and flirting for days.

She was full of life and grace but held darkness fast within her. Like we all did.

We hadn't fully claimed her yet, though, and there was a chance we could lose her. She was like a shooting star in the night sky, hauntingly beautiful, yet could quickly disappear into the darkness if we didn't find a way to bring her to earth.

Perhaps bringing her to earth wasn't the answer. Maybe we needed to join her in the sky.

She finally nodded into my chest, and I breathed a deep sigh of relief, pushing reassurance at her and letting her feel my joy that she had let me in.

I only hoped she felt the same because I was hers now, forever. Claim or not.

Twenty-Four

We were on clean-up duty, having let everyone go back to their cabins on a high note. It was the least we could do, given how hard everyone had been working.

There was just Lexie, Max, and me left, cleaning and joking around. I didn't mind. We didn't get much time just to hang with Lexie lately, and I missed it. She was cool, and I was proud of everything she had accomplished in helping abused women. She was discreet and subtle about it in many ways, which suited what she was doing, but she was also far too modest about it, in my opinion.

I couldn't shake the feeling that something was wrong, though. Something was coming, and I wasn't seeing it. I had been trying to shake off a growing sense of foreboding all evening. Everyone was relaxed and having fun, but I'd gotten increasingly jumpy the longer the night wore on.

I didn't know if it was because Maia wasn't here since she had snuck off with Hunter. Our growing bond was new, and while she was unclaimed, my alpha instincts were riding me to get it done. But it felt like more than that. As much as I wanted her near, she and Hunter deserved this time, and I was happy for them.

This sense of danger felt external to us.

I had the urge to check the gate, but I didn't want to seem overbearing. Damon was there and was more than capable of watching a gate. Max came over and hugged me, sensing my unease. The radio on my hip crackled to life suddenly, startling us both.

"Alpha 1 to all. We have a vehicle on the main road, stopped just before the farm. Need Alpha 3 here, stat. Out."

I looked at Max as the feeling of danger crystallized in my veins, and all my senses sharpened. We waited for Hunter's response, but there was nothing.

"Alpha 1 to Alpha 2, do you have eyes on Alpha 3? Out.'

I pulled my radio off my belt. 'Alpha 2 to Alpha 1. No. Out.'

"Alpha 1, where the fuck is Alpha 3? Out." I could hear his frustration through the radio and feel his fear lightly through the bond. He was breaking protocol with that statement which showed his level of strain.

Max and I had felt Hunter join the bond faintly earlier. We knew what it meant and what Hunter and Maia were doing. We just didn't know where.

I was about to respond that I was on my way and send Max to look for Hunter, but the radio crackled to life again.

"Alpha 3 to Alpha 1, on my way now. Need Alpha 2 to intercept on the pond path for handover. Out"

I felt Damon's relief. Both Hunter and Maia were together and okay.

"Alpha 1 to all. Roger. Going radio silent at the main gate until danger has passed. Alpha 2 has comms. Out."

I was halfway to the back door before Damon finished speaking and took over comms control as soon as he switched out.

"Alpha 2 to all units. Code red for everyone until further notice. Out."

"Beta 4, to Beta 1. We're having trouble with the main gate camera, need you at security HQ now. Out."

Max had been heading to the back door with me already. He had set up the security office in an empty studio cabin out the back of the dining hall, and I knew he'd want to be there watching.

He upped his pace, overtaking me with only a backward glance as he went. His radio was still clipped to his belt but was off, so he switched it on as he went.

"Beta 1 to Beta 4. Roger Wilco. Out."

I called out to Max as he disappeared out the door, "Sweep for visible lights on your way, Max. Shut down any you can see fast. That's prime one right now. The camera is second."

"Got it." He called back.

I turned quickly to Lexie, who was right behind me. Only the guards and our team had radios. We didn't have enough for everyone, so no one living in the cabins would be aware of the potential danger. I needed to do a sweep while I intercepted Hunter.

"Lexie, you stay in here, grab the kitchen radio off the wall and keep an ear out. If there's trouble before anyone gets back, head for Max."

Lexie grabbed the kitchen radio sitting on the charger as she kept moving. I sighed deeply. My days of stashing Lexie somewhere safe when there was danger had long passed. She was coming with me.

"Three sets of eyes are better than two. We're going to have to sweep for lights, and I'm more help out there than sitting here pretending to be helpless," Lexie said, giving me a dark look over her shoulder. Fair enough.

I knew she had trained hard and could handle herself. I had seen her defend women against bigger men before I could reach them, but my instincts still drove me to protect her.

I knew my need was holding her back rather than helping her, so I had learned to let her do her thing and watch from the shadows. My protectiveness still slipped out sometimes, and she called me on it every time.

We ran out the door together and raced down the pond path, intercepting Hunter and Maia. Hunter was racing towards us, carrying Maia, who was holding her heels. I grinned at Hunter. I couldn't help it. I was so happy for them, for all of us.

He smirked back at me, but I could feel his joy, too. He gave Maia a rough, passionate kiss as he lowered her to the ground, sliding her down his body, and then he took off up the hill towards the gate. All his humor was gone. He was a focussed predator now.

Maia stumbled slightly, with a massive grin on her face, holding her heels in her hand. Lexie rolled her eyes at her. "I don't need sexed-up

Maia right now. I need warrior goddess Maia, which means we both need to get rid of these heels and skirts."

She turned to me. "Head back down the path, start your sweep. I'll take Maia to my container. We'll change and meet you in two minutes at the vantage point. Got it?"

I nodded to her, grabbing Maia in my arms and giving her a second passionate kiss before letting her go and racing off down the path. I had zero problems taking orders from my sister.

I heard her mutter behind me, "I need to find my own harem." Maia just giggled in response.

It wasn't too dark, and the guys all had excellent night vision. We had trained ourselves to work without night vision goggles as much as possible. It gave us an advantage over our enemies. Plus, alphas tended to have enhanced senses, which was why so many alphas gravitated to the military, where they were useful.

I could see the path clearly in front of me, although it would take 10-20 minutes of being outside for my night vision to reach optimum levels. I reached the vantage point in no time and swept the hill. There were no visible lights. I didn't bother reporting it, everyone was on-task, and this was my job right now.

It wasn't long before Maia and Lexie joined me. They were stealthy but fast, especially considering they were untrained and on a gravel path.

They now wore plain black leggings, hoodies, and joggers and they blended into the darkness. They were probably better outfitted than me. I wore dark jeans and boots, but my bright, white t-shirt was glowing under the moonlight.

Lexie threw an oversized black hoodie at me, and I grabbed it gratefully. She also had night vision goggles looped around her wrist that she used to scan the hillside.

I needed to check out what she was storing in that container. I had thought it was mostly women's and children's clothing, along with baby stuff and toys. Things fleeing women and young families would need. She clearly had some other stuff going on in there, though.

I shook my head at them both in amazement, but I could feel my shoulders relax at having Maia and Lexie near me, where I had eyes on them. I felt Maia's hand graze mine lightly like she needed the contact.

I grabbed her hand and twined her fingers with mine. I heard a small sigh and felt her relax alongside me. I loved how much she seemed to relish my touch. I realized how tactile omegas were and wondered how she had survived so long without touch.

"Okay, both of you relax your eyes and scan slowly without focusing on anything in particular. We're going to scan for people as well as lights. Let your eyes catch any movements. If we see anything suspicious or out of place, Lexie can zoom in on it."

"Okay." They said in unison. I watched the girls carefully while also keeping an eye on the hill.

They stood together, with much the same stance, keeping an eye out on opposite sides. It was uncanny how in tune they were. Like they could have been twins in another life, or at the very least, sisters.

Lexie had been alone in our cold house for most of our life until she escaped my father's schemes with my help. As much time as she spent helping other women, she didn't have a lot of close friends.

Seeing them interacting together so strongly, two women who meant the world to me, gave me hope and filled my heart with quiet joy.

Max's quiet voice on the radio snapped me out of my thoughts.

"Beta 1 to all. Two people stopped at gate. One got zapped. Have separated. Following fences on each side. Hunter trailing east side. Damon west. Both radio silent. Rear needs eyes. Out."

I jumped in quickly, "Alpha 2 to all, on my way to rear. Out."

I turned to the girls, but Maia had dropped my hand, and they were already moving away quietly. "Oh heck no. You both need to go back inside now." I whispered, following after them, trying and failing to be firm, but I couldn't with them. They were both inside my defenses.

"Don't be stupid, bro. We're short on security, and you know it. I can handle myself, and I'm pretty sure Maia can too."

"We'll be fine inside the fence, Lexie and I can find a good tree and go high while you take the ground. Nothing is going to happen to us up a tree. And if it does, we'll call for help, and you won't be far." Maia said.

I sighed deeply, feeling my shoulders tense again. Maia had a good point, and we didn't have time to stand around arguing. Picking up the radio, I said, "Alpha 2 to, Beta 1, L and M are going high rear corners for extra eyes. Out."

Max's terse reply came back. 'Beta 1 to Alpha 2. Roger that.

I could hear the strain in his voice. I knew he was angry at himself that Maia and Lexie were in the path of danger. I knew the feeling.

I needed to make sure we had eyes on the cabins if we were moving out. I knew Dave would be listening in. "Alpha 2 to Beta 2, 5, and 6, watch cabins and stay on call. Radio silence unless you need backup. Out."

"Beta 2 to Alpha 2. Roger that. We're alert and in position. Out." I knew Dave would have anticipated the call once it was clear the strangers hadn't moved along.

I put the radio back securely on my belt and tried to find the zone where everything calmed, and I could focus. I took a deep breath, then another slower breath. Then I opened my eyes, and I was there.

"Okay. Lexie, you go east. There's a tall tree close to the fence near the lower guest cabins. Go only high enough to get a good view over the fence. Stay against the trunk. It will give you cover. Put your hood up to hide your hair. If you see movement, don't attempt the tree. Just stay near the cabins and watch."

"Your job is not to engage, only to watch and let us know if he finds a weak spot in the fence and makes it through. Watch for movement on both sides, just in case, and make sure your back is covered, okay?"

Lexie nodded, quiet and serious, which was unusual for her. She put her hood up straight away. I was grateful she had reined in the sass for the moment. Maia just watched me with big eyes.

"Go fast but quietly, Lexie. Watch your footsteps. He may be on you by the time you get there." She turned and ran, and I had to trust her to do precisely what I asked.

I turned to Maia. "You'll need to follow me to the fence, then head west until you hit the fruit trees near the bottom corner. Climb one near the fence. They should help mask your scent. Same as what I told Lexie about the tree, only attempt it if you see no movement up the hill. If you do, get low and watch from cover."

"I'll find a spot near the middle. If you have any trouble, and I mean anything, no matter how small, whistle, and I'll come. Damon and Hunter will be following on foot inside the fence line. Got it?"

She nodded.

'Okay. When we get close to the fence, I'll signal you with my left hand, and you take off in that direction. We won't be able to talk."

She nodded again, quiet as a mouse. We took off, and she kept up with me. She was nimble and quick. When we neared the fence, I signaled, and she turned, only glancing back at me once. I pulled up short and watched her go, torn and wanting to follow her.

She blended into the shadows like a pro, as if she had done it many times before. I wondered, not for the first time, what she had been hiding from. I shook my head and forced myself to turn away. I had a job to do, and it would help keep her safe.

I found a shadowy spot near the fence and stepped in. I was too big to hide in a tree effectively, but I crouched down low, changing my mass and blending into bushes, then waited.

It wasn't long before I spotted a flashlight coming from the east. I saw it long before I heard the footsteps, which, if you somehow missed the light, were loudly advertising his presence.

The guy was clearly not military or any kind of law enforcement. He was entirely untrained in surveillance, watching the fence, looking intently for any holes, but not paying attention to anything else in his surroundings.

I followed him, but not too close. He didn't appear to be looking through the fence or gaps in the foliage, trying to figure out our crops or buildings, so I didn't think he was interested in our set-up.

He seemed solely intent on getting through the fence, which suggested he knew what, or who, he was looking for on this side. He was also focused on his footing on the rocky river bed that formed part of our rear border, on the far side of the fence. He was keeping his distance from the fence and seemed hesitant to get near it, so I assumed he was the one that got zapped and wasn't the leader of this expedition.

We were passing the fruit trees on the west corner when we came across the other person. He was standing scenting the air—looking around wildly. He moved forward, stopped, and scented the air again. Then he moved back up, trying again like he had lost a scent.

He grunted loudly in frustration. He seemed fixated on the spot, like he could sense something. I could feel Maia's unease and wondered if she was close. I looked around quickly but couldn't see her.

It was hard to get a good visual of him. I could tell he was big, but not as big as me, with dark hair, but that was about it. He appeared to be wearing a suit, but surely that couldn't be right. Something flickered in my memory, but I couldn't put my finger on it.

The shadows and moonlight lent him a menacing vibe. The breeze picked up for a moment, and I got a hit of mushrooms. He was an alpha, but his scent was fungal and off-putting, with a hint of sour decay.

"I didn't find anything, boss. This place is locked up tight. I don't see how she would have gotten in unless they let her." The beta shouted as he approached, not trying to be stealthy.

The hairs on my arms rose. They were looking for a woman. The alpha growled, low and ugly. "I know she's in here somewhere. I thought I scented her a minute ago, oranges and pineapples. She always smelt like them."

I froze as a hint of fear and panic hit me, but it wasn't coming from me. I was feeling it through the bond.

The beta had been swinging his torch around wildly, but he turned and suddenly spotlighted the alpha.

Rage and possessiveness threatened to overtake me. I knew this alpha. I had watched him stalking and harassing Damon when he visited the Palace. I knew the depths he was willing to sink to get what he wanted.

Ronan. He was looking for Maia, my Maia, and she was afraid of him. She was nearby if she was reacting to him, and he had scented her. I wanted to rip him apart. How could I have let this happen?

The beta spoke, sounding tired. "I can smell oranges too. It seems to be a farm, and those are orange trees." He gestured over his shoulder as he spoke.

"I don't give a fuck about the orange trees," Ronan screamed, getting up in the beta's face. "She's mine, and I'm getting her back. Do you hear me?" He was unhinged. He had no concern about being discovered out here.

"Yes, ah, yes, sir," the beta mumbled, remembering his place, but he stupidly pushed on.

"Maybe we should come back with more backup. There are electric fences and more than one alpha here. I could smell them in places. Something big is going on here."

The alpha lost his shit and started punching the beta, then kicked him viciously when he fell.

I could feel Maia's horror through our bond, but I didn't dare move and go to her for fear I would draw attention to her.

Ronan eventually calmed and turned away from the beta in disgust before stalking back up the hill the way he had come, flashlight swinging in the air. The beta slowly picked himself up and followed, limping behind him.

When they had moved far enough away not to see or hear us, Damon and Hunter suddenly materialized at my side out of the darkness.

The look on Hunter and Damon's faces mirrored my rage, but Damon was struggling to shut it down.

"Where is she?" Damon asked with a quiet fury.

Hunter looked over his shoulder like he'd known all along. "I'm here," Maia said hesitantly and dropped out of the tree next to us, hardly making a sound. I hadn't even seen her there.

I strode over to her in two giant strides and pulled her into my arms, squeezing her like maybe if I could tuck her into my body hard enough, I could somehow keep her safe.

"I love hugs, Leif, but I need to breathe," she said, whimpering slightly.

I released her a little, and she took a deep breath. I could feel a slight tremble in her limbs that defied her bravado.

I stroked her arm, and she flinched when I brushed over her forearm. I raised it gently, and even in the darkness, I could see her skin was red and bruised. I knew it hadn't looked like that when Hunter had brought her back earlier, so there was only one explanation. "Did you hurt yourself to cut off your scent, Maia?"

She just shrugged as she pulled the sleeve of her hoodie down. I grit my teeth and let it go for the moment, as she didn't seem to want to talk about it.

She had a small, white, orange blossom flower stuck in her hair, and I reached out to pluck it out gently while she snuck a quick look at Damon.

Hunter was alternately staring up the hill, monitoring the men's progress away from us, tracking the torches as they blazed in the night, and watching Maia warily.

Damon hadn't taken his eyes off Maia. "I take it, you know him?" he asked, a low growl he couldn't stop vibrating through his voice.

"Yes," she said, tensing up in my arms. "I'm sorry, I didn't think he would follow me after I escaped."

Damon was silent. He took a step towards her, then stopped. Like he wasn't willing to talk or get closer to her while he couldn't dial back his emotions. I don't think she realized his rage wasn't directed at her, though, and that was bad.

"I think I should go," she said, quiet as a mouse and trembling like one, too.

I latched onto that idea. We needed to get Maia out of the trees and away from the fence in case that monster returned. "Yes, good idea. Let's head back to the house where we can keep you safe."

She flinched, and I didn't know what that meant until her next words ripped me open. She stepped away from me, forcing me to let her go, and said, "No. I mean, yes. Let's head back to the house, but then I need to grab my stuff and go."

Damon glared at me, and Hunter whipped his head around toward her while I felt the world fall out from under me.

We were screwed.

Twenty-Five

R onan was hunting Maia. The same Ronan from the Omega Palace, who had hated Damon instantly and who had tried to destroy us by claiming we were a pack.

Only my family stepping in had saved us from being carted off to who knows where, and they only did it for their reputations. Ronan was unhinged and was fixated on Damon at the time. He went to extreme lengths to try and destroy him. Now Ronan was after Maia. I needed to know why. It couldn't be a coincidence.

I wanted to go to her and hold her, then fight all her battles for her, but she had stepped back from Leif and was keeping her distance from us all. I could feel her fear faintly through the bond, but it wasn't clear if she was afraid of Ronan, something else, or both.

I could feel Damon drowning in emotions. I instinctively wanted to go to him as well, but I was pulled in too many directions, and I needed to keep my clear focus while Ronan was still in sight and an immediate threat. Keeping an eye on him had to be my priority right now. It was my job.

"Escaped from where?" Damon asked, his voice sounding forced out over frozen tundra.

"The Omega Palace," she said slowly, with great hesitation.

"I really need to go," she said, the fear in her voice tinged with longing and desperation.

"Maia, no." I could see Damon take a step towards her out of the corner of my eye but stop in hesitation when she flinched. He knew he couldn't force her to stay if she wanted to go.

"Are you afraid of me right now?" Damon asked. I could sense his desperation under his cool tone.

He seemed to both want and not want to know her answer.

"Is that why you want to leave?" he asked, a growl creeping into his voice.

She shook her head, but he just stared at her intensely, like he could force answers from her through sheer force of will. I turned more fully and noticed she was trembling slightly. I also saw the space between us all. There had always been one of us touching her before now, almost from the moment she got here.

Leif looked stricken, and Damon looked like he was about to lose his shit. He was hanging by a thread, with emotions battering him. He was desperately trying to fix it, all his focus on Maia.

I returned my focus to the hill as the lights slowly retreated towards the top. I knew I should be following. This was madness, trying to surveil them from a distance, but I couldn't make myself go.

We had only just had a breakthrough, a tentative understanding between Damon and Maia, but it seemed to be unraveling fast.

Damon took a deep breath, trying to calm his voice and emotions. 'I know I'm not in control right now, but I'm not mad at you, Maia. I'm just trying hard not to chase him down and tear him apart with my bare hands.'

"I know that," she said, her voice quiet and shaky like she was barely holding it together herself.

"I'm sorry, but I have to go, and I have to go now."

This wasn't working, Damon wasn't getting through to her, and he was missing the focus of her fear. He was so fixated on the source of his fear that he couldn't figure out hers. I had to step in, or we were going to lose her.

"I hear you, Maia," I said, and the guys all turned to look at me.

She looked at me quizzically, but I gave her no more right now, and she slowly turned to walk away through the avenue of fruit trees. She looked like an ethereal shadow fae I had read about in a fantasy story once, disappearing into the gloom like it was a second skin. Like she had never really existed, and the last few days had been a dream.

The thought had panic beating like a drum through my veins, trying to drive away my calm focus. I had a plan that was more of a desperate gamble, and I needed to let Maia play this out for a moment. I had one chance to get through to her, and I couldn't mess it up.

The guys were both watching me with concern, so I gave them the "quietly follow" hand signal. They both turned and moved behind her in unison, and I took the rear for the moment.

There was no way any of us would stand here and watch her walk away, but I was relieved when they both followed my lead without question. It showed how messed up Damon was right now after seeing Ronan appear out of nowhere and lay claim to Maia.

He was usually a calm and focused leader in the field, but this situation was intensely personal, setting off all his triggers.

"Alpha 3 to all, two men heading back to gate, west side outside fence. No breach. Need eyes from beta team. Alpha 1, 2, and 3, and Beta 1, standing down. Beta 1, meet at home now. Out." It was an extraordinary call.

Maia whipped around to face me. "What are you doing?" I didn't answer. I kept walking, moving in front, and taking the lead.

The reply was immediate, "Beta 2 to all. On our way. Beta team taking over." I knew Dave had this. He would watch the men until they left and deal with any interactions, calling us only if necessary.

Max replied quickly with a "Roger Wilco." He sounded panicked, even over the radio. I figured he could feel Leif's and Maia's emotions through the bond. I have no doubt he was watching through cameras as well.

Leif grabbed his radio and directed Lexie to meet up with Dave. She replied with a brief, "Roger Wilco," proving she had quickly picked up the lingo.

We all kept walking back to the house without exchanging a word, and Maia had no choice but to follow us now.

We reached the house just as Max came charging down the path at full speed, sliding to a stop in front of us, scattering gravel, and looking around warily for any danger. He instinctively grabbed Maia in a bear hug when he noticed she was standing alone.

She stiffened slightly, and he looked at her in concern, letting her go reluctantly and turning to us. "What's happening?"

"We're bugging out," I said, using a term Max would understand.

Max followed us into the house, asking, "What alert level?" He picked up quickly that I was still in military mode, and the guys were following my lead.

"Code 2," I said, which meant no immediate danger, but we needed to move fast. I was calm and in command, and he responded like I knew he would.

"Okay. I need to know a destination and how long we'll be gone so I can get us packed. I have go-bags for all of us but not for Maia yet, so we'll need to sort her first if we're moving fast." He instantly assumed she was coming with us without having to be told.

I loved him so much right now. Max had to be so confused, but he followed orders like a pro. He had complete trust in us as a team. So did I. I knew we would follow each other anywhere.

I turned to Maia, standing just inside the back door, her face half in shadow with the moonlight behind her and the darkness of the house pressing in on us. "What's the destination, Maia? Do we need to pack to sleep on the road, or are we heading somewhere we can reach tonight?"

Maia just looked at me in silence. I raised an eyebrow, tilting my head in a silent question. She still seemed half fae shadow, half human, one foot with us, and the other already gone back to her realm.

"We need bug-out orders, Maia, and you're in charge here. I'm just directing the troops."

It was a risky play, but I needed to back up everything I had promised her earlier. It was the only way to get through to her and to bring her back to us. If we tried to beg or force her to stay, ignoring her true fear, she would run, and we'd be chasing her into unknown territory and certain danger.

I needed her to know this was on her terms so she could face her fear, and I needed her to trust that she was stronger with us.

"I don't know," she admitted, looking confused, but at least she was communicating. I needed to get her talking more. When she went quiet, it usually meant she was censoring herself or holding herself back, and I needed her to open up.

"I need to go, but I don't know where I'm headed."

"Okay, well, maybe we can take a minute and make a plan so we can all stay safe." I said calmly.

"You can't come. You have to stay here and protect the farm," Maia blurted out, panic bleeding into her voice. She snuck a guilty glance at Max as if she had just remembered the impact her leaving would have on their mate bond.

"Dave has the farm, and we have defense and evacuation plans if needed. He can handle it. So, where do we need to go?" I asked again, still projecting calm confidence.

She just looked at me. "Hunter," she seemed to beg, that note of fear creeping back into her voice.

"Maia," I said calmly in reply.

"I can't," she said, louder now, her voice rising with fear and panic. She knew I was on to her.

I moved up so I was right in front of her, in her space, but not in her face. I was not letting her back away.

"You can," I said in a calm, firm tone. I took a deep breath and squared my shoulders, not looking away from Maia for a second and holding her complete attention.

"You can because I hear you, and I see you, Maia.

"You can because I told you that you only have to tell us what you need, and we'll find a way to make it happen.

"You can because you promised less than an hour ago that you would give us time and honesty.

"And finally, Maia, you can, because the only thing I can't do," and my voice broke for a second before I shored up my resolve, "the only thing we can't do, is let you face this out there alone."

"So either we all stay and plan our defense here, or we all go and make our stand somewhere else if you have a better plan."

I moved in impossibly closer, and I could sense all the guys holding still, hardly daring to breathe, not wanting to break this moment.

I moved my arm up slowly and caressed her cheek.

"Do you hear me, Maia? Do you see me? You said you did. This is me."

She nodded achingly slowly, holding her breath too, before she whispered, "I'm scared."

"I'm not," I said.

"We've got you, and we're not going anywhere. This is us showing you that. Lean into us, Maia. Don't let your fear drive you away. We'll only follow." I spread my arms wide to indicate the guys and let her know where she belonged, in our arms.

"I'm not scared for me. I'm scared that asking you to do this will mean losing one or all of you, and I can't face that. You all mean too much already." Maia said.

"And I brought this here, Hunter. He followed me, and if I leave, it will keep you safe."

Her voice was shaking, her fear plain to see. Her eyes were begging me to understand, but I did, all too well. It didn't mean I would let her give in to her fear and tear us apart.

The guys were all a solid presence around us, silently backing me up.

"That's the beauty of this Maia. You're not asking. I'm telling you. You need to go or stay. It's simple. That's all you need to decide, and we'll make it happen. It doesn't matter how he got here. He was here, and we'll deal with him here or somewhere else."

"Time and honesty, Maia. That's what I asked for, and you promised. I'm going to hold you to it. The place is irrelevant, and so is the why."

"We're stronger here. We already have defenses in place and can strengthen them. We also have friends who will back us up, but if you have a better plan, or what you need isn't here, tell us now, and we go."

"I'm asking you to look past your fear, dig deep and tell me, Maia. Where do you honestly need to be right now?"

She took a deep, shaky breath, and it felt like my heart stopped beating, hanging in suspense. Like it only beats for her.

"Here," she whispered, oh, so softly, "with you."

"That's our girl," I told her, pulling her into my arms. The guys finally moved, like a spell had been released, moving to surround us and encircle us in their strong arms.

Maia in the middle, our heart, where she belonged.

Twenty-Six

I had never been more thankful for Hunter than I was at this moment. We might have lost her tonight if it had been down to me. Everyone made such a big deal about my natural dominance, but it meant nothing against the things that truly mattered, like love and trust.

I couldn't force someone to feel either of those things. They had to be earned. It was at the core of what was wrong with alpha society. I desperately hoped we had a chance here to build something better.

I had already felt instinctively that there was something very wrong with how alphas lived, forcing people to our will, but meeting Maia had shown me how different it could be. She made it seem so easy. Or, she had before tonight, but we all had our demons.

I eventually motioned the guys to step back and release Maia. Their touch had anchored both Maia and me. I could feel it through the bond. She was much more settled, as was I. She wasn't pulling away anymore.

I would be forever in Hunter's debt for jumping in and rescuing the situation tonight when I had been floundering. I would add it to the list of things I owed him.

I had misread the source of her fear, my judgment colored by my issues. It was a lesson I needed to learn and stop repeating.

She was afraid of losing us. Not afraid of us. Or of me. It was a revelation—my second in as many days.

I motioned us all over to the couch, and away from the door we had barely made it through earlier. I pulled the heavy curtains closed before I turned on a single lamp, not wanting to risk a lot of light just yet. It cocooned us in a cozy glow, making the scene feel intimate.

Hunter and I shared a glance, and he nodded. He was happy for me to retake the reins now that I was calmer.

We all settled into the couch, with Leif and Max cozying up on either side of Maia. They were unwilling to let her go, and I was okay with that. We weren't over the worst of it yet.

The thought of her leaving had terrified me, and I wasn't wearing her bite the way Max was. I don't think she had thought about what her going would do to him, not because she had dismissed him, but because her fear had overwhelmed her. I could relate to that.

"I know that was tough for you, Maia. I'm grateful for your honesty, but we need to know exactly what's coming at us. So I have some questions I need you to answer, okay?"

She nodded, looking at Hunter and me where we were sitting on the opposite side of the couch a little warily, but Hunter nodded at her, and she relaxed slightly.

I knew I was being far too formal, which could feel to her like I was distancing myself again, so I tried to relax.

I took a deep breath before getting straight to the point.

"Is he your mate? Has he claimed you?" I asked, some of my rage leaking back into my voice.

Hunter's eyes snapped to Maia at the question. I could see he hadn't considered the possibility.

She didn't have an apparent bite mark, and I'm assuming one of the guys would have noticed one by now, but I had to know. Why else would he follow her this far?

"No," she replied. Then, when Hunter remained quiet, and I didn't say anything, she added, "I rejected him. I rejected them all."

"You rejected them all?" I asked, what the hell did she mean by all? "How many?"

"I don't know. All that tried, it became a bit of a game. I lost count." Something tweaked at the edge of my consciousness, but I couldn't put my finger on it. I couldn't wrap my head around what she was saying.

Leif picked her up and shifted her into his lap, pulling a blanket over her, needing more contact and needing to comfort her. He hugged her gently as if she might break, or he would if she denied him.

Max settled her legs over his lap and stroked them gently as he took off her shoes, getting her comfortable.

She didn't resist or pull away this time. She just put her head on Leif's shoulder, leaning into his neck, and he started gently stroking her hair. The motion seemed to calm her.

It calmed me, too, even though it wasn't me touching her, as desperately as I wanted to. I needed more contact too, but I needed to get through this first.

There was something more going on here. I could sense Hunter felt the same.

"What happened after that?" I asked, trying to keep calm.

"They tried to force me with their alpha bark, but I resisted. For Ronan, it became an obsession. He tried over and over."

"How did you resist an alpha bark?" It was incredibly rare for an unmated omega to be able to resist a bark from a dominant alpha.

Some low-level alphas without a lot of dominance might struggle, but not most of the alphas who frequented the Palace. They were all vetted pretty heavily to get in the door.

"I don't know, I just can. They bark at me. I don't know why they call it a bark. It's way more of a roar usually."

"Some use words, and some just use intent. I can feel their dominance and compulsion pushing at me, almost like a physical weight on my body forcing me to comply."

"It's painful to resist, but I can do it. My mind doesn't enforce it, kinda like it challenges it instead. None of the alphas were dominant enough to force me."

That surprised me. I knew Ronan was highly dominant and wasn't used to being told no. Omegas were genetically designed to be susceptible to an alphas bark, so why can Maia deny it?

"What happened after you rejected them?" I asked, persisting with questions despite her clear hesitation in answering.

Leif gave me a warning look, but I stared back at him with determination. There was something more here, something I wasn't getting, but I couldn't put my finger on it.

"You don't have to tell us if you don't want to," Hunter said, reassuring her.

Maia looked up at me with fear and memories swimming in her eyes, seeing I wasn't going to let this go, before snuggling back into Leif. I didn't want to dredge up bad memories, but I needed to know what we were facing.

"They punished me," she said, so quietly I hardly heard her, burying her face in Leif's neck again. He held her to him gently. "Mostly with isolation, but sometimes beatings, then they would do tests on me...I...."

Every word felt like a splinter working its way into my soul. I didn't know how I would bear it without bleeding out.

"Enough, Damon," Leif said, a note of firmness in his voice he rarely used with me.

I nodded at him. I got it, I was pushing, but we were almost there. I could feel it. I was so close. "Just one more. I need to know how long you were there."

Leif and Max looked at me in shock, and Hunter went incredibly still.

"Three years." She said as she kept her face in Leif's neck, breathing him in deeply as if it would make the memories disappear.

And, there it was.

My arms ached to hold her, and from the faint feelings I was getting from him, Hunter felt the same.

I closed my eyes. I couldn't bear to feel this devastation and watch the dawning horror in Leif's and Max's eyes. I didn't know what this would do to us.

"Oranges and pineapples," I said, my voice breaking. "I kept smelling hints of them, it was faint and elusive, but I couldn't find the source. I asked them once if they had an orchard or a kitchen garden."

"It was you. The whole time, it was you."

I wanted to break, but I couldn't lose my shit again. I needed to face this for me, Maia, and all of us. I was done letting my stronger emotions ruin me or color my relationships and my view of the world.

Maia looked at me in confusion as Hunter instinctively moved closer to me and dropped his head onto one of my shoulders before wrapping an arm around my back. He knew what this meant.

"I remember you talking about oranges and pineapples when you came back once, man. You said you couldn't get the smell out of your head," he said, sadness spilling into his voice.

I looked at Maia again, and realization slowly spread across her face as she lifted her head from Leif. It didn't hold the same horror. It held understanding.

"Rain and lighting," she said. "For a while, I kept going to the windows and claiming there would be a storm because I could faintly smell the rain coming, even when there were blue skies. They kept directing me away and acted as if I was crazy. Then it just stopped one day."

"It was you. I was scenting you." Such a simple statement for a sentiment that felt so profound.

I was gutted. Maia had been right there and had scented me the same way I did her. I had been so deep into my own bullshit I hadn't realized I was scenting my mate, as she was being tortured right under my nose.

How had she survived while holding onto so much light and empathy? I could feel it bursting from her, even now.

"I'm so sorry, Maia." They were pointless words, but I said them anyway.

"Why are you sorry?" She seemed confused as she looked around the room and saw the devastation on all our faces.

"I didn't attend the socials. I went to one and couldn't stand it, but I heard a rumor about an omega everyone tried to claim with no success. My Palace handler dismissed it as idol gossip that was blown out of proportion. I believed him because it didn't seem possible. But it was you, and it was real."

"I was there, and I should have helped you," I growled, a hint of how truly broken I felt creeping past my defenses.

"Listen to me, Damon. What happened to me was not your fault. You are one man, and you can't save the world. As big and as badass as you are, it can't be done."

"I know I can't save the world, but I should have saved you." I closed my eyes. I couldn't even look at her at that moment.

How can she be consoling me right now? She should be yelling at me, hitting me. I would take it all. I felt my emotions trying to spiral and pull me down.

"Damon, look at me. Please." I couldn't, but she was suddenly right in front of me, grabbing my chin roughly.

"I will not sit here and let you blame yourself for something that wasn't your fault. I know you are driven deeply to protect, which has left you with heavy burdens in life, but this is not one of them. What they did to me was not your doing."

I knew what she was trying to do, but she was wrong. It was my burden, and I would carry it. What I wouldn't do is let anyone hurt her, ever again.

I glared at her in my rage and desolation. She yanked my chin roughly again, looking like she wanted to slap me. She looked fragile and fierce at the same time and so fucking beautiful.

"I don't care about what happened in the past," she said, sounding angry. "I'm not there anymore. I got myself out, and I won't ever go back. I fought hard to survive and stay true to myself, and I won't let anyone take that away from me—even you. You don't get to own that journey. It's mine. What I care about now is the future."

I took a deep breath and pulled her into my arms, where I had wanted her all night, cutting off my spiral and calming my turbulent emotions.

"I hear you," I growled, my throat feeling thick. I mimicked Hunter's words from earlier. They resonated deeply with me. I needed to listen to my team more. I was learning, but I had a long way to go.

'But I need you to hear me too. I swear I will do better. I know I promised you that on your first night here, and I've repeatedly broken it. I'm not perfect. I'm going to fuck up, probably more than once, but be patient with me, please.'

'I can do that,' she said, gentling her hand to caress my face lightly. 'We'll be patient with each other. I'm not perfect either, Damon. None of us are. Don't be so hard on yourself.'

'I had my own meltdown seeing Ronan tonight, but we've both come so far in just a few short days. Don't jeopardize our future by focusing on the past.'

I nodded, and she leaned in, breathing in my scent. I knew I would do anything to keep her safe from Ronan or anyone else who tried to hurt her. I'd even let out my beast if I had to.

I needed to tell her the rest of it, though, so she truly understood. I took a deep breath, looking over at where Max was hugging Leif. They both nodded at me, and I felt Hunter squeeze my shoulder.

'Maia, Ronan is the same alpha that accused us of being a pack and tried to destroy us a couple of years ago.'

'I don't think it's a coincidence that he was here tonight. I think he became fixated on you when he couldn't break you. Then either someone at the Palace suspected we were mates when we kept scenting each other, or Ronan was worried my higher dominance might break you when he couldn't.'

'Either way, I think they hid you from me when I was there and accused us of being a pack to get me out of the way. It all makes sense now. We could never figure out why he hated me so much when I never paid him any attention.'

'You did nothing wrong by coming here. You didn't bring anything to our door. I need you to know that.'

'So this is about both of us, not just you and not just me?' she asked. 'Is that what you're saying?'

I looked at the guys before answering. 'Yes and no. This is about all of us. We're all building a bond, you, me, Hunter, Max, and Leif, and that's where our strength lies.'

'I thought we were a strong team until we met you, but you've brought us all impossibly closer. You're making us an even stronger pack. You are the gorgeous, irresistible piece we were all missing.'

'We're all more vulnerable alone now, Maia. All of us, even me.'

'We have targets on us, and not just from Ronan. Our strength is together. We've got your back, and we need you to have ours. You bring your own strengths to this team, this pack, but we need to trust you're not going to run if things get tough unless you're running towards one of us.'

'That's how this works, and we need you to do your part. Do you understand?'

She nodded at me, but it wasn't enough this time. 'No more running. I need to hear you say it.'

She smiled at me gently. 'No more running unless it's towards one of you. I hear you, Damon.'

I breathed deeply for what felt like the first time in hours and nuzzled into her neck, soaking up her scent and letting it ground me further. She felt so damn perfect in my arms. The more I was around her and touched her, the more our bond strengthened. I could feel it like a glowing warmth in my chest. I was dying to kiss her but now wasn't the time.

'I wasn't trying to run away, though. I just wanted to lead Ronan away from you and this home you have built together.'

'I wanted to find my friends, too. I need to know they got out. I feel like I've abandoned them while I'm tucked up warm and safe in here with you. It's not sitting right with me. If Ronan is searching for me, he may find them instead. I can't have that happen. I can't. Ava has managed to stay innocent and kind. She's pure light. I won't let them destroy her.'

Hunter jumped in. 'I was already forming a plan to find your friends, Maia after we spoke earlier. I was going to talk to the guys about it tomorrow morning.'

'Also, if you're leading Ronan away, it will be because it's part of a plan, and you're leading him into a trap where Damon and Leif are waiting while I cover you from a high spot with my rifle, and Max follows you with a drone gun. Got it?'

She laughed, and I knew we were going to be okay.

'I like that scenario.' Then she sobered a little and fidgeted with her hoodie string. 'You were already coming up with a plan to find my friends?' I heard her voice tremble a little.

'Of course I was, pussycat.' That made her smile again. So I loosened my hold and let her climb off my lap and into Hunter's. He immediately did the same thing, nuzzling her neck and taking a deep breath, only to give it a cheeky lick while he was there. She shivered and arched her neck, giving him more access.

Dammit, I needed to get my shit together so that I could spend more quality time with Maia. My dick pressed painfully against my pants as I watched him licking and sucking on her neck. I felt like a creeper, but I couldn't look away.

Her scent started to get deeper, with that hint of cake she only got when turned on. I could see Leif and Max adjusting themselves where they sat across the couch, watching intently.

'So, what's the plan then, Hunter?' Leif said, his voice a little strained.

Hunter groaned lightly, and Maia sighed. 'Yeah, Hunter, what's the plan?'

He reluctantly pulled his head back from Maia, leaving a hickey in his wake. It was like a neon sign announcing 'Hunter was here.' I was desperate to do the same, I wanted to mark her in any way I could, but I knew she and I weren't quite there yet. We kept getting stuck in the heavy stuff and hadn't figured out the fun.

I was going to make it happen soon. I needed Maia's complete and utter trust for what I had planned when I finally took her. My desires ran a little darker than the other guys.

'I think we can talk about the plan in the morning. For now, I think we all need to crash. It's been a big night and a long day. Maia is still recovering from exhaustion, and she's been on the go all day.'

I looked over at Maia and realized he was right. How had I missed how tired she was? Her head was resting on Hunter's shoulder as if she could hardly keep it up, and her eyes were half closed. It probably hadn't helped her shock and meltdown earlier. Exhaustion tended to heighten emotions.

We all looked at each other, thinking the same thing. We all wanted to be close to Maia right now, but no one wanted to be a dick and call dibs on staying with her.

'How about a sleepover?' Max suggested. I was curious about where he was going with this.

'I think we'd all like to stick close tonight. Leif, grab the coffee table and move it out of the way. Damon, help me grab Maia's mattress, and we'll put it on the floor in the middle. The rest of us can sleep on the couch. It's comfy enough, and we've all done it occasionally.'

We'd designed it that way on purpose. When we couldn't sleep, we often crashed out here watching a movie. It's why we had so many cushions and throw blankets scattered around.

Maia perked up as Max talked. 'We're going to have a sleepover? Out here? I haven't done that since I was a little kid, and it was usually only when our parents forgot to come home. Can we do that, please?' She was practically bouncing now.

'We need lots and lots of squishy pillows and soft blankets,' she said eagerly.

Dammit, how had she survived so long and still have so much life and joy in her? Every time she let something about her life slip, it made me realize why she fit so easily with us. She had many of the same scars, yet she bore hers with much more grace. I wasn't worthy of her, but I was going to be.

We all sprung into action, willing to do anything that would help bring a smile to her face. Hunter stood up, still holding her, and Maia grabbed onto his neck. 'Come on. We'll grab more blankets.'

'I can walk, you know.'

'Walking is overrated. Trust me, if I could convince one of these guys to carry me around, I would,' Hunter said with a cheeky grin as they disappeared down the hallway. I noticed he managed to grab a handful of her ass as he went. Lucky bastard.

We brought back the mattress and all the blankets and pillows we could find in our rooms. Maia piled them up around the mattress and couch, changing things up when she wasn't happy with the placement. We all went to help, but she growled playfully at us whenever we moved anything. It looked like a giant, comfy nest when it was ready.

Maia loved it, looking over it with a massive grin before diving into the soft pile of quilts and pillows on the mattress and calling dibs. Leif and Max followed close behind and yelled dibs, too, while laughing.

Hunter looked at me and rolled his eyes, but he was smiling. We could hear Maia giggling under the quilts, and I didn't care if I was on the couch as long as I could listen to that sound.

'We can't risk the noise of a movie on the big screen, but I don't think any of us would last that long anyway.' I said, watching as Leif threw back the soft blue quilt from Maia's bedroom to reveal Maia snuggled into Max underneath. Her eyes were half closed, again, looking like a little kid about five seconds away from zonking out after a tough day running around at the playground.

Max was stroking her back, and even as I watched, her eyes slipped closed, and she was out. We all settled in around her, and while we had always been close, I couldn't remember a time I had felt this connected to the guys. I could feel contentment coming from all of them.

I couldn't wait until we could claim her and make her ours permanently.

I would give her the world if I could. But first, I needed to kill all her enemies.

Twenty-Seven

Maia

I stretched my legs out sleepily and then snuggled back into the warmth of my cozy nest. Strong arms surrounded me on both sides. We were squished in tight, but I was in heaven. I opened my eyes slowly to find Damon sharing my pillow, squashed between me and the edge of the couch, snoring lightly.

I felt a hand move up my stomach to squeeze my breast lightly, and I smiled, guessing who was behind me. I looked over my shoulder, and sure enough, Leif was snuggled in behind me with a sleepy smile, and his eyes closed.

I saw Max's arm around him from behind. He seemed to be curled tight around Leif and squished into the other side of the couch. He was the big spoon to Leif's little spoon, and the thought made me smile wider.

I noticed movement and saw Hunter watching me from the couch. He looked gloriously rumpled in the early morning light, with his blankets pushed down and his toned abs on show, one muscular arm thrown up behind his head.

It was the first time I'd woken up with them all together, and I wanted him down here with us too.

He smiled lazily at me. "We need a bigger mattress," I said.

"Hmm, I like that idea. Damon started on the couch last night, but it seems he didn't stay there. Are you okay? Are you too squished?"

I shook my head, rolling over with a little careful maneuvering so that I could face Hunter. Damon shifted in his sleep, gripping my hip and pulling me back into him. He ground into my ass lightly while Leif threw a heavy leg over me. My eyes widened, and Hunter chuckled.

"Come here, pussycat," Hunter said, lifting his blankets. Oh, yes, please.

I gently lifted burly arms and legs to extricate myself and slid out from under the guys, crawling over them to reach Hunter. I may have given each one a quick sniff on the way, don't judge. They all smelt delicious. I clambered up onto the couch and straddled Hunter before leaning down to kiss him lightly.

"How did you sleep? You crashed pretty hard last night."

"Good," I said as I nuzzled into his neck, taking a deep breath of his delectable scent too. "But I'm hungry."

"Of course you are. We keep interrupting your meals. We need to make sure you eat more regularly. You're still getting your energy back," Hunter said as he ran his hands up and down my back.

"Do you want to head to the dining hall before the guys wake up? I'm sure we can scrounge something up."

"No, I'd rather eat here." I was too busy licking my way across his delectable neck.

"We don't have much here. We ate all the energy bars the other day. We could raid Max's go bags, but he'd probably murder us." He was rambling and seemed distracted by my kisses.

"That's okay. I feel like something with honey for breakfast," I murmured, sliding my lips over Hunter's skin as I spoke before kissing and licking my way across his hard, delectable chest. Making sure I kissed each freckle. They were like constellations on his skin, and I decided I needed to get to know every one.

He tasted salty, earthy, and mine. The need to claim him, claim all of them, was building. It was a steady drumbeat in my blood that was growing louder and stronger every day.

I kept kissing down his chest before licking over his hard pecs, which gave him goosebumps.

"Oh?" he said, a little confused, before figuring it out. For a guy, it took him a long time.

"Oh!" I had finally reached his abs and nudged his sweatpants aside to lick and suck my way down the hard ridge of his adonis belt.

"Maia," Hunter breathed out harshly. I'm not sure if he was trying to ask me something or tell me something, but he never finished as I yanked his sweats down quickly, and his hard cock instantly sprung free.

Sex with the guys had been intense so far, and I hadn't had a chance to explore any of them. I had been so desperate to feel them inside me we had skipped over the exploration stage. Now, I wanted to play with my food a little.

Hunter's cock was hard, yet felt so soft, as I ran my fingers lightly up his length. His honey scent spiked, and his abs went taught as he held himself back from thrusting against my hand. We'd see how long that lasted.

He was bigger than I thought. I don't know how I had fit him inside me last night with so little preparation. It's no wonder I was a little sore this morning. I was still up for some playtime, though.

"Hmmm," I sighed as I tripped my tongue up his hard length with the lightest contact, returning the teasing he had made me suffer last night. If only I had some whipped cream.

I lightly licked over the tip before blowing on it gently.

"Fuck, me," he said with a harsh, desperate tone, shifting his hips restlessly. I didn't think it was a request, more a general exclamation.

"Not yet," I said, smirking up at him. His eyes were hooded and watching me intently, and his face was flushed. He almost looked feverish.

I decided to put him out of his misery. I wrapped my hand firmly around the base, stroking upward slightly while putting my whole mouth around his head and sucking on the sensitive tip.

His hips jerked off the couch, and he groaned loudly.

"Shhh," I said, "you'll wake Max." I don't think anything was waking Max, though. I glanced down, and he was still sound asleep, using Leif as a giant teddy bear to cuddle.

"Fuck Max," Hunter said with a sexy rasp while he threw his hands up behind his head, making the muscles in his upper body jump and flex. It was quite a show.

"Maybe later," I replied, giving him back one of his cocky winks.

He had no comeback as I slid my mouth down along his length as far as I could go and started bobbing up and down on his cock in a slow rhythm, gently easing myself further on each downward stroke and massaging the base.

Hunter started thrusting into me, encouraging me deeper, so I obliged, learning what he liked from his movements and moans. I hummed low in my throat to help relax it. A trick I learned from one of the Palace textbooks. He seemed to lose his mind as I adjusted my angle, took him all the way in, and deep-throated him while continuing to hum lightly.

I was so turned on, with my half-naked ass waving in the cool morning air, that I needed something to grind on.

The humming drove him wild. He groaned as he brought his hands down to my head and held me gently as he thrust up into me. I reached down with my other hand to caress his balls and lightly rub his taint, and his thrusts quickly grew more erratic. He exploded in a frenzy and came hard and fast down my throat, groaning deeply and raggedly.

I pulled off him, licking my lips with a satisfied smile. I liked knowing I could drive the guys crazy and make them lose it before they were ready.

"Fuck, Maia," he said again, breathless this time, as he brought me up to kiss me gently.

"Fuck me, fuck Max, fuck Maia. You need to make a decision and stick to it," I teased him while licking across his plump lower lip and giving him a quick nip.

He laughed and flipped me underneath him. The soft leather of the couch was warm from his body, and I wanted to snuggle into it and him, but he was sliding down me while keeping eye contact, and I couldn't look away.

"What are you doing?" I asked as I stretched my body out indolently.

"Having my breakfast," he said, with a wicked gleam in his eyes.

He pushed up the t-shirt I was wearing. I'd abandoned my yoga pants at some point in the night when I got hot and was only wearing yellow lace panties. He ran his nose up the length of my pussy, breathing deeply, and I never knew how erotic that could feel, a guy just enjoying my scent from such an intimate place.

He slowly teased one side of my panties with his finger, and I started to wriggle underneath him. I was already wet and turned on from the taste of him.

"Hunter," I groaned, and his wicked smile matched the gleam in his eyes.

I could feel my whole body shiver, and I yearned for him to touch me more intimately. It felt like every nerve in my body had moved down to my pussy and was begging to be stroked. I started gushing slick, and he had barely even touched me.

"Fuck, yeah," he said darkly before yanking my panties aside, not even bothering to take them off, and pulled my folds apart. He roughly licked up my length and then teased my clit lightly with his tongue.

"Hunter," I warned or begged. I wasn't quite sure. He was quickly driving me mindless with need.

"Shhhh, you'll wake Max," he said.

I groaned quietly, grasping at the quilt lying thrown to the side and trying to keep my need contained, but it was no use. Hunter's light teasing flicks on my clit grew slowly firmer and firmer, moving at his own pace. Then he started in on maddening circles until I was desperate. He finally slipped one finger deep into me and started thrusting in time to his licks.

I clenched around him, needing to be filled. One finger wasn't enough. It was just more teasing. I thrust against him desperately, waves of need rolling through me, building in a delicious surge as my legs fell completely open on the couch.

He used the access to his advantage. He added another finger, quickly followed by a third as he stretched me out and increased the friction against my inner walls, making me shiver and moan.

The feeling of arousal intensified, but it wasn't just coming from me. My head rolled to the side, and I noticed both Leif and Damon watching me with fevered focus.

Leif had rolled onto his back and had his hand down his sweats, jerking himself off furiously. Damon looked pained and was gripping his hard dick over the top of his sweats like he was trying and failing not to touch himself. He was thrusting into his hand gently and almost unconsciously in time with Hunter's movements.

I eyed their hands, and my need skyrocketed, sparks of light bursting inside me. Leif seemed to know what I wanted. He pulled his sweats down and exposed his enormous cock. It was engorged, angry, and glistening at the tip, and he was handling it roughly.

Hunter used that moment to stroke against my inner walls with his index finger, finding that rough, sensitive spot easily and causing violent tremors to set off inside me. He sucked my clit, hard, and I exploded in a frenzy of light and sensation that made me moan and almost weep from relief.

I was panting hard, with aftershocks wracking my body, watching Leif come all over his stomach. Damon followed a little more discreetly but with a deep groan, a wet spot staining his sweats.

Hunter chuckled lightly as he kissed me gently and licked me clean. He used a tee to wipe his face before throwing it to Leif.

"Nice of you to join us for breakfast," he said to the guys.

"That was hot as fuck. I haven't come without direct touch since I was a teenager," Damon murmured, almost to himself, before looking me in the eye. "I hope you didn't mind us watching, Maia?"

I shrugged. "If I minded, I wouldn't have done it while you were lying next to us."

"I can't believe Max slept through that," Leif said.

"Slept through what?" Max mumbled sleepily, looking at Leif and noticing the mess, then looking over his shoulder at Hunter, where he was pulling my panties back into place while I stretched like a cat, a satisfied smile on my face.

"Why the fuck didn't you guys wake me up, you jerks?"

"You guys are very sweary in the mornings," I said as I yawned. I was ready for a nap, even though I had just woken up. I was feeling lazy and content. Hunter snuggled against me on the couch as he wrapped me up in his arms and breathed me in deeply.

Damon looked over his shoulder at the early morning rays staining the sky. Leif must have opened the curtains after I fell asleep last night. The pink and gold-painted sky was stunning as it washed across the horizon.

I heard Damon say, "Shit, we're late. I wanted to help the girls in the kitchen this morning. They worked so hard last night and some overindulged a bit when they got to relax. There might be some sore heads this morning." I snuggled further down into the couch, hoping he wouldn't notice me.

Damon jumped up and went to grab his shoes where he'd kicked them off last night, but Leif stopped him in his tracks. "You may want to grab a new pair of sweats first."

Damon looked down at himself, then over at Leif. "Good call, thanks," before dashing up the stairs.

"Grab me a tee, too, please," Hunter yelled at his retreating back. Damon just gave him a thumbs up over his shoulder.

Leif grabbed his tee where it was hanging over the back of the couch and threw Max his while Max was rubbing his eyes and muttering to himself. Then Leif disappeared. I couldn't see where he went.

"Up you get, pussycat, no time for napping," Hunter said, pulling me up with him.

I grumbled, but I enjoyed the show of all his muscles flexing as he pulled me up while standing over me.

I was up and looking for my yoga pants as Damon came bounding down the stairs, throwing a hot pink tee with a unicorn on the front at Hunter.

It hit him in the face, and I heard him chuckle from underneath it. "Fuck you, Damon. I'll get you next time."

Damon just smirked when I looked at him in question. "Hunter kindly bought it for me when we were at an airport, and my luggage got lost. It's been a rule ever since. If someone chucks it at you and it touches you, you have to wear it."

Leif returned and handed me a bag. "I grabbed some more stuff from Lexie for you, so you don't have to keep wandering around in our clothes."

"I like her in our clothes," Max said as he winked at me.

"I know, right! Me too," Hunter said as he slapped Max on the back.

'Thanks, Leif," I said as I kissed him sweetly before dashing off to my room to give myself a quick wash and get changed.

I picked out a dress that was dark blue, like my eyes, with big colorful flowers, and I loved it. It had short flutter sleeves that would help keep the sun off my shoulders but not be hot or constrictive. It also hit mid-thigh on me, not too short that a breeze would be a problem, but not so long I'd be sweltering in too much fabric. It also had pockets which I loved.

It was a little tight around my girls and pushed them up a bit. The buttons looked like they might pop at any moment, but I didn't care. The dress suited me perfectly. Girly but practical. I was usually a jeans and t-shirt girl around the farm, but I liked to put on something pretty now and again.

The guys all stopped and stared at me for a moment before they seemed to shake themselves and get moving.

"Let's go, people," Hunter said thickly as he unlocked the door and headed out, proudly wearing his pink unicorn tee.

Max took my hand as I looked around, enjoying a walk through the slowly waking farm. I was happy to be here with a group of men who were quickly snapping up the pieces of my shattered heart and making it beat in a way I never thought it would again.

I took a deep breath of the rich morning scents, freshly turned earth, and the flowers they had dotted around for the bees as the world slowly appeared out of the darkness at the bottom of the hill.

The morning light hadn't quite reached down here yet. This section of the path was overhung with big trees, their canopies meeting at the top in places. I heard a splash from the pond and wondered what had jumped in for a swim.

I smiled at Hunter as he walked, balancing along a short timber border wall along the path instead of on it. With the pink unicorn t-shirt, he looked like a giant five-year-old with too much energy.

"We should probably talk about the plan while we walk this morning. I think it's going to be a busy day," Damon said.

"Where were you supposed to meet your friends, Maia? And where were they when you separated?" Hunter started.

"They were at the Palace, in my sanctuary in the library. Ava gave me this bracelet." I held the bluebird bracelet up to them that I was still wearing on my wrist. "She told me to head for her uncle's farm in Greensborough, that he would recognize it and take me in. She said he helped hide omegas."

The guys all looked at Max. "Interesting," was all Max said.

"Why didn't they run with you?" Damon asked.

"We didn't have time. Cary came to tell me the alphas were at the gates, led by Ronan, and the guards had abandoned us. Cary insisted I run. I had to grab what I had in the room and go. That's how I ended up bringing the book with me rather than supplies. It was in my hands when I ran, and I had seconds to get out."

They all asked me a lot more questions, and I told them what I could, but I didn't know more than her uncle's name. I shook my head in frustration. I could see them all look at Max again.

Leif leaned over and put his arm around me. "Hey, we'll find them, sunshine."

"Hunter has a plan to find them, okay? Just give me today to research like we talked about," Max said, squeezing my hand lightly.

I stiffened in response to their reassurance. I knew I'd been an emotional mess since Damon blew my defenses apart and let my omega out, and I wasn't being helpful by providing many details right now. But I wanted them to know that I could handle things, and I needed to know what we planned to do. I could deal with things better if I knew what was coming. I hated to be blindsided.

"I need to know the plan," I said, a little sternly. "You asked me to tell you what I needed, and this is it. I'm not used to relying on others to do things for me. I know you guys want to protect me, but I'm never going to be a demure little omega who sits in the corner and waits patiently to be told what to do."

"If you're expecting that, we will have a problem."

"We know, pussycat, we don't expect that. We're just so used to working in sync with each other we're not really used to explaining what we're doing," Hunter said, jumping down and stepping in front of me to stroke my arms lightly like you would a pet cat. It was kind of nice. If I could purr, I probably would.

"I plan to start with the Palace. That's the last place we know they were. Max is a genius at hacking and digital tracking.

"Max will find Ava's uncle's farm, and we'll check that out as well, but I want to see if, or when, your friends left. We can follow a trail online from there, so we have a good idea of where to go when we leave.

"If we go out without any idea, we're likely to miss them and expose ourselves to unnecessary danger. We don't want to be driving around out there aimlessly. It won't do your friends, or us, any good."

I nodded reluctantly. I got it. I was just frustrated and wanted to feel like I was doing something to help.

Damon also stepped up to me, draping his arms around Hunter from behind, like he wanted to be part of our huddle but needed a buffer between us right now.

"There are two different people or groups out there right now trying to infiltrate this place, and we know at least one is after you. So we just want to make sure whatever move we take next is calculated, with the least risk, okay?"

"Two groups?" I asked.

He nodded slowly, narrowing his eyes like he was trying to figure out how much I could handle hearing right now. I waited him out with my eyebrow cocked, taking a leaf out of Lexie's book. I'd seen her do it with them, and it seemed to work. My omega brought out her pom poms and started cheering as Damon kept talking, but I kept my face neutral on the outside.

"The person probing the fences on the first night was stealthy, military trained. We only caught him because he didn't seem to be expecting the level of surveillance we have around the farm, thanks to Max."

"The two on the second night weren't aware of our security either, so clearly hadn't been warned and didn't appear concerned about being spotted. Or even know how to be quiet, let alone stealthy. They were arrogant and untrained." Damon said.

"So I believe they are from two different groups." I felt or saw all the guys nodding. Shit.

"Do you have any idea who the first person could have been? Is there anyone else you are running from or who might be looking for you?" Hunter asked as he shifted in place restlessly under Damon's arm like he wanted to be doing more, too.

I shook my head as Leif gave a low rumbly growl that I felt through me more than heard. As if the thought of someone else looking for me caused an instinctive alpha response. I felt him gently nuzzle my hair, and his arm subtly squeezed me tighter. Like he could keep me safe if only he could keep me close enough.

I leaned back into him more, rubbing my head lightly on his cheek in response, and the rumble quietened.

I took a deep breath and was suddenly distracted by the guys' scents and the heat of their bodies where they were touching me and crowding me as Max and Leif shifted closer. I could feel my nipples rapidly hardening in response. Shit.

"Is it hot?" I asked. I suddenly felt constricted, like I needed to take off all my clothes as Hunter swayed towards me while eyeing off my cleavage, and my scent spiked.

Damon pulled Hunter out of the way, elbowed Leif aside, and pulled me clear of the guys, forcing me to drop Max's hand as he stood in front of me protectively.

"Give her room. You're crowding her." Damon growled, and the sound vibrated through my core and lit me up inside.

"Sorry, Maia. We'll go ahead and let you breathe for a minute, okay?" Leif said, dragging the other two away while Hunter looked at me knowingly over his shoulder.

I nodded without looking at them, feeling even more frustrated. I couldn't keep up a serious conversation if my body went into instant sex kitten mode whenever one of my guys touched me. My omega started pouting and pulling at me, wanting more contact with Damon right now.

I groaned as I leaned into Damon's back, grabbing onto his t-shirt and battling to control my hormones while he stood still and waited for me to ride it out. It didn't work, though. All it did was give me a lungful of his stormy, electric scent that had spiked in response to mine.

His scent sent shivers over my body like it was calling to me, wanting to drag me out to play in the maelstrom. I dragged my hands down his back and around his waist before I slipped my hands under his t-shirt to skim my nails over his rock-hard abs. I heard him groan and felt him flex under my hands.

We had gotten more comfortable with each other, and I was trying to respect his boundaries, but he hadn't kissed me yet, and it was honestly driving me insane. The electricity kept building between us the longer we circled each other.

I slid my hands back around and ran them up his taut back, pulling his t-shirt up with them, before I dragged my lips lightly over his back. At the first touch of my lips, he whirled around and pushed me up against a tree as he growled low in his throat, not in warning this time, but in need.

I remembered how Hunter had done the same the other night, pushed me up against a tree in his desperation for me, and I decided I really liked having trees around the farm.

Damon grabbed both of my wrists suddenly and pinned them over my head. "Don't move," he growled. "I've wanted to kiss you since the first moment I saw you, but I'm not sure I can stop at just a kiss after watching you with Hunter this morning. I'm on edge, and I will lose control if you touch me right now. Neither of us wants that. Do you hear me?"

I nodded my head slowly, trying to keep still. He was wrong, though. I wanted him to lose control. I trusted him not to hurt me, but I needed him to trust himself first.

I needed his kiss with a burning ache, so I stayed perfectly still. He was so close I could feel the heat from his body caressing my skin, but he was only touching my wrists. He stroked one lightly as he held it, and I shivered. His body tensed, and his pupils dilated further in response.

I was his prey, and I was caught. I trembled as I waited to see what he would do next.

He leaned in so slowly that it felt like time stood still, and he brushed my lips so delicately with his own I barely felt it. It was like brushing up against a butterfly wing, more air than substance. I keened lightly, needing more but holding still like he asked.

He leaned impossibly closer, and I felt his breath on my lips before he parted his own lips slowly and kissed me softly, dragging his lips over mine before licking them gently. I felt light explode around me, and our bond strengthened at the contact, filling me with an intense bliss. I opened with a gasp, and he dove in, unleashing all of his pent-up need on me.

He ravaged me with his lips and tongue, stroking me intimately. His stormy scent turned tangy and wild as his carefully controlled need exploded through it, tasting like salted toffee on my tongue. I was lost, like a rowboat in a storm, riding the giant waves, completely at the mercy of a higher power.

The light splintered with sweet, dark heat as he invaded me ferociously while maintaining contact only at my wrists and mouth, holding the rest of his body away from me. Until he pulled back suddenly, exerting steely control over himself again with monumental effort. I ached for him, but I stayed still, as he'd demanded.

He nuzzled into my neck, breathing hard, and twined his hands into my own before he brought them down beside us.

I was achy and desperate, but he pushed into my body lightly and started up that buzzing purr that made my limbs go weak and brought instant comfort.

It was a hell of a first kiss and well worth the wait.

I could feel contentment coming from him, too. Our tenuous bond had strengthened. I had never felt this close to him. I had never felt this close to anyone before I met the guys. I ran my hands up his arms and pulled him closer, snuggling into him. The intense heat and need dissipated with his comforting rumble.

We had been circling each other warily for days, electricity charging between us, but I felt more settled now that we had established a physical connection beyond some discrete neck sniffing and hugging.

He shifted back and smiled at me in a way that transformed him from a fierce and dangerous creature into something boyish and light. His face both lit up and softened at the same time. He reached up and stroked my face, and I could feel his joy thrumming through our bond.

"Mine," he growled lightly, and I smiled.

"Ours," came Hunter's reply from around the bend, and Damon's grin grew until it felt like it rivaled the sun. His stern glare was panty-dropping, but his pure grin was sunshine on a winter's day. It was so blinding that it almost hurt to look at. I wanted to soak it up and bask in it.

I smiled widely, too, knowing this was a hint of the man he might have been and the boy Hunter had been drawn to before he endured so much trauma and took on so many burdens.

We walked around the corner, holding hands, and found Hunter, Leif, and Max all waiting.

"Sorry, I...," I didn't get very far before the three men instinctively moved toward me but pulled up short like they didn't want to crowd me again.

"Don't even think about apologizing, sunshine. You don't owe us anything, not even your time and especially not your body. We all want this, and I know figuring out how will take some time, but none of us is going anywhere," Leif said, looking serious.

"We should apologize to you for crowding and overwhelming you," Max added.

Hunter just wandered over to Damon, threw his arm around him on the other side, and said quietly, "I like this smile on your face, bro."

I breathed deeper and let their reassurance wash over me. I felt centered with them all near, like I was where I belonged.

I would just have to get used to the intensity when they surrounded me with their scents and warm, hard bodies. But, you know, I'd deal. There were far worse problems to have, I thought. My omega was a smug bitch right now, but her gloating was interrupted when my stomach rumbled loudly, and the guys all laughed.

We dashed up the last stretch to the dining hall. There were a lot of people around when we walked in, with Damon still holding my hand. Most were chatting while finishing up their breakfasts, but they all went quiet. Again.

I needed to learn to sneak in the back door here.

Damon led us to a table in the back, glare already back in place as he surveyed the room protectively and kept me close. We were almost there when the doors swung open, and Sirena stepped out.

Oh, hell no.

Twenty-Eight

When Sirena saw us holding hands, she gasped and turned to Damon as he stiffened. I could only imagine what she was about to say, but I wouldn't let her harass him any longer.

I stepped into her space, put my palm up in front of her, and said, 'No.' Like she was a naughty puppy.

She just stood there with her mouth open. When she went to speak again, I said, "Nope, no, nada communicando with Damon. That shit you pulled yesterday was a disgrace. I'm revoking your girl club card."

She winced, almost apologetically, but still tried to talk for the third time and dodge around me. I stepped back into her space, put my hand back up, and said again, "No, sorry, it's been revoked already, and customer service is busy now. If you want to complain, you'll have to come back and see me later."

"If you ever want to get your girl card back, I'll give you a hot tip, just this once. You need to change your attitude. I don't know what your damage is, we all have some, but you don't get to pull that shit on other people."

"Figure it out, show you can do better, and we'll talk. Until then, turn your Manolos around and head back into the kitchen, or continue on your way past, but you don't get to talk to Damon."

I heard clapping and turned to see Lexie and the other girls from the kitchen standing by the food table, where they'd been stacking up bowls and dishes. Lexie had a massive, shit-eating grin on her face.

I needed to spend more time with these chicks. They seemed cool. I took a bow, and they all laughed before I grabbed Damon's hand again and pulled him past where Sirena was back to standing with her mouth open.

Damon pulled me down onto his lap as Lexie dashed over with a few bowls of food.

"Here, I saved you some breakfast. I was hoping you'd be up soon. You deserve a feast and people laying at your feet for that performance with Sirena, but all I have is porridge. We kept it simple this morning.'"

"Porridge is perfect. I'm starving. Thank you, Lexie. I'll give you girls a hand as soon as I've eaten something.' I was a little embarrassed about my impromptu performance. It had been instinctive, but I wasn't used to drawing attention to myself.

"Sure thing, we could always use a hand," she said. As she walked back, she called out to Sirena, who was just standing around awkwardly, not so subtly watching us and glancing around the room nervously.

"Sirena, grab some bowls, please. We need them back in the kitchen."

Sirena huffed but went to follow her, grabbing bowls and cutlery noisily. I heard her grumbling lowly, and someone else warned her, "I'd give it up, honey. She's an omega."

Sirena shrieked loudly, "She's an omega?"

I could feel eyes on us. Lots of eyes. So many eyes.

I turned to Damon, wanting to snuggle into him and disappear for a moment, but the most intense eyes were coming from him. He stared at me fiercely while completely ignoring Sirena and everyone else, like they didn't even exist right now.

"You just defended me, as a true mate would," he growled so quietly I barely heard him as he pulled me tightly against him, securing me to him with a firm grip on my waist and the other on my thigh, edging the hem of my dress.

"That's because you're one of my true mates," I whispered back as I felt his dominance rising and his fight to keep it contained. Every word felt true as they reverberated through me, and an intense need to claim slid through our bond.

"Maia, I...," he growled as his grip tightened almost painfully. I was hanging on to his next words but got distracted as Max suddenly jerked his head and made a frantic abort motion to someone behind us, but it was too late.

Damon whipped his head around when he sensed the person behind him. He growled low and deadly, glaring at the poor guy menacingly. A feeling of electricity flooded the room, making my nipples harden painfully, and his scent turned instantly stormy.

The guy froze in his spot, unwilling to move forwards or backward. I'm not sure he was even breathing.

I was suddenly yanked off Damon's lap and pulled into Leif's arms. I was panting hard. I half expected Damon to growl and lunge at Leif as he rose from his seat. A beast I could almost see shadowing his movements. All sweetness was gone now. He was all predator again.

"This is going to happen," Leif said in a firm, unyielding voice, "but not in the dining hall at breakfast. Take a walk, Damon."

Damon gave me a look so filled with heat I was surprised the dining room didn't burst into flames. It was either a promise or a threat, and I was okay with either.

He reined himself in with difficulty, his nostrils flaring before he gave Leif a curt nod and turned to stride out of the room without looking at me again. Hunter followed him closely. I could feel Damon's wild emotions through the bond and knew we both needed some distance.

"Are you okay?" Leif asked me.

"Yeah, uh, that was intense," I said, trying to slow my breathing and remember why claiming me here on the table was a bad idea. "Thanks for saving my reputation."

He nodded and stroked me lightly, attempting to reassure me, but any touch right now was just stoking the flames. I stepped back from him. He let me go reluctantly, but I sensed he understood.

We were on the cusp of something powerful that I knew would change us all forever, but we weren't quite ready yet. I could sense it intuitively. Damon had come so far in a few days, as had I. But he hadn't fully embraced all the parts of himself, and I needed him whole. I wanted all of him, with nothing held back.

Damon and I together were explosive, with both of our emotions set to volatile ever since we had met and blown each other's walls apart. But there were moments of tenderness and a deeper connection in there, too. It was all just a little overwhelming at times.

Hunter returned and let me know Damon had calmed down once he got outside in the clear air. Or was at least back to his usual level of gruff dominance. He went to get an update from all the team leaders about the upcoming farm yield.

I was curious to see what Leif, Max, and Hunter would do next. I didn't think they would let me wander off on my own right now without someone sticking close to me. Honestly, I wasn't sure I wanted that either. Except for my brief attempt to flee, we'd all been attached since the moment I arrived, and I'd gotten used to their presence. They were starting to feel like an extension of me in a way that was comforting.

I watched them as I shoveled my breakfast down quickly while standing next to the table. Max had already planned to do research today. I could see he felt torn. Part of his brain was already in the security office. I figured he was about to go down a rabbit hole, and we wouldn't see him for a while.

Leif decided he would go over security with Dave, seeing where they could modify or reinforce areas and help train some of the younger guys.

Hunter announced he was going to do a food stock-take. Damon would need the information once he got the farm updates, so they could plan for the next few months and determine where they had any supply gaps.

The function center was fully stocked for some upcoming events, plus they had the eggs, fruit, and vegetables they usually sold at the weekend markets. They had plenty of food on hand, but it would run out quickly, with everyone working and living on the farm needing three meals daily.

I smiled to myself. There had been plenty of pointed looks during their conversation, and it seemed Hunter was nominated to stay nearby. A sensible choice, he was always good at de-escalating situations.

Max looked at a camera and made an 'I'm watching you' motion while I kissed him goodbye, while Leif reminded him he was up at the gate if

I tried to run again. I just laughed at them both, their antics calming me down.

I needed some girl time, so I wandered into the kitchen with my plate. Hunter grabbed the guys' plates and followed me, dropping them off to be washed with a thank you to the girls before heading to the cold room next door.

Lexie squealed when she saw me, jumping up and giving me a big hug. "Wow, that dress looks great on you. I'm impressed you managed to get out from underneath that lot in it. They are seriously losing their shit over you, girl."

"I heard that," Hunter yelled.

"You were supposed to!" Lexie yelled right back.

Sirena was hanging around, moving bowls around on a bench like she was re-organizing things, but was really watching me closely as she said, "I just wanted to–"

Lexie just put her hand up and interrupted her to ask, "I'm sorry, can I see your girl card? Did you get it back already?"

Sirena huffed, and a few of the girls laughed. I kind of felt bad. I knew she had been horrible to me, but I didn't want her to get bullied. I was hoping she'd learn to be nicer, but you couldn't force people to change.

"So, I'm Maia," I said a little awkwardly. The girls all chorused, "We know."

Lexie introduced me to all the women, and I tried hard to remember their names, but I knew I'd probably have to ask again later. I was terrible at remembering names and making small talk.

"Um, why are all the women in the kitchen and the men out in the field? It seems a little old-fashioned to me, and I lived in the Palace," I blurted out without thinking.

I realized belatedly that I could have very well just insulted them all. Lexie just laughed at my expense.

"Most of the field hands worked for Damon's grandfather. Some have worked here all their lives. Now their kids work around the farm, too. Some women are in the fields, but it's a hard grind. None of us were keen."

"A lot of the women working on the farm have joined over the last few years since the guys took it over. Damon set up the function center and farm-to-table markets to give us work," Lexie said.

Isabella, one of the younger women, was washing dishes and said with feeling, "Damon and his friends took us all in, one by one, without question, when Lexie found us and rescued us. Most of us fled abusive situations, often at the hands of alphas, and dragging kids in tow, with nowhere to go and no prospects."

I felt terribly sad all of a sudden. Looking around the room, I realized many women had that skittish look that abused women often have, like they were waiting to get kicked. I'd seen too much of it at the Palace, especially in the older girls who'd experienced the dark underbelly of alpha society.

I walked over, picked up a dish towel, and started drying dishes in a silent show of support. My heart was aching for these women, but I didn't want them to see me cry for them. They didn't need my tears. They were survivors.

"Lexie rescued you?" I asked, looking over my shoulder at her with newfound respect. It seems she had downplayed her role and just how much she worked with the women she taught self-defense.

Sofia, who was maybe in her forties and was washing dishes at the next sink, nodded and said quietly, "This place isn't just a farm. It's a safe haven, a refuge."

"It's why there is so much security around here. Even before the crash, the guys were trying to keep everyone safe and keep problems out," Lexie explained.

"I don't know what we would have done without Lexie, the guys, and this place. None of us expected a handout, and we all wanted to work. Damon asked the first of us what we could do, and I'd run a restaurant before. He came to me a few days later and asked me to help him set up the function center, and I was glad to help," Sofia said.

"The farm-to-gate started when some women started making jams and other things to sell. It never felt like Damon was giving us busy work, more like he was giving us the tools to build something ourselves, to give us stability and a future. Something we could share in and help give us back our pride. It was more than I ever dreamed would be possible."

Lexie also picked up a hand towel and came to help dry dishes, giving Sofia a friendly shoulder bump and a smile.

Isabella added. "It's why a lot of farm workers avoid the kitchen. Some of us who haven't been here as long are still a little skittish around men. With the Crash, we converted the function center to a dining hall. The plan was to keep all the food in one place and make sure everyone was getting fed, but they've all been very respectful about giving us space unless we approach them."

"Leif scared the hell out of me when I first got here, but I felt so bad about it later when I realized what a teddy bear he was. He's so good with all the kids. He gives them plane rides and piggybacks all the time," Sofia said.

I could picture Leif doing that, a gaggle of kids following him through the fields, and the thought made me smile.

"Hunter is always so sweet when getting each of us settled. He puts everyone at ease, even though he's an alpha," Isabella chimed in.

One of the other ladies piped up. She was doing some lunch prep at one of the counters, cutting up carrots. I think her name was Marcie. "Hunter sat with me for hours when I first got here and just let me talk and cry it out," she said. "I'd never known any man to sit and listen to me before."

"Max was amazing, too, setting us up with new accounts and phones, giving us new lives and sometimes identities," Marcie said as she passed me another dish and smiled gently at me.

Lexie looked pointedly at me. "It's one of the reasons Damon holds so tight to his dominance. He has other reasons, too, but when he's here, he doesn't want to scare any of us unnecessarily. I worry about the cost to him, though."

I knew my guys were special, but hearing about them from the perspective of these women, made me realize I had barely scratched the surface.

"The guys have always been different, especially Damon. Most people can't see past his stern facade, but he wasn't always like that. Life made him that way." Lexie said. "Underneath it all, he's one of the most protective people I know."

"I know I haven't known them for long, but I can see how special they are. I know how lucky I am to have Damon, Leif, Max, and Hunter all wanting to be a part of my life," I told them.

I figured there was a reason the girls were telling me all this. They obviously cared about the welfare of the guys and didn't want to see them get hurt. So I knew I needed to be honest with them.

"I was running myself when I landed here, and I tried to keep running when I met them. They scared the shit out of me. But they weren't having it. They asked for a day, then another, and another," I sighed.

"I'm still here because I can't imagine walking away now. I can't imagine my life without all of them. Just the thought is the worst kind of pain."

"I know it's fast, I know I don't deserve them, and I know society will judge us if we're all together. But I couldn't ever choose between them. They all mean the world to me already, and they feel like the most right thing that has ever happened in my short, shitty life."

I couldn't make eye contact right now, so I dried my plate furiously even though it was bone dry.

I felt someone move behind me and hug me from behind. I saw a tendril of bright hair fall past my face. Then I felt more arms coming around me from the sides, layers of them until I was centered in a tender swell of solidarity.

This place and the group hugs, they were killing me. I dropped my plate and grabbed what hands I could, squeezing hard, my emotions all pressing under my skin and my scent turning tangy with my sudden angst.

"Fuck society," I heard Lexie mumble behind me, and the other girls laughed.

"My sister was an omega," Isabella said from next to me, and she squeezed my hand in return. "She was so beautiful and sweet. I adored her. When she presented, they sent her to the Palace. I didn't see her for years, but she was so changed when I finally did. Like all her light had been sucked out, she was just an empty shell."

"I don't know what the fuck they do to omegas there, but it's nothing good, and if the world needs to burn for a better one to rise, so be it, I say."

I couldn't hold it in anymore. I started to cry quietly, for me, for these women, and for Isabella's sister. For all of us who had been abused in a way our society condoned. I was a mess. I never cried, not even as a kid, and now I couldn't seem to turn the waterworks off.

"It's okay, honey," another woman said from close by, "it's usually only when we feel safe that we break down and let it all out. We're too busy surviving the rest of the time. We've all been there."

They all tightened their arms around me in silent support, and I felt wet tears on my arms that weren't mine.

I could feel the guys' concern through the bond. I tried to send reassurance back to them.

We stood that way for a few minutes before Isabella said, "So, all four, hey? That sounds like fun."

I started to laugh. I recognized her voice suddenly from my first day here.

"Oh yeah. Since I know you were wondering, Max and Leif are definitely into women and happy to share. It's one hell of a man sandwich."

She burst out laughing, and I heard a deep, masculine chuckle behind us. We all turned round to see Hunter casually lounging in the doorway.

"Sorry to intrude, ladies, but I could feel our girl getting upset. I just wanted to make sure she was okay before the cavalry arrived."

I saw Lexie tilt her head curiously, looking between us, but I didn't have time to explain how we could feel each other through our bond before he strode forward and enveloped me in a massive bear hug. I melted into him as he lifted me off my feet, taking a big breath of his woody scent.

Isabella and Sophia sighed dramatically, and I giggled. Yeah, I know. I was one lucky girl.

Lexie was having none of it, though. "Nuh, uh, no boys allowed. It's girl time. Out with you, we got this.'

She started whacking him with her dishrag, and he play-acted having an injury before giving me a wink and backing out of the room.

"Okay, okay, witch, I get it. You need to perform your pagan rituals."

She turned and threw a carrot from the counter, but he caught it mid-air and said, "Thanks" before taking a giant bite and sauntering back out the door, all cocky attitude.

Lexie tapped me on the shoulder when I short-circuited, watching his delectable ass in his tight jeans as he strutted away. "Earth to Maia, do we need an intervention?"

"Maybe," I sighed. "My pheromones are rioting after being locked down for so long. The guys just have to look at me sideways, and my omega bends over, lifts her skirt, and yells, come and get me."

Lexie waved her hand in front of her face to clear my scent and said dryly, "Yeah, we know."

"Oops, sorry. Omega occupational hazard," I said.

We turned around, and I was startled when I noticed Sirena standing awkwardly by the bench on the other side of the kitchen. Her eyes were glassy, as if she were holding back tears, and her brows were pulled together.

Sirena opened her mouth like she was going to say something to me, but then shut it again with a sigh and looked away, wrapping her arms around herself. She looked sad and conflicted.

I had completely forgotten she was even here. She seemed different, a bit raw and vulnerable. Her whole posture had changed. I was tempted to ask if she was okay, but before I could, Lexie grabbed my arm and said, "Okay, we need some air. I'm taking Maia for a tour of the farm."

I shrugged, figuring I was the last person Sirena would open up to after my little performance earlier. Maybe the other girls could work their magic on her.

I yelled to Hunter, "We're going on a farm tour, Hunt. See ya later."

Hunter popped his head around the doorframe, still munching on his carrot. "You know Damon won't be happy if I let you wander the farm alone."

"She's not alone," Lexie said as she reared back, then narrowed her eyes at Hunter with her hands on her hips, like she was gearing up for an epic smackdown.

"You don't *let* me do anything. I'm not your princess to be kept cosseted in a palace or a cabin, but if you're worried, just tell him I overpowered you." I crossed my arms over my chest and smirked at him.

"How exactly would you do that?" Hunter asked, subtly flexing his muscles.

"Knee you in the balls, of course," Lexie answered, crossing her arms and leaning against me in solidarity. Giving him a cool, "Come at me, bro" stare.

Hunter paled and grabbed his junk while the other women whooped and hollered. I felt like these women were going to be my tribe.

"Carry on," he said, backing away and disappearing into the other room.

Lexie waved goodbye to the other girls while I mouthed thank you to them. They knew what for, as they nodded and smiled. I glanced at Isabella and subtly jerked my head in Sirena's direction with a raised eyebrow. I knew they were currently bunking together. She gave me a subtle thumbs up, and I felt better knowing she was on it. I smiled gratefully at her.

We wandered up the main path, heading for the upper fields. I wanted to check out what crops they had planted on the terraces and how the irrigation worked.

Then I wanted to see the creche the women had set up to take turns watching the younger kids and where they made those amazing honey and goats milk products I had been using in the shower. I wanted to see it all.

I still had Ava and Cary on my mind, but I knew Max was working on it, and I just had to be patient. The farm was a good distraction.

Lexie's brow was furrowed as we walked. She seemed pensive like she was thinking about something that was worrying her. I asked her what was up, thinking she needed to talk about something.

"I was just wondering about your scent and how that worked. I mean, you didn't have one when you got here, but now you do. I don't get it. Can you turn it off and on?"

"Not really. My scent was always subtle, and I could disguise it by wearing other strong scents like leather and perfume. I used to wear my gramps' old hat and one of his shirts whenever I was around people. They smelled strongly of him."

I shrugged, taking in the view while we walked, happy to meander and chat for the moment.

"I noticed early on that stress seemed to make it fade further, so I would make myself physically stressed by causing pain if I noticed my scent spiking."

"When Damon touched me the first time, though, it was like my scent exploded everywhere, and I haven't been able to get it back in the bottle again."

"Huh, interesting," she said, kicking rocks on the path as we walked.

She went to say something more, but at that moment, Dave came jogging around the bend towards us wearing black camo pants, boots, and a snug black tee that showed off all his toned muscles.

The man was built, and that salt and pepper hair gave him an air of authority. If I had a daddy kink, I would go there.

No, bad omega, down girl. Dave is a friend. I felt like I was lecturing a naughty puppy while I talked my omega down.

Dave stopped short when he saw us.

"Let me guess. You're our bodyguard?" Lexie asked dryly, giving him some serious side-eye.

He had a radio on his belt, and Damon's voice suddenly blared, "Alpha 1 to Beta 2, do you have eyes on them?"

Dave looked a little flustered. "Pretty much," he answered honestly before responding to Damon in the affirmative.

"Hi, Dave. Don't worry. I'm not going to accost you again this time, so you don't have to worry about Damon getting all growly when you're covered in my scent."

He smiled at me and nodded absently, but his attention was on Lexie, who was looking everywhere but at him. Interesting.

Lexie sauntered away, swinging her hips while looping her arm through mine and dragging me with her. I snuck a peek at Dave, and he was mesmerized by her ass the same way I had been by Hunter's not five minutes ago.

Very interesting. Dave looked away quickly when he noticed me watching.

Oh, this was going to be a fun afternoon. I cackled wickedly inside my head.

Twenty-Nine

I strode down to the security room, feeling impatient. This morning had been intense, and I'd been trying not to obsess about Maia's movements all day.

It was easier feeling her through the bond now, though, and knowing she was getting along so well with Lexie filled me with quiet joy. Lexie needed a sister as much as Maia did, and we were all keen to let them spend time together.

While my connection to Maia was growing, I was able to feel each of the guys lightly through the bond, too. I loved the sensation, and I hoped it intensified when we all claimed her. But right now, the emotions I was picking up from Max had me concerned.

We'd all given Max space to work today. We knew he would disappear once he started his research. Sometimes we needed to pull him out for his own good, but otherwise, our presence interrupted his flow and thought process, so we left him alone as much as we could.

He usually called me whenever he found anything significant, though. His emotions had swung wildly from his initial excitement to fear, then bounced between nausea and horror this afternoon. I kept expecting a call any second, but it never came.

I finally headed for the security office. It was time to pull him out or sit with him through whatever was distressing him. I couldn't stand to feel it and be so far away.

As I got closer, I noticed Leif sitting outside the cabin, leaning against the wall with his eyes closed.

"You okay?" I whispered, crouching down next to him.

He nodded before opening his eyes to look at me. He looked wrecked. "Max's emotions have been pulling at me, but he hasn't called. I just wanted to be nearby when he did. I got someone to fill in at the gate."

I sensed movement behind me and spotted Hunter coming out the kitchen's back door. "It's time," he said, mirroring my impatience.

I pulled Leif to his feet before I turned and knocked loudly on the door. It was Max's protocol to always knock before anyone entered the security cabin, even me.

Nick, one of the young guys who helped Max monitor security at the farm, opened the door and paled when he saw me.

I could feel the frown on my face and knew it made me look stern, but I was agitated about Max and couldn't wipe it off. I needed to know he was alright.

I stepped into the space quickly, followed by Hunter and Leif. I scanned the room and breathed a sigh of relief when I saw Max look up, startled, from behind one of the monitor banks. He looked like he was trying to figure out when and where he was. He was deep down the rabbit hole.

It was dim in here, without any natural light and only a few lamps on. Keeping the blinds closed was another of Max's security measures.

Leif flung himself on the couch. I could feel his relief, but he wouldn't go and hug Max while he was working, as much as I knew Leif wanted to. It was a regular couch, but Leif made it look like kiddie furniture when he draped himself across it.

Hunter slouched against the door jamb as he propped the door open and kept watch for anyone approaching. His casual pose belied the fact we were on high alert, as did Leif's. It was a camouflage we had perfected while working undercover.

Having three alphas in here took up all the space and air. It was like having too many scented candles burning at once. Having the door open would help Nick. Max was used to our scents by now.

I looked between Max and Nick, unsure if I should ask the questions I wanted while Nick was there.

"Stop freaking Nick out, Damon. You scared him enough when you growled at him this morning at breakfast," Max said. There was a lightness to his tone that masked his roiling emotions.

I was confused at the reference to this morning, and Hunter laughed. Hunter was well-liked around the farm, and Nick looked to him now. I suddenly remembered Nick approaching us at breakfast. Had I growled at him?

Clearly, I had frightened Nick without meaning to. Twice. Today. Shit.

"It's okay, Nick. Why don't you take a break while we chat with Max?" Hunter said, giving him a playful shove out the door, which he was still lounging against.

Nick looked relieved and turned to escape, but I called out, "Nick, before you go can I have a word?"

Nick stopped abruptly, already half out the door, and reluctantly turned around, taking a small step back inside.

I put my hands in my pockets and attempted to relax my posture to look less intimidating. I smiled at Nick to try to get him to relax. I didn't want people around the farm to be afraid of me. The farm was our home, all of our home.

"I appreciate all the help you're giving Max here. He said you're doing a great job and learning fast. He left you in charge the other night because he was confident you could handle it and trusts you, and we trust Max."

"I just wanted to thank you for jumping in when we needed it and apologize for growling at you this morning."

I tried to get it all out calmly without growling at the poor guy this time. Nick looked like he was going to pass out. He looked around the room at us, a little unsure, like he thought it was part of a prank.

Hunter grinned at Nick, and Max nodded, reassuring him, but Leif was focused on me with a curious look.

I didn't give out praise unless it was earnt, but surely I did it enough that it wasn't a surprise to people. If not, I needed to work on that.

"I'm not sure if Max has told you, but Maia is our mate, and finding her has thrown me off a bit. My instincts are going a little wild. It wasn't personal, and I'm trying to rein it in. So please, just be patient with me."

Nick stood with his mouth slightly open, watching me warily like he didn't know what I would do next. Like I might change color or grow a tail. I know I had been very closed off in the past, so changing everyone's perception of me was going to be difficult. This was awkward as fuck, though.

I started to get a little uncomfortable when Nick didn't respond. I figured the guys could sense it through the bond as Hunter nudged Nick subtly.

"Oh, yeah, sure, of course," Nick mumbled, spouting random affirmations and shifting on his feet. He was a good guy and smart as hell, but he was a watcher. He liked to hang back in the shadows. It made him nervous when people noticed him.

"I think we need a code word for when Damon is being intense, or a dick, something that will snap him out of it," Hunter said.

"The word biscuit always works with dogs and kids. Just yell biscuit at him next time," Leif jumped in quickly, side-eyeing me and trying not to smirk as he stretched out on the couch.

I tried to glare at Leif but failed, breaking into a grin at Hunter and Leif's antics, which always weirdly calmed me down. I knew they used it to their advantage sometimes. They were sneaky fuckers when they wanted to be, but I didn't mind.

Nick seemed unsure and turned to leave again but stopped himself this time. He looked a little pale but squared his shoulders and looked me in the eye.

"About the whole mate thing, we figured it out, and we all agree, nobody here cares that you're all her mates. We think she's good for all of you, and you deserve to be happy."

"Some of the old timers here, they know what that means." Nick bounced his foot as he spoke, betraying his nerves, but he looked determined to say his piece.

"You've been more than good to us, all of us, especially the women you've taken in. If you ever need us to back you, we're all in."

Nick turned to leave again like he wanted to get out before we could respond, but Hunter straightened from his slouch and put out his hand to block him. I was too shocked to speak. I was having trouble processing everything he said. I was thankful Hunter seemed more on the ball.

"Hang on a sec. Thanks for the support, we all appreciate it more than you know, but you said the old timers know what it means?"

Nick looked a little uncomfortable. His family was native to the area, as were many of the original farm teams that worked for my grandfather. They had worked the land for generations and had close ties to it, with multiple generations of some families living and working on the farm.

They taught me a lot about the seasons and working with nature rather than against it. The old timers used to talk and tell stories around bonfires at night, whenever they burnt off farm cuttings and waste, and my gramps always took me when I was here. I still loved to go along and listen as much as I could, as did the guys.

"Yeah, it means you're Pack." He looked between us, his expression wide open and honest, no guile in sight. "Uh, you know that, right?"

It felt like the whole world ground to a halt, first Maia with her book and now Nick. I heard Max and Leif both inhale sharply, but I was speechless. Hunter looked like he'd won a winning hand in a high-stakes poker game. He was rubbing his hands together with glee.

"Your family knows about packs, about how they work?" Max asked.

Max stood up from his chair, then sat down again, like he wasn't sure if he should stay or come closer. It was the first time he had spoken since scolding me earlier. Leif was watching all of us carefully.

Nick just nodded slowly, looking thoughtful.

"We didn't know until Maia showed us a book she found," Hunter clarified.

"We thought we were just close friends, like adopted brothers, until Maia showed us we were more," I said. I was trying to keep my breathing and voice level so I didn't freak Nick out and stop him from talking.

"Well, that's interesting. We figured you were just hiding it because it would get you in trouble with the military," Nick said. His shoulders finally relaxed, and he had some color return to his face. He seemed more comfortable discussing this than anything else I had said earlier.

"Can we talk to one of your family, who knows more, sometime?" I asked while holding my breath.

"Sure," he said, shrugging like it was no big deal, "they've been waiting for you, Prime Alpha."

Thirty

I could hardly breathe, and Damon looked like you could blow him over, just whispering in his direction. Leif jumped up and put his arms around Damon, hugging him from behind. Damon sunk into him without saying a word.

Hunter had the biggest grin on his face. I wouldn't have been surprised if he'd done a little touchdown dance.

Instead, he slapped his hands on Nick's shoulders and said, "You've dropped a couple of bombs, and don't get me wrong, you've made our day, but right now, we've got some shit to discuss."

He turned Nick around and pointed him out the door. I called out, "Thanks, Nick, I'll buzz you when we're done." Hunter handed Nick his radio before Nick finally escaped out the door, and Hunter closed it behind him.

Hunter and I walked over to Damon and Lief, joining in and making it a group hug. That whole conversation with Nick was staggering; we all needed contact to ground us in who we were. It was instinctive, like the need to breathe.

Hunter was vibrating, and Leif was projecting calm reassurance, but Damon was deathly still. I leaned back and looked at him.

"Damon?" I asked, needing to know where he was in his head.

"Do I need to slap him? Can I slap him?" Hunter asked me.

I don't know why he felt he needed my permission. He had never pulled his punches with us before.

Damon groaned suddenly, taking a massive shuddering breath.

"No, no slapping," he said to Hunter, who pouted like a kid who'd been denied a frosted cupcake with sprinkles.

"This is a good thing, Damon," Leif said. His tone was hushed, like he didn't want to spook him.

"I know. It was just a shock to hear someone address me as Prime Alpha. Maia said the word like she was reading it from a book. It almost felt like she was talking about someone else."

"Nick addressing me like that so casually was weird and overwhelming. That shit just got real, and it's going to take a bit to adjust to."

We all chuckled, and he relaxed more. Something felt like it was missing, though, and I realized it was Maia. Thinking about her made me remember what I had been doing when they all walked in, and I felt myself stiffen.

They all turned to look at me, and the day's tiredness swamped me. My eyes hurt, and my head ached. I'd been sitting in this darkened room obsessively staring at computer screens all day, but I hadn't been able to turn away.

What I had found chilled me to the bone.

"Tell us," Damon said, reading me perfectly.

"I don't know if I want to," I said honestly, "but I know I need to."

"Is it that bad?" Leif asked, finally reaching for me and taking my hand.

"Worse. Take a look." I knew I could only say so much. Some of this they needed to see for themselves.

I let them all go reluctantly and returned to my desk. Hunter and Leif dragged over chairs. Hunter sat backward in a way that made me smile. He could never just sit normally. While Damon perched himself on the edge of my desk.

"First off, I briefly checked out Maia's brothers. Ben is still running the farm, but it wasn't doing so well even before the Crash. There's not a lot we can do about him right now."

Hunter had told us what Maia had revealed to him briefly about her younger brother the night before. We had all wondered how she ended up at the Palace and wanted to know more. He was on the list of people we would hunt to protect and avenge Maia, but he wasn't a priority right now. Every time Maia mentioned something about her past, and the guys looked at me; I added a name to it.

"Sam is a ghost. From my quick search, it's like he never existed. I'm going to have to spend some serious time trying to unravel that mystery another day." The guys just nodded in understanding and didn't push it.

"Is that the Omega Palace?" Damon asked, pointing to the closest of the six screens I had running.

"Yeah," I sighed. "It's a live feed."

I'd start with what was going on at the Palace. I needed to work my way up to Maia.

The Omega Palace had been easy to hack. They had upped their security sometime recently. Probably due to all the shady shit they were up to. I had hacked them before when Damon was visiting, and I'd left a back door open in case I needed to do it again. It seemed nobody had found it.

At the time, I'd wanted to track him through their internal cameras when Ronan started causing him trouble, having a bad feeling about it. I had never looked at anything else while there. I just followed Damon's movements. That was a mistake I'd have to live with for the rest of my life.

"The Palace is way more than it appears," I started. "They have long-standing ties to the military. Some documents suggest they knew from military sources that something was coming. They just didn't know when or how bad."

"Are you suggesting the military might be behind the Crash?" Damon asked.

"Yes, does that surprise you?" It shouldn't. There was a reason we had retired early, as had Dave. The military's corruption was rife, and too many of our orders had been questionable.

"It would explain why they haven't mobilized to help the people," Leif said.

I turned to the satellite feed of the compound.

"A military unit has barricaded themselves into the Palace. It wasn't just Ronan and civilian alphas that turned up at the gates the day Maia fled."

They had a lot of trucks and equipment, some of which appeared to be solar panels, but most were lying around like they weren't quite sure what to do with them. I pointed it all out to the guys.

"Shit. How many?" Damon asked. I could feel his anger through the bond. None of us had wanted to join the military, but we had hoped that by doing so, we could help people. Seeing members of the military hiding out now, instead of protecting the community like they were supposed to, made me rage.

"I've been watching them on and off all day. The best I can tell, there are maybe half a dozen civilian alphas and three dozen military personnel. The military is an even mix of alphas and betas. That's assuming there aren't any out on patrol or a mission today."

"Where are all the omegas?' Hunter asked with a chill in his voice. Hunter didn't get loud when he got angry, he got scary quiet. He was sitting as still as a statue right now, barely breathing. All his humor was gone.

I showed them some of the other feeds from inside.

"They have all of the younger omegas sequestered away. Some of the older omegas are working in the kitchen, but I think they're rationing food to the omegas.

"There's a huge truck of food parked out front, and I saw a bunch of alphas come back earlier with more supplies. They were only gone an hour or two, so I think they're raiding the surrounding villages for the time being to supplement what they have.

"They're not set up to survive long-term without more resources, especially once winter arrives. It's like they thought this would be over in a few days or weeks. I'm afraid of what they'll do when they start running out of options."

"You think they'll start trading omegas?" Damon asked, death riding his voice.

I clenched my jaw, hesitant to say it, but it was what I was thinking. "Possibly, we've seen it happen in warzones before."

"Shit, shit," Hunter cursed, getting up and pacing in the small space. He knew we couldn't leave all those omegas at risk, but we didn't have the numbers against so many alphas.

"It gets worse," I warned.

"I found Luke Fischer's farm, and it's not too far. I've written down directions, but it's not going to help us right now." I pulled up a recording from earlier and showed the guys on one of the screens.

"I found Maia's friends. They're still hiding out in the library at the Omega Palace. There are no cameras in there, but they snuck some food from the omegas in the kitchen earlier."

"They seem to have evaded notice so far. I don't know how, but they either don't want to leave or can't figure out a way to escape the Palace without notice."

Hunter got up to peer closer at the screen. I knew he was committing what he could see of Maia's two friends to memory, not just their features but how they moved and their mannerisms.

The guys were all quiet for a moment. They knew what it meant. We had to rescue them. Damon stopped pacing and turned to me.

"None of that is good, and we're going to have to figure out a plan, but it doesn't explain your emotions today, Max. You were horrified. What aren't you telling us?"

It was usually me being blunt and direct when the guys were avoiding something, it was weird to have the tables turned. I took a deep breath. Here comes the hard part.

"They have reams of data and files on Maia. Smaller ones on all the other omegas, but they have been studying Maia closely for years."

"They ran a blood test on Maia the day they took her. They have markers pinpointed, but I don't know what they're for."

"They have years of video of Maia resisting alphas trying to dominate her. Then the disciplining after when they tried to break her. Just like she said."

"I didn't watch them all. I couldn't. I only watched enough to see what the videos were. One almost made me vomit, and there are hundreds of them."

"I..." I took a deep, shaky breath, and each of the guys reached a hand out to me. Cold fury etched into the lines of their faces.

"She never gave in. She fought every time. The alphas bark at her, and you can see the strain on her body in the way it shakes. Her body wants to comply, but she refuses with sheer will. It looks painful. She's sweating and groaning, but the fierceness, the determination in her eyes. It's palpable, even through a screen.

"In every awful, brutal attempt to dominate her and dehumanize her, she stands firm and holds to herself. It's sickening. But she's fucking magnificent, even looking half destroyed. It drives the alphas feral.

"Each attempt to dominate her has a file. There are a lot of different names at first, but then it's Ronan every time."

Watching Ronan try over and over to dominate her, his escalating psychosis and obsession, had left me feeling destroyed, and I knew the guys would be picking up on it, as they had been all afternoon.

Leif got up abruptly and punched the wall, putting his fist right through it. I could feel his rage through our bond. I didn't tell him off. I'd come close to doing the same myself, but watching my gentle giant do it had me rattled.

"I want names," Damon growled. He was so still he almost looked carved from stone, and he had dropped his hand from my arm to clench his fists hard.

Hunter reached over and grabbed one of Damon's hands, rubbing the back in what I'm sure was supposed to be a calm and reassuring way but it looked more like he was trying to rub off an instant win scratchie. None of us was calm.

"I already added them to the list," I said.

"I have no idea how much money Ronan spent, but his attempts became more frequent and unhinged, and the attempts to break her became more extreme. I think he was funding it all by the end."

"It looks like they were trying to break her using negative reinforcement type punishments, a type of behavior modification training. Every time she refused to submit to a bark, she would have things taken away or something bad would happen."

"They were hoping her mind would eventually associate resisting with negative consequences, and she'd start complying. They initially used light forms of torture like isolation and starvation and analyzed the results."

I gripped my hands tightly to try and stop them from shaking and tried to breathe shallowly as the guys' scents all darkened.

"But then, more recently, they started using more extreme and physical methods like tying her down, and sound torture. They never hit her but they were using military torture techniques, guys, to break her mind. The kind we always refused to use."

"I'd heard rumors the Palace conditioned and brainwashed young omegas rather than trained them, but by using positive reinforcement. This is beyond anything we've ever heard being done to an omega. They seem to have escalated their tactics with Maia."

I rubbed my chest, feeling the echoes of her terror I'd seen on the screen.

"I have no idea how she survived for so long. She withstood it for years. She's tougher than all of us combined. I don't know if any of us would have lasted as long," I said honestly.

Hunter dropped his head into his hands like he didn't know how much more he could hear, but hearing about it was nothing compared to what Maia had lived.

They had tried to take something vital from her, her sense of self, and although she had hidden it for years, she had held fast to it in the end.

"I don't know what they want with her, but there's something about her that's unlike the others. At first, I thought it was because she was so much older when she arrived, and they had to work harder to break her. Looking at all the blood tests, I think it's more than that."

'Strangely, from what she said about fear and pain keeping her omega scent at bay, I think maybe what they were doing to her was helping her resist and hide her true abilities. It's fucked up, but I don't think they understood how her resistance worked at all.

"I knew she was special from the start, but the way she was able to claim me and link Leif and me. She's different, and they either suspect or know something about her. I need more time to figure it out."

I would be eternally grateful that Leif had convinced her to stay, that he had taken her under his protection that first night and she had let him. From what I could see of her treatment by alphas at the Palace, I wasn't surprised she had run from us initially.

"I won't show you the videos or data without talking to Maia first, though."

"What videos and data?" Maia asked calmly from behind us, and we all spun around, shocked.

Thirty-One

Goosebumps broke out over my skin as all the guys stared at me.

I heard Lexie speak quietly from the doorway like she could sense the sudden tension. "We knocked, but no one answered. Maia said she could feel your distress, so we opened the door. It wasn't locked."

She sounded almost apologetic.

"I'll go," Lexie said softly like she didn't want to intrude.

"No," I said, waving her in. "You're family. I have no secrets from you, Lexie."

"Lock the door," Damon said without looking at her, not taking his eyes off me for a second.

I heard the door shut, and the lock click in place, and then Lexie took a few steps into the room, but I hadn't taken my eyes off Max.

"What did you see?" I asked Max. I was proud my voice stayed even.

Max stepped up but didn't touch me and told me what he had found. I could see the truth in his eyes. They were tortured.

I closed my eyes and dropped my head. I couldn't look at him for my next question. With my eyes closed, I could scent all my guys even stronger. Their scents had sharpened to create a heady, potent mix, with electricity crackling through it.

"Does it change how you feel about me?"

"Yes," he answered. At least he was honest with me, but it felt like my heart was running through a paper shredder.

I went to step away. All I could sense from Max in the bond was turmoil, but I felt him caress my cheek so softly, and I paused.

He lifted my head gently with his calloused hand. The thought that it might be the last time he touched me almost broke me. After everything I had survived, that would bring me to my knees. I couldn't go back to a life without their touch.

"Maia, after watching some of that, I realized how strong you are. I'm so fucking humbled that you chose to claim me."

"You're a warrior, like us. Forged in fire." His eyes were burning into me with a rare intensity from my easy-going beta.

"I'm amazed that you were brave enough to let us in. We don't deserve you. I will worship at your feet for as long as you'll let me, and if you ever banish me, I'll worship you from afar."

Hunter, Leif, and Damon all got up and surrounded Max and me, hugging us tightly. I took a deep breath, letting my fear go. I knew that if Max still cared for me after seeing the extent of my damage, he would care for me through anything. So would the others.

"Why are you all here?" I deflected, not wanting them to ask questions about what Max had seen.

"We could feel Max's emotions, and all turned up one by one when we couldn't stay away anymore, just like you did right now. We haven't been here long," Leif said quietly. I could feel a slight tremor in his body that showed his emotions were running high.

"Do you mind if we watch some of the videos and read the reports, Maia? We won't if you say no, but I'd like to know what we're up against," Damon asked.

I turned my head to look him in the eye, feeling conflicted, even though I was surrounded by their warmth and strength.

"What's in those videos could give us clues about why they were watching you so closely and why they were trying so hard to break you. I think there's more going on than just Ronan becoming obsessed with you," Damon explained, watching me earnestly.

I thought about it for a moment, and they let me quietly figure myself out, sending me reassurance through the bond. I knew if I said no, they would honor it and figure out another way to get the information they needed.

I nodded slowly. "If you think it would help, I'm okay with it. But I lived it. I don't need to see."

I waited for a beat before I asked. "Why are you sitting over there like a weirdo, Lexie? Get in here." I managed to wriggle an arm out between hard bodies and wave her over.

She squealed and said, "Really?"

"Yes," all the guys yelled at once. Hunter coughed out a "weirdo," then smirked at her.

Lexie dived into the mix, and we all stood for a few minutes, enjoying the group connection. Until Lexie muttered, "This is lovely, but it stinks in here."

We all laughed and broke apart. I was drawn to their scents, as they were to mine, but I got that it could be overpowering to other people, especially betas.

Leif and Lexie squished onto the couch together. She picked up his hand, which looked red and angry, then glanced at a hole in the wall and looked back at him in question. He just shrugged, taking a leaf out of my book.

"Okay, moving on. We need an extraction plan," Hunter said. He shook his hands out like he was physically trying to shake off the heaviness and focus.

"Extraction plan for who?" I asked. The change in the topic had made my head spin a little, and I wasn't keeping up.

"Max found your friends," Leif said, his eyes shining with pride.

"They're still at the Palace, with the military." Damon said with a grim tone and a determined set to his shoulders.

Well, shit. "When can we get them?" I was almost scared to ask. Could they even get them out?

The guys all looked at each other and said, "Tonight."

They jumped into action, and Lexie and I scampered to get out of their way. We headed to Lexie's storage container to pull some things together we thought Ava and Cary might need, then set up a guest cabin near ours.

I didn't know whether to be excited or terrified. I was a giant, raw bundle of both, with a side of nausea, like an overshaken, fruity cocktail. The next few hours were excruciating.

Later that night, I sat on a chair next to Max, watching his hands fly over his keyboard and work his screens like a magician. Lexie had opted to go back to her cabin. She couldn't stand to watch, but I couldn't stay away. I needed at least one of my guys close while the others were all in a dangerous situation.

Seeing Max in his element, all intense focus while wearing hot as fuck, thick, black rim glasses, had built a simmering need in me. I was fantasizing about riding his dick while he continued to work. It would be naughty and wanton, and just the idea had my lady bits sizzling.

He was in mission mode, though, so I was trying to be a good girl and not make a sound while we watched the guys surveil the Palace.

Damon had asked me if I wanted to go with them in an effort not to treat me like a princess, but I could tell they were worried about exposing me to Ronan.

Honestly, I knew how to be stealthy and keep to the shadows, skills I had learned out of necessity. I appreciated the offer, but I was nowhere near the level of the guys. I knew I would only distract them and hold them back, potentially putting any chance of extraction at risk tonight if they found an opening.

Watching them on the satellite feeds, I knew I had made the right call to stay with Max. Hunter was a ghost I could barely track. Even Leif, as big as he was, showed a level of stealth I could only dream about.

Damon was a deadly predator on the hunt. His every movement was precise and controlled, with no unnecessary energy use. He had the scent of his prey and was entirely focused on it. He was like a jungle cat, stalking its quarry through the underbrush.

I was amazed Max could follow them so closely from the satellites. I had no idea technology was that good. Or maybe Max was just that good.

We had no audio, but the guys were in silent mode anyway. Using hand signals I couldn't begin to understand. They all seemed to react with barely a glance. They were a team, focused and unified.

I had naively thought they would go on foot and be gone for days, but they had trotted out the work ute, as Damon called it. It was his baby and was a monster of a vehicle.

It was a dual cab with an open tray on the back. It was also all black, with tinted windows and black rims, so it all but disappeared into the night when the lights weren't on. It was fully electric, so it ran silently and had enough range to make it to the Palace and back.

I had already nicknamed it the ghost truck. I kind of wanted one for myself.

The security at the Palace was sloppy, at best, tonight. They didn't appear to expect anyone to challenge or attempt to infiltrate them with so many alphas on site. The alphas were busy drinking in the main hall and harassing omegas, Ronan included, and there were only a few betas on patrol.

Luckily, the Palace was within range of the amplified CB radio Damon had in his truck, and Max could tell him what was happening inside.

Damon had gone radio silent when he decided it was too good an opportunity to pass up, and they had gone in.

Max had told me he could do simple things, like crash their security if something went wrong, but it would leave us blind as well. It would also betray that we could access their system remotely, and they would likely find a way to shut us down permanently.

So, for now, we could only watch.

The guys started out checking the equipment abandoned outside.

They stopped and messed with a hulking vehicle that I couldn't make out well. I couldn't tell what they were doing. "Hot damn, that looks like a PMV. I hope the guys are disabling it somehow."

I poked him in the ribs, and he jumped. "What's a PMV?"

"Sorry, it's a Protected Mobility Vehicle. It gets troops into the field and can operate alone for up to three days before needing re-supply. It's armored and has a gun turret. We don't want it turning up at our gates."

I cringed and let him focus back on the screens. The guys finished whatever they were doing and headed inside. We lost sight of them. Max had shown them where all the blind spots were, and they used them to their advantage.

The wait was agonizing. I could feel cold sweat running down my back, and my stomach was in knots. I'm pretty sure Max was grinding his teeth.

As soon as the guys went dark, I felt Max's stress levels surge, and he became hyper-focused. I could feel his frustration at not being there to back up his guys.

Nick was here with us, watching the farm security feeds while we focussed on the Palace. He kept sneaking furtive glances at us and our screens, though. The tension was impossible not to pick up, even for a beta.

Where the hell were they? The library complex didn't have cameras, which is how I had managed to hide so much, but we should have seen something by now. They were taking way too long.

I had a death grip on the arms of my chair, and Max was flicking a pen between his fingers in agitation, swiveling his gaze through all six monitors obsessively.

Finally, Damon came into view from the darkness on one of the external cameras. Max was confident no one else was watching the feeds right now. He monitored the feed outside their security room all day, and no one had gone in or out. I held my breath anyway, waiting for alarms to sound.

Damon was followed closely by a man and a woman, who could only be Cary and Ava. They sprinted for the fence, and Damon helped them over before they raced for the van parked just out of camera range.

I breathed a small sigh of relief, but where were Leif and Hunter? I started to tap my hand furiously on my leg. My heart was pounding so hard it felt like it was going to punch through my chest.

Max looked at me, startled, then gave me a crooked smile and pulled me into his lap. I don't think he was used to having someone hovering over him while he worked, but I couldn't back off.

"They'll be fine." He sounded calm and almost convinced me, but he was squeezing the life out of my hand.

We both turned back to the screen as two more figures emerged from the side of the building, moving much slower. One was carrying a heavy bag. It looked like Hunter, but the outline of what I assumed was Leif was misshapen. There was something big slung over his back, making him hunch forward.

"What the hell is he carrying?" Max muttered, peering closely at the screen like the pixels would suddenly improve, and he could see clearly if only he got close enough.

"He looks like a giant turtle," I said, twisting my head from side to side, trying to make sense of the image.

"Is that a chair?" Nick asked. He had leaned over and was watching our screens.

"Oh shit, they wouldn't," I breathed out, then started laughing.

"Is it a chair? We have plenty of chairs. Why would they take a chair?" Max asked, his brow crinkled as he looked at me.

"I think it's my chair from the library. I was talking to Hunter about objects that hold meaning to us. I told him I missed my chair." I shook my head. "Those idiots!"

Nick looked shocked that the guys would risk their life for a chair, but Max nodded as if he got it.

"They're our idiots, though," he smiled affectionately at the screen.

They made it to the PMV they had been messing with earlier, opening the doors and putting the chair and bag inside. Hunter raced to the front and hopped in while Leif ran silently towards the gate, keeping to the shadows.

What the hell were they doing? It was supposed to be a stealth mission.

I was hardly breathing, waiting for flashes of gunfire from the guards at the gate or someone else to dash out of the building.

Damon approached the gate from the other side, and my heart clenched. I leaned over and put my arms around Max, clinging to him.

Leif suddenly leaped out of the shadows, taking one guard to the ground with a vicious punch before he even saw him. He grabbed the guard's head when he went limp and gently lowered him to the ground.

The other guard whirled toward Leif, gun raised, but Damon dropped to the ground behind him and rendered him unconscious with some kind of ninja pressure point hold to his neck. It all happened so fast that it was mostly a blur. My guys were deadly. Was it wrong that it turned me on?

"Are they dead?" I whispered to Max.

"No. Damon and Leif won't kill indiscriminately, and there was no reason to kill the guards. They just needed them neutralized. The guy Leif hit will have a wicked headache in the morning, though."

Damon sent Hunter some kind of signal, and he powered up the vehicle, driving it through the gate that the guys opened and closed for him, securing it behind him. I knew they wouldn't want to leave the other omegas vulnerable. It was the same reason they hadn't touched any food in the truck.

We checked all the feeds. Nobody followed them or even seemed to notice they had been there. The party continued as if nothing had happened.

The relief felt like a sack of potatoes had lifted off my chest. I could breathe again. My guys were on their way home to me.

I turned to Max and looked him up and down. "The girls were right."

"About?" He looked adorably confused.

I shifted in his lap slightly so I could run my fingers through his hair, messing it up, then ran my finger along the edge of his glasses. I leaned in close, pressing my breasts against his chest, and whispered in his ear.

"How sexy these glasses are on you."

Max in glasses went from hot to smoking hot. He had the sexy nerd look down pat.

I ran my hand down into the opening of his button-up shirt, and his breathing picked up speed.

I shifted my mouth from his ear to his neck, taking a deep lungful of his natural, musky scent that still carried a hint of both Leif and me, chocolate oranges. I moaned slightly and gave my mate mark on his neck the tiniest lick with the tip of my tongue.

He shivered almost violently, and I felt him instantly harden under my thigh. I tried desperately not to moan louder as my scent flared hot and fierce in the room. I squirmed on his lap. I was impossibly wet and felt suddenly empty inside like I needed to be filled.

One lick of his mate mark had me completely and instantly undone.

"Max," I begged on a low moan.

"Maia, why don't we take a break and head back to wait for the guys at the house?" he said as he ran his hand up and down my bare leg, inching a finger under my dress.

"Can't, too far," I all but growled at him. I was so turned on I couldn't even form complete sentences. I started undoing his shirt as I licked and sucked at his neck, and I felt him thrust into my thigh subtly, then slide me up his lap instinctively until my ass was grinding on his hard cock.

"Uh, Nick, how about you take a break? Maybe take the laptop to your place and watch the local feeds from there until the guys return?"

Nick grabbed the laptop and bolted out the door like the building was burning down. I had completely forgotten he was here.

"Maia, sweetheart, we need to slow down, get somewhere more private."

"No, need you here." I desperately wanted to mess up his tidy office.

I bit down lightly over his mate mark, and he groaned long and low, panting hard suddenly, and a light sweat trickled down his chest. It was like an on-button. His mate mark seemed to be incredibly sensitive. Good to know.

"Fuck, it feels like you're licking my dick when you do that. Like it's directly connected."

I had his shirt half off and ripped the other buttons off with a strength I didn't know I had. He pulled it off his arms while I licked his neck and chest like he was candy.

He was broad and muscled across his chest and narrow in the waist, like a swimmer. I wanted to taste every muscle, every inch of skin. I dragged my lips across his chest until I reached his tattoo. I kissed it lightly, smiling briefly, remembering the night he told me about it and how badly I had wanted to kiss it then.

I remembered how close I had felt to him as he told me what it meant to him and how it resonated with me.

A burst of need hit me at that moment that was so intense it left me panting and dizzy.

I pivoted on his lap, so I could straddle him and ground down on him hard, moaning brokenly. He tasted so damn good, but I needed more. Now.

My clothes suddenly felt itchy and too tight. I shrugged off the long cardigan I had thrown over my dress when it cooled down earlier this evening.

Max instantly started undoing the buttons down the front of my dress as I ground on him, leaning up to kiss me firmly, biting my lip, and then kissing the delicious sting better.

"Max," I urged, wanting him to move quicker before I ripped my dress off myself.

He finally got it all undone and tugged it down my arms, so I was straddling him in just my underwear and bra. He ran his hands back up my arms and down my chest to cup my breasts in his hands.

I thrust my chest into his hands, needing more. He was being too gentle. It was a shadow of what I needed. I ground down on him harder, feeling his stiff cock underneath me through the rough fabric of his jeans. He groaned louder before unsnapping my bra and slipping it off my arms.

He was breathing hard as he stared down at my breasts. I leaned back slightly so he could get a better view. I felt wanton and desired, utterly unashamed of my body. For the first time in my life, I wanted to be seen.

He leaned down to lightly and reverently lick a breast, too lightly.

I thrust my chest up into his mouth, chasing his heat. He leaned me back further and scooted us closer to the desk so I could rest my elbows, thrusting my chest higher and wrapping my legs around him for support.

Yes, this was almost what I had imagined earlier. Only his dick had been deep inside me.

I started grinding on him furiously as he licked and sucked each breast, giving them equal attention, biting each lightly and then licking the sting like he had my lips.

It was driving me insane. I didn't want Max to think about what he was doing. I wanted him as wild for me as I was for him.

I pushed up off the desk and jumped off his lap suddenly. Pushing the keyboard aside as I sat on his desk, spreading my legs wide.

"Fuck me, Max," I pleaded. I wasn't above begging at this point. His eyes were dark, and his glasses were starting to fog, so he took them off.

"I'm not letting you rush this, Maia. I'm going to enjoy devouring you this time."

He grabbed my underwear, pulling it down my hips as I pushed up slightly to help him before he dragged them down my legs. My pussy was wet and clenching on nothing as he spread my legs wide again.

He started to kiss back up my legs again, and I almost lost my mind. Each kiss and lick felt like a heated promise connected directly to my core. I was aching for him.

Feeling his desire feeding back to me through our bond as he kissed up my legs only intensified my need.

I tried to slide myself forward to the edge of the desk, trying to hurry him, but he clenched my thighs hard, keeping me in place.

"I've got you, Maia. Just let me taste you first."

He turned his head too slowly for my liking. The anticipation of his hot mouth on my core was killing me. I was thrusting against his hard hands, moaning wantonly, as my slick started.

He groaned long and low when his tongue connected with my folds, parting them gently.

"That's what I wanted. You taste so fucking good," Max said, his voice more gravelly than I had ever heard it. I could feel his intense satisfaction as he tasted my slick.

He started licking and sucking me with the lightest touch, teasing me, and I couldn't stand it. It was heaven. His hot tongue was sending sparks washing through me. I needed to be filled in a way that felt almost feral.

I had lost all sense of my surroundings. Only Max's hands, mouth, and body existed at this moment.

"Max, please, please, I need you," I begged.

He sensed my desperation and straightened after one last, long lick up my core that had my eyes closing and my legs clenching with need.

He popped the button on his jeans and slowly drew down his zipper with an arrogance I would have imagined from Hunter instead of Max. This was a side of Max I hadn't seen before, or maybe hadn't existed before I bit him and made him feel complete.

"Is this what you want?" he asked as he pulled his jeans down enough to let his long, hard cock spring free. His Jacob's Ladder shone in the low light of the room.

I remember wanting to lick it the last time I saw it, and I felt the same need now, but I was too far gone. One day. Very soon.

"Yes, please, Max." I spread my legs as wide as possible, giving him plenty of room to move between them. I propped one leg up on the curve of his desk, so I was wide open to him.

"Fuck," he swore as he palmed his length before taking a step forward. 'You beg so sweetly, Maia. I can't deny you anything.'

He rubbed his dick over my entrance briefly, getting it nice and wet, and I groaned at the sensation so close to where I needed it.

I ground against him before he held my thighs in place again and slowly fed his dick into me. I couldn't move, couldn't thrust, and it made the sensation more intense as I had to stay still and take it at his slow, agonizing pace.

He slid in slowly until he bottomed out, his pupils dilated in contradiction to his tight control.

"I'm going to fuck you now, Maia, just like you asked." My sexy nerd had a dark side, and I was here for it.

I didn't have time to respond before he pulled out and thrust into me hard. I cried out as he did it again and again, setting a firm brisk pace that built with each thrust.

His grip on my thighs still immobilized me, but I was writhing my upper body, my tits bouncing, and his gaze was devouring them.

His pace increased rapidly now, and I could feel my core clench around him as my orgasm built. A wildfire was burning in my veins, and I was so close to immolation.

His thrusts became erratic, and he let go of my thighs, gripping my ass, lifting me, and throwing my legs over his shoulders.

His firm and confident handling of my body had my omega in raptures.

The new position changed the angle and deepened his thrusts so that he hit a sensitive nerve every time, making my entire body buzz. I was entirely at his mercy, unable to move without falling, barely able to maintain my grip on the table while he lifted me and thrust into me wildly.

All the monitors and equipment were shaking, and I heard something crash as I yelled, "Yes, yes, Max, fuck, me, yes," in a litany that spurred him on until he thrust so hard I saw light burst behind my eyes and my whole body ignited.

The sensation was so overwhelming I almost cried in relief as he followed me into his orgasm, groaning hard and repeating my name like a pagan prayer.

I could feel him spurting hotly, deep inside me as he ground against me, wringing every ounce of sensation from our bodies.

I dropped my legs and wrapped them back around his waist as he picked me up fully. He wrapped my arms around his neck instead and fell back into his computer chair.

"Fuck, what are you doing to me?" he panted. "The guys are never going to let me live this down if they find out. I'm usually so paranoid about keeping this place clean and strictly business. I don't even let the guys online game in here."

I chuckled. "Well, if it makes you feel better, I take what we just did very seriously."

He smiled affectionately at me, but whatever he was about to say was interrupted by a knock at the door. We both stilled as we realized neither of us had locked it when Nick escaped.

Thirty-Two

"**N**obody's here. Come back again later." Max raised an eyebrow at me, and I shrugged. It was worth a shot.

"Nice try, pussycat," I heard Hunter reply as the door opened and closed again quickly.

Max spun his chair sideways to hide me from the view of the door while I clutched myself to him, not sure who might be with Hunter, and I got the giggles.

"Shit, don't giggle while my dick's in you, Maia. You'll get me hard again."

"Well, well, what have we here? Breaking a few rules, are we, Mr. No Messing Around In the Security Office?"

Max sighed. I looked up and over the back of the chair at Hunter, who winked at me.

"Hi, pussycat, are you having fun?"

I just nodded at him, grinning like a fool. I wanted to run to him and jump him, but I was in an awkward position, still sitting on Max's slowly softening dick.

"Do you know how hard it is to hold a conversation with strangers and drive a car while I can feel you two getting frisky through the bond?" Hunter said as he sat casually on the edge of Nick's desk, legs spread wide like he was ready for a show.

"Shit, sorry. I didn't even think about that," Max called out over his shoulder.

"I figured, but I hope you're done because I have some friends of Maia's here who insist on seeing her before they'll believe she's here, unharmed by us big, bad alphas."

"Should I bring them in, so they can see you're okay, Maia?"

"Shit, Hunter, why didn't you say sooner?"

"Sorry, I was a little distracted by the Eau De Maia Just Got Fucked, which made my already uncomfortably hard dick into a battering ram the second I opened the door."

"Then there was this view of your bare legs peeking out from behind that chair you're straddling Max on,' he gestured towards me, swirling his finger around in my direction. 'It's like a naughty peekaboo show giving me all kinds of ideas."

I stood brazenly, sliding off Max, and Hunter's eyes widened.

"Now we're talking. On second thought, I'm telling your friends to fuck off for a while." His eyes devoured me, and he adjusted the impressive bulge in his pants.

Max jumped up and started grabbing clothes, passing me my dress and bra.

"Nope, sorry, the show's over. You missed it. Maybe you shouldn't be so tardy next time and get home quicker," Max teased.

I pointed to my underwear lying by Hunter's feet. "Can you throw me those, please?"

He picked them up and stuffed them in his back pocket, shaking his head.

"Nope, if I don't get to watch the show, I'm at least keeping a souvenir."

Crap, if these guys kept ripping or stealing my underwear, I would have to revisit Lexie's storage container before the week was out, and I didn't want to explain to her why.

"Sure," I shrugged and feigned nonchalance. "If you're okay with me going outside to talk to a hot, male omega with no underwear on, I'm cool too."

Max laughed out loud as Hunter scrambled to grab my underwear out of his pocket and threw it to me. I winked at him as I ducked into the bathroom for a quick clean-up.

"Fine, but you owe me a pair of underwear," he called after me.

I came back out a minute later, running my hands through my hair, trying to get it under control and reduce the just fucked look I was rocking.

"Did you leave them alone out there?" I asked Hunter.

"No. Amos, one of the young security cadets, came down with me. He's watching over them in the kitchen, getting them something to eat."

"Where's Leif and Damon?" Max asked as he came out of the bathroom after ducking in quickly.

"Leif stayed up at the gate. Ava and Cary seemed nervous about having all three of us close, and he wanted to brief Dave. Dave was waiting for us up there in case trouble followed us home. They'll stay there until Amos gets back to make sure we weren't followed."

"Damon has gone to get Lexie and the supplies for your friends."

"I don't think either of them has had a decent wash lately. Damon figured they'd appreciate a change of clothes after a hot shower."

That's my Damon, always protecting people and taking care of them.

"Okay, let's do this then," I motioned towards the door.

"Aren't you forgetting something?" Hunter asked, from where he was still propped against the second security desk. All cocky arrogance and charm, a lethal combination.

When I just shrugged and shook my head at the same time, he crooked his finger at me. When I got close, he grabbed me and pulled me into him, taking a deep breath.

"This room is saturated with your scent, but there's nothing like the feel of you pressed against me while I breathe you in. Did you even miss me while I was out risking my life to save your friends? I'm feeling kind of insecure here."

"Hunter, if you want a kiss, you never have to ask."

"Good to know," he said as he pulled me flush against him and ravaged me with a kiss worthy of a standing ovation. He was all tongue, heat, and need. He stroked the inside of my mouth the way he had stroked between my legs the other night.

"Smooth bro, real smooth," Max chuckled from behind me.

Hunter shrugged, letting me go. Max instantly grabbed my hand, leading me away while I was a little dazed.

"It worked," Hunter said, his cheeky smirk back on his face.

I had missed him. I'd missed all of them in a way that had torn at my insides. I hadn't wanted to say anything, but it had felt like pieces of me had broken off and left jagged holes when they drove out those gates without me. I didn't like it and wasn't ready for a repeat.

We headed to the kitchen, and Ava launched herself at me the minute I walked through. Cary stood up from where he'd been sitting on a stool, watching Hunter warily.

It seemed Hunter hadn't worked his charm on Cary yet. I wasn't that surprised. Cary was a tough nut to crack. Like macadamia, encased in armor.

"Maia, thank god, I've been so worried."

I let go of Max's hand and hugged her tightly to me. After having had so little human touch for so many years, I would never knock back a hug.

"Are you okay?" she whispered in my ear.

"Yeah, more than okay. Great, actually."

She pulled back and looked at me closely. When she saw the smile on my face and my relaxed posture, she relaxed too. I noticed she was wearing her bluebird bracelet again. I had given it to the guys with strict instructions not to lose it in the hopes that if they saw her, it would convince her to go with them.

"You're safe here, both of you, for now," I looked at Cary to make sure he knew he was included in that. He was now standing warily against the wall, watching all the exits with his arms crossed and his hood over his head, all brooding, dark protector. He lifted his chin at me briefly in acknowledgment.

I didn't approach him directly for fear of setting off my guys.

"Nobody here will hurt you, and we have security to keep out anyone who wants to try."

"I can't believe you have electricity and food here. How the hell did you find this place?" Ava asked.

"That's a story for tomorrow. For now, we'll get you some showers, a change of clothes, and a comfy bed. Okay?"

Ava and Cary looked at each other, and Ava nodded. "That sounds good."

Damon, Lexie, and Bear walked through the door. Lexie made a beeline for Ava while I turned and shot over to Damon. I rose on my toes to wrap him up in a fierce hug and kiss him soundly. He growled and pulled me in tight against his body.

"Missed you," I whispered into his ear as we broke for air.

He smiled with a dark possessiveness but took my hands, spun me around to face Ava again, and hugged me from behind. I figured Damon wasn't ready to let me go just yet but he didn't want to put on a show in front of my friends. I felt him lean down and take a deep breath of my scent as he pressed up behind me.

I wiggled against him, and he held me still with a rough chuckle.

Ava was distracted by Lexie approaching. Her eyes were wide and fixed on Bear, but Cary watched everyone with a guarded focus like he was just waiting for one of the alphas to pounce on Ava.

My guys kept a respectful distance from my friends but watched Cary and me just as closely.

"Hi, I'm Lexie. My brother is one of the alphas who rescued you, the big, hulking one who grunts a lot." She chuckled to herself, even though he wasn't here to hear the dig.

Bear ambled over to Cary and Ava, giving them a good sniff, and making Ava tremble as the giant dog got close. "Sorry about Bear. He needs to vet all newcomers. I won't say he's harmless. He's very protective of his tribe, which is pretty much all of us, but he's never attacked anyone without provocation."

"He's a great judge of character. You'll be fine if you have Maia's approval already." Bear finished his sniff fest, nudging Ava's leg with his big head until she gave him a cautious pat, then wandered over to me for scratches behind his ear, which I happily provided.

"I brought you some stuff for tonight, and we can figure out some more tomorrow." She handed them each a bag, and Ava thanked her before taking a peek inside.

Cary grabbed the bag without looking at it, nodding thanks to Lexie, but kept his focus firmly on Damon. Cary was too smart and watchful not to have noticed I had also been holding Max's hand when I walked in, and Max had two bite marks on his neck.

"Have you guys had enough to eat?" Lexie asked, seeming oblivious to the tension between the guys, but I knew she was just trying to keep things light and not cause waves.

Cary and Ava both nodded. "Okay, I'll take you to your cabin now, so you can get cleaned up and sleep."

"We're not staying with you, Maia?" Ava asked me, trying to hold back a massive yawn. She looked almost as exhausted as I did when I first arrived.

"Oh, uh, no. I'm staying with my friends, and all the bedrooms in our cabin are taken," I said. It sounded lame even to my ears.

Hunter didn't make it any easier when he scoffed and asked, "Friends?" Max punched him lightly on the shoulder for me.

Cary narrowed his eyes even further and Ava's widened. I reluctantly extricated myself from Damon and walked back to Ava, taking her hand before this situation spiraled.

"A lot has happened since I last saw you, and there's a lot to tell, but it's late, and everyone's tired. I'll explain everything to you in the morning, okay?"

Ava agreed readily, but Cary wasn't having it. "I'm not risking Ava's safety when something is happening here that you're not telling us."

I sighed. I had hoped to put this off until tomorrow. "Okay. Short version. Ava, Cary, I would like you to meet my mates, Damon, Hunter and Max. I also have a fourth mate, Leif, who you met earlier. The big grumpy one," I said as I winked at Lexie.

Ava's eyes widened further until they were huge in her face, like a cartoon character. It was almost comical. She squeezed my hand, but I didn't know if it was in support or shock.

Cary crossed his arms, glaring at the guys. "Explain."

"Look, like I said, it's a long story, but they aren't like any alphas I've ever met. They took me in when I was lost, exhausted, and half-starved. They asked me to stay, and they've done nothing but help and protect me."

"I promise you, I'm here by choice, and these are my true mates." I gestured at my guys. They were all standing straight and proud, watching me intently as I publicly claimed them.

"Are they your pack? Like in your book?" Ava asked quietly. I sucked in a breath, shocked.

"I read it while I was waiting for you to reappear sometimes. It was all about packs and mates, and I thought how beautiful the world would be if it were just like the book."

My eyes were misty as I nodded to her. "I felt the bond as soon as I met them, Ava."

She hugged me fiercely and whispered in my ear, "I'm so happy for you."

I looked at Cary. He was the one I needed to convince. He was rubbing his jaw like he was thinking hard. "Have they tried to claim you yet?"

"No," Damon growled in answer for me. "We're waiting for her to be ready. We would never force her to do anything she doesn't want."

"Maia claimed me, though," Max said, chest puffed and chin jutting proudly. Damon and Hunter looked at him, and I could see and feel their affection.

"Show off," Hunter teased him, laughing.

Cary looked curious at that. Then he turned to me and nodded as his tense posture relaxed. "We'll stay for now because I trust your instincts, Maia. You've always had a strong sense of self-preservation and good intuition about people."

"Not everyone," I sighed, thinking about my brother.

"Okay, then, let's get this welcome wagon moving." I grabbed Ava's hand and led her towards the door, knowing Cary would follow.

Ava explained on the way that they had stayed to try and grab intel for her uncle in the hopes he would help them rescue the rest of the omegas.

After we got them settled and walked back into our cabin, I eyed off my mattress longingly, but my curiosity wouldn't let me rest until I had more answers.

"So, did you guys get me a present?" I asked, with a cheeky little sass in my tone.

"We got you more than one." Leif said as he grabbed my hand and let me through the kitchen to a door I hadn't paid any attention to on the other side. I assumed it was a pantry or storeroom.

I lost my breath as I walked through. "How did you guys build my dream room?"

"It's Damon's bat cave, where he likes to hide from the world." Hunter said. Damon just rolled his eyes at him.

"It's just our study," Damon said, watching my amazement with a tender look.

It wasn't just a study. It was a room straight out of my fantasies. It had high ceilings and shelves filled with books lining the walls. There were wooden ladders to reach the upper levels. A wall of glass windows and a sliding door led out to a small deck with a view down to the river that let in the moonlight.

It also had old comfy chairs around a coffee table in the center that looked like they had all been rescued. They had stories to tell, these chairs. I imagined a lot of life had happened in and around them.

And there, sitting next to them, like it belonged, with a big bag next to it, was my chair.

I ran to it and jumped into its warm embrace. I looked up with tears in my eyes. It was the best present in the world, better than useless diamonds or sparkly things.

"You look good in here." Damon said roughly. "Like it was made for you."

Hunter walked around beside me and lifted the bag, unzipping it to show me the whole series of old books mine had come from. He had found them on the shelf and brought them all back for me.

My heart was so full.

"Max told us your book said alphas who want to claim an omega traditionally brought her courting gifts. These aren't much, we'll figure out something better, but it's a start." Hunter said, unusually serious for once.

"No, they're perfect. I don't need gifts, but if I could have asked for anything, it would have been these."

I stood up and grabbed his hand, reaching out for the others, and they all encircled me in the way I loved, touching and stroking me as we stood together in the moonlight. I could feel everything I wanted but couldn't yet say, reflected in our bond.

"These and maybe a PMV as my new wheels." I teased, and they all laughed.

Thirty-Three

I opened my eyes slowly the following morning, feeling cozy and warm. I was burrowed under soft blankets on the mattress in the living room. We'd crashed quickly last night when we eventually made it to bed.

I was snuggled between Damon and Hunter this time. I could get used to waking up surrounded by warm, muscled bodies.

I looked out the doors through the open curtains. I liked the way Leif opened them at night and how it let in the early morning light.

The world was only just waking up, so it was early. I looked behind me to see Max asleep on the couch, but Leif was missing. I could hear a shower running somewhere and decided that was a great idea.

I eased myself out of the pile of men and blankets and tiptoed up the stairs, following the sound. From what I could see from the top of the landing, there were four bedrooms with a fifth closed door at the end of the hall.

It was the first time I had been up here, so I took a peek into each door as I went. I could tell who each room belonged to by the scent.

Damon's was minimalist, with lots of solid timber furniture and few personal touches. He seemed to keep most of the stuff he cared about in the study. Hunter had said it was his retreat from the world. I was humbled that he would share it with me.

Hunter's room was a messy jumble, with an eclectic mix of keepsakes, old circus paraphernalia, and bawdy art that made me smile.

Max had a lot of photos stuck all over the wall behind his bed. Most were of the guys at different ages and in lots of places. I wanted to explore them in detail one day.

The last bedroom was Leif's, and he had a massive timber bed that looked handmade. I figured he needed it with his height and size. He had quite a few plants in his room, which surprised me. I'm not sure why, though. He was very nurturing.

He also had pictures on his wall that looked drawn by young kids. Many showed what looked like a giant playing with a bunch of little stick figures. Looking at them made my heart swell for this man.

I spied a box on his bedside table, with the lid half off and something green nestled inside. I stole over to have a peek, my curiosity overcoming propriety. I lifted the lid and found two dried green leaves and a white flower snuggled in tissue paper. I wasn't sure what they were, but they seemed to have some significance for him.

There were no bathrooms in any of the bedrooms. It seemed mine was the only one with an ensuite, and the guys all shared. There was only one door left at the end of the hall. It had to be the bathroom.

I stopped outside it, a little nervous all of a sudden.

Leif called out and startled me, "Are you coming in, or are you just snooping around out there?"

He must have caught my scent, or he could sense me through the bond.

I peeked through the bathroom door, and the sight was glorious. Leif was naked and standing with his arms crossed over his head, gripping the top of the glass shower frame while leaning slightly against it. The flex had all those muscles on top of muscles popping out, with rivulets of water mapping them slowly.

Fuck, yes. I loved that pose on Leif. I remember him doing it with my bed frame and his shirt riding up my first night here. I had imagined him naked then. I didn't have to imagine it now.

The shower glass framed him perfectly. He was all powerful muscle with a long, thick dick that was half hard already. I wanted to take a picture and keep it forever.

He looked at me in bemusement, and I realized I hadn't answered.

"Coming in?" I had no idea why there was a question in my tone. I was absolutely coming in.

"Good," he said as he turned around. I almost passed out. The view was just as glorious from behind. His ass was a work of art I would happily hang on my wall, or maybe Hunter's. It would fit right in with his other art.

I stripped off quickly. It was lucky the shower was oversized. It took up most of the room and was designed for multiple people, with four rain shower heads and hand showers on the walls. I don't think we'd fit inside a regular shower together.

It was all warm navy tiles, with timber cabinetry and black fittings, very masculine yet cozy, like showering in a hidden cave. I could seriously bliss out in here for hours.

He pulled me under the water of the showerhead he was already using, and it was the perfect temperature. He got me all wet before pulling out a bottle of shampoo and lathering it into my hair.

I was seriously in heaven. I thought the hair brushing was bliss, but this was even better. He gently kissed the back of my shoulder while he worked, like he couldn't help himself. Other than that, he was a perfect gentleman.

His dick had been half-hard when I first spotted him, but it had sprung to attention once he got his hands on me. He was ignoring his hard-on like a champ, though.

Once my hair was shampooed to his satisfaction, he rinsed it off before adding conditioner. I lost any coherent thought when he soaped up a sponge and started washing my body next. I wasn't sure what to make of it, and I tensed up a little.

"Don't overthink it, Maia. I just want to take care of you."

I had to admit, it felt strange at first, having someone wash me, but having the sponge and his hands run all over me felt decadent. I almost felt drugged from all the touch and the attention combined with the warm water and the soothing honey scent of the body wash.

I closed my eyes and breathed deeply as he finished washing me, trying just to enjoy having someone pamper me. He was paying a little more attention to particular areas, like my boobs, but I wasn't complaining.

When he finished, he rinsed me off, then shut off the water and grabbed a towel from a folded bundle next to the sink. He wrapped me in it, and I felt blissed out.

There was no way I was moving on my own. My body felt like it was made of playdough, all soft and malleable. He picked me up, chuckling as he did, and sat me on the sink as he grabbed another towel and thoroughly dried me.

He was sporting a tented towel, but he had made no move to seduce me since I'd entered the bathroom, and I'd practically gift-wrapped myself. I was confused.

I reached out tentatively to touch his chest as he started combing out my hair. I ran my fingers over him slowly, following the path the water had taken earlier, then leaned forward and kissed him over his heart while breathing in his comforting campfire and s'mores scent.

He breathed deeply and wrapped me up in a big hug. I leaned into him, happy to share this moment, but I needed to know if something was wrong.

"Don't you want me?" I could feel my hands against his chest shaking slightly. I'd never had a conversation like this with someone before.

He pulled back suddenly to look at my face, but I couldn't meet his eyes, not sure what I'd see there. I knew in my head that Leif had shown me nothing but care and support since the first moment I'd met him, but sometimes my thoughts turned dark.

It was hard to let go of the corner of my brain that feared not being wanted or loved, thinking he or the other guys would pull away or leave at any moment. I was trying, but sometimes my fear won out over reason.

"What makes you think I don't want you?"

"Um, I'm sitting here naked, and you're not trying to have sex with me?" Crap, I sounded like a petulant child who had been denied a rainbow-flavored ice cream cone. My emotions were all over the place lately, like I had let them out, and they were running riot. I was a mess.

"Sunshine, there's more to a relationship than sex. Of course, I want you. It took everything in me not to push you up against the wall and sink my cock so deep in you you'd feel me for days."

My omega perked up her head in interest. That sounded fun.

"Every alpha who has ever met you has wanted you. I want the small moments too, where I get to just be with you and take care of you. I think those moments are just as important."

I finally looked up at him and felt like I was drowning in strong emotions I couldn't name, both mine and his. This man got me in the feels every damn time.

He fidgeted with his towel a bit and looked away before looking back at me, seeming conflicted all of a sudden, and I was curious now.

"Tell me," I urged him. "I want to know what's going on in that beautiful brain of yours." I reached up and stroked his face lightly, following the contours of his firm cheek and jaw.

He searched my eyes for a moment while stroking my legs lightly like he was trying to reassure himself I was here. My ass was cold sitting on what felt like a marble benchtop, but I wasn't moving for the world right now. There was no way I was risking interrupting this moment.

"Damon told you about this driving need we all have to claim you."

His face creased like he was in pain. I smoothed the lines out with my hand.

"I read parts of your book this morning. I woke up early, and it was on the couch. It made me realize just how much alphas have twisted and corrupted the claiming and mate mark."

He looked down at his hands on my legs, like he was trying to memorize the sensation of touching me in case he lost me. The thought made my heart crack open a little further.

"In the past, they didn't bite an unwilling omega to force a bond and dominate them. We've turned what should be a profound, arcane connection between people who love each other into a form of slavery."

He paused, and I waited quietly for him to fully purge what was bothering him, ignoring the goose bumps spreading across my skin.

"I just, we were horrified when Damon visited the Palace, and it was about more than what went down with Ronan. None of us felt we could do what they were pushing Damon to do."

"I couldn't even go in. I kept thinking, what if my sister had been an omega? I've spent my life trying to keep my sister safe from a monster, and she's a beta. I can't stand to even think about what omegas go through, what you've gone through."

Leif picked up my hand and held it over his heart, covering it with his own in the way I loved. I hardly breathed, waiting for what he was going to say next.

"I want to claim you. I want to feel you in every part of me, but I don't want to claim you how society says we should. A part of me is worried that if I claim you in a frenzy, I'll break this beautiful, fragile thing between us. I want to make you stronger, not cage you."

My heart bled for this strong man who was such a gentle spirit. The world may see him only for his physical strength, but he was so much more. I felt the urge to protect him and cherish him.

He always called me sunshine. But he was my lighthouse, a shining light in the darkness that would always point the way home. I struggled to express that to him, though. I wasn't good with words the way he was.

I took our joined hands, turned them, and put them over my heart.

"I don't think you could break what we have, Leif, because you're already in here. You break down every wall I build and do it so gently, like they're made of cotton candy."

"I trust you, I trust us, to figure out a way to do this that works for us. I don't give a shit about what anyone outside the five of us thinks or says we should do. This is ours, and we'll do it our way, okay?" I said.

Leif finally smiled and let out a deep breath. "'Okay."

"So, does that still mean no shower sex just yet?" I asked. "Because the whole shoving me up against the shower wall and impaling me with your cock sounded hot. I'm just saying. Can we take a rain check on that?"

He laughed a deep, bellowing laugh that made my skin tingle and lit me up on the inside. I needed more of those in my life.

He picked me up again and carried me out and into his bedroom, sitting me gently on his bed while he rummaged through drawers. He pulled out a yellow hoodie and tossed it to me. It wasn't as big as the last one he lent me, but it covered my ass.

"Put this on for now. It's one of Max's and should fit you better. Plus, he likes seeing you in his clothes." I grabbed it and took a deep, happy sniff of the warm smokey campfire scent with the hint of s'mores. It was Max's hoodie, but it smelt like both him and Leif, as if he had been cuddling Leif the last time he wore it.

"We'll go downstairs and grab those yoga leggings Lexie gave you that you like so much. I put them in the wash and dried them for you last night when we got home, along with your bra and underwear."

I dropped the towel, slipped into the cozy hoodie, and hugged him again. Yep, my man mountain was a keeper.

"Thanks, Leif."

He just shrugged and looked embarrassed.

Thirty-Four

We got downstairs as Damon and Max were stirring. Hunter was awake and watching us with a mischievous smirk as we came down.

Leif grabbed my yoga pants and underwear from the dryer and handed them to me before he plopped down onto the couch, pushing his hair out of his face. I noticed his hair was drying all tangled.

"Uh, can you do that every morning, Maia?" Hunter asked.

"Do what?" I asked, looking around me, confused as I pulled on my pants.

"Come down the stairs with only a hoodie and no underwear while I'm lying on the floor."

I looked over my shoulder at the stairs, realizing they were timber floating steps with gaps. I must have given Hunter a peep show.

"Pervert," I chuckled as I dashed back upstairs again.

"Hey, no fair, it's pants off Friday."

I heard an "oomph," and I assumed Leif had thrown something at him or someone had punched him.

"It's Thursday, you idiot," I heard Leif say with laughter in his voice.

"So, tomorrow then?" Hunter called out to me.

I bounded down the stairs and said, "Only if it applies to everyone."

"I'm in," Damon mumbled sleepily.

"Me too. I'm not missing out this time." Max said as he stretched and yawned on the other side of the couch.

I flopped down on the floor behind Leif, slipping my legs down either side of him on the sunken couch. He looked over his shoulder at me, a question in his eyes, and I held up the hairbrush.

"My turn?" I asked. I hoped he'd let me.

"You don't have to," he said gruffly, squeezing the cushion he was hugging.

"I want to, as long as you don't feel unmanned by a chick brushing your hair."

"I don't believe in manliness, only humanness. Besides, you make me feel more confident in myself than I ever have in my life, Maia."

Aww, shucks. This guy.

"Cool," I answered, deflecting my feelings like a pro, "we'll do manicures next."

He just shrugged. "I'm game. I have no problem with some sparkles."

I figured he would let me, too. And really, who would call out a man mountain about a bit of glitter polish?

Leif closed his eyes as I started to brush his hair, and I felt joy swell in our bond. I could also feel the warmth coming from the other guys while they watched.

"That's it. I'm growing my hair long so that Maia will brush it for me," Hunter said, watching my hands running through Leif's hair and the look of satisfaction on Leif's face.

"He deserves it after washing me and pampering me in the shower."

"You're getting your hair brushed, and you got to rub her all over with a sponge?" Hunter asked, throwing up his hands in mock outrage.

Leif just nodded, a smug smile spreading across his face. Hunter threw a cushion at him, which Leif caught, even with his eyes closed.

We all just lay around comfortably for a while, enjoying each other's company without really needing to fill the space with noise, which was nice.

I got the feeling they were usually busy and didn't get the chance to just lay in together much. Hunter and Max both seemed to doze off again, but Damon watched me intently the whole time.

I finished brushing Leif's hair and moved on to weaving some small plaits into it, just like I'd pictured the first night I met him.

I looked up as movement caught my eye outside to see Lexie, Bear, Cary, and Ava coming up the path.

"Incoming, you may want to put some clothes on."

Hunter popped up quickly to look over the floor and out through the glass wall-to-ceiling windows.

"Crap, it's a pesky little sister, a slobbery dog, and two suspicious omegas."

The guys all scrambled to find shirts. Leif put his hand under the couch cushion and threw one at Hunter, who grabbed it without looking.

When they saw the unicorn, Damon and Max laughed. "Shit, why is it always me? You're going down, Leif," Hunter said, but he pulled it over his head good-naturedly.

"Knock, knock," Lexie sang as she opened the door and walked straight in, followed a little more hesitantly by Cary and then Ava.

"Well, this is new," Lexie said, eyeing off the mattress and all the blankets with her hands on her hips. "Did you guys have a sleepover party and not invite me?"

I shrugged. "I think it's more of a semi-permanent fixture until we can figure out something better."

I was feeling oddly territorial, and I couldn't figure out why. These people were my friends, but I instinctively didn't want them in this space right now. I had the insane urge to snap at her to back off.

Damon piped up, "Already working on it." I looked at him curiously, but he just winked at me.

"Oookay," Lexie said. "I spotted Cary when he was wandering around early this morning. I figured I should take them up for breakfast, introduce them to a few people, and then give them a proper tour so no one freaks out seeing a strange man wandering around."

Cary stiffened like he was expecting a lot of questions or accusations about what he had been doing poking around so early.

Even though I felt increasingly anxious, I tried to put him at ease. "It's okay, Cary. I know you like to run the perimeter, like me. That's how we met if I recall." I smiled at him with what I hoped was a reassuring smile, and he nodded at me.

The man was gorgeous but overdoing the "strong silent type" persona. Then again, I had been the queen of the shrug until I met my guys, so I couldn't judge.

Ava looked at Leif and me in fascination as I kept plaiting his hair. I got it. My guys didn't act like any alphas we met at the Palace.

"We'll join you guys for breakfast, but first, why don't you sit for a second, and we can chat about some of the things we'd rather not talk about in the dining hall," Damon said, playing the gracious host.

Cary and Ava stepped forward to walk down the steps into the lounge area but stopped as I let out a low growl. Lexie raised her eyebrows in surprise.

I tried to choke it off, but it was vibrating from deep in my chest, and I had no control.

My guys all leaped into action instinctively. Damon jumped clear across the mattress and pulled me into his lap on the couch, while Hunter and Max boxed me in from either side with their arms, and Leif crouched protectively in front of me while reaching back to put a hand on my leg.

"Uh, what the hell was that?" Lexie asked. She looked shocked, and Ava and Cary took a quick step back.

My low growl continued but cut out abruptly as Damon started purring.

"And what the hell is that noise? Is that Damon?" Lexie asked, an edge of panic entering her voice as she waved her arms around.

This was bad, really bad. Cary looked like he was a heartbeat away from grabbing Ava and bolting. Ava just had her head tilted to the side and looked at me curiously before inspecting the mess of blankets on the mattress around me. She showed no fear or panic at my aggression, which surprised me.

I didn't know why I reacted the way I did. They were my friends. I cared about them. I just didn't want anyone near the couch or my guys, especially omegas.

I could feel a faint tremor through my limbs, and my temperature spiked rapidly. Shit, shit.

"It's okay, Maia. I'll stay back here on the steps. Cary and Lexie, I need you to move back to the wall," Ava said. Cary shot her an incredulous look, but she narrowed her eyes at him and said, "Move, please."

It seemed my sweet friend had some hidden bite. I liked it. I got the impression she had secrets and layers we hadn't seen yet, but I was here for it.

Lexie grabbed Cary and pulled him back. He went begrudgingly. Bear pushed past him and moved over to our group. He nudged his way past Leif so he could all but jump in my lap, licking me softly.

If Bear was unconcerned, I knew there was no real danger, but I couldn't take my eyes off the perceived threat.

"Maia, honey, you're going into heat and nesting. It's perfectly natural." Ava said sweetly.

"She's what?" Leif asked Ava in a deep rumble, all his protective instincts in overdrive.

"Oh shit. Ava, you're right. I should have picked that up." Max said as he relaxed slightly, looking around the room as well.

Ava sat down where she was, but she shooed Cary and Lexie back more, so they shuffled back and sat down against the wall under the television.

"We're not going to move closer, Maia. I just want to talk to you from over here. Is that alright?" Ava asked gently but firmly.

I nodded and relaxed slightly. My guys all breathed a little easier as I did.

"If you guys can, you should move back from her a bit, give her some room now, or we may set off her heat," Max said. Leif and Hunter moved back from me stiffly, grimacing as if it pained them, but they didn't go far.

"What the hell is her heat?" Damon managed to grind out through his purring.

"A true-mated omega will have a heat a couple of times a year. It's when she's highly fertile. She'll get increasingly emotional and extremely turned on until the heat manifests. Then she'll mate non-stop until it breaks," Ava explained.

I almost blushed. Max made it sound like we were going to have an orgy or something.

"It's essentially one giant, insatiable orgy that can last for days," Ava stated matter-of-factly.

I almost swallowed my tongue, and Lexie sputtered out a laugh.

I wasn't a prude, but I'd never discussed sex openly with anyone in my life, so this was awkward as hell. It explained a lot about my recent teary meltdowns and horniness, though. I remembered reading that section but hadn't paid much attention to it, never thinking I would find a true mate.

All the guys were staring at each other with their faces lit up in excitement. I rolled my eyes at them, but my omega was on her back on the floor with her legs in the air, ready to go already.

"I'm guessing this was all in the book?" Hunter asked dryly.

Max shrugged. "Yeah, sorry, I only skimmed that section. I figured I'd read it after we claimed her. I thought it only happened afterward. I was more interested in the bits about packs and prime alphas at the time."

"An omega approaching her heat will start to nest," Ava looked pointedly at the mess of blankets, quilts, and pillows on the mattress between us. "I read that section in detail. The true alpha claiming and the heat interested me the most."

Cary leaned forward, a dark look on his face like he wanted to drag her into a cave and keep her there.

"You need to bring her the softest fabrics you can find. Anything scratchy or tight will start to irritate her."

"She's got pretty much every blanket and pillow in the cabin here already," Hunter said defensively. I squeezed his shoulder lightly, and he leaned back towards me slightly.

Ava ignored him. "She won't want anyone but her mates near her nest either. She'll get territorial, and she's likely to attack."

No shit. I wish I'd recalled that bit earlier. "Sorry."

"It's all good." Ava said with her usual sweetness, giving me a small smile. "I used to read that section a lot when you were gone. Imagining what it may be like to have a space I felt completely safe and adored, with a group of protective mates around me."

I noticed Cary slump slightly behind her as if he felt defeated, and my heart broke a little for him. Lexie looked intrigued by the whole thing, like she was eating it up.

Bear ambled back over to Lexie, now that things had calmed down, and lay on the floor next to her. She ruffled his fur but didn't take her eyes off us.

"She's going to be highly fertile?" Leif asked.

"Yep," Ava chuckled. "Not just her, the build-up to the heat sets off your pheromones, too. By the time it starts, you guys will be supercharged sperm bombs."

I felt Damon tense underneath me.

I looked over to Max, who was gently playing with the plait I had woven in Leif's hair while Leif was sitting on the floor in front of him, and the realization hit me that they would all make great dads. The thought shocked me. Did I even want kids?

I had assumed I would live alone in hiding on my gramps' farm all my life. Or be found and mated against my will. Either way, pregnancy amongst omegas was so rare these days that I had never thought about it. Our fertility rates have been dropping for decades.

Max touched my leg gently when he noticed me watching him. "Are you okay, Maia? It's a lot to take in. Do you even want kids?"

I nodded. "I'm not opposed to the idea of kids, Max. More intrigued. I hadn't considered it as a possibility."

Damon was frowning when I looked over my shoulder at him. He squeezed me tighter, and his purring cut out.

"Damon?" I asked hesitantly.

"It was almost impossible not to fuck you senseless on the path the first time I kissed you. So if the heat is even more intense, I don't know if we'll be able to stay away from you, Maia. We need to know now if that's going to be a problem for you. If it is, we'll figure out a way to slow this down or not be here."

The thought of them not being here made me feel like I couldn't breathe. Plus, Damon was talking about this as if I was the only one who got to make a decision.

"Do you guys even want kids? It's not just me who gets to decide."

KNOT YOUR PRINCESS

"The thought of you all round and pregnant with a little one of us? I vote heck yeah," Leif said, smiling widely at me.

I looked at Max, who nodded eagerly. "Me too."

When I glanced at Hunter, he grinned just as wide, flashing a mouth full of teeth. "I think the world needs another little Hunter running around. I vote yes, too."

I smiled before looking back at Damon. He was still watching me intently. I turned around and straddled his lap, taking his face in my hands.

"There's no right or wrong answer, Damon."

He gently slipped his arms around me. "All of us had shitty childhoods, Maia. We know exactly what we wouldn't do with our kids, and we've all got a lot of love to give. If you're asking about kids, the questions should be how many and when."

"I'm just worried we're rushing you into something. I'm not sure you're ready for us to claim you, much less knock you up."

My sweet, protective alpha, constantly worrying about everyone else and trying to take on everyone's burdens. Damon still hadn't figured out I was only waiting for them to be truly ready.

"Damon, let's just take it one day at a time. But know that if one of you knocks me up with super sperm while I'm blissed out on heat hormones, I'm more than okay with it."

Damon let out a long breath and kissed my forehead tenderly.

I felt a tear track slowly down my face. Hunter, Leif, and Max moved back closer, surrounding me, stroking and reassuring me.

Leif said, "No crying, sunshine." At the same time, Max grabbed my hand and squeezed it. Hunter just licked the tear away, which made me laugh.

I knew they could feel through the bond that I was full of joy rather than sadness.

I glanced over at Ava; she looked like she was about to cry, too, but she smiled at me happily. Cary looked like a portrait of pained longing as he watched her. His repressed need was etched into his face.

Bear had perked his head up, and he and Lexie were looking out the door, with their heads tilted, listening.

"That sounds like our herd dogs," Lexie said.

I finally noticed the dogs growling and barking in the distance. Hunter jumped up and ran to the study. Damon picked me up and settled me back on the couch, giving me a quick peck before my guys, Lexie, and Bear, all leaped to their feet and followed Hunter.

I looked at Cary and Ava, shrugging before we jumped up and followed too.

Max grabbed a pair of binoculars off the shelf, passing them to Hunter as we walked in.

"The cows were due to be grazing nearby, in the forest on the other side of the river this morning. The sheep should be a little further out," Damon told Hunter. Bear pushed Hunter to the side, determined to get a spot at the window, and Hunter cursed him.

"Why are the cattle and sheep out in the forest?" I asked, always endlessly curious about the farm and how it worked.

"We use silvopastoral farming methods, so we don't have to strip more land for pasture. We manage the forest to promote suitable undergrowth for feed," Max said, although he was still looking out the window and sounded a little distracted.

"The trees provide shade and shelter, so the animals don't suffer from temperature extremes. The trees absorb methane and nitrous oxide, so it's better for the environment. We also use a hell of a lot fewer chemicals for pest control. So it's a win-win-win," Damon said. "It's not a common method. Max did a lot of research into it, so we could try it here."

"How do you manage them out there? Won't they get lost?" I asked. I was intrigued, as I was by everything to do with their farm.

"We have collars on the herd and the dogs so that we can track them via satellite, and we use drones to monitor them. We also have a team that goes out to do health checks regularly and sow areas they have grazed with native seeds to help speed up the process."

"We also use a pack of Anatolian Shepherds to guard the herds overnight, the same breed as Bear. They're intensely loyal to their herds, often bonding with them and getting aggressive when anything threatens them. Only Bear kind of adopted Lexie instead."

"That sounds interesting, and I'd love to see how it all works, but I want to know more about how you just kinda called Lexie a cow." I side-eyed her with a smirk, and she rolled her eyes at me.

Hunter laughed from his spot at the window, lowering his binoculars to look over his shoulder at us. "Yeah, I tried that joke with Lexie. It didn't go over so well." He rubbed his ass like he was soothing a remembered pain.

"Ha, I remember that. I gave you the biggest wedgie," Lexie gloated.

"She almost ripped your junk clear off." Leif said. He had a massive grin like he was proud of his sister.

"I would have liked to see that," I said, winking at Lexie. Hunter glared at me before turning to look out the window again.

"Are you allowed to feed the animals out in the forest? Isn't it public land?"

"Damon owns over a million acres on the other side of the river. He inherited it from his grandfather. He's the biggest landholder in the area, probably the whole country. He just doesn't farm it all," Leif said.

Damon looked uncomfortable and wouldn't meet my eye.

"Technically, I don't own it. The farm cooperative owns it now," Damon grumbled.

I eyed Leif, hoping he would translate.

"Damon made us all partners in the farm, and not just Hunter, Max, Lexie and me, but also the original workers who worked for his gramps and lived here too.

"The five of us own twelve percent each, giving us sixty percent. The long-term workers all got a share of the remaining forty percent. We run the business aspect of the farm, but we vote on major decisions. So if the workers want to do something big, like introduce a new crop, they just need to get one of us onside to get a majority vote."

I was speechless. I knew Damon was generous and caring, but to give away most of his inheritance to his friends and the people who had worked for his grandfather. That was a whole other level.

He looked at me cautiously. "It didn't feel right to inherit it all when people had lived on and worked this land for generations, and these guys are my family. Grandpa would have approved. He just wanted me to have a home and choices."

I took Damon's face between my hands and kissed him gently. He searched my eyes like he was worried I'd reject him for giving his inheritance away.

Before I could tell him how I felt about him, the radio blared to life, and a panicked voice yelled about men near the cattle.

Thirty-Five

"Shit," Hunter spun into action, grabbed the binoculars up again, and stepped out the door onto the deck, looking towards where the workers had directed.

"Report, Hunter," I said, following Hunter out the door, moving swiftly into military mode.

"Two men. They look military, in all black, up different trees. They don't appear to be hiding. They have their hands up in a surrender pose. They have guns, they could have shot the dogs, but they haven't. I think they're trying to get our attention."

I buzzed the animal team and told them to hold until we arrived.

"Hunter, grab your sniper rifle and cover us. Pick your spot. Max, grab a drone, circle, and see if you can spot anyone further out. Leif, you're with me. Maia, wait here, then stick to Max like glue when he gets back with the drone."

She nodded at me and planted her ass in the chair to wait. I could have kissed her for not arguing with me, but we didn't have time, and I needed to focus.

"Lexie, I need you to take Cary and Ava back to their cabin and stay with them until we know more. They don't know our protocols or emergency procedures, so you're responsible for them. Got it?" For once, Lexie didn't argue either.

She grabbed Cary and Ava, but Cary pulled back. "I can help."

"I appreciate the offer, Cary, but I don't know your training or skills, and we don't have time to figure it out right now. Next time, I'll use you. I promise. Right now, we've got this covered, and I need you with Lexie. If things go south, she'll know what to do, but she'll need help."

He nodded begrudgingly before he followed Lexie and Bear out the door with Ava.

I slapped Leif on the back, and we both took off. Hunter passed us guns from the locked cabinet as we went.

When we reached the back gate, I signaled for the electricity to be shut off to this section. Then Leif and I slipped through, both of us shifting into military mode as we did.

I approached the dogs cautiously, giving them the sit command. The dogs were independent and fiercely protective. They would often choose which orders to listen to and ignore others, just like Bear, especially if their herd was in danger.

They ignored me, continuing to howl and circle. So I growled low at them and gave the sit command again, pushing some dominance into it and letting them know I was pack alpha. The dogs obeyed, for now, but they were all watching closely.

I signaled for the men to drop from the trees, and they complied, watching the dogs and us warily. The one closest was an alpha. He was a big guy with short blonde hair. He was almost as big as Leif, but his hair was lighter. He had the same golden hair and skin color as Maia.

I felt a chill run over the back of my neck. I wasn't sure if it was a ghostly warning or an intuition.

The second man was an alpha as well. He had curly brown hair with highlights from the sun and darker olive skin. They both looked like they had spent a lot of time outdoors recently, with scruffy beards and dirt-marked clothes.

I heard a buzzing noise and knew Max had intentionally flown the drone close by so these men would know we weren't alone out here.

The first alpha didn't flinch or move, but the second took to his back and watched the drone circle, keeping it in his sight. They were highly trained and coordinated their actions without any signals that I could see. Which meant they had worked and trained together for a long time.

They moved the same way we did.

I didn't say a word. I just watched closely, waiting for them to fill the silence.

"We're not here to cause problems. We're just here for my sister and to let you know trouble is headed your way," the blonde alpha said.

I felt Leif tense at my side, but I kept myself still and calm, not giving anything away.

"What kind of trouble?" I was deliberately ignoring the comment about his sister for now, even though it sent a spike of fear through my heart.

"The Omega Palace. An alpha from there was sniffing around here a few days ago. And either your raid last night has been discovered, or he's finally rallied troops to get what he wants from inside your fences." He narrowed his eyes at my silence.

"He's on his way, and he's bringing friends." He ground out as if he'd rather be somewhere more important than talking to me right now.

I narrowed my eyes right back at him. "Where are you getting your intel?"

"Part of my team has the Palace under surveillance. We're in communication."

They must have working satellite phones. Something I'd wished we had more of since the Crash happened. While we had bought some tech privately, we'd been retired when it happened and didn't have access to the kind of resources we'd used in the past.

Max hadn't had a chance to go through the PMV yet and see what we could use. It made me wonder what else these two guys had access to and what they might be willing to trade.

"Why would he come at us in the daylight? That's not a smart strategy. Maybe they're just on a supply run."

"I didn't say they were smart. There's a civilian directing them. My teammate overheard them talking. I'm pretty sure it's a snatch and grab, and they're not after your supplies. They're looking for an omega, and I'm worried it's my sister."

His mate looked over his shoulder and said, "We're wasting time. We need to get her and go now. They'll be here soon."

"How soon?" I asked.

The first alpha ground his teeth harder and spread his feet like he was preparing to fight. "It seems like I'm doing all the talking, and you're doing all the asking while avoiding any mention of my sister or the omega, who I'm pretty sure are the same person."

Damn. I couldn't put this off any longer. I shifted on my feet to mirror his stance.

"Who is your sister, and why do you think she's here?"

"My sister's name is Maia, and Claudio is pretty sure he tracked her here." He jerked his head towards the alpha behind him. "I need to find her."

I fought to keep my calm. No way was I giving Maia up. "Surely you'd know her from her scent. Why aren't you sure it's her?"

He looked like he was about to crack his jaw. He was clenching it so hard.

"I haven't seen my sister in a long time, but I've always tried to keep watch from a distance. If she's here and trouble is coming for her, I'm not leaving without her."

"I'm almost out of patience with asking nicely, Damon."

I didn't react to the use of my name. I just stepped forward into his space. We were evenly matched in height and build, but if he knew me, he knew my reputation.

"You seem to have me at a disadvantage, Sam. You know me, but I don't know you or where you were when your younger brother betrayed your sister, and she was sent to be tortured for three years at the Palace." I was taking a wild guess that this was Sam, but it wasn't a stretch. He looked a lot like her.

Sam's eyes widened, and he sucked in a shocked breath. Claudio whirled and put his hand on him. Interesting.

"What the fuck are you talking about? Who hurt Maia?" Sam demanded hotly.

"Do you mean your sister harm? Because there's no way I'm letting another member of her family hurt her more than they already have." I tilted my chin, all but inviting him to come at me.

Sam stepped into my space, Claudio following and keeping a hand on him while all our scents flared. It was a potent cocktail of lightning, smoke, whiskey, and chili popcorn.

"I would never hurt my sister," Sam said vehemently.

"Really? You think leaving her without saying a word or even leaving a note didn't hurt her? She worshiped you, and you abandoned her, just like the rest of your family. It left scars."

He paled and seemed to wilt slightly before my eyes. Claudio grabbed onto him the same way Hunter often grabbed me, with an arm around his chest. It was eerie.

"He left a note and sent letters all the time, as well as money," Claudio said, a frown marring his face.

"Well, she never got them."

"I need to see her, and I'm not saying another word until I do." Sam's anger and brashness were gone, and his voice sounded raw, but he had a determined set to his shoulders.

I was about to deny him, but I felt Leif's hand on my shoulder, from where he'd been watching my back the whole time.

"It's not our place to make the call for her. It's up to her if she wants to see her brother or not."

I nodded. I wanted to know how Sam knew me, but it had to wait. Maia was my priority, then the imminent threat.

"Let's move then, Leif. You take up the rear."

"The infamous Leif, it's nice to meet you finally. You're kind of a legend in some parts of the military," Claudio said, in a friendly tone, smiling at Leif.

Leif just quirked his eyebrow at him.

"Not the time, Dio," Sam growled. Claudio just shrugged and walked casually with his hands in his pockets, like he didn't have a care in the world.

"Just making conversation," he said calmly.

As we headed back towards the gates, and I signaled for the electricity to shut off in this section, I picked up my radio and requested Max to bring Maia down to the gate.

"If Max is here, then you may as well call Hunter down too. He's gotta have a scope on us from somewhere around here."

He looked around and pegged Hunter on the roof of our house, waving at him.

"Jesus, Dio, cut it out," Sam groaned. "Do you want to ask for an autograph next?"

"Yeah, do you want me to sign your chest, Claudio?" Leif deadpanned.

Claudio just laughed and slapped him on the shoulder while I radioed for Hunter, too. No point keeping him up there if he was made. I was impressed Claudio had spotted him, I had trouble making him out, and I knew where he was.

Although, I was getting irritated with not knowing who these guys worked for, where they had come from, or how they knew so much about us. I kept focusing on Maia and getting details on the imminent threat for now. I would ask questions later.

The drone came over our heads to set down in front of us, and then Max and Maia stepped out from the other side of the barn.

I stepped away from our guests and walked toward her quickly. She ran at me and jumped into my arms, kissing me soundly. I felt her joy at seeing me, and it settled me instantly. I relaxed into her, needing her close for a moment before I heard Leif cough discreetly behind us.

Maia looked up and seemed to notice the strangers for the first time. Her face paled as she zeroed in on her brother. I'm sure he looked a lot different now if he was a teenager when he left, but she seemed to recognize him.

I felt her tense in my arms, and her heart rate sped up rapidly.

"Sam?" she whispered on a breath.

Thirty-Six

Maia

I t couldn't be. I had to be imagining it.

I let go of Damon and took a step towards the apparition in front of me, then another. I felt numb, and a sense of disbelief overcame me.

I looked at him closer. He certainly had the same features as my brother, the blonde hair a shade like my own and the same dark blue eyes. But my brother had been a young boy just starting to go through puberty when I last saw him.

This was a man. Who was staring at me intently but not saying a word. Neither was anyone else, which was weird.

"I'm sorry for staring," I said quietly. "You startled me. You look a lot like a brother I haven't seen or heard from in a long time."

I stepped closer to him and held out my hand to shake. "I'm Maia. If the guys are letting you in the gate and you're not all beaten up, I'm guessing you're a friend or a good guy?"

His eyes roved all over my face like he was searching for something. He looked at my outstretched hand, then back to my face again. I dropped my hand and looked to Damon quickly, who was watching us closely but not intervening.

I turned to the man again.

"Mai?" he asked, in a gravely masculine voice I didn't recognize.

I took a step backward, breathing fast, feeling dizzy like I might faint.

He stepped towards me, following me.

"I've waited for this moment for so long, and I knew you must have grown up, but in my head, I still pictured you as a twelve-year-old girl in pigtails."

"Sam?" I asked again, and he nodded, tears welling in his eyes.

I froze in place. This was my brother, who I had hero-worshiped, but had left me without a word.

Over the years, I've made up many stories about why he may have left when my gramps refused to talk about him. I always imagined he was desperate to come back to me. Yet he never had, and eventually I had let him go.

Now here he was, standing in front of me. Big and powerful, definitely an alpha. But with the same kind eyes he'd always had. Eyes that were boring into me like he was begging me for something, but I didn't know what.

I wanted to run to him, but I also wanted to slap him, and a small part of me wanted to turn tail and run away. If he was here by coincidence and wasn't expecting me to be here, I wouldn't cope with the devastation I would feel.

The indecision left me completely unable to move at all.

He raised his hand, like he wanted to reach out, but stopped.

"Mai, Damon told me you never got my note or any of my letters. I have written to you every week since the day I left. You never wrote back, but I kept trying. I never gave up hope I'd make it back to you," Sam said.

"I never would have left you if I had any choice. I left to keep you safe." He stepped towards me, shaking so bad I was amazed he didn't crumble.

I just stared at Sam, a tremble starting up in my limbs. He was saying everything I ever wanted to hear, but it felt too good to be true.

I touched his face, feeling a rough beard under my hands instead of the smooth skin I remembered as a child.

"Am I dreaming, or are you real?" I asked.

He shook his head, and a tear fell down his cheek, landing on my hand. I wiped it gently and felt him shake, or was that me? I couldn't be sure.

"I'm here. I'm so, so sorry, Mai. Please forgive me."

He didn't wait for my reply. He grabbed me in a fierce bear hug like he couldn't hold back another second. I took a deep breath of leather and sandalwood. I realized suddenly why I gravitated toward that scent.

My chair hadn't just reminded me of my gramps' old hat. When Sam's scent had come in just before he'd left, he had smelled like old leather. I must have blocked that out.

I thought I had let him go, but I had just shoved him down in a box in the deepest part of my heart and kept him there, waiting and unconsciously looking for him wherever I went.

Loud sobbing tears broke from me like they were spilling from my soul, no longer able to be contained. The box cracked wide open and what came out was messy and real.

I hugged him tightly, remembering all the times he took care of me when nobody else did. The way he would always shield me if he sensed danger, even when he was a little kid.

"I'm here, Mai. I'm sorry," he repeated. He sounded broken, and he squeezed me so tight I could hardly breathe.

I don't know how long we stood like that, while everyone just let me cry into my brother's shoulder, and he held me—silently supporting us in our pain.

I felt my guys sending me comfort through our bond, and I finally looked up to see Leif and a strange man over Sam's shoulder. The man was crying openly, too, and Leif looked like he was only just keeping his shit together.

I sensed Hunter had joined us, and I looked over my shoulder to see Damon, Max, and Hunter all standing with their arms around each other. They sent me wobbly smiles. They sensed what this meant to me.

I looked up at Sam finally, feeling raw and vulnerable as I did it.

"Why are you here now?" I asked, needing to know.

"I came for you," he said. Such a simple statement, but it had such a profound effect on me. I had to choke back the sobs that threatened to start up again. My brother had come for me.

I had dealt with my father and grandfather's deaths, mourning them. I had even dealt with my mother's abandonment and Ben's betrayal, partly understanding why they had done what they did. But I had never really healed from or been able to comprehend Sam leaving, and it had left a hole.

It made me fear that anyone who loved me would do the same. I knew it wasn't going to be simple, having Sam back. I was sure we had both grown up and lived very different lives. Yet he was here. Finally.

"As soon as the Crash happened, I came home, and my team came with me, but you weren't there. We've been tracking you ever since," Sam said as he gently wiped the silent tears still running down my face. "We just missed you at the Palace."

"A few nights ago, someone tripped our perimeter alarms. Was that you?" Hunter asked from behind me. His voice was detached, like he was reserving judgment until he knew more.

I heard the strange man, who Leif appeared to be guarding, pipe up.

"Uh, that was me. I was impressed. Those alarms were well placed. I never even saw them. Good job, Max."

I saw Leif's eyes narrow. I was confused. I dropped my arms from around Sam and stepped back. He watched me as if he was worried I was going to disappear.

"Do you guys all know each other, or not?" I asked.

"They appear to know us quite well, but we have no idea who they are, apart from Sam being your brother who's been missing without a trace for over a decade."

I noticed Sam tense and sensed wariness from my guys in the bond. Yeah, this was not going to be easy at all.

"This is Claudio, but we all call him Dio. He's a member of my team. He's been with me for most of that decade or so I've apparently been missing, and I trust him with my life."

"Wow, Claudio, well, that explains a lot. Your name means one who stumbles, so it's no wonder you tripped the alarm," Max teased. I sensed Max was trying to ease the tension. It worked because Claudio burst out laughing, and everyone relaxed a little.

I took a closer look at Claudio, standing casually with his hands in his pockets and seeming unconcerned with Leif's hulking proximity.

"You look familiar for some reason. Do I know you from somewhere?"

"No. I've heard about you endlessly for years, but we've never met. I would have remembered you," Claudio said as he looked me up and down.

All of my guys growled, and Leif took a threatening step closer to him. Claudio chuckled and said, 'Interesting.'

"Stop messing with them, Dio." Sam said with a sigh.

"No. I remember you from somewhere recently, I'm sure." I said as I shook my head like I was trying to shake a memory loose.

"From the Palace?" Damon asked, a dark tone to his voice that promised pain. His dominance started seeping out, and everyone went on high alert, including Sam and Claudio.

Shit. "No, not the palace."

I wracked my brain, trying to focus on his face, but it was bright, and the sun was shining on my face. I took a deep breath and smelt popcorn faintly. I put my hand up to block the sun, and the sudden shade and scent made me remember.

"That's it. It was dark, but you were standing in the middle of the road in a tiny town between here and the Palace. I saw you, and I backtracked, then went around the town."

He clapped slowly like he was congratulating me. "Well, no wonder I had so much trouble tracking you. Your little sister has some skills, Sam. I sensed an omega nearby, but I couldn't scent her. How did you do that?"

"It's a long story, one for another day," Damon interrupted, cutting him off. "Now that you have seen your sister, we need to know how long we have before we come under attack."

"Attack? What attack?" Hunter asked, straightening up from where he had just relaxed against the barn wall, glaring at Sam and Claudio.

"Ronan is coming for Maia, and he's bringing some of the team from the Palace with him," Damon said. "Sam and Claudio came for Maia and to warn us."

"What the fuck do you mean came for Maia?" Hunter asked. He was ignoring the other threat for now, but he looked like he was settling into that calm, deadly zone everyone feared so much. I could almost see a death count starting in his eyes.

"We intercepted a communication that implied a snatch and grab at the farm was going ahead. We don't have any details of when, but we have eyes on the Palace. We haven't seen anyone leave, so you probably have some time," Sam said.

"Look, I appreciate you taking Maia in, but you need to see to your people, and we need to get Maia away from here," Sam said as he took my hand.

Oh no. This was going to go south, fast.

"Thank you for everything you've done to help her, but we'll take it from here," he added, giving me a not-so-gentle tug and jerking me forward.

Oh shit. I could see Hunter's hand go to his gun on his hip. Max wasn't far behind. Damon was leaking dominance everywhere, with murder in his eyes, and Sam swung me behind him.

"Not going to happen," Hunter said with deadly calm.

I needed to do something before my guys did. I felt a hand on my back and then a gun click.

"Easy there, tiger," I heard Claudio say as I looked over my shoulder to see him standing behind me, touching my shoulder, and Leif with a gun pointed at his head. I heard two more guns click and assumed it was Hunter and Max.

Okay. Too late. Now I was mad at all of them.

"Okay. Down boys, all of you." I snapped my wrist out of Sam's grip and stepped away from him and Claudio. They both tried to reach for me, but I dodged them.

I stood in front of my brother with my arms crossed. "Nobody makes decisions for me, not anymore and never again. Are we clear?"

"Guns down, now." I glared at my guys, pushing my anger at them. Max and Hunter quickly lowered their weapons. Leif hesitated.

"Sunshine, he touched you," Leif tried to start, but I didn't let him finish.

"Now, Leif," I growled, sending *Don't Fuck With Me* glares at him.

I'm sure I looked as threatening as a hissing kitten, but he dropped his gun and stepped back.

I spoke directly to my brother, my tone now even and firm. "I appreciate you coming for me if you thought I was in danger, but this is my home now, and I'm not abandoning it or this community."

"Mai, you've only been here a few days," Sam said

I put my hand up. "Sam, I love you, always have, always will. But I've found my home and my mates here. I'm not going anywhere with you, now or later."

"Mates?" Sam asked. His face was a picture of surprise, I could hang it in an art gallery, but Claudio just chuckled.

"You never were very good at picking up social clues," Claudio said to Sam.

Damon, Max, Hunter, and Leif stepped away from my brother and his friend and moved over to stand behind me. I took a deep breath, feeling them in the bond.

"You seem to know them already, but I'd like to formally introduce you to my mates, Damon, Max, Hunter, and Leif."

Sam looked at Max's neck and then at mine before raising his eyebrow in question. "If you're their mate, then why has no one claimed you?"

"Because she just escaped a traumatic situation, and we're not assholes," Damon snarled, repeating what he told Cary last night and clenching his fists. "Make no mistake. She is our mate, and we will claim her as soon as she's ready."

"Read the room, Sam," Claudio stage whispered to him while putting his hand on Sam's shoulder. I could have hugged him right then, as Sam relaxed, but I didn't think it would help the situation.

Instead, I silently mouthed "thank you," at Claudio, and he winked at me. I got the feeling that if they hung around, he and Hunter would be trouble.

"If you want to leave again, Sam, you're welcome to, but I'll be staying here and defending my home with my mates."

There was a sudden quiet, and I realized I didn't know if staying here was the plan. 'We are staying and defending our home, right?' I stage whispered quickly to Hunter, who was next to me. He had a twinkle in his eyes like he was trying not to laugh but just nodded.

"We could use the help, though. We're likely to be outnumbered," Max said, watching Sam and Claudio carefully.

"If Maia stays, I stay," Sam said decisively.

Claudio grinned. "Well, alright then, I've been itching for a fight with those wannabe alphas at the Palace for a while. What's the plan?"

Hunter finally laughed, walked over, slapped Claudio on the back, and said, "Come with me, my friend."

They started to walk up the path towards our house, but Sirena came barrelling around the corner towards them, running full pelt, carrying her heels in her hand and her gauzy skirt flying out behind her. Her hair was messy, and she was breathing heavily.

She spotted Hunter first and barrelled into him, grabbing his shirt and looking around with wild eyes. "Hunter, they're coming," she panted, breathing heavily. "You have to do something. They're coming for Maia now."

Thirty-Seven

Maia

Damon instantly stepped in front of me, laser focused on Sirena, while Leif, Max, and Sam ranged out behind and around me, watching our surroundings.

"I thought you said we had time," Damon snarled at Sam and Claudio.

"Our intel said we did," Sam growled back.

I wasn't sure what Sirena was playing at, but I didn't trust her. She'd been quiet since our showdown. I didn't know if she had been licking her wounds, plotting her next move, or just painting her nails.

Hunter was deadly calm. He had his hands up at his side and was trying not to touch her, knowing it would set me off. I could see Claudio had instinctively jumped into place to watch Hunter's back, with only a quick sideways glance at Sam.

"Who's coming?" Hunter barked at Sirena, putting a bite of alpha into his tone.

Her gaze locked onto him, and she froze, "My brother is coming. He could be here now."

I tried to duck out from behind Damon to see what was going on, but he reached back with one arm and pulled me up tight against his back. I could feel a fine tremor running through his body, but he was also tense like a bowstring pulled tight just before it released death in a whisper.

"What the hell is Ronan's sister doing at your farm?" I heard Claudio ask harshly.

"Ronan's sister? How the hell did we not know that?" Hunter snarled.

"Not many people do. I'm only a beta. My family doesn't acknowledge me publicly, and I use my mother's maiden name."

I peeked out from behind Damon and saw Sirena swallow hard. Her gaze was still fixed on Hunter, but she had dropped her hands from his shirt and taken half a step back. "My father made me seduce Damon to get information on what you were doing here."

"When you all quit the military, it made him nervous. He thought Damon was building support and planning a coup, especially after your run-in with Ronan. He wanted you either brought back onside to use as part of his plans or destroyed."

I felt Damon start to growl, low and fierce. Sirena's lifespan might have been reduced to seconds if he wasn't guarding me.

Sirena's eyes flicked our way, but Hunter roughly grabbed her by her shirt and jerked her attention back to him. "You don't get to look at them," Hunter growled at her.

"We don't have time for this. I know you don't trust me, but I'm not the only one my father sent here. Allegro and Manuel are his men, and they've been watching my every move."

"Why the fuck do you think I was so desperate to keep Damon's attention when he didn't want it? The consequences for failing my father are deadly, even for me, especially for me."

Her voice was high-pitched and angry while her hands scrabbled at Hunter's hold on her. I was conflicted. This Sirena didn't match the one I thought I knew.

"Shit, I'm pretty sure Allegro and Manuel are the two men Lexie was talking about when Maia arrived. When she said there were only two men here she didn't trust," Max said from behind me. "I've been meaning to talk to her about it, but there hasn't been time."

"I never gave them anything they could use, and I tried to misdirect them, but it's too late for all that now. Allegro has gone to sabotage the fence and let Ronan in. I hit Manuel with a shovel, but I don't know how long he'll be out. You have to move, NOW."

Sirena was yelling now, more afraid of her dad's henchmen and her brother than she was of Hunter, trying to jerk out of his grasp. He let her go suddenly before he ripped her shirt, and she stumbled toward me, "Maia, you have to hide."

"Let me out, Damon," I growled, in my kitten growl. It was nowhere near as effective as any of the guys' but surprisingly, Damon let me go, swinging me around in front of him but keeping his arm around me.

"Damon," Sam growled in warning. His was much deeper than mine, but it didn't affect Damon.

"She has earned the right to fight for herself. I will protect her with my life, but I won't cage her," he snarled at Sam.

I stared Sirena down, "I'm done running from Ronan, and I'm done letting people beat me down. Do you mean to harm me, Sirena?"

"No, I swear. I know I treated you badly, and you have no reason to believe me, but I was acting like a bitch to keep women at arm's length and protect them. Allegro and Manuel were told to take out anyone who was competing for Damon."

"I've watched all the women here discreetly, even before you arrived. They're so strong, and they've been through so much. I can't sit by while any of them get hurt again. Even you. I can't."

Tears ran down her face, and mascara mixed into the mess. She was pulling at her hair in a desperate mix of fear, frustration, and anger. She was a shadow of her usual glamorous self, with all the artifice stripped away. She was raw and bleeding emotionally all over the place.

"I swear, Sirena, if you're lying and you get anyone here hurt, I will kill you myself." She just nodded at me, looking resigned.

"My life is forfeit now anyway. My father won't let this stand," she said as she slumped slightly, the adrenaline of her wild dash ebbing away.

"Please, please, just hide, Maia." She looked like a broken doll that someone had smashed and thrown away.

I took a deep breath and reached for her hand, gripping it tightly. I still didn't know if I trusted her, but things hadn't been adding up with her since Damon had publicly ended things.

Either her old persona was fake, or this one was, but I wasn't going to waste time figuring it out right now. "We won't let Ronan or your father get to you, Sirena. I'm not letting another woman get hurt, either. Even you. The rest, we can sort out later, okay?" She nodded at me, but she didn't look convinced that I meant what I said.

"Tell us everything, Sirena. How is Allegro letting Ronan in?"

"I don't know. He had some kind of note from Ronan. He said he was turning off the electric fences, but I don't know how. He just took off."

We all swiveled to Max, but he stepped forward before anyone could ask.

"You can only turn off all the fences from the security office. Individual sections at the top and bottom gates can be turned off manually from inside the fence."

"Nobody has come past us to the bottom gate, so he's got to be at the top or at the security office."

Just as he spoke, a sudden quiet fell over us, and the hairs on my arms lay flat. The electric fences aren't generally noisy, but this section around the gate emitted a steady clicking noise I had noticed earlier, and the fences always seemed to make my hairs stand on end when I got close. But it was all gone suddenly.

"Fuck," Max grabbed a long blade of grass and touched it to the fence. "It's out. He's at the security office. Ronan could come through anywhere."

Hunter grabbed his radio off his belt and tried to radio the security office, but there was no response. Suddenly faint yelling and screaming filtered down to us from the top of the farm. It seemed to be coming from the fields on the east corner.

Damon turned to the two farmhands who had been quietly watching us all from the corner of the barn. They were young, maybe in their late teens.

"Take Sirena and get inside the barn. Grab whatever you can to defend yourselves and secure the animals. Keep an eye on the bottom gate, and if you see anything come through or over, call us. Don't try and stop them if they're not threatening you directly. Leave them to us."

They nodded and ran for the barn, one of them giving a piercing whistle that had the dogs outside the gate herding the cows and moving them further into the forest.

Sirena shook her head and turned back towards the path. "I'm not hiding or running anymore either. There are children up there. I'm heading for the nursery."

I moved to take off after her, deciding I liked this new Sirena, even if I still wasn't sure if she was lying. But Damon's light bark had her stopping in her tracks.

"Can you shoot?" he asked when she stopped short and turned around. He took a keyring off his belt, and at her nod, he threw it at her. "I'm trusting you, Sirena, only because Maia is. If you fuck with us, you won't like what happens."

She just nodded again and straightened her spine.

"There's a gun cabinet in the garage. Take a gun for yourself, grab a bag and take as many as you can carry. Arm any workers who know how to shoot and want to help on your way. Send the rest to the barn."

She nodded yet again and took off without another word. I didn't like bitchy Sirena, and I wasn't sure about wild, crying Sirena, but I could get behind silent kick-ass Sirena.

"Was that wise?" Sam asked.

"We don't have a lot of choices right now. All our workers are unarmed and defenseless. It'll either help or go badly, but we need all the help we can get right now." Leif answered, knowing how Damon thought and that Damon wouldn't bother to explain himself right now.

"If Ronan hurts a single person on this farm, I'm going to fuck him up," I growled lightly, fingering a gun Max had given me, and I currently had stashed inside my waistband under my hoodie. Sam looked startled, but Claudio just rubbed his hands together and whispered to Sam, "I really like your sister."

This was my home, and I would defend it and my people. I had promised the guys no more running, and I had meant it.

Damon was riding the edge of his beast and smiled darkly at me. "That's my girl."

"Max and Hunter, head to the security office now. Neutralize the threat, and get it back under our control. Max, radio us a location if you see anything we need to deal with. Hunter, go wherever you're most needed after you secure the office."

They turned to go, but it was my turn to yell, "Wait." When they all turned to look at me as one, I gulped, but I put on my big girl pants and said, "I have a plan."

"We're listening." Damon growled, tense and alert. I knew now that he wasn't angry at me, though, he was ready to rip the heads off anyone who threatened me, and it was kinda sexy. My omega purred. *No, bad omega. Focus, Maia.*

"If they have the security room, will they have eyes on us here? Can they hear us?" I asked Max.

"Eyes, possibly, but from a distance. Ears no." He shifted on his feet, eager to be doing something but not sure what I was suggesting.

I breathed a small sigh of mingled fear and relief, my crazy plan just might work, but it was insane.

"It's Hunter's plan, really," I said as I looked at Hunter and winked. "He came up with it the other night when Ronan first visited."

When they all looked confused, I elaborated. "Hunter said if I'm ever leading Ronan away, it will be because it's part of a plan, and I'm leading him into a trap."

Hunter paled and said, "No." Damon just straightened and stared at me intently.

"That's crazy. Hunter was joking," Max said. He spun away and yelled, "Fuck," when he saw Damon was considering it. Leif just put a hand on him, looking determined.

"No way in hell," Sam growled, his whole body tightening with tension.

Claudio just looked at me, impressed. "You've got some big balls, little sis."

"Does anyone have a better idea?" Damon asked, never taking his eyes off me.

Sam pulled out a satellite phone and started talking to someone in code while Damon watched me carefully, looking for signs of uncertainty or fear. But I had this. I was done running.

"Help is coming, but they're thirty minutes out. We need to hold the fort until then," Sam said.

"Everyone could be dead in thirty minutes. I can do this, Damon. Let me help. I may even be able to get him talking. Didn't you guys say you thought there was more going on here? And didn't you also just say I've earnt the right to fight for myself? I trust you to have my back." I stood strong and sure in front of him, planting my feet. He'd asked me to do my part, and this was it.

"Maia's plan it is then," Damon said, as he nodded at me like I was one of his team.

"We're blind and potentially outnumbered. We need to get the upper hand, and this may be the only way.

"Maia, I'm going to direct you to the house to follow Sirena. Sam, Leif, Claudio, and I will take the other path to head for the upper field, but we will disappear into blind spots.

"Once we're gone, Maia, you're going to veer off from the house and head for the back of the dining hall. Don't go inside. Lean against the building like you have a stitch, or you're going to throw up if you get all the way there," Damon said, I could almost see his brain strategizing how to keep everyone safe and defend the farm at the same time.

"There are lots of places to cover you there. Stay on the main path, and they'll have you on camera most of the way. We'll disappear and cover you.

"Hunter, you and Max are still headed for the security office, do exactly what I said earlier. Cover us in any way you can once you get it secured. You need to go first, so you're ahead of Maia. Allegro should have directed Ronan to her by the time you get there. We all need to move fast."

They hesitated, not wanting to leave me. I could feel their anguish through our bond, but Damon barked lightly, "Go," and they both took off at a fast run up the hill.

Leif grabbed me and hauled me into him, giving me a quick, brutal kiss that was nothing like his usual gentle sweetness. He whispered, "I'll be watching you, sunshine," before he partnered with Claudio and took off on the other path.

Damon spun Sam and directed him to follow. Sam wasn't happy, giving me a quick look over his shoulder, but he was a soldier and knew the stakes. It was a desperate, stupid plan, and so much could go wrong, but we had no time or options.

I waited for them to disappear out of sight, heading up towards the house, then veering up the path. My blood was pounding in my ears, and my adrenaline was pumping. For the first time, I wasn't afraid. My pack and my family had my back.

I had just turned the bend into the yard behind the dining hall when a rough hand grabbed me around the waist from behind, and a revolting scent of mushrooms I had hoped never to smell again swamped my senses, right as I felt cold metal touch the side of my head.

They had seen me coming on the security footage and had lain in wait. My plan was working.

I had no time to rejoice as I was dragged into the clearing and saw a flash of purple and red hair when someone was roughly pushed to their knees next to me, followed by two more familiar heads.

Oh shit, no. Ronan had Lexie, Ava, and Cary, too. The hot adrenaline in my veins turned to ice.

Thirty-Eight

"Is this who you were looking for?" Ronan asked as he held a gun to my head and gripped me under my chest with his other arm. He had seven other alphas with him.

Lexie was on her knees on the ground. She was bleeding and looked dazed. She had put up a fight. So had Cary, from his looks. Only Ava appeared unscathed.

I pointed my finger at the ground discreetly, urging them to stay down.

"No. I'm pretty sure she was looking for you. She has a score to settle," Damon said as he, Leif, Sam, and Claudio stepped out at different points in front of me, guns raised.

I could feel Damon and Leif raging through the bond, but they couldn't react, not with a gun pressed against my head. Leif also felt torn. His sister was being held hostage alongside me. Going after one of us could mean the death of the other.

Max and Hunter were a distraction in the bond, too. Their energy was intensely focused. It felt like they were fighting.

"Oh, there you are, Damon. I had some friends keeping an eye on you, too," Ronan said as two more alphas stepped out behind my guys. Sam and Claudio swiftly pivoted towards them, guarding Damon and Leif's backs.

Suddenly a gunshot could be heard from the direction of the security office. Ronan chuckled as I flinched. 'Well, either Allegro, Max, or Hunter are dead. I wonder who it could be?'

"It doesn't matter either way to me. It's just one less person I have to kill when I clean up this mess," he said.

I searched our bond and got calm focus from both Max and Hunter. I tried reaching out to them, and they sent reassurance back to me. I was relieved. Damon's beast would have slipped his leash too soon if one of them had died.

Ronan would have no idea we could feel each other through our growing bonds, so we had an advantage. I knew Max and Hunter would have eyes on us quickly and figure out a way to back us up. We just needed to give them some time.

"I'd say it's nice to meet you again, Ronan, but it's not," Damon growled, finally taking his eyes off me to glare at Ronan.

"Always so arrogant, Damon. Thinking you're the smartest, strongest person in the room. You have no idea how my family has been playing you for years. Now I have you right where I want you, completely at my mercy."

Damon didn't respond, happy to let Ronan monologue while we waited for our moment.

"It seems my little princess slipping her leash worked in my favor because she's brought me you and your friends on a platter,' Ronan gloated as he caressed the side of my face gently with his gun. 'I've wanted you dead for years, Damon, but you were always too well protected.

"Ever since we were teenagers, everyone always talked about how powerful you would be. My father watched you closely. He wanted to see you reach your potential, so he could figure out how to use you."

Damon still didn't react, but his jaw clenched slightly.

"He told your father to make sure he could control you by any means," Ronan said with a note of smugness. I could almost feel him puffing out his chest behind me, thinking he was now the bigger man.

"There's only us here now, and no one's watching with the power out. I can finally kill you, thanks to my princess."

I knew hearing the abuse he had suffered growing up talked about so openly and so maliciously had to burn, yet Damon was the picture of calm control. His gun was firmly fixed on Ronan without wavering.

"She's not your princess," Leif ground out, but Damon stayed quiet, not giving anything away.

"Interesting. It seems my little princess has been playing the field while she's been having a little holiday out here." Ronan pushed the gun harder into my face, and I saw both Leif and Damon tense. A slight growl escaped Damon before he could rein it in.

"Did you whore your mate out to your friends already, Damon?" Ronan asked, ignoring him completely, his entire focus on me now. "What fun."

"You would know about whoring people out, wouldn't you, brother?" Sirena said as she stepped out from the bend in the path. Her gun was raised and focused on her brother. She must have heard us and detoured. One of the alphas behind Ronan swiveled to get her in his sights.

Ronan looked her up and down dismissively before he snarled at her. "Well, don't you look lovely today, sister." The last word was said with a sneer.

"Are you going to betray your family? I should have known. You're nothing but a worthless beta who can't even follow simple instructions."

Sirena planted her bare feet, not moving closer, but her hands shook slightly. "No, because I no longer recognize you as family. You don't even know the meaning of the word."

"And these alphas do?" Ronan asked. "Their families have all but disowned them. They have no power anymore, and they have no idea what's going on out there," he bragged, thinking he had the upper hand.

"We chose our own family," Damon said finally, trying to bring Ronan's attention back to him and away from Sirena.

"You chose a pack," Ronan said, turning his head and spitting in Damon's direction. Some hit me on the side of the face, and my skin crawled. "There was always something off about you. I sensed it even when you were younger."

"Maybe you should have done the same," Hunter called out from the roof, where I figured he was lying with his sniper rifle. "Instead of being a whiny little bitch who did whatever his father wanted." A small smile escaped me.

"Pack loyalty is stronger than family loyalty, it seems," Max added as he stepped out from behind the building and pointed his gun at the alphas behind Ronan, backing Sirena up.

Leif gave Ronan a chilling smile that promised a brutal end. "It seems it was Allegro who bit the bullet. He never stood a chance against my pack mates, and neither do you. You're dead already. You just don't know it yet."

Ronan snarled. I knew that sound. I could picture the mask of rage he would wear as he eyed Leif. No hint of the rich, charming facade he presented to the world would be left. Only the madness and violent appetites that were his true nature. I knew that snarl and that face well.

"Allegro was expendable. That's why he was here. All he had to do was keep an eye on you and make sure you were busy fucking my whore of a sister and staying away from the Palace."

I felt Ronan's arm tighten possessively around me, and I wanted to gag. His touch and his nasty fungus smell always made me feel nauseous. Memories threatened to swamp me of Ronan trying to bark me into submission. I felt a cold sweat break out along my spine, but I kept my face neutral. I didn't want to set my guys off.

"You know, I figured out the delectable Maia here was your true mate when she kept scenting rain and lighting around the Palace on clear days whenever you visited.

"I kept you away from her because she was my toy to play with, and I'm not going to stop until I break her." Ronan was breathing heavily, and his scent turned moldy and rancid. I knew from experience he was always unpredictable when he raged. And stinky.

I kept perfectly still, my gaze fixed on Damon.

"Such a special little omega, the Palace was very interested in her. They let me do whatever I wanted with her, as long as I kept funding all their little tests. They think she's different, a stronger, more powerful omega. That she's the future. I didn't care about her blood or any of that, though. I just wanted her submission."

"Such a pity you didn't claim her when you had the chance these last few days, Damon, but it will make it easier for me now. Once her mate is dead, I'll be able to claim her finally, and I'm going to breed her just like the Palace wants. They want to see if she'll have strong alpha or omega babies if she mates with a dominant alpha, so they can study the babies, too."

I felt sick, and I could feel the guys' horror through the bond.

"So you wanted to claim her, but you didn't care if people tortured her?" Damon asked, trying not to react to Ronan's revelation.

"You're not listening, Damon. She's my toy, not my mate. I don't care if others play with her, too. Now the lovely Ava will get to join in our games."

I ground my jaw at the mention of Ava, and Cary let out a low, soft growl that earned him a kick to the ribs.

"We've been waiting so long for Ava to be ready. Her blood tests were surprising. They indicate she's almost as strong an omega as Maia, but she appears to be more submissive. We don't have any tests from Maia at a young age to compare, though, so we needed Ava to reach maturity."

I stayed calm on the surface, but inside I was raging. I would never let Ronan get his hands on my friend. No way was she suffering what I did.

I needed to show my guys that I had this. Ronan had terrorized me for so long, but facing him with my guys surrounding me and backing me up, gave me strength. I had always resisted, but up until now, I had never fought back. That changed today.

"You couldn't claim me, Ronan, because you're not alpha enough. That's never going to change. When Damon is ready, he'll show the world what he's capable of, and I'll be right beside him cheering him on," I lifted my chin slightly and taunted my personal devil.

All the while, my eyes were locked on Damon, trying to send him trust and love through the bond. If anyone was going to get us out of this without bloodshed, mine, my packs, or my friends, it would be down to Damon.

If Ronan's blood, or any of his followers, was spilled, I didn't care. I would happily dance in it.

Damon narrowed his gaze on me slightly, like he was confused about what emotions I was sending him and what I wanted him to do.

Ronan was oblivious as he leaned forward to whisper in my ear, "Are you sure about that, Maia? I've come close before. All I need is the proper motivation for you. Maybe I should offer to spare your mate's life and claim you right now in front of him. Would that make you submit?" He slipped his tongue out and licked my ear. I shuddered and tried to lean away, but he held me fast.

I could feel Damon's beast rattling the bars of his cage through the bond, not wanting any part of Ronan touching me. Like his beast himself was trying to reach me.

Damon clenched his fists around his gun like he wanted to wrap his hands around Ronan's throat and growled louder, trying to bring Ronan's focus back to him again.

It felt like power was running through our bond, building into a savage storm ready to wreak carnage on those who persecuted innocents. Instead of raging through Damon and destroying him, it was filtering through all of us. We were channeling it back to him, making his power burn bright and steady.

We were almost there. I could sense it. Damon just needed to trust himself now and join with his beast. I knew Damon felt like he was losing control, but I instinctively knew he just needed to fully take control of both sides of his nature for the first time. He needed to embrace his prime alpha, and we'd have his back when he did.

I could smell lightning singeing the air, and my scent reacted, spilling a fruity tanginess into the air, calling to my mates.

"Not being able to claim her is your weakness, not mine, Ronan. That's all down to Maia. It had nothing to do with me. She's just stronger than you," Damon goaded Ronan, a dark smile painting his face with deadly intent.

Ronan roared, spittle flying out of his mouth and hitting me. I flinched before I could stop myself. I almost heard Damon's beast bellow through the bond and his cage tremble.

"Are you okay, Lex? Where's Bear?" Leif asked in a quiet, dangerous voice.

I noticed her nodding out of the corner of my eye. "I'm just pissed these morons got the jump on me. I think they knocked out Bear. He took off in a hurry when he seemed to sense something. I found him unconscious but breathing just before they jumped us."

At the sound of Lexie's voice, Sam and Claudio spun towards her, forcing Leif and Damon to pivot and get the alphas behind them in their sights.

Suddenly there were too many guns crossed over and pointed in too many directions. If someone fired now, it was likely to end in a bloodbath, and someone I loved might get caught in the crossfire.

"Sam," Damon barked roughly as I tried to figure out what was going on and what had made my brother and his friend switch focus so quickly during a heated stand-off.

"I need you to focus," Damon growled when Sam didn't respond.

Sam and Claudio were fixated on Lexie. They were ignoring Damon, with their guns pointed at the alphas behind her. Lexie was holding her stomach and panting like she'd had the wind knocked out of her. Her eyes were unfocused and glazed, but she suddenly took a deep breath and went completely still.

Ronan started laughing maniacally. "It looks like you're not as dominant as you think, Damon."

I felt Ronan's whole body shake, and his arm loosened slightly. I breathed deeply, relaxed my body and waited.

"There's no way you're getting out of this alive. You may be able to dominate one of us, maybe even me, but you'll be dead before it makes a difference," Ronan said as if he didn't care if he lived or died. "You can't dominate us all, and I know you won't risk us shooting the people you care about in a crossfire."

Ronan's gun slipped off my temple as he gestured with his hands. He seemed to forget me for a moment as he taunted Damon in his mad glee, thinking he had won. I knew this was my chance. This moment was mine, and I had to take it.

Ronan seemed to want me alive, which I hoped meant they wouldn't shoot me. But he wanted my mates dead and to take Ava. I wasn't going to let either of those things happen. I had to free myself, so my guys could save my friends.

Damon looked over his shoulder at me, sensing my intent. I mouthed, "Now," slamming the command into him. The bond lit up with Leif, Hunter, and Max sending the same energy, following my lead.

Then I dropped all my weight, elbowing Ronan hard as I knocked him off balance. I slipped out of his grasp while reaching for the gun at my waist as I went down.

As I dropped, the alpha alongside Lexie pivoted towards me and pointed his gun at my chest. I guess the not shooting me theory was wrong, but I was already in motion and couldn't halt my fall or aim my gun quickly enough. My life was now in my mates' hands.

The whole world slowed to milliseconds as the alpha started to squeeze the trigger, and I felt Damon's beast erupt from his shattered cage.

Damon roared his bark with all the unbridled strength of a prime alpha freed from his restraints, pushing dominance out towards everyone who was a threat. It was an icy storm of command, and all ten of the Palace alphas surrounding us dropped to their knees alongside me and froze in place, including Ronan.

I felt the command slide around and past me, caressing me as it went, promising me wicked things and making my body light up.

A heartbeat later, a sniper shot rang out from the roof as Hunter took out the alpha that had been about to shoot me. I guess there was no leniency or second chance for anyone who tried to shoot me. That should probably concern me, but it didn't.

At the same time, Damon surged forward. He yanked Ronan away from where I'd landed on my knees and snapped his neck in one smooth motion before Ronan could even register Damon coming at him.

No questioning. No opportunity for escape. No mercy. In one quick, powerful motion, my tormentor was dead, and I was free. I almost moaned.

"Drop your weapons," Damon barked deep and guttural, like boulders crashing together. It was a pure command to the rest of the alphas, with nothing held back. They instantly complied, and the heat in my body amped up another level. There was something very wrong with me.

I felt Leif and Max jump into action around me, checking and removing weapons from frozen alphas. They were fast and efficient. It wasn't their first rodeo.

Damon released his hold, and the world seemed to speed up again as the remaining alphas cowered and lifted their hands in surrender.

Someone came running around the corner just then, and everyone tensed. It was just Nick, though, brandishing a broom like a sword and carrying duct tape.

Damon swiveled to him and glared. Nick pulled up short, yelling, 'Biscuit, Biscuit, BISCUIT!' Leif and Max burst out laughing before pulling him over to them to help duct tape the alphas' hands together.

No known alpha had ever dominated more than one person at a time. Alphas were no longer strong enough. The ones who could were the stuff of legend, and these alphas knew it.

Damon had always had the potential, but he had kept it leashed and spent most of his life afraid of it. But now, despite his rage, he felt centered and whole for the first time through the bond. We were both free.

He was a dominant, possessive predator as he stood over Ronan's dead body, claiming his kill. He hadn't even broken a sweat. He had dropped every enemy alpha and left his friends untouched. He had protected us through sheer will.

His body was coiled tight like he was ready to strike at anything that moved while his mates secured the area. Damon's beast was out of his cage. He was all prime alpha, and he was magnificent.

Was it bad he looked sexy as fuck, glaring savagely at everyone who had threatened us? Was it the wrong time to lick him?

I started pulling at my clothes restlessly. They felt too scratchy and tight. I was so hot all of a sudden.

Damon's dominance was still running beneath the surface of his skin, like an electric current, in a way it hadn't before. His beast was vibrating under his skin and leaking through his piercing gray eyes.

I could feel the vibrations throbbing in a primal beat as they stroked over my skin. It was like a siren call to me.

I jolted as I noticed Sam and Claudio move to help Lexie, Ava, and Cary, but Lexie waved them off. I had almost forgotten they were here.

"Anyone here looking to avenge Ronan or cause more trouble?" Damon barked lightly as he spun, glaring at each alpha in turn. They all shook their heads, looking terrified of him. Poor alphas, they'd finally met someone they couldn't push around.

He looked to Sirena, who had moved closer and was staring at her brother's body. Not in shock. More like her brain was trying to catch up. She shook her head, and a look of profound relief crossed her face before she shut it down.

I didn't think any love was lost there, and I suddenly felt bad for her. I knew those emotional scars, and I finally recognized a fellow survivor. One that was still deep in the trenches, though. Lexie and I needed to talk to her, but not now.

Suddenly, Hunter dropped down from the roof like a ninja, barely making a sound. The way his big body moved so silently, every muscle taut as he crouched, balanced on the balls of his feet for a moment while he scanned for threats, had heat rocketing through me.

He was stealth incarnate, and when his murderous glance landed on me, where I was still kneeling amongst the carnage, it sharpened into a possessive snarl. My body burst into flames.

He headed straight for me, helping me to my feet and pulling me into an embrace. I instantly forgot all about Sirena or anyone else.

"Pussycat," he murmured into my hair. I leaned into him, breathing him in deeply. My body was shaking as I tried to hold back my need. A hug from one of my guys usually made me feel better, but now it was just stoking the flames.

I needed to get out of here. I moaned lightly, and Hunter asked, "Are you okay?"

I shook my head as I felt him take a deep breath and go still.

"Your scent has changed, thickened. It's musky and almost syrupy. It's like a dessert wine, and fuck, it's potent," Hunter whispered. "I feel almost drugged."

I peeked up, and his pupils had dilated. He leaned into me like he was drawn in and couldn't fight it. He tightened his arms around me, and I felt his hard cock press against me. I thrust against him slightly. I couldn't help myself either. I was burning for him.

"Damon," he bit out sharply in a snarl.

I felt Damon approach behind me, his wild energy stroked the skin of my back, but Damon didn't touch me.

"Are you hurt?" he growled. I shook my head while keeping my face pressed into Hunter's neck, breathing in his woody scent that was spicier than usual from his anger during the attack and had sweet honey undertones from his lust. Every breath felt like a stroke of my clit.

He hesitated slightly before asking quietly, "Are you afraid of me?"

I spun around, reached up and touched Damon's cheek. I hated that he was still unsure how I felt. He'd asked me that question before, and I never wanted him to ask it again.

"Never, Damon. I'm in awe of you. Every day you show me more of who you are, and I fall more in love with you. You think you're a beast, but if you are, you're my beast. I could never be afraid of you."

Damon stilled underneath my hands, and his entire being focused on me, his piercing, light gray eyes bore into me like they owned my soul. It was a dark, possessive gaze that had me squirming and rubbing my legs together as his scent flared, lightning spiking the air. My simmering need ramped up a thousand percent.

I almost whimpered just from that intense gray gaze on me.

I dropped my hands, but he caught them fast as my beast stared back at me. He was all predatory intent, and he had me trapped against the hard wall of Hunter's body.

"Did you just say you love me?" he growled, low and dangerously sexy.

Thirty-Nine

My whole world, my entire life, narrowed to this moment. Everything but her fell away.

She had eviscerated all my barriers already, but I had still been holding my beast at bay from claiming her, waiting for this, for her to be ready to claim us all too.

Now she wasn't just claiming the guys and me, she was claiming my beast as well, and it made him roar in my head.

She was wide-eyed and trembling in front of me. Her scent was intoxicating, and it spiked headily when I growled lightly at her in encouragement. I wanted more of her scent, body, heart, and every desire. I wanted it all.

I felt Leif and Max draw in close. I could feel their focus and intensity reflecting mine in the bond. We were building off each other, circling her like the predators we were, scenting the air for the right moment to pounce.

But a noise, someone yelling my name, was splitting my focus. I shook my head, trying to clear the noise, when Sam tried to intervene and grab Maia.

I growled and blocked him roughly. I knew Sam was her brother, but my beast was in control. It wanted to rut and claim our omega. Whatever Sam wanted could wait.

"Damon, snap out of it," Sam demanded.

I growled at him again, a vicious warning, and this time, Leif, Hunter, and Max joined in.

"Fuck, Maia, you need to try and back away from them," Sam urged.

"She can't and doesn't want to anyway," I heard Lexie intervene. "I'm pretty sure she's in heat."

"What the hell is a heat?" Claudio asked her, looking between us all, intrigued. He leaned closer, sniffed the air, and caught a whiff of Maia's sultry scent, which was growing stronger by the second.

His pupils dilated, and he adjusted himself uncomfortably while taking a giant step back. "Oh shit, what the fuck is up with her scent? It's like sexual napalm, and it's pulling at me."

"I'll explain later. I don't know where you guys came from, but you need to back away now before you lose your heads," Lexie demanded.

Ava stepped towards us but halted when Maia started to growl lightly. Cary limped to her side, ready to pull Ava away if needed.

"Shit, even I can feel that. This is bad," Cary said, trying to talk and hold his breath simultaneously. He turned his head away to get some clear air.

"Damon, you need to get her out of here now. When the heat starts, it deepens her scent and draws alphas in," Ava said. "She's definitely in heat now, and she's going to set off every alpha in the area that's unrelated to her. We don't need an alpha frenzy on our hands."

Shit. I nodded to Ava in thanks. I could feel an intense draw to Maia that was intoxicating. I didn't want any alphas around her right now who weren't pack.

"Lexie, you're in charge," I ground out around clenched teeth. "Get Dave down here and let him know Sam has back-up on the way."

"Keep people away from our house. Feel free to smack around any guys who get out of line. Get the other women on board if you have to. We're relying on you."

"I'll help her," Sirena said quietly.

Lexie raised her eyebrows at Sirena but nodded at us quickly before I grabbed Maia and swept her up in my arms. She immediately moaned and started kissing and sucking my neck. My knees almost buckled as her syrupy heat scent enveloped me and made it feel like her hot mouth was tonguing my dick. We needed to move fast.

Max stepped to Sam. He was barely in control and breathing hard, but he was doing a little better than Hunter, Leif, or me. Leif looked a hair's breadth from throwing fists while Hunter was glaring death at everyone around us, holding one hand protectively on Maia's back.

"Can you back up Lexie and Dave to help secure the farm? Lexie is our sister."

"Can you promise me you won't hurt MY sister?" Sam demanded.

Max got in his face, a ballsy move for a beta. "We would NEVER hurt your sister. She's our mate," he growled, low and angry.

Leif instantly stepped up behind Max, but Claudio got in the middle of Max and Sam first, pushing Sam back. "We know nobody is hurting anyone here, except maybe a few sneaky kicks into the dickwad alphas behind us. Okay. We got this, Max, go."

Maia swung herself around in my arms to wrap her legs around me and started grinding against me as her syrupy orange and pineapple scent exploded and flooded the area in a wave of pure need that demanded action. We were out of time.

"Move, now," I yelled to the guys and took off. I heard scuffling behind me, but I had to trust Sam and Claudio had it handled.

"Grab a gun. Point and shoot if anyone moves," Sam yelled.

I heard Cary respond, "With pleasure," and Lexie yelling, "Take that fuckers," before we were around the bend and moving out of earshot. I didn't hear any gunshots, though. I had no idea what the hell Lexie was doing, but she sounded gleeful about it.

It took only minutes to get back to the house at the fast pace I set, but they were some of the longest minutes of my life. Maia was moaning my name and grinding on me, begging me for relief.

I almost stopped to fuck her on the path, but my purr started unconsciously, easing her moans. She was still humping me like I was her battery-operated boyfriend, though, and damn if that wasn't a turn-on.

The purr had been able to calm her pre-heat lust, but it seemed only to have a slight effect on her heat.

Hunter dashed ahead. He was the fastest of us all and got the door open just before I barreled through.

I jumped onto the couch, not caring if I broke it, and placed Maia onto the mattress in the middle of the room. She immediately burrowed into the blankets, rubbing herself all over our scents on them.

Leif closed all the curtains, and Max turned on a low lamp, making the large space feel more intimate.

Her scent suddenly spiked again, and she moaned loudly, grabbing her breasts and rubbing her legs together.

"Holy shit. Somebody needs to fuck her now," Hunter groaned, grabbing his hard dick through his pants.

"Not yet," I growled at him as I watched her every movement with intense focus.

"Tell me we can claim you, Maia. I need to hear you say it."

Maia moaned something unintelligible into the quilts. She seemed past all coherent thought. But I needed to hear her words, loud and clear, or I'd remove myself from this situation, as painful as that would be.

I had been so afraid of letting my beast out and hurting people. But I knew now that he was me, we were one, and we only wanted to protect. Especially her.

At this moment, we had one thought. Claim Maia, rut her and make her pack. But we would never force her or take away her choices.

"Maia," I growled, low and dominant. Her body arched in response, her breasts pushing into the blankets and her legs spreading open. Her responsiveness to me almost drove me over the edge.

But she was spiraling, and I needed her to break through her lust haze and focus on us for a moment.

"On your knees, now," I barked lightly, directing just enough bark at her to get her attention without compelling her. She dragged herself up, as she kept her eyes on me, and kneeled in front of me, panting hard.

"Good girl," I crooned at her, and her eyes almost rolled back in her head. Seeing her on her knees in front of me nearly undid me. It brought out every dirty fantasy I had of her submitting to me.

"I know you're feeling overwhelmed with heat and having trouble focusing, but I need you here with us. So I'm going to help you, okay?" She nodded at me with dazed eyes.

"Lie across my lap," I demanded, and my dick became a steel rod when she complied. The guys were all watching with intense focus, barely breathing.

I ran my hand smoothly down her back. This usually worked better naked, but I wasn't ready to see her skin yet. I wanted to take my time with that part.

I stopped at the fullness of her delectable ass, rubbing my hand across it and over the junction at the top of her thighs. She moaned lightly. I slapped her across one ass cheek, then the other quickly, before rubbing over the sting. Not hard enough to hurt, but enough to focus her through her lust.

"Maia?" I growled at her, and she groaned unintelligibly again, thrusting back against my hand. So I repeated the motion, adding a smack directly across her mound, and she moaned long and low.

"Maia?" I growled again.

"Yes, Sir?" She rasped. I had to breathe deeply to focus after hearing those words coming out of her luscious mouth. They threatened to drag me down into the madness of her heat with her, but I needed to be present right now.

I sat her up, grabbed her chin, and forced her to look into my eyes. They were clearer than they had been a moment ago but burning with lust and life.

"Tell me you want this, and we can claim you. Or tell me to back off, and we'll leave Max to see you through your heat. But I need to hear the words."

Hunter and Leif growled low in their throats, but I knew they would comply if I demanded. And I would, for her. My dominance was now running hotly below my skin, thawing all my ice. I knew I could call it up at any moment. It was a part of me now.

"I want this, Damon. I choose you all. I need you all to claim me, the same way I'm about to claim you," she said, looking deeply into my eyes, and it was everything I wanted from the first moment I saw her standing in the kitchen.

That this strong, beautiful woman, who had submitted to no one and had been tortured for it, was now giving herself willingly to me, to us. It finally made me feel like I was worthy. I felt my chest swell with pride and love for her and our mates.

"Do you want me to take over and direct us?" I asked roughly, edging forward slightly. I was dying to take control, for her as much as me, so we made it enjoyable for her rather than descend on her all at once in a hormone fuelled rut.

I wanted her to submit to it willingly, though, and I would give up control to her in return if she needed it. That's how a pack worked. I may be a prime alpha, but we were all equal and gave each other what they needed.

She nodded and said in a breathy voice, "Yes, please, Prime Alpha."

That one whispered phrase had my beast roaring and all my dominance pounding inside my bones, like a demand for action. I growled intently at her. She moaned louder in response, widening her legs and rubbing herself against the soft blankets underneath her.

"Leif, Max, strip her," I demanded as I released her, with a slow stroke across her lips with my thumb.

They lowered her to the middle of the mattress again. Then they both knelt and started running their hands over her, but kept to safe zones, teasing her. They laid her down before sliding her pants down her body with long strokes, then running their hands up her sides to lift her hoodie.

"Fuck me," Max whispered. Underneath, she had a pale pink lace bodysuit that barely kept her luscious tits encased and gave us a teasing glimpse of her hard nipples pushing against the semi-sheer fabric.

I had a sudden image of her dressed only in that, welcoming me home one day while draped over her chair in the study, and I wanted that moment fiercely.

I groaned, running my eyes all over her skin as Leif, Max, and Hunter stilled what they were doing, to do the same. She was magnificent, with her golden hair splayed all around her and her body on show for us like a work of art.

She moaned again and begged, "Please."

"You are so beautiful," Leif moaned as he and Max moved in unison, completely enraptured with her, and bent to kiss and nibble at her bra straps, slowly sliding them down her shoulders and arms with their teeth.

"Oh god, yes," she groaned as the lace dragged over her breasts, exposing them slowly to our gazes.

"That's fucking hot," Hunter whispered from the couch next to me. I couldn't agree more, but I was momentarily unable to form words.

They dragged the scraps of lace down her body slowly with their teeth, over the curve of her hips, as she raised her body slightly to help them, then down her legs. It was the most exquisite torture watching her be revealed to us.

When she was completely naked, she looked up at us, returning our hungry gazes.

"Knot me, please," she moaned as she panted heavily. Her scent spilled into the room. I almost came in my pants as the guys all groaned in unison.

"Not yet, kitten," I growled. "Leif, Max. Get naked, now."

They both stood and stripped off their pants and boxers hurriedly, not questioning me and not bothering to put on a show. Maia watched them hungrily, all the same, licking her lips as their hard cocks sprung free.

"You and Hunter, too," she demanded, and I felt a wicked smile creep over my face. I liked my kitten getting bossy.

Hunter and I both stood and removed our pants, a little slower than the others had. Her scent spiked again, and I knew she was getting desperate to feel us against her skin from the way she was shifting restlessly.

"I need to feel you all touching me," she moaned.

"Touch her, but only with your mouth," I commanded.

We all moved in unison, like we had one mind, one goal. To please her and worship her. We were completely hers.

I slipped to my knees on the mattress while Hunter moved to kiss her neck and Leif and Max worked in tandem to caress her breasts gently with their tongues.

She thrust into their mouths as she arched to give Hunter better access to her neck. Her legs fell open before me, and her wet, glistening folds were like an open invitation to ravish her.

The time for teasing had passed.

Forty

Maia

The exquisite feel of three sets of tongues worshiping my body had me losing my mind. Hunter was licking slow strokes up my neck and biting me gently while Leif and Max licked teasing strokes up the sides of my breasts and around my nipples.

I arched my chest, thrusting it into the air, silently begging for more. They obliged as I felt two hot mouths close over my aching nipples.

I moaned deeply, and my legs fell open naturally, exposing my soaking wet pussy to the room's cool air and Damon's scorching gaze. I could scent his salted toffee lust saturate the air and dominate the other scents mingling in the nest as his desire consumed him.

I looked up, past a dark and blonde head intent on devouring my breasts slowly, to see Damon's wicked grin as he licked his lips and bent towards me. The beast was free and ready to play.

He parted my folds slowly and blew a hot breath against my wet core, causing me to thrust at his face as he sniffed my scent deeply. He groaned loudly as he licked a hot line up my pussy.

"You taste just like your scent," he growled low and sinfully before he dived in and devoured me. He thrust his tongue deep into my core as I frantically thrust against his face in return.

I was so primed and ready that I was set to explode, and he knew it. He ran a line of fire with his hand down my stomach, over my mound, then grazed it over my clit slowly before rubbing gentle circles in time with his tongue.

I thrust harder and cried, "More," as Hunter, Leif, and Max all picked up their intensity. Hunter sucked on the sensitive spot in the crease of my neck with hot, open-mouthed kisses while Leif and Max lathed my nipples interspersed with tiny nipping bites.

I thrust into Damon's face wildly as the sensations built rapidly, making me mindless with need. I felt my slick gather as Damon moaned, lost to my taste and scent.

Sparks fired off all over my body, and the swirling, rushing feeling in my belly dropped between my legs as pure pleasure pulsed through me in a blinding wave. I cried out sharply and squeezed Damon's head between my thighs as I came hard.

Damon teased out my orgasm, lapping at my slick, as Hunter kissed me passionately and Leif and Max stroked my body lightly, settling me but keeping the fire simmering.

"That was just to take the edge off, kitten," Damon said as he sat back on his heels, his eyes blazing and roaming over me like he wanted to lick every inch of my skin.

I wanted to do the same, staring at all the tanned olive skin stretched tightly over his heavily muscled frame and all of it on show, just for me.

He wasn't as bulky as Leif or athletic as Hunter or Max. He was built like a god, a perfect specimen. Beautifully broad in the shoulders, before his muscular chest tapered down to a narrow waist and a defined adonis belt that pointed at his thick cock.

The orgasm had momentarily tempered my need, but I still wanted them all. I wanted to feel each one of them moving deep inside me.

"Need you, Damon," I moaned. I was half a breath away from demanding. I needed him desperately. Now.

"You have me, kitten, all of me," he reassured me.

"I want a taste of her," Hunter said as he moved around to sit on the couch behind Damon. I was confused for a second, unsure how he could taste me from there, but he grabbed Damon's face in a firm grip, twisting it towards him, and then licked across his lips.

"Oh god," I moaned while Leif and Max chuckled darkly.

Damon looked startled but didn't pull away, and Hunter smirked as he let him go. "Don't worry, bro, that wasn't about you. I think our girl liked it, though."

They both looked at me, and I nodded eagerly. I was so getting inside that sandwich one day soon.

Then Damon reached down and stroked his hard dick roughly, and every other thought fled.

"Is this what you want, kitten?" I stretched out my legs and wrapped them around his waist, trying to pull him towards me as I nodded, not taking my eyes off the harsh handling of his dick for a second.

My body started to burn again, and my slick flowed out freely. I wanted that dick inside me right the fuck now.

"Uh, uh, kitten. I'm in control here." He grabbed my hips, dragged me towards him, and lifted my ass to his waist. Then he jerked his hips forward slightly and rubbed his dick through my slick lightly.

I almost came again just from the feel of his hardness against my soft folds, but it wasn't enough. It wasn't nearly enough.

"Damon," I moaned in desperation, needing him inside me now and wanting him to lose control the way I was. I could feel light tremors running all over my body like a junkie needing a fix, even though I had an orgasm moments ago.

I wanted them to claim me so bad I could almost feel the bite marks on my skin already. The teasing and spanking had been deliciously sexy and had driven my heat-induced lust to levels I had never known. But my need felt like a brand under my skin. I needed Damon inside me, or I was going to burn into ash and disappear.

When he still held back with a wicked smirk on his face, I pulled myself up to sit in his lap, rubbing myself all over his cock. I looked my beast in the eye and growled, "Fuck me, Damon, or I'll find someone else to do the job."

Hunter shot his hand up into the air like the teacher's pet, but Damon roared possessively, losing all reason and his calm control.

Damon lifted me roughly and speared me with his hard cock. He was wild, unrestrained, and thrusting furiously to shove himself all the way in, inch by glorious inch, to push through my tight, slick channel. And. I. Was. Here. For. It.

The burn stretched me out in the most delicious way, and I cried out in pleasure.

"Yes, fuck me, Damon," I rasped out as he grabbed my hair and yanked my head back, holding me in place. I loved how they handled my body when they were lost deep in their desire for me.

"You. Are. Mine," he growled at me before giving me a sharp smack on my ass, harder this time. My slick gushed at his display of dominance. He slipped deeper inside me on one quick, hard thrust before setting a viciously fast pace that had me moaning wantonly.

"Ours," I heard Hunter growl, low and dominant, feeding into Damon's frenzy. I sensed Hunter shift around and close in behind me, drawn in by our maddened heat.

"Our omega," Leif and Max growled as they pressed in closer to my sides, licking every inch of skin they could reach like they were trying to mark me.

"Hold her," Damon snarled as he released his hold on my hair to Hunter. I felt Hunter twist my hair around his fist and pull me back against his chest behind me, kissing and biting at the sensitive spot on my neck as he did it.

Lief and Max reached out, securing my arms around their necks and supporting my back, positioning me exactly where Damon wanted me. Leaving Damon free to run his hands down my body and tweak my nipples hard when I arched into him before grabbing my waist in his big hands and slamming me up and down on his cock in time with his wild thrusts.

Damon was snarling savagely, and I could feel all their needs building in the bond, stoking each other higher and higher until they all burned with need.

I was trapped between the walls of their bodies and held firmly in place for Damon's pleasure. He had been orchestrating all our movements, like a maestro, in complete control. But now he was lost to his lust for me, and it made me burn brightly.

I had no choice but to submit completely, and I did it willingly. Not just with my voice or my body this time, but through the bond. I completely let go of every wall I had ever built, and every fear, and gave myself to them.

The moment I did, I felt Damon roar through the bond, and the other guys all growled possessively as they stroked themselves roughly while keeping their mouths on my body.

Max reached down and stroked a long finger over my clit, making my slick gush. Damon took the opportunity to drive into me savagely and thrust his engorged knot into my already full pussy, causing the most delicious friction as it kneaded a sensitive nerve on my inner walls.

A few more harsh, frantic grinds as he was locked with me, and I came violently on his knot. My muscles clamped around it, squeezing hard. He roared again, in triumph, as he spurted hot come deep inside me.

All four men bent forward in unison. Then sank their teeth into my neck, shoulders, and breasts, claiming me hard as they all came, painting my body with come, inside and out.

Their bites sent liquid fire running through me, turning my orgasm explosive. I twisted my head on instinct and bit Damon just as hard while I convulsed, claiming him as my prime alpha. His roar sent vibrations skittering through my body.

It felt like every atom in my body shattered apart in pure rapture and rearranged around the delicate bonds connecting me to my mates. The connections burst into bright, white lights in my chest, strengthening my connection to each of my mates and filling me with warmth.

I felt their love and desire pour into me, strong and bright. It made my orgasm crest endless waves on Damon's shallow thrusting until I was wrung out and slumped against them, breathing hard.

Damon collapsed against me too, both of our bodies slick with sweat. Hunter bundled us gently in his arms while Max and Leif embraced us to form a giant pack hug.

"My pack," I whispered. Because that's what we were now, there was no denying it. We were a pack. I was home.

We stayed there for a few minutes, basking in our shared bond. I kissed and stroked all of the guys in turn. I was murmuring comfort to Leif, remembering how worried he had been about breaking our bond if he claimed me too soon.

Leif nuzzled into my neck as Damon caressed me tenderly and asked, "Are you okay?"

I didn't answer. I just turned my head and licked over the raw bite mark I had left high and proud on his neck.

"Oh, fuck," he groaned as his dick jerked inside me where I was still locked on his knot.

"Yeah, feels like the bite mark is connected to your dick, right?" Max groaned.

"More, please," I whispered into Damon's neck as I continued licking my bite mark. The heat rose in my body again, turning me liquid with need. I was insatiable.

"You're going to kill me, kitten," Damon groaned. Hunter shifted out from behind us, and Damon laid me down on the mattress as he started gently grinding into me at a slower, gentler pace that lit every nerve back up again.

He kept up the pace as a languid, slow orgasm spread through my body, making me shiver and tremble. He kissed me passionately like he wanted to taste every part of me, inside and out, before he came again with a long, heaving sigh.

His dick softened inside me, but I stayed cuddling him until I heard a soft moan and glanced over to discover Max and Leif kissing passionately on the couch.

I watched in fascination for a few moments, feeling like a voyeur. While Leif ran his hand down Max's body, making his muscles jump and stroking his pierced dick lightly.

Max moaned into Leif's mouth, and I was suddenly hot and ready again. Damon shifted back and slipped out of me, whispering, "Go get 'em, kitten."

As I crawled over to them I heard Hunter growl quietly behind me. I looked over my shoulder to see his gaze firmly on my pussy while he stroked his dick softly, teasingly. He flicked his gaze up to meet mine when he noticed me watching, and I winked at him, which made him smirk.

He shrugged. "It seems I like to watch."

"Good to know," I said as I arched my back, feeling his gaze like a caress. It seemed I liked to be watched, so win-win.

I turned my attention back to Max to find him and Leif watching me intently. I resumed my crawl towards them and pulled myself up on Max's knees until I was at eye level with Max's dick.

I licked my lips, and he panted heavily. I had wanted to do this from the first time I had seen his pierced dick. I was fascinated.

I leaned forward and ran my tongue slowly up his Jacob's Ladder, exploring the feel of the cool metal against his hot skin. Max's abs clenched as he sucked in a breath. When I reached the top, I swirled my tongue over it, lapping up the bead of pre-cum that had already gathered there.

Leif slipped off the couch and moved in behind me, running his hands over my ass and squeezing lightly before running a finger along my folds and gathering my slick.

I blew a breath onto the glistening head of Max's dick, and his legs trembled before I took it into my mouth and sucked gently. He reached out and stroked my hair, moving it out of my way and holding it back so he could see what I was doing.

I gasped around Max's dick as Leif rubbed his slick finger around my ass before he slipped it inside me. Max took the opportunity to gently thrust his dick further into my open mouth, so I closed it again and sucked him down further.

I bobbed my head up and down, swirling my tongue around the piercings, loving the feel of the cool metal in my mouth. I moaned when Leif scooped up more slick and thrust a second finger into my ass, stretching it wickedly.

Max shook as my moan vibrated over the tip of his dick, and he gently pulled my head off him. I looked at him in question, and he said, "I want to come with you and Leif."

I nodded at him and Leif released me, then grabbed me, twisting me around to face him.

"Let him get wet inside you, sunshine."

I nodded, and Leif helped me balance on Max's lap backward, sliding down onto his dick with a sigh.

Leif kissed me in a frenzy as Max thrust into me a few times before pulling out and notching his dick against my ass.

"You need to relax your body," Leif murmured as he ran a hot trail down my body, flicking my nipples with his tongue before spreading my legs wider and slowly sucking on my clit.

It was my turn to gasp as I thrust into Leif's mouth while Max worked his dick into my ass, sinking all the way in slowly.

When he bottomed out, I groaned and started bouncing lightly before Leif popped his head up and grinned wickedly at me.

He raked his hot gaze over me for a moment and watched me bounce up and down on his lover while Max ran his hands up my body and cupped my breasts, tweaking my over-sensitive nipples lightly.

"So fucking beautiful," Leif swore.

"Need you, too, Leif," I moaned, and he happily obliged. He hopped up and pulled Max and me to the edge of the couch with brute force before hoisting my legs over his forearms and thrusting his hard dick into my pussy.

He set the pace, fucking both Max and me at the same time. The feel of them both moving inside me and rubbing against each other through the thin inner wall separating them had us all moaning.

I faintly heard Hunter mumble, "Fuck, that's sexy," and Damon chuckled.

My heat had me so primed, despite the multiple orgasms I had already had. I needed more. I felt wanton and needy, surrounded by their heat and intoxicating scents coating my nest.

"Harder, Leif," I begged. "I need your knot."

"So tight," he groaned, "I'm going to fuck you so hard while my dick rubs Max's inside you." I heard and felt Max groan behind me.

"Do it, I goaded." Leif twisted us on the couch, so Max was lying down, and he was lying on top of us fucking into me ferociously and making the couch creak in protest.

Max met each thrust, and the feel of them both pounding into me relentlessly nearly tipped me over the edge.

Leif moaned wildly. He hoisted my legs up further and thrust furiously until he worked his knot into my tender flesh. I clamped around him, squeezing his knot tight as he ground against me. Then, I grabbed his hair, pulled his head sideways, and latched onto his neck.

"Motherfucking, yes," he roared as he came hard and fast, dragging both Max and me into an orgasm with him. I felt his bond light up, sure and true in response to my bite, securing my connection to my gentle giant.

He managed not to collapse on us, continuing to hold himself up with immense strength as both of their dicks spurted hotly inside me, and my body shook. His arms started to wobble as his orgasm subsided. "Roll onto the mattress, Leif," Max directed him.

Max pulled out as Leif and I rolled, still knotted together. I got the giggles as I landed on top of Leif while he absorbed the fall.

"Fuck, don't giggle when I'm inside you, sunshine. You're going to get me going again." Max snickered at that, and I remembered when he told me the same thing.

"I'm telling your grandma you swore," Hunter teased, and I laughed harder.

"Your secret's out, big guy," I said. Leif just sighed and rolled his eyes.

"Sex doesn't count," he claimed, but the mention of his grandma softened his dick, and he slipped out of me quicker than he wanted.

"Now look what you did, man. You owe me a knotting," Leif grumbled at Hunter.

"You want me to knot you, big guy?" Hunter asked, winking at him salaciously.

"That's not, I mean, I didn't say, I was...." We all burst out laughing, and he just shook his head and smiled.

Damon came back into the room with his hands full of damp cloths, water, and snacks. I hadn't noticed him leave.

"What did I miss?" he asked.

He threw the damp cloths at the guys. I reached for one, but Hunter said, "Here, let me."

He gently started washing down my arms and body, and the cool cloth felt divine, running over my heated skin. When he got to my lower half, he spread my legs and wiped gently before deciding he could do a better job with his tongue.

He lapped at me gently, softly spreading my swollen and sensitive folds, starting a slow heat building up in my core again until I started moaning and writhing underneath him.

"We can take a break if you're too sore," he said, but I shook my head. I was ready to go again. The ache was building incessantly and making me whine.

"Need you too much, Hunt."

He dropped the cloth onto the floor before laying down next to me and rolling me on top of him.

"Go at your pace, pussycat."

This man was patient and generous, always watching and stepping in to lighten the load when needed. Then holding back and letting everyone else shine. He had my heart completely, as they all did.

I straddled him gingerly, and he gently reached up to massage my breasts. I eased down onto him, my slick still flowing, and he sighed in rapture.

"Ours," he growled mindlessly, closing his eyes, lost in the sensation.

"Yours, always," I said breathlessly.

At my words, his gaze snapped open, and he cupped my face gently.

"My home," he whispered reverently, kissing me gently while starting a slow thrust and grind. He was topping me from the bottom, but I didn't mind.

"My heart," I moaned, half delirious, as I shifted my head to the side and latched onto the soft, sensitive spot between his neck and shoulder, biting gently as he thrust into me again.

He groaned and thrust harder, his knot slipping inside and rubbing me at a deliciously slow pace.

I bit down harder, and we came together, sweet and intense. Hunter's bond glowed warmly in my chest and completed the circle, making all the bonds light up like a fireworks display as Hunter gasped.

I felt intense joy flow through me, and a golden, shimmering connection between us all that I knew meant I would never be alone again. I felt each of the guys clearly as they opened to me completely.

We were a part of each other now. We were a pack. Forever.

Hunter's big brown eyes were damp as he burrowed deep into my heart, claiming his place, and said, 'Love you, pussycat.'

"Love you too, Hunt," I murmured as I stroked his face, my own eyes feeling damp.

We stayed that way for a moment, locked together and gazing into each other's eyes, enjoying the feel of the bond thrumming in our chests. Before the guys joined us, their eyes dampened, too, and they collapsed around us in one big puppy pile of love.

"Love you all," I murmured to Leif, Max, and Damon.

A chorus of "Love you," echoed around me, and I smiled tiredly, feeling joy bouncing amongst us.

"I can feel love from you all so strongly, but more than that, we all feel interconnected. Like I can sense where you are as well as your emotions. We're so much more than a team now, or even a family." Leif said, a note of quiet awe in his voice.

"We're a pack," Damon said simply, in a way that felt so right.

My eyes slipped closed as I felt hands stroking my body languorously while I was still lying on top of Hunter and locked on his knot.

"Let her nap," Max whispered beside me, and I decided that was a great idea. I could still feel the heat, making my nipples hard where they were pressed against Hunter's solid chest, but it was banked for the moment, and I was exhausted. Group sex was hard work.

Someone grabbed some blankets and slid them over us, and I was out.

Forty-One

I stretched out, sensing my guys all around me and feeling content in a way I'd never known. I could feel our pack bonds glowing warmly in my chest, solid and secure, making me feel safe and loved.

Leif had opened the curtains during the night, and the early morning light was spilling through the windows. I used to hate early mornings on my gramps' farm, but lately, this has become my favorite time of day. Waking up early and snuggled in with all my guys.

Damon had told me last night he had plans underway to knock out a wall upstairs and make us a giant shared bedroom, away from prying eyes and people popping in. He wanted me to turn into a permanent nest. They had enough leftover materials from building the workers' cottages to get the job done.

I couldn't wait. I didn't want to go back to sleeping in a room by myself. I may have also wanted to watch the guys getting all sweaty with power tools while building it, but that was my omega talking.

I winced as a muscle in my back twinged. My heat had lasted two days and a night of marathon sex, broken up with snack and water breaks and a few naps. I needed to work more cardio into my daily routine and build stamina before my next heat.

Overall, I wasn't complaining. My body was flooded with endorphins, and I was feeling pretty good. I had four bright, glowing bonds in my chest that made me feel whole in a way I had never known.

I no longer worried about Damon, Hunter, Max, and Leif disappearing on me. I knew I would always be able to feel them, no matter where we went or what happened to us. Our bond was permanent and secure. I would go through all the horrors again if this was where I got to end up.

I had no idea what was happening with the farm, apart from a few notes from Lexie when she had dropped off food supplies, letting us know everything was fine.

Just knowing my brother was out there, waiting, and Ronan was gone. I couldn't ask for more. A family that openly loved me was the only thing I had ever really wanted in life and something that had eluded me up until now. Yet here I was, surrounded by a family I had chosen, and a returned loved one was waiting for me somewhere outside.

I wriggled out from between my guys, lifting arms and legs gently, wanting to let them sleep longer while I hit the shower. We had wiped ourselves down, but I desperately needed to wash my hair and give myself a good clean-up.

The hot water was heaven on my sore muscles, but my stomach started growling. So I rushed through my shower and got dressed in another one of Lexie's summer dresses with a long knitted cardigan over the top. Then I slipped out quietly to head to the kitchen through the back door. I wasn't making a spectacle of myself in the main dining room this morning.

The women were already there, preparing breakfast, including Lexie and Ava. Lexie was teaching Ava how to scramble eggs. I couldn't see Cary nearby, which was unusual.

Bear noticed me first, he ambled over to sniff me thoroughly and nudged my legs with his giant head. I patted him affectionately. He was a good dog. I was glad to see he was okay after whatever the Palace alphas had done to knock him out.

Lexie squealed 'Maia' loudly when she finally noticed me and came rushing over. Ava smiled at her softly. It made me happy to see them getting along. I got a chorus of "Hi" and "Hey" from the other women as they rushed around busily. I noticed Sirena was working away alongside them.

Nobody seemed bothered at my appearance, though, which made me happy.

Lexie wrapped me in a giant bear hug, and I almost choked. She'd gone a little heavy on the perfume this morning. She instantly started teasing me mercilessly, hardly taking a breath.

"Damn, girl, that was some marathon sex. Are you sure you should be walking?

"Are those bite marks I see? Did they all claim you?

"Watching you climb Damon like a tree and dry hump him while your brother freaked out was hilarious. I could have used a heads up that he was your brother, by the way.

"So where are the guys?

"Did you wear the whole pack out? Oh no, did you break them?"

She only stopped when footsteps approached the dining room door, and Dave, closely followed by Claudio and Sam, stepped in. They all looked menacingly sexy in their tight-fitting clothing and focused determination. Except for Sam, of course, because, eww, he was my brother.

They reminded me of how my guys dressed and moved, especially how they moved in sync. Including Dave, oddly enough. A moment later, Cary stepped through the door, too. He hung back, though, keeping away from the alphas.

"Maia, I thought I heard Lexie yell your name. Where's your pack? Are they here?" Dave asked, looking around the kitchen and moving towards the back door.

I put my hand on his arm to stop him and shook my head. "I let them sleep."

"Damn, I'm going to have to wake them. We need them if your heat's broken. We've still got trouble."

I was a little flustered at how casually everyone was talking about my heat and our status as a pack now, but I didn't miss Dave's mention of trouble.

"What's going on?" I asked him, practicing my eyebrow powers. I wasn't as expert as Lexie, but it sometimes worked. I think I looked more startled than threatening, though.

Dave looked skeptically at me, but Claudio jumped in before he could say anything. He was leaning casually against a bench and munching on a stolen piece of bacon.

"The trouble with the Palace isn't over. Ronan said they've been studying you, and they think you and Ava are both important. We're worried they'll try and grab you both again. It sounds like they had been waiting to start their tests on Ava and they won't be happy she's gone.

"Plus, we need to figure out what to do with the men we captured during the attack."

Sam glared at Claudio, who just shrugged innocently, but my attention wasn't really on them.

I had forgotten what Ronan said before he died. I had been so relieved he couldn't hurt me anymore and then completely hijacked by my heat. I hadn't thought about it since, but it matched with the documents Max found about me when he hacked the Palace.

What Ronan had said about the Palace wanting to breed Ava and me to study our babies, sickened me. Especially considering I had just gone through my first heat. I would never let that happen.

There was no way I was ever going back there unless it was to burn the place down. What about the other omegas that were still there, though? Were they secretly testing all the omegas? I didn't like the idea of leaving them there with monsters. I needed to talk to my guys, and we needed to get more help.

I looked over at Ava. She looked like she was thinking the same thing.

"We can't leave them there. We need to get them all out," she said quietly. I nodded at her before looking at Cary, who matched my nod.

Sam approached me and ruffled my hair like I was a kid again. "Are you okay, Mai?"

I nodded, taking a deep breath. "Of course."

He eyed the bite marks on my neck, two were fully visible, but the two on my breasts were only partially visible. I shrugged. "My pack claimed me."

If my friends were okay with us openly being a pack, I wasn't going to try and hide it or my bite marks. I was proud of my pack and wanted the world to know they claimed me.

He took that in his stride, and I assumed Lexie or Ava had been filling him in. I was a little surprised that he seemed okay with it, but I had no idea who he was as a person now and what he had been through over the last decade. I wanted to find out, though.

"Have you been helping Lexie and Dave secure the farm?" I asked him, wanting to know what had happened since we had disappeared so soon after he arrived. I still could hardly believe he was here. I reached out subtly and stroked his arm lightly, just wanting to make sure I wasn't hallucinating.

I noticed Lexie blush furiously at the mention of her name before she turned away. Sam eyed her back with a familiar intensity that confused me a little, as Lexie was a beta. They didn't get looks like that from an alpha.

I turned slightly and noticed Claudio smirking at Lexie. While Dave had narrowed his eyes, and was glaring at Sam and Claudio from his spot near the back door.

I looked at Ava and raised my eyebrows in a silent question, but she just shrugged. Most of the other women were too busy preparing breakfast to worry about our drama, but some gave them curious looks too.

I was intrigued. It looked like things had gotten even more interesting around the farm while I was busy.

I had felt the guys wake up a little while ago and panic at my anxiety. Our bond was so strong and bright that I could feel them all clearly. I had tried to send them reassurance back through the bond, but I could feel a pounding need to touch me and make sure I was okay coming from all four of them.

"Uh, incoming," I said vaguely.

Before anyone could ask questions, thumping footsteps came barreling through the dining room, and the door was flung open. All four of my guys came bursting through, attempting to get through at once, looking panicked and only half dressed.

"Sunshine," Leif growled as he manhandled the others out of the way and stomped over to me, wearing only one shoe and no shirt. He picked me up, wrapping me in his giant teddy bear embrace. "We felt your anxiety. It woke us up, but you were gone."

"Who upset you?" Damon growled from behind me, where he had his arms wrapped around both Leif and me but was glaring at everyone in the room.

"Claudio did," Sam piped up with a smirk. Claudio choked, spluttering out protests, along with half his stolen bacon.

Max and Hunter crowded into us, knocking everyone else out of the way.

"Who the hell are all the military guys in the dining room?" Hunter growled as he and Max joined our group hug.

"Uh, they're with me," Sam said. "It's the rest of my team."

I noticed Max was wearing the hot pink unicorn tee, but no pants, only his underwear, and I laughed, leaning over to kiss him lightly. I was surrounded by warmth and my pack's hard, half-naked bodies. My omega perked up, and I gave her a quick scolding as Sam coughed pointedly.

"I'm fine, guys," I said. "I was just getting some breakfast and Claudio was bringing me up to speed on some things we needed to talk about." I winked at Claudio and he grinned.

"You might want to put on some more clothes before you meet Sam's team." I suggested, eyeing off Max's toned legs as he blushed. I heard one of the ladies catcall, and I laughed.

"We need to add Nick's family to the list of things to talk about," Damon said. "They know about packs and prime alphas. We need all the information we can get about our new dynamic. We also need to know if there are more people like us out there."

His words were serious, but he smiled softly at me in reassurance. Damon had dropped all of those alphas to their knees before we had fully claimed each other as a pack. I had no idea what he, or we, were capable of now. If there were other prime alphas out there, we needed to know that too.

I took a deep breath as I felt Damon purr lightly behind me and my whole body relaxed. No matter what was coming for us all in the future,

I knew I could handle it with my pack, my family, and my friends by my side.

I'd finally found my tribe.

If you've made it this far, thank you. You're my new favorite person in the world for reading my first book. If you liked the story, please consider giving it a review. I'm a new writer, so I need your help getting the word out.

Thank you to Alicia, Colleen, Jill, Kimber, Cassandra and Casandra. My amazing beta readers who volunteered to wade through my rough first draft. Your feedback was insightful and your positive vibes got me through the grind of the editing process. You guys rock.

Would you like a **free bonus scene** for Knot Your Princess? Do you want to find out Damon's plans for Maia's nest? Or read about Damon letting his beast out to play a little more, and two of Maia's fantasies from the book getting fulfilled (this scene was written with you in mind, Alicia).

If so, subscribe to my newsletter through my website at www.laclyne.com. I promise not to spam you, I'm busy writing so I'll only be sending out newsletters every other month or so, when I have something to tell about upcoming books.

If you're keen to find out how I see characters and settings in my head, check out my Pinterestmood boards. I have a mood board for all three planned books in the Pack Origins series.

You can also stalk me on Facebook and Instagram, or join the private Facebook group L.A. Clyne's Tribe. The tribe is where I plan on giving sneak peaks into the next books, and will happily chat about spoilers, books and all kinds of smut. Anyone looking for a tribe is welcome.

Printed in Poland
by Amazon Fulfillment
Poland Sp. z o.o., Wrocław

30484810R00226